Manley: Conjoined

Ariane Amann

First published by AA Publishing, Ariane Amann,
Ammensleber Weg 1f, 39179 Barleben, Germany.

No instances of artificial intelligence have been used during the creation of this novel.

1. Edition, 2024

ISBN print book 978-3-9826484-1-5

The Author:
Ariane Amann is a freelance journalist and author,
wife, and mother of two children.
She lives in rural Germany and cannot not write.

"Manley: Conjoined" spent 20 years in her digital drawer, as a draft of 15 pages. After some courses in creative writing at the University of Oxford's department of continuing education, the author found the tools to make this into an elaborate story about trauma, friendship, and new beginnings.

To Alison, Amy, Hannah and Hoyt.

This would never have happened without you
and your ongoing support.

Chapter 1

Once upon a time...

The Claver Mansion was a fortress. The two-story mansion with two impressive wings built in sandstone with floor-to-ceiling windows stood on a hill on Enkil. It was surrounded by a park with blooming trees and a menacing security line with walls, barbed wire, and laser spring guns. Darren Halloway and Amy Carter hardly ever saw any of that. They usually entered the estate through the giant gate at the main entrance to the south, absently nodding to the guards with their machine guns, and followed the paved, grey road leading to the mansion. Darren and Amy occasionally went to visit and hang with Landon Claver, who Darren went to school with. His family was rich, and sometimes he showed it off with an attitude that Amy wasn't particularly fond of. But he was funny and intelligent and Darren liked him, so she went along.

While they were walking towards the big gate, Amy glanced sideways at the boys, who where in the middle of a semi-heated discussion about the best path for some mission in a computer game. Darren was so handsome with an inch of dark hair on his head and those intense green eyes. And when his eyes locked with hers, she felt seen and safe, at least when the fluttering of butterflies in her stomach took a break for long enough for her to calm down. She felt like nothing could ever go wrong while he was at her side. She didn't care much for Landon Claver, she just enjoyed being anywhere with Darren. Her parents were trying to talk her out of marrying him right now. They had to give their approval because she was underage, and for the time being, they were completely refusing cooperation in that matter. But right now, Amy and Darren had an afternoon to themselves and that was what counted.

Amy closed her eyes for a moment and enjoyed the slight breeze wafting through her auburn hair. She shook off the memory of slamming the door when she left her parents' house this afternoon. Her mother had begged her not to go, to talk to her about Darren, to think about getting married this young. Amy didn't want to hear this. Her parents hadn't been much older when they got married, so how could two years make such a difference? She sighed. There was no use in going there now. She was determined to have the best day with Darren, and her parents would come to get her soon enough. They had done this a few times too many, showing up unannounced and taking her home with them.

She skipped a step and made Darren catch her. He had his arm around her in an instant, so she did not fall. He looked deep into her eyes and took the opportunity to kiss her. The world around her vanished, as it did every single time he did this. Amy closed her eyes and dreamed of a future with him, him alone. She could see a house somewhere at the foot of these hills, with a lovely garden lined by flowering shrubs. Two smaller children were playing in the garden, a little girl and an even smaller boy. Both had Darren's dark hair.

"Are you done yet?"

Landon's arrogant voice pulled her out of her daydream. Amy rolled her eyes and snorted, "Thanks to you, yeah."

Darren chuckled and pulled her up. He looked deeply into her eyes, his hand still on her waist. He could still feel his own body reacting to her, making his face feel heated. Letting her go right now wasn't something he appreciated, but the touching would have to wait. "We'll continue this later." He took her hand and pulled her with him. Landon had promised a new computer game they could try, on the big screen, with no parents around limiting their screen time or intake of unhealthy foods. Hell, they might even down a couple of beers when no one was watching. Darren let go of her hand and playfully slapped Amy on her bottom, the touch leaving a hot mark on his hand, promising more, demanding more.

Amy laughed, a sound that was both surprised and delighted. She swatted at him lightly, her eyes sparkling with mischief. "Behave yourself," she teased, though she couldn't hide her smile.

"Come on, let's go." He gestured towards the mansion.

She looked at him for a moment, considering a snarky response, then started trotting towards the house. He walked behind her, amused by the way her hips swayed. She was wearing an innocent white shirt, short enough to see her skin above the waistband of the green skirt that was the perfect length to show off her thighs. Who knew what the day still held? There were many rooms in the Claver mansion. One of them might be perfect to have a little quiet time with Amy. Again. Darren smiled quietly. He could see them in ten years, raising their kids together. That was a vision he knew none of his friends would ever understand which was why he kept this to himself. Most of their visions included seducing as many girls as possible, not committing to anything except their own pleasure. He was right in the middle of his exams, planning his career in interstellar banking. He knew Amy wasn't as sure about her own line of work, but she still had a year until her exams. There was no rush to make that decision. Maybe she would venture into trading like her father and become his confidante in banking. And maybe she would be a mother and wife, with all of that filling her day perfectly. For now, he walked into the mansion with her, looking forward to a day away from all the learning. He and Amy followed Landon through the great hall that was the entrance to the house. Their footsteps echoed off the white, marbled walls. Landon turned around and motioned to his left. "Let's go in over there. I'll just make the kitchen get us some food and drinks in there", he said and walked towards the back of the house.

Amy and Darren looked at each other and giggled, opening the huge white double doors to the salon that went right off the hall. They closed the door and Darren pulled her towards the rich red velvet couch opposite the antique fireplace. Everything about this place was opulent and expensive. Amy let Darren guide her onto the couch. She was still giggling. He pulled her close up against his body, moving his hand under her shirt with complete confidence.

Amy shivered and let her head fall back while Darren's lips were tracing her neckline. She could feel his tongue on her skin, making it tingle. The tingling moved from her skin to her core, changing into solid desire. She started fumbling with his black belt. The piece of leather didn't yield as easily as she had expected. Then she opened Darren's pants and felt his lips wander towards her nipples. Before she could focus on the pleasure that was ahead, the door flew open. Landon walked in, a plate of leftovers from the kitchen in his hand. It was remarkable, Amy thought, that he was carrying this himself instead of having someone bring it in for him. She casually put her shirt back in place while Darren scrambled to pull up his pants. "Ah, you're back", she stated matter-of-factly in Landon's direction. His expression changed for a split-second, and she wasn't sure what to make of it. He looked puzzled, hurt, surprised, and furious all at the same time. And then the curious expression disappeared, and Landon was his usual, arrogant, sleazy self again.

"I see you've found a way to pass the time", he snarled with a forced grin, setting down the plate on one of the smaller tables beside the couch. He tapped a wall panel and the gallery wall on the far side of the room morphed into a giant video wall. He threw a control pad in Darren's direction and looked directly at Amy. "What do you wanna do?"

"Ah, never mind me. I'll just hang around here. You got wine?" If she had to pass the time while the boys were playing video games, she might as well amuse herself.

Landon nodded. "Kitchen will bring some." He was used to being waited on. Then he turned around and joined Darren on the couch, cutting her out of the action.

Amy sighed. This would probably take some time. She found herself a lounger a few yards away from the boys. When the kitchen help brought the wine, Amy found herself drinking too much too fast out of sheer boredom. Darren and Landon were concentrating on their game, not even looking in her direction every once in a while. They were tapping and hacking away at controls, engaging in galactic firefights between fleets of spaceships. The game, "Stellar Conquest," was a blend of strategy and real-time combat, set in a galaxy teeming with vibrant nebulae and distant star systems. Darren and Landon were locked in an intense battle, their grey, slim spaceships darting and weaving through asteroid fields and around planets. Each ship they encountered, from the small fighters to the colossal battleships, was rendered with exquisite detail, their hulls gleaming under the harsh light of the nearby stars. The game demanded not only quick reflexes but also tactical skill, as they had to manage resources, build outposts, and forge alliances to gain the upper hand.

The boys communicated in a flurry of jargon and strategy, their faces bathed in the constantly changing light of the screen.

"Deploying interceptors to sector seven!" Darren shouted, his fingers flying over the controls. Landon responded with a quick nod, his eyes never leaving the display as he manoeuvred his ship into a defensive formation. Explosions lit up the virtual cosmos as ships collided. The stakes were high; every move could mean the difference between victory and defeat.

Despite the intensity of the game, the boys were completely immersed, their world reduced to the on-screen battles and the pursuit of supremacy in their make-believe galaxy.

Amy yawned and kicked off her shoes. Within a little time, she felt sleepy and gave in to the temptation to just close her eyes. When she awoke, the sun was considerably lower in the sky. Darren and Landon were gone. Someone, probably Darren, had put a blanket over her. She carefully propped herself up. Her vision blurred, and she squinted her eyes. Her head was throbbing a bit. She probably shouldn't have had that much wine, let alone in such a short amount of time. She had no idea how long ago the boys had left. Amy looked around. They had just left everything as it had been when she fell asleep. The food was still on the plate, the game on the video wall was paused. Landon was a little behind, Darren was leading. Maybe that was why Landon had proposed something else. That would be just like him.

Amy closed her eyes again and let herself sink back on the couch. She couldn't think of a sensible reason to get off the couch. She certainly was in no mood to go back home. Her mother would want to know why she had been out this late and why she was drunk, and Amy didn't feel like arguing with her again. There had been so much of that lately, ever since Amy had told her parents that she wanted to marry Darren. They had said so much about her plan. That she hardly knew him. That she could hardly know what she really wanted in life at her age. Her age. What a presumptuous phrase that was. In earlier times, kings and queens had reigned over their realms at her age. Empires had fallen because of 17 year-olds. Her parents seem to be inclined to not let that happen. They insisted she finished school and turned at least 18 before she should get herself married, and preferably to someone who wasn't Darren. They didn't agree with her choice, and they made no effort to hide their disapproval. They said they didn't like his attitude, though Amy couldn't quite figure out what that was about. Why couldn't they see what she saw in him? His determination, his ambition, his ability to make her laugh even in the darkest moments. To Amy, Darren represented a future full of possibilities, a partner in every sense of the word. Her parents' insistence on her finishing school first felt like an arbitrary barrier, a way to control her decisions and keep her tethered to their expectations. He was finishing school, he was planning to become a banker, so he would certainly be able to provide for them even if she decided to just be his wife without a professional career. And she wasn't even sure about that. She had little to no idea about what she was going to do with her life after school. Her grades were excellent, but there wasn't a single subject that she truly loved. There was no fun in school for her, and she doubted that finding a career of her own would be something that came easy to her.

Amy sighed again and sat up. She was going to find Darren and ask him to go to his place. She didn't feel up to the usual teasing Landon used to fall back upon when things didn't go his way. She stood slowly, not too sure on her feet, and walked out of the room into the great hall. It seemed to stretch endlessly before her, its walls adorned with portraits and tapestries that blurred at the edges of her vision. Each step felt as though she were walking on a ship at sea, the ground swaying gently beneath her. The chandelier overhead cast shimmering patterns of light that danced across her path, adding to the disorienting effect. Her head was light, and a soft, insistent buzzing filled her ears. Amy's fingers brushed against the cool, smooth surface of the wall to her right, seeking support. Her breath came in shallow, uneven gasps as she tried to focus to find the boys.

The air in the great hall was cooler, carrying the faint scent of fresh flowers from the arrangements placed strategically around the room. Amy took a deep breath, hoping the crispness would clear her mind. With each of her steps, it took her a small effort to maintain her balance. She paused for a moment, closing her eyes and letting the coolness wash over her, grounding herself just enough to continue. If only she would find Darren. He would steady her in every way possible.

But neither Darren nor Landon were anywhere to be seen. She knew better than to shout out for them. The Claver mansion was so enormous that they wouldn't hear her on the upper floor or even at the end of the corridor in the wing opposite the hall. Amy was about to head out the front door when she heard footsteps coming from the back of the house. But those footsteps couldn't be Darren's and Landon's. What she heard sounded like at least half a dozen people, with heavy boots and weapons clanging on their belts.

Her heart quickened, the dizziness momentarily replaced by a surge of adrenaline. Amy crept towards the front door, each step measured and deliberate. She was insanely glad that earlier, she had thrown off the shoes that might give her away. She could still hear the heavy, purposeful tread of the intruders drawing nearer. She pressed herself against the wall, the cool surface chilling her overheated skin, and crept towards the door, trying not to draw any attention to herself. The scent of the flowers seemed more pronounced now, as she was drawing near to the staircase. Amy's pulse pounded in her ears, a steady drumbeat of fear. She could sense the front door just to her right. She turned her head a bit, still keeping an eye on the back of the hall. The brass handle on the front door gleamed faintly, beckoning her to come.

Carefully, she continued her silent advance, her naked feet barely touching the ground. The footsteps had stopped momentarily, as if the intruders were reassessing their surroundings. Amy swallowed hard, willing herself to remain calm. The front door was only three steps away now. She reached out, her fingers brushing against the wood of the door first, then against the smooth, cool metal of the handle. She heard the footsteps resume, faster and more determined than before. She knew she had only seconds to act. She didn't look in their direction and ran out the door. Someone grabbed her from the right, pulled her aside and put a hand over her mouth, all in a matter of seconds. With wide, panicked eyes she tried to scream but a hand in front of her mouth silenced her.

"Shhhhhhh!"

She turned her eyes to the right and met Darren's gaze. Her heart was pounding wildly in her chest, and her instincts told her to run hard and fast. Darren seemed to be guessing her thoughts and shook his head silently. He pulled her down behind a large shrub that stood in front of the mansion walls, his hand still over her mouth. He motioned her to stay down and slowly removed the hand from her mouth.

"Man, I was just about to come and get you. Something's up, we need to get out of here", he whispered, looking from left to right with panic in his eyes.

Amy felt anger rising up in her. She could hear her heart pounding a little more loudly, and she took deeper breaths than before. So he knew something was odd and let her sleep? "What were you waiting for? For all you knew I could still be in there, asleep", she hissed.

Darren's hands went up in defence, "I know, I know, I'm sorry. I don't even know where Landon is. He went to check on something. I haven't seen him since. His father's around somewhere. He's carrying a weapon. There are three trucks with soldiers in the back. They're marching around, looking for something. I don't think we should be here. We really need to get out of sight." He paused for a moment. "Amy, I'm scared."

Amy's breathing was laboured, stressed. She was desperately trying to think. Out of here. They needed to get out of here. The obvious way went out the front gate. That seemed to be out of the question with armed soldiers around and the need to keep out of sight. Her eyes darted from left to right. Maybe if they made their way along the walls to the back of the mansion. Maybe — no. She shook her head. Darren said there were three trucks of soldiers over there. Also, they probably couldn't just waltz into the house again and pretend they didn't notice the soldiers. Their presence was usual even for the Claver mansion. From inside the house, she could hear heavy footsteps again, metal clanging on metal. They were walking faster now, and their weapons clanged louder. Someone was shouting orders she could hear but not understand. Their words sounded distorted by the distance and their movement. Amy pushed herself harder against the wall, her heart racing so violently she feared it might give her away. The shouting inside the house grew louder, more urgent, punctuated by the staccato rhythm of boots on marble. The clanging of weapons was a harsh, dangerous sound. She could hear the soldiers moving through the house.

Maybe her mother had been right, and she shouldn't be out and about after school. Someone was barking something, and she thought she heard Landon's father. He'd know how to set an end to this. Before Darren could stop her, she had turned around to the window on her left and carefully glanced inside the mansion. What she saw entered her mind, but she couldn't process what she saw.

Two men clad in black were kneeling in the middle of the entrance hall, their hands bound behind their backs. About a dozen others were standing behind or beside them. Facing them from about six feet away, Kirk Claver, Landon's father, was saying something she couldn't hear. He was holding a weapon in his right hand. He was looking from that weapon to the two men on their knees. The men exchanged looks and shook their heads without a word. Landon's father shook his head, too. Then, without further ado, he raised his weapon and shot.

First, the black-clad, kneeling man towards the house entrance dropped dead. The other one followed with the next shot. Amy screamed. Darren grabbed her, forcing his hand back over her mouth. He pulled her to the ground violently, hoping no one had heard her through the general mayhem. But luck wasn't on their side. One of the soldiers ran out the front door, looked around. He found them, of course. It wasn't like they were invisible behind the shrubs. He silently motioned them to stand up with his gun. Amy's hands started shaking uncontrollably. Her eyes darted from left to right, looking for Darren's eyes. He was avoiding her. This felt so wrong. She could see that the soldier's lips were moving, but she couldn't hear what he said. Her ears were ringing, and she thought her head would explode. She couldn't find Darren's hand. She didn't dare to look away from the nameless soldier with the gun who was looking more annoyed by the second.

"Sir, I've found something", the gunman shouted. Someone answered with something Amy couldn't hear. He motioned the two kids to walk inside.

Amy set one foot in front of the other as if she had just learnt to walk. She knew enough about mercenaries to be scared. The men inside the mansion were all clad in black, including the two that Landon's father had just shot. Their lifeless bodies were still sprawled on the floor, their legs pointing away from their torsos. Their hands were still bound, and each one had a small dot of blood on the side of his head where the laser gun had seared the skin and tissue beyond. Amy couldn't take her eyes off the wounds. She couldn't help but think she'd be the next one to have a hole like that in her head. The soldier pushed her towards Claver. "Found them outside listening in on us."

Kirk Claver smiled sardonically. "Now look who we have here." Considering the solders in front of him, he looked completely out of place. He was wearing a green dinner jacket with matching pants. His shirt was white, his brown shoes were highly polished. She couldn't quite make out what they were made of, but it didn't really matter now, anyway, did it? Claver was still smiling. "Amy Carter and her boyfriend Darren." And without really waiting their answer, he continued, "Well, you've got yourselves into quite some trouble. You see, no one was supposed to know about the little encounters that have occurred here today. I'll have to think about what I'm going to do with you." And with that, he turned to the soldier who was still aiming his gun at Amy and Darren. "Put'em in the room next door. I'll decide what to do with them later. Get the dead out of here and dispose of them." No one was asking any questions. Apparently, people just did what Kirk Claver told them.

Amy suddenly felt someone poke her in the small of her back with something hard. A gun. She hadn't even noticed that a soldier was now standing behind them. She turned with Darren and faced back towards the room she had just emerged from mere minutes earlier. In a haze, she walked in there and listened silently as the soldier locked the door. Darren stood still for a moment, then he raced towards the giant double doors leading to the next room. They were locked. He pushed down the handle on both sides violently, but the doors didn't budge.

The room seemed to close in around Amy, the walls pressing in on her. The dim light cast long shadows that kept moving on the edges of her vision.

Her breath came in ragged gasps, her mind struggling to comprehend the sudden shift from dangerous confrontation to grim entrapment. Darren's frantic efforts to open the doors amplified her sense of dread. The rattling of the handles echoed through the air.

Amy's eyes darted around the room, looking for an escape route. The lavish furnishings now seemed menacing, obstacles in their path to safety. The screen still showed the paused game Darren and Landon had been playing. Her empty wine glass sat on the small side table. The whole room in its seeming peacefulness was mocking her. She felt a sob rising in her throat, but she swallowed it down, refusing to give in to the rising panic.

She could not believe what was going on. Surely this whole spectacle was some sort of improvisational theatre Landon had ordered for entertainment. Surely she hadn't watched two men getting shot out in the hall. Surely the men outside hadn't locked Amy and Darren up because they were witnesses to the crimes committed and needed to be gotten rid of. All of this went through Amy's head in seconds while she was watching Darren trying to find a way out of this room.

Darren stopped his assault on the doors and turned to face her, his eyes wide with a mixture of fear and determination. "We need to find another way out," he said, his voice strained but steady. Amy nodded, her mind racing. Before she could say anything, the door behind her, the one through which they had entered, flew open again. She whirled around and faced Claver. Next to him was a dark-skinned mercenary carrying an even larger gun than the one used to shoot the men in the hallway.

"Take the boy", Claver barked, not even looking at her. He shoved her aside hard. She fell and hit her head on the table behind her. She bit her tongue, trying not to scream. She scrambled to the side, moving away from him. Claver made two others grab Darren, who tried to fight them. He didn't stand a chance against two trained mercenaries. He tried to pull his arms from their grip and received a blow to his head from one of the weapons the soldiers were carrying. Darren slumped down, barely conscious. Amy put her hand over her mouth to keep herself from screaming again. Tears filled her eyes. This was no dream. This was real. She could hear her blood in her ears, and she could have sworn she could hear her own muscles trembling. The soldiers took Darren, and there was nothing she could do about it. She tried to run after them, but she was too late. They shut the door in her face and locked it. She heard something big slumping to the floor. She imagined that the mercenaries had let Darren fall to the ground, and he wasn't able to control his body. She heard herself breathing faster, and her throat was becoming dry. What were they going to do to him? She put her ear to the wooden door, so she could listen to what was happening on the other side. There was talking, but she couldn't make out the words. She didn't know who was talking.

It dawned on her that she didn't even know if Darren was still alive. She had no idea if she was going to get out of here alive. The more seconds ticked away, the more she feared she would not make it home.

"I didn't see anything! Landon, no!"

Darren's voice rang through the hall, echoing off the walls. Metal clanged on stone, something scraped across the floor. There was screaming and laughter. She couldn't take it any more. She rushed towards the window and heard someone scream, "Run, Amy! RUN!"

It was Darren's voice.

She ran. Fumbled frantically with the unlocked ground floor window. She heard a blaster sound and a muffled scream. In her heart, she knew that Darren was gone. Claver had killed him because of what they had seen. And Amy kept running. Running away from the mansion, away from the laughter and the blasters. She needed to get to the green wall in front of her, so she could hide. She heard noises behind her in the building but couldn't place them. Her ears still rang. She ran. The trees and shrubs were suddenly shielding her from being seen. She could hear louder orders and shouts from the mansion now, but they weren't coming toward her. Amy kept running. Sprigs and branches were hitting her face and body, bruising and scratching her, but she didn't stop. She knew that she was going to be dead as soon as she stopped running. So she ran. She ran for her life until she almost hit the security wall on the outskirts of the mansion grounds. Amy looked left and right in panic and realized that there was a door on her right, as if someone had placed it there to give her a chance to survive. She couldn't believe her luck. She tried the handle breathlessly. If this one didn't open, she was dead. The handle gave and opened the door to the outside of the wall. Amy looked back one more time, but she couldn't see anyone chasing her. The noises disappeared on the far side of the mansion. She took a deep breath and stepped through the door in the wall, careful to close the door again behind her, so maybe they wouldn't find her way out right away. Then she took up her running speed again, ignoring the sharp pain that pierced her bare feet every now and then.

She had no idea where she was going. She just tried to put as much physical distance between her and the wall as possible. She knew her life depended on it. Little did Amy know that she would never go back to the life she knew. She kept running, too scared to stop to catch her breath. Her legs just kept moving forward, twigs constantly lashing at her. She didn't even try to protect her face. She knew she had to keep moving if she ever wanted to get to a place where she was not in mortal danger. She ignored the fading light and only stopped when she felt herself almost crashing head-on into a tree. She had no idea where she was and how far she had managed to get away from the mansion. What happened there felt far away, like a dream or a story someone told her. She might have slapped herself to see if she could wake up from this nightmare if she hadn't been so tired.

Amy leant against the tree for a moment in the dark, breathing hard, trying to get some air into her lungs. This was insane. Apparently, she was running from her friend's house where she had witnessed two strangers and her boyfriend getting shot to death. She had escaped with her life, barely. Her legs and arms started shaking now, protesting the intense strain they had been under. She sank down to the ground for a moment, just to give in to the sensation in her legs, and closed her eyes.

Next thing she knew, the sky was lit again and birds were singing in the branches above her. She wasn't propped up against the tree any more. She had rolled over to her side and curled up into a fetal position. Yesterday's events rolled over her as a giant wave when she opened her eyes. Before she knew it, she was back on her feet, breathing hard and running from what happened. Branches snapped underfoot as she pushed through the underbrush, hurting her feet. Twigs and leaves were scratching at her legs and arms. Minutes became hours, hours stretched into days. She drank handfuls of water from puddles a few times while the sun was in the sky. From time to time she passed out under a tree when she paused to catch her breath. When the third day drew to a close and the sky was falling grey again, she broke through the wall of green and found herself in a clearing.

She paused, not knowing what to do next. She looked around. There was a ship parked at the edge of the woods on her right. She stared at it, expecting someone to shoot her. When no one did, she ran again, heading for the other side of the clearing. Before she hit the wall of trees and shrubs on the other side, someone caught her by her shoulders, stopping her in her tracks. Amy screamed, kicked, and hit out at whoever or whatever was holding her. She managed to shake off the grip and tried to run back across the clearing.

The man holding her was silently wondering where the girl had come from. His name was Daxton Faris, and he was a young ISA commander out on his very first mission as a team leader. ISA was the interstellar security agency which handled legal and not-so-legal matters concerning the general safety in this part of the galaxy. He was hiding out in the woods, trying to figure out how he had lost two men from his command three days ago. He had seen the girl run from the other side of the clearing. Her face was dirty, and she had cuts on her face, arms, and legs. The blood was dried, and she looked horrified, haunted, in terror. Her eyes looked right through him. Her breathing was laboured. When she broke free, he set out after her and caught up with her in no time. She was clearly exhausted, she looked like she had been out in the woods for days. He held her tightly in his arms, protectively, so she could catch her breath.

"Hey! Stop running, I'm not hurting you!" he said in the most soothing voice he could command. This wasn't easy, considering that he was trying to get to terms with the loss of his two colleagues.

Amy's body trembled against his, her muscles tight with fear and exhaustion. The night air was filled with the sounds of the forest, the rustle of leaves and the distant calls of animals. Her mind was a whirlpool of confusion and panic, the events of the past days blending into a surreal nightmare. She felt the man's grip tighten, holding her, while she tried to break free again.

Daxton Faris could feel her rapid breaths against his chest. He looked down at her, his expression softening despite the turmoil inside him. The girl looked so fragile, so broken, and something in her eyes struck a chord within him. "You're safe now," he murmured, his voice barely above a whisper. He wasn't entirely sure he was only speaking for her good. "I promise, you're safe."

But his soothing words seemed to fall on deaf ears as the girl continued to struggle against him, her movements frantic and uncoordinated. She fought against his hold, her body tense with fear and adrenaline. Daxton, clad in his dark uniform with a small blaster at his side, maintained his grip, his arms wrapped securely around her.

Amy's heart pounded wildly in her chest. The stranger's grip was unyielding, his strength overpowering her own, weak attempts to break free. She couldn't run, she couldn't hide. Her blood boiled with fear, every nerve on edge, as she wanted to run but couldn't.

With each new onset of struggle, her muscles screamed in protest, her body pushed to its limits by her running and her panic. The stranger's voice, though gentle, seemed distant, lost in the chaos of her own racing thoughts. She felt him steadying her, his lips forming words she couldn't comprehend over the pounding of her heart.

Despite her best efforts, her resistance began to wane, her limbs growing heavy with exhaustion. She realised, with a growing sense of defeat, that she was no match for her captor's strength and determination. Her struggles slowed, then ceased altogether, her body finally succumbing to the overwhelming weight of fear and fatigue. Her resistance weakened and finally, inevitably, she stopped struggling. It was no use, she was sure this one belonged to the armed men in the mansion. She was probably going to die anyway. And she was so tired from the running. And hungry, and thirsty.

She let her head hang and closed her eyes, awaiting the blaster. She probably wouldn't even hear it through the ringing in her ears. But nothing happened. The arms around her didn't let go, and she was suddenly aware of the young man who was holding her. She felt his body behind her, still holding her tightly. His arms were blocking hers from movement, and they were both still standing. Her breathing was finally slowing down, but that did nothing to reassure her. All she could think was that she had to get out of here. She just had to. And still, she couldn't.

Amy had no idea how long they were standing this way. It felt like hours. When the light around them was starting to fade, the man started to ease his grip on her. He whispered something in her ear. She could feel his breath, but she couldn't make out any words. She could feel his hands moving away from her. And the next thing she felt were her legs giving in. There was nothing she could do, she just fell to the ground. And when she hit the ground, she closed her eyes and welcomed the blackness.

When Amy finally emerged from the deepest sleep she could remember, she found herself in a small bunk bed in semi-darkness. Her ears had stopped ringing, and she could finally hear again. What she heard was a low humming. She couldn't place the noise but at least she didn't hear anything else. The walls were grey. Someone had put a grey blanket over her. It was worn, but it felt soft on her arms.

Her throat ached, and she felt ravenously thirsty. She tried to keep quiet so as not to alert anyone to the fact that she was awake. And then it dawned on her that this had been no ordinary sleep. She had passed out after three days of running away from the Claver mansion where she had witnessed at least three men being killed, her boyfriend Darren among them. She gasped for air involuntarily, and tears welled up in her eyes, spilling down her cheeks. The horror of those few minutes was vivid, playing out in her mind as though it was still happening. She could hear Darren's scream echo in her ears. She could feel her muscles tense. That man who had caught her in her running stride was nowhere to be seen, but she was sure he was close. She suddenly became aware of distant talking, and she stopped breathing. Her eyes widened. Amy lay still and listened. She could hear footsteps coming closer, towards her. She couldn't move, her arms and legs didn't obey her. She couldn't even close her eyes. The footsteps kept approaching, and suddenly, right in front of her, was the young man who had held her in the clearing in the woods before she blacked out. He knelt down beside her and softly spoke to her.

"Easy there," the young man said in a gentle voice, his words meant to be reassuring, but they did nothing against her panic. "You're safe now."

Amy was still expecting a fatal blow, her heartbeat pounding in her ears like a war drum. She could almost see it happening in her mind's eye, the man snapping her neck or aiming a gun at point-blank range. Every fibre of her being screamed for her to run, to escape the impending danger, but her body remained frozen in place, paralysed by fear. She couldn't even look away from him. She could feel the weight of his gaze upon her, his eyes filled with concern and compassion, but all she could see was danger looming over her. Her breath came in shallow gasps, her chest tight with the grip of fear. She wanted to scream, to beg for mercy, but her voice remained trapped within her throat, choked off by the sense of dread that consumed her.

Seconds stretched into minutes as Amy waited for the inevitable, her mind a whirlwind of terrifying possibilities. She knew she couldn't let her guard down, couldn't afford to trust him.

"I'm sorry I wasn't here when you woke up. I wanted to be here. How are you?" He kept looking at her with what seemed like genuine concern.

Amy couldn't react. She couldn't remember how to will her tongue to speak, to communicate with him. She just kept looking at him, trying to figure out a way to make him understand.

"What's your name?" He raised his hand casually, reaching for the edge of the bunk bed.

Amy, awaiting a fatal blow, kept looking at him with her eyes wide in terror, unable to respond. His hand barely touched her arm, softly stroking her.

He sighed. "Okay. You're still terrified of me. I get it. Believe me, I won't hurt you. I'll fly you back to ISA central, and we'll see where I can take you. I take it you don't want to go back where you came from." He seemed to keep his tone and movements calm and non-threatening. There was no trace of impatience or frustration in his voice, only a quiet understanding of the fear that gripped her. He continued to look at her with compassion, his gaze unwavering as he waited for her response.

But Amy remained silent, her mind still reeling from her recent trauma. She wanted to believe him, to trust in his assurances of safety, but she couldn't. She stared into his blue eyes. No, she didn't want to go back. She just couldn't tell him that. Her body seemed to be in shutdown. His gentle touch sent a shiver down her spine, a bittersweet reminder of the kindness that existed somewhere out there. As he withdrew his hand, she wanted him to stay. But she remained rooted to the spot, unable to move, unable to speak, lost in her fear.

The man sighed again. "Alright. First things first. My name is Daxton Faris, I'm a commander with ISA. We're still parked on the clearing where you ran into me. We'll be flying back to ISA headquarters. Can you tell me your name? Are you hurt?"

Amy's thoughts were running wild. What was she supposed to tell him? That she saw Claver murder two men and heard him execute another? That she ran away instead of trying to help? That her parents had no idea where she was? That there were probably mercenaries out looking for her? That she didn't feel like she was ever going to be safe again anywhere? And still, her lips didn't move, and neither did her tongue. She just stared at him, blinking occasionally.

Faris frowned. This was becoming more and more difficult. Obviously, she was still in shock. He had no idea when she had been through but whatever it was, it was something far beyond the ordinary for a teenage girl. At least that was what he guessed age wise. She was certainly no older than twenty, and definitely a few years younger than himself. He sighed again and addressed her, "I'm going to touch you now. I'll heave you up and carry you to the bathroom where you can yourself clean up a bit."

He hesitated, waiting for a reaction, even though he was sure there would be none. He was right. The girl with the mud-caked hair just kept looking at him. He stretched his arms out and put them through under her body, so he could pick her up. She didn't fight him. Her head rolled against his shoulder as he turned the corner to the tiny bathroom on his ship. He looked down at her face, seeing her absent eyes look towards something he couldn't see. She still made no movement of her own, and he was sure that she would even have stopped breathing if her brain hadn't been ordering that constantly. Faris gently set her down on the floor, carefully propping her up against the wall into a sitting position. He took his hands away and slowly established eye contact with her. "I'll leave you alone for a moment. If you need help with anything, just give me a shout, I'll be right outside."

When he had finished speaking, he noticed how ridiculous that sounded. The girl was clearly traumatised and unable to respond to anything he did or said, and he had just told her she was supposed to call out for him. He shook his head. "You know what? I'll lend you a hand. I don't know why you can't respond to me, but you can't stay like this. I'll help you clean up. If you can, please let me know if that's OK. Or not OK."

She kept staring at him blankly. Faris knew he had to act. She wasn't going to get out of this catatonic state on her own. His training kicked in, and he went into support mode. When he was done, she was cleaned up, her hair was wet, and she was wearing clean clothes. His pants and shirt were too big on her slim frame but at least they were dry and clean. He hadn't found any serious injuries on her, just superficial scratches. No bruises, no gunshot wounds, no knife marks. In general, she seemed unhurt on the outside. But something must have clearly terrified her. He picked the girl back up, as gently as he could, and put her back into the bed. He needed to talk to his boss. This was something he couldn't handle on his own. He was an agent, not a psychiatrist. He gently pulled the blanket back over her. "I don't know who hurt you, but I'll find out. I promise."

With that, he turned and walked back the cockpit. He fired up the engines. He had no business in this part of the planet any more. His men were dead, and he urgently needed to go back to ISA's headquarters on Enkil and face his superior officers. He had no idea what he was supposed to tell them. He had messed up. He had completely underestimated the situation at the Claver mansion, and two men were dead because of him. Faris sighed. This might as well be the end of his career in the agency. He opened the communication channel on his PAC. "Faris to headquarters." It took a few seconds to establish the connection. Then he could see his supervising agent's face. Mark Millan didn't look amused.

"Where have you been? We've been waiting for you for days, Faris." His voice sounded sharp.

Faris sighed again. "I know. I'm sorry. Tonk and Headen are dead. I messed up. I hid in the woods for three days." He felt the blood rise into his face. His cheeks started burning. The cockpit suddenly felt a lot hotter that it had a few minutes ago.

Millan frowned. "We were wondering why their PACs had stopped transmitting. What happened?" His voice changed to a tone of concern below the obvious anger.

"I'm not sure. There were a lot more soldiers than we expected. They must have got caught. I assume they were executed." Faris almost bit his tongue saying this.

"But you don't know for sure."

Faris shook his head. "I think it's safe to assume. Their PACs are destroyed, I haven't spotted any human life signs coming towards the ship except-"

Millan cut him short. "Except what?"

"Except who." Faris inhaled deeply. Millan wasn't going to like what he had to tell him now. "There's a girl in the back. I caught her running past me in the woods. She's traumatised, not communicating. I haven't managed to get a word out of her. I don't know what's happened to her, but I'm bringing her in."

Millan's frown deepened. "You're doing what?" The sharpness had returned to his voice.

"I'm bringing her in", Faris said with determination. "Something happened to her and I want to find out what it is. Maybe she has intel on what went on in the mansion."

"How do you know she's not a sleeper? She might kill you as we speak."

Faris had to admit that Millan had a point. "You're right. She might be. But she hasn't tried anything so far. In fact, she hasn't even moved since she blacked out in front of me. I had to clean her up because she wasn't able to do it on her own."

Millan raised an eyebrow. "I assume you're on your way already."

Faris nodded.

"So there's no use talking you out of this."

Faris shook his head.

"Be careful. Bring her in, we'll have medical evaluate her. I'll see what we'll do with her after that." Millan shook his head, too, possibly in frustration. "I'll see you in a bit. Millan out."

With that, the tiny screen on Faris's wrist computer went black. He leant back in his chair and exhaled sharply. He wasn't sure what he was getting himself into. And had he known that the events to come wouldn't only change the girl's life forever, but his own as well, he might have made different decisions. But in that moment, he had a hunch that something big was happening and that he was doing the right thing. He stood up and went back to the sleeping cot behind the cockpit. The girl was still in the same position, but she had closed her eyes. Her breathing was calm and her head had rolled to the side, looking away from him. Apparently, she had fallen asleep. He had no idea if and what she might be dreaming, but he hoped that she could gain some strength from her rest. He didn't know much about recovery from trauma, but he knew enough about it to guess that it wasn't going to be easy. She would need all the strength she had.

Daxton Faris was right. When he returned to headquarters, he learnt from Millan that a 17-year-old teenage girl named Amy Carter went missing from the Claver mansion the day Faris's men had been killed. Her parents were devastated and had launched a media campaign to find her. The pictures they had given the news stations proved that the girl in Faris' custody was indeed Amy Carter. For some reason that he chose not to disclose, Mark Millan didn't think it was a good idea mentioning to the public that one of his agents had found the girl. That was something Daxton Faris wondered about from time to time over the course of the years. But he didn't in the early weeks.

Millan assigned him to the girl he found in the woods. She was still silent. A few days into her time in ISA headquarters, she started reacting to him. Only him. He first realised it when she responded with a barely noticeable nod to one of his questions. He hadn't given up asking her things from time to time. And one day, when he wasn't even looking for it, she nodded decidedly when he was talking about fresh air and a walk. She didn't get far because she had spent too many weeks inside, barely moving from the chair she was sitting on, staring at the opposite wall. But she left the apartment building she had been placed in and walked around it for a few minutes. The steps she took towards movement and healing were small and not enough to raise actual optimism in Faris. Whenever another person was near, she fell back into her catatonic state and ceased all human interaction. Doctors, psychiatrists, nurses, all finally gave up on her and said they couldn't help her as long as she didn't cooperate.

Millan knew that there had to be a reason for it. He also told Faris that Amy's boyfriend Darren had been found dead not too far away from the Claver mansion and the place that Amy had run into Faris. And Millan said that one needed to be particularly stupid not to see the connection between those events. Millan handed Faris everything he needed to get close enough to Amy, so he could find out what she knew, what she had seen. He lived in an apartment with her, in some anonymous block on the outskirts of the city. Nothing but flat countryside was opposite it, so it was hard to spy on. Also, no one could look inside without using drones or other technology that Faris would be alerted to.

The days all seemed the same in the first few weeks. He woke her up in the morning, he placed her in the bathroom where, after a few days, she at least took care of herself. In the meantime he made breakfast. More often than not, she left it untouched. Just had coffee and water. Faris was watching this with growing concern. She had lost a lot of weight already and was on the verge of being seriously underweight. The dark circles under her eyes were not fading. He didn't know how much she really slept at night. Eventually, he always nodded off himself, catching a nightmare of hers or two before he did so. The days stretched into weeks and months. Each time he thought they were making some serious progress, there was a setback of some kind. Like the one time he thought she was actually going to say something. He had made it a habit to just talk about things, like he would to a responding human being. He talked about the weather, and the cooking, and the food. He talked about it when he felt bored, tired, or full of energy. He even talked to her when she was asleep. And one day, she had looked like she was going to say something. When she caught herself with that, she stopped in mid-movement and headed for her bedroom. She sat on the bed, hugging her knees frantically, crying silent tears. Faris knelt in front of her, trying to take her hands, but she pulled away, silently begging him to let go. "I'm sorry, Amy, I'm so sorry", he said quietly.

He was at a loss as to what to do. He wanted to take her in his arms and make her feel that she was not alone, but she didn't let him. She suffered in her own world to which no one else had access. And who knew what she was suffering from? Faris sighed. He was tired of all those weeks of trying, and he felt rage rise in himself. Rage directed at her. At her inability to work with him, at her trauma, at her, period. His stomach started aching, and his diaphragm was tensing up. Faris stood and left the room in a hurry, alarmed by this unexpected reaction. He didn't want to hurt her, to inflict any more pain on her than she was already going through.

Considering everything he and Millan had found out in the meantime, his men being killed might well have been the reason for her to run away. Also, the dead boyfriend must have added to the trauma. Faris closed the door behind him and leant against it, breathing heavily. This needed to stop. He'd call Millan and ask to be relieved of this. He couldn't stay in this apartment with her any longer. Not alone. From the other side of the door, he heard nothing. Whatever she was doing, she was doing it in silence. He couldn't even hear her breath. Faris let himself slide down until he sat on the ground, hugging his knees, too. He hung his head and closed his eyes. Seeing numbers of collateral damage or death on duty on a computer screen wasn't easy, but it was at least bearable when they were anonymous.

This, now, was something completely different. Even if she never said a word again, and even if they never fully knew what happened to her, Faris couldn't shake the feeling that the mission he sent his men on was at the core of this. That he was to blame for what she was going through. It had been three months since she had run into him, and he didn't have a clue as to whether she would ever go back to her old self, whoever that might be.

Faris sighed. He couldn't stand the waiting any more. It could take weeks or months, even years, until Amy found a way out of her trauma. He didn't have the time to wait for that. But he had no idea how to help her. This mission was a lot harder than any other he had been on before. He opened the door to the bedroom where Amy still sat on her bed, looking out the French windows, focusing on something he couldn't see.

Amy heard him enter again, but she couldn't bring herself to react. She was busy enough steadying her breath, not being dangerously close to panic all the time. The sun was shining outside, but Amy was still sitting in the shade of the building around her. Soon enough, it would be time for her daily walk. She could feel that it helped her body. She didn't feel as weak as in the first weeks here, and she knew she had to work her muscles if she ever wanted to get her strength back. Faris had told her that her parents were still looking for her, that she hadn't been declared dead yet. He was constantly talking to her. He was probably waiting for a reaction. But she couldn't. She just couldn't. She felt like her voice was going to betray her every time she tried to say something. How could she know she wasn't going to scream? How could she know Claver and his men weren't just waiting for her next door, waiting to jump on her when they recognised her voice? No, she couldn't. It was probably for the best if everyone thought she was dead. Her parents would never understand her grief for Darren, after all, they hadn't even wanted her to see him again. They didn't think he was appropriate company for her. And since he was dead, she didn't want to live that life any more. Of course, she couldn't tell anyone. Her mind was beginning to play tricks on her. The rustle of the leaves on the trees outside was turning into voices every now and then, muttering something she could hear but not quite understand. The shadows were distorting themselves at night, turning into soldiers and trees.

There was so much going on in her head. Her brain never stopped, like she was still running. Running away from Claver, from her old life, from everyone she ever knew. And she ran with Faris, the one person whose company didn't freak her out. She didn't know why she felt remotely safe when he was around. Amy closed her eyes for a moment. The world was silent, all she could hear was her own breath and heartbeat. Faris was probably still standing on the other side of the door, not making a sound either. She kept breathing and opened her eyes again. The view out the window hadn't changed. The sun was still shining and the few trees she could see in the distance weren't moving their leaves at all. The world didn't seem to take notice of her inner turmoil.

On a grey day a few weeks later, Amy's world changed again. Faris entered the living room in the afternoon. He had just come home from running an errand. She saw him from the corner of her eye. He walked towards her and sat down in the armchair next to her. "Amy, we need to talk." He paused. "Actually, I need to tell you something." He paused again. This wasn't going to be easy. He reached for her hand but she withdrew, inching away from him. She looked at him, wide-eyed, as if she knew what he was going to have to say. Faris sighed. "Amy, authorities have declared you dead. It's too dangerous to allow you to go back to your parents. We've got you covered, we'll set you up for a new identity in our witness protection programme." He wasn't sure what kind of reaction he was expecting.

Amy wasn't sure she understood. What he had just said was that everybody was supposed to believe she was dead. That she was really dead. That she was never going back. That she would never see anyone she knew again. That she would be dead to her parents. To everyone she ever met, except for him. She stared at Faris in disbelief. This couldn't be true. No, there had to be some kind of mistake, she had surely misheard this. She started shaking her head. Slowly at first, then more determined.

Faris didn't know what to say, how to give her any kind of solace. "I know it's hard", he tried. He saw her facial expression set in disbelief, and he couldn't blame her. Again, he tried to touch her hand, but she pulled it away. She moved backwards on the sofa until she was cornered on the other side. "Amy, this isn't something I have chosen. This decision was made without me, without you. They didn't even ask me what I thought was best for you. But this is bigger than you and me. I'm sorry. So sorry." He could see that his words didn't seem to have the slightest effect on her.

Amy could feel panic rise up in her. Her heart was beating a little faster right now. She felt like she couldn't breathe as before, and her hands started sweating. The temperature around her seemed to drop dramatically, and the room started spinning ever so slightly. No, this couldn't be. Her world couldn't be wiped out like this again. She could see Faris move towards her on the couch, talking to her, as he always did, but she couldn't hear what he was saying. Her ears were ringing, and her reality was breaking into pieces. She could almost hear shards of glass crashing on the floor. She had to get out of here, she needed some space. When she moved to jump off the couch, Faris moved with her, trying to intercept her in a half-hearted attempt. She moved away and ran into her bedroom. She let herself fall on her bed, breathing heavily, curling up into a fetal position. She didn't care if Faris came after her, she didn't care what he did to her. If she was pronounced dead anyway, what was the point of caring? Amy's breathing was getting more and more laboured, and she could see flashes of green before her eyes. She didn't hear Faris come in, and she hardly felt it when he climbed into her bed with her. He wrapped his arms around her and held her tight.

He could feel her whole body in motion, she was breathing hard, and she was trying to reign it in. He whispered in her ear, "Amy, I'm so sorry." He didn't remember how many times he had said this already in the past few months. She had never reacted. She also didn't say anything now. But he could feel her body tense even more. "Amy, I'm here. I've got you. You're not on your own", he whispered.

And that was when he heard a muffled sound from her. An uncoordinated croak left her throat, and her breath became even more laboured, if that was possible. And even though this wasn't close to actual good news, Faris was relieved that she was finally losing control. That she couldn't keep her emotions bottled up any more as she had done for almost half a year. Amy's laboured breathing mixed with her sobs. By now, Faris wasn't insecure any more about what to do. He knew he couldn't help her, he couldn't pull her through. He could only be there, supporting her in whatever she was going through. And that was what he did. When he remembered this moment later in his life, which he did from time to time, he had no idea how much time passed until she fell asleep in his embrace. He only knew that it felt like forever.

Amy couldn't remember anything of those moments. What she remembered later was waking up in her bed, still feeling him close. He had turned away from her, and he was clearly sleeping. Her face felt weird. She remembered crying before, and when she softly touched her face below her eyes, the skin was dry and rough, and she could still feel the salt that her dried tears had left behind. Her whole body felt sore, as if she had run three marathons in the woods in no time. Her throat was dry, and her lips felt cracked. She needed to hydrate. A lot. A big glass of water appeared in her mind. Yet she didn't dare to move because she didn't want to wake up Faris.

She tried hard not to think about where she was heading. She knew she had to talk to him about what he had said. About not going back to her old life, her parents, her friends. There would be a time for that, and that time wasn't right now. She needed to gather some more strength first. Amy slowly moved over onto her back. She knew that whenever she was ready to face her demons, and to go back to what he had said, and to recall what she had been running from when they met, that he would be there. He would be there and listen and hold her and reassure her that none of this was her fault, that she had done nothing wrong. Amy closed her eyes again. Before she knew it, she had drifted off to sleep again.

The following days went in a blur for both Amy and Faris. Thinking back to this time later, neither of them could name the number of days or weeks that went by until they moved out of the apartment building and back further into the city to get used to having other people close by. Amy managed to make it a habit to at least signal yes or no to things Faris proposed, and he made it a habit to leave from time to time, so she had the space for herself. He still talked to her about everything but by now, he had the feeling that she understood what he was saying. It took Amy a long time to accept other people close by, and she always felt uncomfortable in company other than Faris'. But with time, she was able to appear halfway decent and normal again whenever other people were present. Only Faris saw her shrink or pull back half an inch when she wasn't comfortable.

To other people, the young woman he kept entertaining seemed perfectly normal, if a little reserved. The lot of other people consisted of Faris's colleagues even a year after they met in the aftermath of the killings in Claver' house. And it was with them, in their selected company, that Amy slowly managed to accept another name and background story. They wrote a whole biography for her that she could learn by heart. That she could follow until she found her place in the world again. Her world that had so cruelly been wiped out twice within the span of a year. When Faris offered her an office job at ISA, she didn't hesitate. This was the straw she had been needing to grab for. Faris had assured her that she didn't need to talk to people, that she just needed to assist him in the office. Do some research on the computer, far away from the rest of the agency, without other people. She just needed to store her research results in a couple of digital folders and leave when she was done for the day.

One night, after a particularly uneventful day, Amy, whose name was now Dana, sat quietly on the sofa in their flat, waiting for Faris to come home, too. She was lost in a trail of unsorted thoughts when she heard the front door hiss open. She raised her head and looked straight at him when he came into the living room. "Faris, we need to talk." Her voice sounded sandy, hoarse, from not being used for so long.

Faris looked surprised. He certainly hadn't expected this. He was about to say something about his surprise, then thought better of it and sat down opposite her. "What's on your mind?"

Dana swallowed hard. She wasn't sure how to say what she thought. She also wasn't sure at all as to how he would react. She had a feeling he wouldn't take this lightly. She inhaled, stopped, and spoke as firmly as she could. "I need to go see my parents. One last time." She saw him open his mouth and knew what he was about to say. "I know I can't talk to them, I know it's too dangerous. I just need to see them. From a distance, from hiding. I don't want them to be in any more danger." She paused and looked directly in his eyes. "Please." And she still knew what he was going to say, and she was afraid of what she might do when she heard it.

Faris couldn't believe what had just happened. Amy, no, Dana had spoken. She hadn't spoken this much since they had met, even in the company of others. She had always been the quiet one, the bystander, the listener who smiled politely without taking any part in the conversation herself. He stared at her. He needed to say something. And quickly. "Dana…", he started. His voice probably gave away what he needed to say as he saw her expression shift and become much more solemn. "Dana, you can't. We've talked about this. Claver is probably having your parents' house watched. If you show up there, he'll know you're alive. And he might come after you to finish what he couldn't do last year." Faris carefully watched her as stopped talking. He could see her heart sink, and tears filled her eyes. He could only guess how much strength it had taken her to speak up to him, and to voice this plea. And it broke his heart that he couldn't grant it to her. It certainly broke hers. He could see the brim of tears begin to spill down her cheeks.

She had known he would say this. She had known it was a futile question, leading to nothing but tears. She had known there was no way back, not even in a glimpse from afar. She stared at him in silence, and the tears rolled down her cheeks. She blinked. She couldn't see anything from all the tears. The thoughts that had been tumbling through her mind were suddenly gone. She felt an emptiness inside that she had never known before. She would never again be Amy Carter. That girl, once so full of life, so happy, so young, was dead to the world. She had been for a few months, and now she was dead to herself, too.

Faris watched her reaction from the other side of the table. When he realised that the tears had blinded her, he gave up his watcher's post and quickly moved to her side. Before he knew it, she had wrapped her arms around him, crying uncontrollably. Her whole body shook, the tears still streamed down her face.

He knew better than to speak. There was nothing he could say that would help. She was mourning her old life, and she needed to do that if she would ever be able to find some closure. He softly moved his thumb in a caress on her back, not knowing if she felt that. It seemed the right thing to do. Eventually, Dana's arms released, and she let herself sink into his lap, still crying, but silently now. With any other woman in the room, Faris would have felt uncomfortable right now. But he had spent so many nights holding her and watching her sleep that she felt a lot more like his sister than a love interest.

He didn't know how much time had passed by the time he could feel her breath slowing down. She didn't seem to have the strength to rise from the couch, so he picked her up in his arms and carried her over to her bedroom. He had done this before, and he knew she was letting him do it. He gently lowered her down on her bed and pulled up the covers for her. He was surprised to feel her hand on his wrist, keeping him from pulling away. She was lying on her left side, not even looking in his direction, but she held his arm tightly. She didn't use force, just the kind of strength you need to get someone's attention. Faris understood and climbed into bed with her. He snuggled up to her back, putting his right arm around her carefully. She didn't let go of his wrist, and he held her tight in his embrace.

He wondered what was different today. This was the first time she had actively asked for help, even if she hadn't used words. Grabbing his wrist was the first time that she had seen her own need and acted accordingly. Faris sighed silently. Maybe she was starting to heal after all.

Chapter 2

Today

Manley sighed. She couldn't believe it. She was actually going on a holiday. Free time during which she didn't have to rummage through files, do research, stalk people and fly dangerous manoeuvres around the sector. As much as she was looking forward to her new job at the Faction, she had to admit to herself that right now, she needed some time for herself to process the events of the past months. Too much had happened for her to simply go back to business as usual. Recounting the events that Owen Harlow had started was something not too many people would actually believe. The public didn't even know half of what had gone down since he had shown up.

She looked at the instruments of her good old Packet once more before making her approach towards Nergal B. She had already obtained permission a few minutes ago. While her ship was descending, she wondered whether other spies, assassins, or similar riff-raff were waiting for her on the planet again, or whether she would really have a relaxed and quiet holiday. She couldn't believe it yet. When her ship gently touched down on the ground at the spaceport, she shook her head. "Wake up, Manley, it's over," she said softly to herself.

She grabbed her suitcase and put it outside, where a spaceport employee was already waiting to relieve her from it. She stepped out of her ship, acknowledged the landing on the employee's pad by fingerprint and left the landing terminal. Under usual circumstances, she might have engaged in a quick chat, but today she just wanted to get out of here. A shuttle was waiting outside the spaceport to take her to her hotel by the ocean. Maybe she would take it easy for the first few days and then disappear into the nightlife of Nergal B. After all, she was planning to have a little fun, too.

The travel brochure had called the planet "the ultimate location for pleasure seekers". Manley sincerely hoped that this planet would live up to the full-bodied promises the travel advertisements had made. During her last visit, she hadn't really seen much of the planet and its advantages because she had been far too busy convincing Privateers of Owen's plan, meeting Haylen, Dixie and Faris, and quietly making sure that Claver's games were finally put to an end to. There hadn't been time for the kind of private pleasures Haylen and Dixie had distracted themselves with.

Manley allowed herself a sly grin. Oh, if only Owen could see her now, he would certainly have been pleased. She had said goodbye to her formal "service uniform" for now, usually dark suits with a white blouse, and was wearing a tight black skirt with a split on the left side that no parent would ever have approved of, and an even tighter black blouse with silver hooks holding it together at the front. With it, she wore high-heeled black leather boots that reached up to her knee. There was only one thing she could not part with — her blaster, which was inconspicuously and very carefully tucked into a small, black holster under her loose-fitting leather jacket. In all those years at ISA, she had made it a rule to never leave home without her blaster. Because she never knew what might happen.

The shuttle that took Manley to her hotel was an exceptionally comfortable one. The seats were soft and cosy and Manley was very pleased that the windows were tinted very, very dark. No one would be able to see her from outside. The shuttle pilot was a tall, handsome, dark-haired man with broad shoulders and a forced smile. He probably spent all day flying tourists like Manley from the spaceport terminals to the hotel and back. Admittedly, that could be nerve-wrecking, and it wasn't anyone's dream of a piloting career.

The flight to the hotel over the city took little more than fifteen minutes. From above, she could see people crowding the streets, looking for pleasure and relaxation. She rested her head against the window and closed her eyes for a moment. Suddenly the shuttle gently touched back down on the ground. Apparently, she had fallen asleep from general exhaustion. She would never admit to that, though.

"End of the line, Ms Manley." The pilot turned to her, and she did not like the way he said that sentence. It sounded like a menace. But she ticked it off in her mind and thought to herself, *If I had to fly people to the hotel or spaceport all day, I'd probably be glad as hell to see them off, too.* She gave him a friendly nod, thanked him and wished him a good day, which he acknowledged with a small, open smile this time. *That wasn't so hard now, was it?* She left her seat and got out, which was not so easy in the tight skirt, and picked up her grey suitcase. She gave the pilot one last smile and turned around — three weeks of promising amenities lay ahead of her.

The hotel was big, admittedly, but it was exceptionally exclusive. You could tell by the colour of the façade, a bright, friendly and undisturbed orange, that it cost a credit or two more than the usual cheap hotel on the coast of Nergal B. Still a little indecisive, Manley walked towards the entrance lined with real palm trees as a liveried clerk rushed towards her to relieve her of her suitcase. She quickly transferred him a few credits and followed him into the hotel lobby.

At the reception desk, she dutifully queued behind a blonde lady who was filing a completely nonsensical complaint. Apparently, she thought the pool was not up to her standards. When Manley looked down at her, she knew why. You could easily have carved at least two Manleys out of that woman, if not three. Provided, of course, you had a knife with you. She stifled a sardonic grin and pitied the receptionist, who took up the complaint with the patience of an angel and even wished the woman a pleasant remainder of her stay. Then Manley stepped up in front of him. "Good afternoon. I have a reservation. Manley."

The receptionist, who wore a cute little sign on his suit that said John Panda, nodded and checked his computer. "Ah yes, here we are. Ms Manley. A quiet room with a view of the ocean for three weeks." He turned and took a key card from a huge, antiquated, wooden shelf behind him. "Your room is on the seventh floor, the lifts are over there. If you have any questions or complaints," he glanced after the lady from just now, rolling his eyes, "we're here for you 28 hours a day."

Manley thanked him quietly and headed for the lift, where the porter was waiting for her. He dutifully accompanied her to her room, put her suitcase on the bed, and wished her a good day. When he left, she locked the room door behind him and checked the room for bugs thoroughly. After turning every piece of furniture and every cushion twice, not finding anything suspicious, she went out onto the balcony. The ocean was incredibly blue, and judging by what she had heard about it, it was also incredibly clean and refreshing. Exactly how much of that corresponded to reality would soon become clear.

Manley took a few deep breaths and decided to unpack her suitcase first and then go down to the beach. She put her clothes in the wardrobe, neatly sorted, and she was sure that she could never have turned up at ISA in any of them without being on the receiving end of a whole range of slippery remarks. Hopefully it would be different in the Faction. She was tired of walking around in a high neck. She opted for an extremely skimpy black bikini in which she looked stunning. Having a good-looking companion by tonight should not be a challenge in this. On her way out, she stopped in front of the mirror for a moment and eyed the result of her holiday mission. She smiled at her reflection. She looked nothing like the agent she had been for so long. Instead, she looked like a confident woman out on her own. Her red hair was down on her shoulders, framing her face perfectly. The little lines between her eyebrows spoke of the stresses and strains she had been under lately, but she was sure no one but her would notice. Only her eyes might have betrayed her sadness about how things went down with Owen, and Claver, and everyone else. But again, no one would know. She smiled at herself, turned, and left her room. On her way to the stairs, she was so engrossed in being happy about her holiday that, quite contrary to her training, she did not notice that someone was approaching from the other side of the corner she was walking towards. And as an unobtrusive observer might have predicted, she collided with that very someone as he stepped up the stairs and around the corner.

Manley dropped her towel in shock and, out of reflex, almost gave the stranger a free flight down the staircase, aiming for his solar-plexus with full force. She barely managed to stop herself as the stranger raised his hands protectively. No telling what would have happened if she hadn't locked her blaster in the safe...

Manley reigned herself in in no time and eyed her counterpart a little more closely as she apologised. He was exquisitely handsome. He had short, light brown hair, which he had made stand up with a little gel. He also had a muscular upper body — and a naked one, too, which she only noticed now. "I'm sorry, I didn't hear you there."

The stranger smiled at her, apparently pretty sure of himself. "No problem. As long as you aren't planning to beat me up..."

Oh boy, he had noticed after all. Well, she couldn't help that now. He certainly looked like he could be a lot of fun, and Manley definitely wasn't thinking about playing cards. He had bent down for her towel in the meantime and handed it to her with a mischievous grin. When she took it from him, he held out his hand to her and introduced himself nicely. "Michael Blake. Pleased to meet you."

She gave him a reserved smile. She wasn't going to make it that easy for him. "Manley."

He smiled at her rascally. "Is that your first name?" Manley just raised her eyebrows and said nothing. Alright, he thought himself funny, then.

"I guess not", he said. Now that their conversation had reached a point of either getting together or going their separate ways, he spoke up again. "I'd be delighted to join you for dinner. That is, if you eat."

Finally. At least he didn't want to come straight to the beach, that made him kind of likeable. And even without knowing it, he had chosen Manley's favourite meal of the day. How delightful!

She nodded. "I'd like that, too. I'll be down in the hall at eight." With those words she pushed past him and walked down the stairs.

Michael Blake watched her go. She didn't look back as she disappeared, but he would most certainly be waiting for her in the hall tonight. Maybe this lovely red-headed someone would sweeten his holiday a little. He had the impression that she was somewhat guarded, as if she suspected danger around every corner. Maybe she had a stressful job and needed to relax for a few days before she would melt a bit.

On the beach below, it took Manley a few minutes to find a free lounger under a palm tree. She spread her towel and settled down. *A drink would be nice now*, she thought. And as if the waiter had been waiting just for

Manley to appear, he suddenly stood next to her and smiled at her.

"Can I get you a drink, Miss?"

Manley smiled back. "You wouldn't happen to have any freshly squeezed orange juice and a sandwich for me, would you?" What would Owen think now? She had barely arrived here and was eating again already. He would definitely be amused. And he would enjoy this free time with her, and he would absolutely be happy for her. With a quick sigh, she chased away the thought.

Manley sat back and enjoyed the sun's rays warming her pale skin. She could not even remember when she had last simply enjoyed a day of rest in the fresh air of an actual planet. After half an hour, however, she had enough and decided to test the waters, hoping they were as refreshing as they looked. Out of the corner of her eye, she saw Michael Blake making himself comfortable on a lounger about 50 yards away from her. He didn't seem to have seen her yet, which in turn meant that he probably hadn't followed her on purpose. Which in turn made him seem a little nicer even. Manley stopped in the shallow water and closed her eyes for a moment. In all likelihood, this was going to be an extremely relaxing holiday. The water was pleasantly warm and lapped at her legs with an inviting splash. Manley waded in further and then submerged herself. A few seconds later she came back up, splashing lazily in the water. She floated for a while, enjoying the sun, before returning to her lounger. She didn't waste a moment with the towel. The water droplets on her skin glistened in the sun and emphasized her slim figure. Manley tried to make eye contact with Michael

Blake, but he had obviously fallen asleep in the meantime. In his place, a passing guest gave her an admiring look. Oh yes, she would definitely enjoy this holiday.

At 7 pm sharp, Michael Blake was waiting for Manley in the hotel foyer. When the door of the lift opened again - he had already been waiting for ten minutes because he couldn't stand waiting in his room any longer - he felt like he was in heaven. There she was, wrapped in a black, shimmering evening gown of semi-transparent fabric that took his breath away and did not make things easy for him in other, more physical ways either. The dress clung to her body as if it had been made just for her. She had put her shiny, red hair up elegantly, only a few strands gently framing around her face.

She gave him a warm smile as he took her hand and breathed a kiss on it. "Good evening, Mr Blake. I see you are awake..." Her eyes glittered mischievously, and she broke into a big grin.

He should have known she would tease him about that. After all, he had only wanted to close his eyes for a few minutes while she was in the water. Unfortunately, he had fallen asleep, and when he woke up, he found her lounger abandoned. "Well, it was so exhausting trying to figure out your first name, I needed some rest", he said.

Manley grinned. "Point taken. Shall we?"

Blake grinned back and let his gaze wander down her body one more time, in a very obvious way. "Shall we what?"

Manley felt herself blushing, unexpectedly. She knew exactly what he was thinking. And if she was honest, she was thinking the same thing. She was thinking about the way his body would move up against hers and the way his hands would make her shiver. She was also thinking about the things that she might do to make him moan not so softly. She bit her lip. She didn't want to give in to him this fast. She hardly knew him, and almost having beaten him up did not count as getting to know each other, even in this part of the galaxy. Also, she had simply spent too much time dressing up to just cave at the first opportunity. "I'm talking about dinner."

"Sure you are", Blake said and offered her his arm. "Well, go on then."

Manley hooked his arm, and together they entered the restaurant where dinner was being served. All the tables were set in white and instead of electric lights, the room was lit by the soft glow of dozens of actual candles, creating an exceedingly romantic mood.

Just what Manley needed right now. She gave Blake a furtive glance when she felt unobserved - and he caught her. She smiled at him and he winked at her, leading her to a table on the terrace that was apparently reserved for them. Blake adjusted her chair and Manley felt a little like she did when... No, she didn't want to think about that now. The moment was too beautiful for that.

She let her eyes wander towards the ocean, the soft sound of waves gently rustling in a natural accompaniment to the music in the background. Nothing in this scene reminded her of the life she was about to leave behind. Nothing reminded her of the horrible things she had seen in the past few months. "Thank you," she whispered in Blake's direction. He didn't say anything, just followed her gaze until the waiter stood next to them with the menus. They were printed on paper in the old-fashioned way and bound in expensive leather. When she opened the menu, something tempting immediately caught her eye — pasta with porcini mushrooms, and even in cream sauce... Manley sighed inwardly with pleasure. This was going to be a very promising start of the night.

The waiter returned after a carefully timed interval, took their orders, nodded his head, and moved away again quietly. Manley turned to Blake. "And what do you do when you're not scaring defenceless women almost to death in hotels?"

Blake held her gaze steadily. "I didn't get the impression you were defenceless." He sipped from his glass of water.

Manley chuckled quietly. This was getting interesting. "Maybe I'm not. You didn't answer my question." She just hoped he wasn't avoiding her question for a sinister reason. Maybe he was an assassin and shared her line of work. Maybe he was one of Claver's henchmen still wanted by Faris. Maybe he was one of the many Privateers whose names she hadn't had the time to learn during the past few months.

"Sorry. I work in a law firm on Hani. Satisfied?" He grinned at her with a provoking wink.

She grinned back. There was no way she was going to let that pitch go by unused. "Not yet. Lawyer or cleaner?"

"Do I have to answer that?" He broke eye contact for a split second, grabbing his drink. Then he settled again, leaning back. "I'm a lawyer alright. Studied on Birdu, got stuck on Hani. Your turn."

Manley hesitated for a moment. He was probably telling the truth. Yet, she couldn't possibly tell him about her life now. She hadn't even run a background check on the handsome stranger on the other side of the table. She'd have to go for a censored version of what had actually happened in her life so far. "I used to be a Privateer, then I worked for ISA, and now I'm just looking for something new. At least when this leave is over." She wondered if he'd buy that.

"That makes you older than you look", he replied dryly.

Manley decided to take his reply as a compliment. "Thank you."

"And why Nergal B?" He looked at her again with that mischievous smile that suggested a clear ulterior motive.

But it took two to tango, and by no means was she a bad dancer. "Well," she replied, "I've heard that the most attractive lawyers can be found here." This comment dripped off Blake like water on the cockpit of her Packet. Not that it rained often in space. But that was the exact effect her remark had. He didn't seem impressed at all, and Manley was wondering whether she might just have ruined her night.

Like being saved by the bell, a plateful of pasta suddenly appeared right under her nose. "Bon appetit," she managed to say before devoting herself entirely to her meal and managing to completely embarrass herself on her first night in front of this image of a man who also possessed (at least a modicum of) manners and decency. This was a treat she hadn't had the pleasure of very often in the past few years.

During the meal, Michael Blake kept looking up furtively from his plate. He was having a steak with potatoes and vegetables on the side, and he was hoping to catch her eye. But whenever he looked up, her gaze was fixed on the meal on her plate. This was strange. He wasn't used to this kind of ignorance, he was used to women trying desperately to catch his attention. He had no choice but to wait until she had finished her meal before she looked at him again. When she finally did, he commented dryly, "I take it you enjoyed that meal."

Manley grinned at him unabashedly. "Indeed I did. It's been a while since the last decent food." The past few weeks and months, there had mainly been rushed fast food in questionable bars and restaurants, if anything at all, while she had been investigating with Owen. Boy, she missed him. She wished she could at least have said goodbye to him, or she could have said something that made him know how much she appreciated his company. Now she would never again get that chance. Owen and Darra were dead, and there would be no second chances with them.

Manley sighed inwardly. Perhaps she should better go straight to her room. Then again, maybe she shouldn't. She was torn between the prospect of spending the night with the man on the opposite side of the table and the prospect of having a long night of peaceful sleep. She hadn't had many of these in the past few months, either. She voted for the quiet night after a few minutes of harmless small talk. There would still be enough time to seduce Michael Blake tomorrow. "Mr Blake, it was really nice to meet you. I'll go up to my room now, the journey today has been quite tiring." Goodness, had she really just said that? Manley could hardly believe it. This sounded wrong even to her own ears.

Yet Blake didn't seem to be thrown off course by that. "Do you mind if I accompany you upstairs?"

Manley shrugged. That wouldn't hurt, after all. She rose from her chair and walked forward, turning the low back of her dress towards him as she did so, completely aware of the effect it had on him. Blake had to pull himself quickly together to avoid an embarrassing situation. He hurried after her, walking the stairs with her. He wondered why she didn't even seem slightly out of breath after seven flights of stairs.

She stopped in front of her door, leaning against it with her full weight. Her heart pounded at the thought of what he might do next. She met his gaze deliberately and took notice of the small laugh lines around them. Blake stopped directly in front of her, his hand gently brushing hers as if by chance, his touch hitting her like an electric shock. She closed her eyes. A soft kiss, like a warm summer day, touched her lips. His body pressed up against hers, making her feel what she had expected from him. Her own stomach felt full of butterflies, and she hadn't felt that in a long time.

Manley thought of the bed beyond that door, of sheets moving over and under two bodies. Trying to retire to her room had been such a stupid idea. He clearly wanted this just as much as she did. But as gently as the kiss had come, it disappeared. When Manley breathlessly opened her eyes again - somehow she had forgotten to breathe - he was gone. He had simply left her standing there. Unbelievable. Manley began to grin. This game was getting more delightful by the minute.

She couldn't wipe the grin off her face as she walked into her room contemplating what she would do with the evening she had started. She let herself sink into the armchair by the window and looked out over the ocean. The possibility of sleep now seemed far away.

So much had happened in these last months. Back when Daxton Faris had sent her to Birdu to investigate Owen's crash, no one, least of all her, had guessed the scale of what was going to happen. But the moment she realised that Claver was deeply involved in the mess, she had found one more motivation. No one but Faris knew that her and Claver's paths had crossed so many years ago, and things had happened then that she could never forgive or forget, even if she wanted to. Her last "encounter" with Claver had changed her life — for the second time–he had been involved in the mission Faris had sent her on with Owen. And she had come face to face with Claver again, but he was been dead when she entered his office in the mansion she had tried to forget for so many years. She had found new friends in Owen and Darra, who had been taken away from her almost immediately. Or had they? Manley didn't know what to believe any more. The image Mr Graham had shown her gave her hope that once again all was not as it seemed. If they were both still alive, they would come forward as soon as they thought it was safe. Until then, she just had to hope that everything would turn out all right.

Manley sighed softly. The sky had darkened and the stars gave the canopy above her a peaceful glow, something that she was glad to see after she had spent most of the last few months on ships in space.

Her thoughts went back to Michael Blake. She had not intended to get involved with anyone this quickly. Could she trust him? Could she ever trust anyone again beyond the physical fun? She sighed. There had been a time when she wouldn't even have thought about seeing him again. She couldn't have risked meeting anyone for a second time. She blamed her past and her training in ISA for checking Blake's background with her personal wrist computer through some not-so-official channels in the following minutes. The story he had given her checked out; apparently he really was who he said he was. Lawyer with his own small firm on Birdu, no record of spouse or children. Workaholic. Good at what he did. No connections at all to Enkil. She stopped reading. She didn't want his whole history right now. She just needed to make sure she could risk allowing him to get a little closer.

She managed to restrain herself for a few minutes longer before searching for Mr Blake's room number. It turned out that his room was almost directly above hers, just one floor up. Manley decided to take that as a hint of fate and made a grab at the bar. She took the bottle of champagne from her room fridge with her and walked up the stairs to Blake's floor. Outside his door, she stopped for a moment and listened. He seemed to be alone, she could hear nothing. Cautiously she knocked. Nothing happened. After a few moments she knocked again, this time a little louder. Then she heard a voice saying, "One moment!"

Inevitably she had to smile. So he was there. Suddenly the door opened in front of her. He was wearing nothing but a towel around his waist. His skin was still wet. She stared at his bare chest for a moment, then her gaze slowly wandered down until she remembered to meet his gaze.

He was grinning at her again. "Ms Manley."

Manley had to clear her throat before she could say another word. "Mr Blake. I thought you might have glasses. For... dessert." She waved with the champagne bottle, clearly aware that she didn't mean the drink.

Blake stepped aside to allow Manley into the room, leaving barely enough space for her to squeeze through. His room looked much like hers, except for the fact that there were men's clothes scattered on several pieces of furniture instead of skirts and bikinis. Hastily, he cleared the small table by the window before thinking better of it. "Why don't we go outside?"

Excellent idea, she thought. Fresh air would help cool things down until she was ready to give in to the attraction.

Blake couldn't believe his luck. He had regretted just leaving at her door after dinner in the meantime. He had noticed how her body had reacted to his touch. She had pressed up against him when he had kissed her, and he had noticed that she held her breath. He was pretty sure that her desire wasn't so very different from his own. Fortunately, the attraction seemed mutual, and here she was. She was still wearing that dress, which made it a challenge for him to control various important parts of his body, and she looked like she had pretty much everything on her mind except talking and crossword puzzles. She briefly turned her delightful back to him as she stepped outside onto the balcony and then gave him a short but very meaningful glance over her shoulder. Elegantly and seductively, she lowered herself into one of the wicker armchairs, crossing her legs in a slow movement that gave Blake a tantalising glimpse of her thigh. When he brought the glasses to the table, he could not take his eyes off her. She leaned forward and opened the bottle expertly. She gestured to him to pour, leaning back again to reveal a little more of her perfect legs.

Manley wondered how many more hints he would need towards what she really wanted? At least he didn't bother putting any more clothes on. Considering Manley's deeply cut-out dress and all the parts of her body that it showed, that was only fair.

He filled both glasses and then took one for himself. "To a... pleasurable holiday", he murmured.

Manley half leaned across the table. She was well aware of the effect of this, following it up by gazing deep into his eyes. "I certainly hope so."

He leaned back and smiled, feeling himself giving in to her charms. Yet, he wasn't too sure about having control over his whole body in this moment, so he tried to stall. "And I've earned this one, that's for sure."

Tell me about it, Manley thought, *tell me about it*... She doubted that his line of work involved people trying to kill him on a regular basis; unlike hers. She didn't give away a hint of this in her response to him, though. "I haven't had a decent holiday in years."

Blake felt his body do something that he might have wanted, but not just yet. He stood up quickly and excused himself. "Just a minute, I'll be right back." He really needed to get his mind off certain things. And above all, he needed to get some blood back into his brain. He practically ran into his bathroom and closed the door behind him. For a moment he leaned breathlessly against it and closed his eyes. He hadn't expected to meet a female being here — or anywhere, for that matter — who turned his head like that. Hell, he didn't know her at all. And yet she seemed to know exactly what was going through his mind, and he couldn't help but figure that she was thinking the same thing.

Manley, meanwhile, sat on the balcony and grinned out into the night. It wasn't really dark with all the stars and no clouds. One of the planet's moons was reflected in the ocean. She had a sneaking suspicion why he had left so quickly. She hadn't been able to see because of the towel, but it was pretty obvious that he felt as attracted to her as she felt to him. The seasoned agent in her shook her head slightly. She couldn't believe what she was doing. Acting just on her physical instincts went against a lot she had learnt during the past 17 years. It went against instincts well-trained and exercised. It went against being cautious and secretive and not letting anyone in. It went against so much she had built in the past 17 years, and yet, it felt perfectly right. She wasn't quite sure what made her act so out of character, considering spending her holiday with just him.

She had a fleeting memory of having acted like this before. In a life far away from the one she was leading now. She had been young and happy, and she had trusted people. She hadn't done this in a while now. So what made her act like a teenaged girl, giggling to herself while she was imagining what she might do with him in that bathroom? She had never felt attracted to a lawyer and complete stranger before like this, and it felt weird.

For the best part of the past 17 years, she had acted on sides of the law no lawyer would or could approve of. She had spied, and she had killed, and she had gone unpunished for all of that because it had happened in the name of the greater good of the public. Actually, it might have been a really good idea if Manley kept away from the lawyer instead of trying to get closer. She would get herself into trouble eventually when she would have to confess what she had really been doing for 17 years of her life. But that day to confess was not today. Today was the day that she would unashamedly hook up with a good-looking stranger simply because she wanted to. Manley silently left her post on the balcony and tiptoed towards Blake's bathroom door, forcing herself to breathe quietly. And then she waited.

Blake, on the other side of the door, was silently contemplating what he was supposed to do next. He certainly knew what he wanted. What he didn't know what whether or not that would be a good idea. While he wasn't the type for a long-time relationship, which was partly due to his jobs and the countless overtime he did, he also saw a lot of betrayal and deceit in his line of work. He was used to only trusting certain people that had earned his trust over time. He knew that his clients mostly weren't telling him the whole truth when they first consulted him. He didn't know whether Manley was telling him the truth about herself and her motives here. He had to make a decision about taking a leap of faith, or to just admit that he would never really know someone the first time he met them.

When Blake had caught his breath and opened his bathroom door again, Manley was standing right in front of him, her face curious. As if she had been waiting for him. And she had. She had been waiting and imagining and anticipating in full colour and grip. She took another step towards him until only a sheet of paper could have fit between their chests. She could feel his body below, his hands gripping her hips and pulling her towards him swiftly and expertly. He knew exactly what he was doing. His touch made her skin tingle, and she felt a familiar sensation rising in her. She lifted her head and looked at him. Without saying a word, their lips moved closer. The tension that had built up between them like electricity began to discharge and multiply as their lips met. Manley let her dress slide to the floor expertly at the same time Blake's towel fell, and before she could take a breath, she found herself on the bed, wrapped around Blake's well-trained body, finally getting what she wanted…

When Manley woke up the next morning, she was feeling a little disoriented. This wasn't her room. And the man next to her wasn't an inflatable luxury gift from the hotel, he was definitely real. Slowly, last night's events started to come back to her. She remembered opening a bottle of champagne, going after Blake when he hid in the bathroom… And after that, events sort of disappeared in a blur. There had been kissing, and more champagne, and — she blushed a little in the semi-darkness. She remembered things she had not enjoyed this much for a while. Yes, there had been encounters with men in the past years. Even pleasurable ones. But not a single one had been this intense, emotionally or physically. Some guys had made her feel good for a couple of nights, and some had just been single-use toys. But Michael Blake had been the first one in a long time to touch something else, beyond the physical pleasure. Oh, and he was good at that. Manley found herself grinning. She wasn't really sure what it was that made her feel so safe with him. By this morning, she was willing to take a chance, so she could find out.

Blake lay with his back to her, still sleeping soundly after last night's exertions. She softly touched the back of his neck, causing him to stir slightly in his sleep. An idea crossed her mind. She snuggled up to him from behind. His soft, warm skin felt good on hers. She moved her right hand under the sheet and to his front. He moaned softly and moved his legs, so she had better access to the body parts she was softly massaging. "It's Dana", she whispered in his ear.

"What?" he mumbled, still half-asleep, clearly enjoying what she was doing.

"My name. It's Dana", she answered in his ear.

Blake yawned, turned his head and grinned at her. "That's good to know. I was afraid I'd have to keep calling you Manley. Also, keep going."

Again, that grin. She grinned back, turned around, removing her hand from what she had been doing, and left the bed.

Michael Blake stared at her naked back while she walked away. This was way too good to be true. He wasn't quite sure he could just get up and follow her, considering what she had been doing before. While he was contemplating this for a few long seconds, she stopped in the doorway and smiled. "If you wanna come", she winked and turned the corner.

Michael Blake could not resist. Nor did he want to. He joined her quickly in the shower without a word. Hands and lips took over, warm water running down their backs.

When Manley switched off the water a good while later, she smiled contently. "What a satisfying way to start a day", she said with the broadest grin. Blake could do nothing but agree. He ordered an extravagant breakfast, which they ate in bed (with another interruption or two) before spending the rest of day on the beach and in the water. And while laws on Nergal B seemed few and far between, there were a couple of passages they quietly did not follow that day. The public place at the beach did nothing to dim their mutual attraction, and at least no one could really see what they were doing in the water with their hands submerged. At least, they managed to leave most of their clothes in place.

Manley couldn't believe how lucky she was. Michael Blake seemed to be not only a joker, but also an extraordinary gentleman who knew exactly how to treat her. He brought her drinks, and more importantly, he brought her little snacks, which she greeted with bright eyes and wide smiles every single time. He brought small, delicious snacks on little colourful plates that piled up next to Manley's lounger as the day went on. Apparently there seemed to be some truth to the claim that the way to a woman's heart went through her stomach. It certainly did with Manley. The shadows of the past few weeks, months, and years seemed to disappear into a gathering mist of forgetfulness. Manley was intent on having a good time, not having it spoilt by memories of things she couldn't change.

Blake was also extremely pleased with the way things were going. He hadn't actually intended to fall in love here, or anywhere for that matter. He had come here to have some non-committal fun with maybe a couple of other tourists, preferably female ones. And then Manley had almost hit him in the chest in the corridor, and she had worked a way into his heart as she did so. There was something about her that made him wish she would never leave. Even though he had only met her yesterday and still knew practically nothing about her, that didn't change his feelings. He handed her another little plate with chocolate-covered fruit and rejoiced in the delighted expression on her face.

She thanked him later that day. With full-bodied effort, even though this probably might have been as much fun for her as it was for him. She pulled him into her room and locked the door with a swift movement. She made him sit on the couch and took off her clothes without a word. They landed in a heap on the floor, beside her shoes. She opened the knot into which she had tied her hair earlier. Her red hair fell on her shoulders, framing her beautiful, happy, excited face again. All of this he watched in quiet amusement. When she came over to the couch, completely naked, he pulled her on his lap and kissed her hard. He held her firmly pressed against his body with one hand and moved the other one downward until she broke free with almost no effort. She slowly moved backwards towards her bed and gestured him to take off his clothes.

Blake complied, careful not to take his eyes off Manley. He threw off his clothes with swift, determined movements and crossed the distance to her in no time. Pulling her up from the bed with one hand, he made sure that their bodies connected without any further delay. He forced his arms under her thighs and heaved her up against the wall beside her bed a little more violently than necessary. "Sorry!"

She shushed him, shaking her head determinedly, and pulled him closer, holding on to him with a lot more strength than someone her size usually had. Before, he had noticed her stamina, which seemed to be above that of the average office agent. He'd have to find out how she hid all that strength in that slender body. But not now. Right now, all that counted was him and her and that inexplicable but powerful connection they seemed to have. He kissed her long and hard and moved his hungry lips across her neckline. She grabbed his hair with her left hand and clearly enjoyed what he was doing. When their erratic, passionate movements were becoming more of a mutual rhythm, Blake carried her back to the bed effortlessly where he let them both carefully slump on the mattress before their passion of hands and lips finally took over their every movement.

Manley threw her head back in pleasure, giving herself over to what he was doing now. Blake was in command in a way that no one had ever been before, and she didn't mind being out of control for once. When it came to the sheer, physical, ecstatic part of this, she could absolutely handle it. And she was certainly entitled to enjoy that someone was actually trying to make her feel good without any hidden agenda. This was just sheer pleasure for him and her, and she wouldn't want it any other way right now. And when she fell asleep in his arms that evening, completely exhausted, she thought she was the luckiest woman in the universe.

Someone shook her by the shoulders. Manley startled up from her sleep, drenched in sweat, gasping. She had trouble placing where she was. She looked up into a man's face. It was Michael Blake. She was on Nergal B, on her holiday.

He looked worried. "What's the matter? I've been trying to get you awake for a while now."

She opened her mouth, but her tongue wouldn't move. Her cheeks were hot and wet, she had been crying. She shook her head. *No*, she thought, *no, no, no, this can't be happening...* She had seen glimpses of faces, people who had died so long ago. She had seen herself running from the killers, running until she had not known where she was. For so long, these memories had left her alone, for so long she had thought she had left the past behind, like an ugly town you only visited once on a holiday that you'd rather not remember. She was still sobbing, willing Michael to hold her by pulling his arm around her waist, until the images in her mind grew paler, disappearing back into the mental box where they were usually locked. She held on to his arm around her for dear life, feeling utterly embarrassed to need his protection but too helpless to let go. "I... I'm sorry," she whispered, "there's a couple of things you don't know about me yet..." She couldn't tell him that she had been the right hand to one of the most powerful men in this part of the galaxy, that she had basically been co-leading ISA with Daxton Faris. She couldn't tell him all the unspeakable things she had done in her years as an agent, all the deaths she had caused and witnessed. She couldn't tell him that she was joining the Faction next month, an organisation the lawyer Blake could hardly approve of.

Blake, locked up in their embrace, wasn't sure what he was supposed to do. He had seen clients cry in his office, men and women, even close to nervous breakdowns. Usually, he handed them tissues and waited for them, politely but firmly, to calm down. Until now, he never had a woman he felt drawn to act so completely out of character, so helpless about herself. He willingly granted her the embrace she so desperately seemed to need after her nightmare. He breathed a kiss on her hair. "Shhhhh, it's alright. I'm right here." Her breathing slowed down eventually. As the new day approached, she fell asleep again, exhausted, in his arms. Her breathing remained shallow, though, her tight muscles never fully relaxing for the rest of her sleep.

Manley's sleep did not last long, nor was it restful. Images from her past haunted her, caught up with her without really exposing the scenes. Forests she had run through. Faces of people she had known, dark rooms she had been caught in. The laser gun connecting to Darren's temple, something she had never even seen. But she heard the orders and the noise of the gun and the sound of Darren's lifeless body as it slumped to the ground.

The next day felt shadowed for Manley. She saw the bright sunlight outside but couldn't bring herself to find it joyful. The light seemed dimmed to her, and she did not touch her breakfast. Even the snacks that Michael brought her lacked aroma. She found herself restless and tired, and her mood was almost anchored at the bottom of the ocean she looked at from her lounger. The palm trees lining the beach were unimpressed, though, seemingly mocking her. Manley kept frowning at the world without even noticing. She couldn't seem to focus her gaze on anything for more than a few seconds. Her head was swirling from all the emotions that were trying to catch a hold of her. Her pulse was racing even though she sat quietly. She felt like she was running from something she could neither hear nor feel, just like she had been so many years ago. She still felt so drawn and connected to Blake who was sitting beside her silently, and yet she couldn't bear the thought of him right now.

She couldn't quite place the confusion. Yes, the past weeks had been stressful, and losing Owen and Darra when she had just started to like them hadn't been easy. But she had been there before. She had seen colleagues and target persons and innocent bystanders die, and while she had been a little shaken after each and every of these deaths, she had not had nightmares about her own past. Not for a long time.

She remembered the first time she had met Faris, back when she had still been in her teens, running into him in the wood and spending the months after with him. She had felt like she was going completely out of her mind after all the things she had been through. She remembered feeling utterly helpless, not knowing what to do next. She even forgot to eat and drink, and he had reminded her constantly to do so. She remembered how she had been sitting on the floor of her small room in the flat she had shared with Faris. It was situated in a safehouse ISA had on Enkil. She had stared at the opposite wall for days, barely taking in enough food and drink to stay awake. Faris had usually closed the blinds for her. For a few weeks, every night, he shut off the light and crawled into bed, making her to join him gently. He had put his arms around her and held her, just held her tight. For just as many weeks, she had not shed a single tear, still in shock, still unable to speak. The sheer exhaustion of keeping up her guard had almost led her over the brink of self-destruction back then.

It wasn't this bad right now, but she felt herself steering in that direction. Yes, other than 17 years ago, she knew she had a decade and a half worth of agent's training. Perhaps she would be able to ride out this wave until the water smoothed out again at her feet. She concentrated on her breathing and pulse, trying to will them to slow down. But the memories flashing up every now and then seemed determined to prove her incapable.

Michael Blake did not ask her questions about what happened last night. He admitted he had been worried when he woke up, finding her in the middle of a nightmare. He knew this was serious. He had been a lawyer long enough to see too many traumatised people. And Dana Manley was certainly traumatised. He didn't know why or when that had happened, but he knew for certain that the cause had to be nothing short of serious crime or injury. So he kept quiet and brought her food and drink from time to time to keep her amused. Except that it didn't work. While the food had brought her honest joy the day before, all it now did was fill her stomach. She looked paler than the days before. Her movements were erratic, her memory unreliable. She didn't care about placing the plates he handed her in a neat little pile like the day before. She put one on top of the other indifferently. She couldn't remember the day or time, he had to remind her several times that it wasn't morning any more. She sat on her lounger and stared at the sea, not moving, not speaking. She seemed to have lost interest in the world. Her eyes were sunken, and her hair had seemingly lost its glow.

Blake noticed that she tried to control her breathing. He also noticed that it didn't work. She couldn't slow it down and was still breathing quicker than someone sitting on a lounger with her kind of training and stamina usually did. Once, he tried to take her hand ever so carefully, but she didn't react, so he kept his respectful distance. He felt like it wasn't a good idea to force physical touch on her now. Watching her carefully from his lounger, he hated how helpless he felt. He hated how unsure he suddenly felt about their connection as she completely cut him off. Had this affair been a good idea after all? Blake wondered what he had got himself into. He contemplated that he had no idea who the shaken redhead on the lounger next to his own really was. He knew she could be funny and sassy and demanding, but she seemed to have a side that had seen or done dark enough things. Things that made her cry and sob after that nightmare.

When the sun started descending towards the horizon and the and the shadows were growing longer, Blake started picking up their things. He would take her up to her room and give her some space. They'd have to vacate the loungers eventually, and he wasn't going to stay out here in the darkness after sunset. After all, this was Nergal B, and you never knew what riff-raff might be about to rip off some tourists.

When she noticed him move about, she looked at him in clear puzzlement, her frown deepening, and her eyes narrowing. He sat down on the edge of her lounger and looked deep into her tired eyes. He wasn't sure if he saw puzzlement, relief, or some deeper distress as he was interrupting her trail of thought. "I'm not sure what last night has done to you. If you want, take your time to recover. I'll take you to your room, you sleep it off. What do you think?"

He wasn't sure what he was expecting from her, but he didn't want their time together to end with a day like the one that was just drawing to a close. He needed to be with her again, after this day was over, after she found a way back to her old self again. He needed to consider they might even see each other again after this holiday. And he couldn't believe that he was starting to think about a future with a red-headed woman he only met two days ago.

Manley squinted her eyes. She didn't seem so sure what she wanted. She didn't look straight at him, rather through him. But she was so tired from sitting with all these emotions, and she nodded. "Thank you."

She moved to pick up her towel and frowned at the plates again that had held all the little snacks. It was a pity she hadn't enjoyed any of them. When they had gathered up their belongings, Blake led the way back to the hotel building and up to her floor. Manley followed him silently, evading eye contact and looking a lot smaller than the days before. He put her key card into her hand when they had reached her door and said, "Good night, dear."

She was about to breathe a kiss on his lips when he moved his head up and kissed her on her forehead. "Not tonight, Dana. Go, sleep it off. I'll still be here tomorrow." He wasn't about to exploit her obvious weakness now for his own pleasure. Manley was in no state of mind to make any consensual decisions about her body. She was probably just feeling a need to numb the pain she was in. Blake had seen this before, and there had been more than one similar offer in his practice. He hadn't accepted a single one, and he wasn't going to start now, not even when they had been intimate before.

Manley accepted his refusal with the relief that at least he seemed to know how to do the right thing. She would sleep off the memories and the confusion, and tomorrow would be better, she was sure. "Will you pick me up for breakfast?" She gave him a smile so weak it was barely recognisable.

Blake nodded. "Will do." With that, he turned and headed up the stairs to his own room.

Manley went in and locked her door when he was gone. She threw the towel in the bathroom and undressed warily, turning on the shower. She longed for the water to burn down on her back before she went to bed. She went into the shower when the steam had started filling the room. The beating of the hot water on her skin made her feel remotely alive again. Tears mingled with the water and steam, and she didn't really know where they came from. She also wasn't sure if the screams were coming from her mind or her mouth. She closed her eyes and remained still, supporting herself on the wall with her forearms, while the gush of water was washing away part of the horror.

The faces in her memories began to slowly drip off her with the water, and the sounds seemed to disappear in the noise the water made when it hit the ground. The images of pain and death in her mind started to slowly fade out, losing their vividness. The scenes receded to the back of her mind again where she had buried them for so many years. The pain she had felt physically in her chest started to dissipate into a soreness that lingered just below her pain threshold. Soon, the only sound was the noise the water made. Her shoulder-length red hair hung down from her head. Her breathing finally slowed down a bit, and she was feeling a little less haunted by her memories from so long ago. She wasn't sure how long she stood like that. At some point in time, she blinked and turned off the water. The bathroom was full of steam. She could barely see the mirror on the opposite wall, and she was sure that she didn't want to see her own reflection right now. She dreaded the sight of puffy eyes and red spots all over her body from the stress of the day.

She dried off her skin and hair a bit and then threw on a loose shirt and underwear for sleep. Her mind suddenly seemed unable to process anything and her head started swirling again. Her hands started trembling, her legs suddenly hurt. Her ribs seemed to cramp, and she found it a lot harder to breathe. She started to see shadows wavering on the edge of her sight, and she knew this was serious. Her body was shutting down from stress and exhaustion and from fighting her instincts to run and hide for a whole day. She had seen this before. She needed rest. She needed to allow her body to calm down, to sleep, to work out the stress hormones and come back to its normal function. Manley quickly let herself fall on her bed and barely managed to pull the duvet around her before she passed out.

A sudden noise startled her from her sleep. Sleep still wafted through her mind, and she wasn't even sure that she was fully awake. She couldn't pinpoint the sound, though it seemed to come from behind her. In an instant, her heart rate shot up again. She held her breath for a few seconds. She opened her eyes, barely noticeable, without moving any other muscle. Her door was open, light streaming in. Someone was there.

Manley decided not to react for now. It would certainly not be in her favour if they found out she was no longer asleep. She heard muffled footsteps behind her. Suddenly someone held a wet cloth in front of her nose. She didn't have to think twice what the biting liquid might be. Chloroforme. She stopped breathing. She needed to be quick now, before her body ran out of oxygen to fight on. In a flash, Manley jumped up and landed with both feet on the floor.

She found herself in the semi-darkness, facing two men dressed in black. Masks hid their faces. If only she had acknowledged her instincts and placed a blaster under her pillow instead of putting them all in the safe. Now she was facing two men seemingly made of pure muscle with her bare hands. On her own. In the middle of the night. Deep breath. Two was a number she could deal with, had dealt with before. Admittedly, with more clothes and a weapon or two, but she knew she could do this. She had to, she couldn't count on anyone coming to help. The sky outside was dark, and she guessed it was the middle of the night. One man moved his head to the left, barely noticeable. Instinctively, Manley jumped towards him and hit him in the nose with the flat of her hand. He held his face in pain and stumbled back while Manley kicked the second one in the chest. Suddenly, she heard a noise behind her and whirled around. Two more men came in. She wasn't quick enough. Before she could react, someone hit her skull with something very hard and heavy, and Manley's world rapidly plunged into impenetrable darkness.

Chapter 3

Day 1

Some indeterminate but significant time later, the darkness enveloping Manley's consciousness began to recede, only to be replaced by the harrowing insistence of a throbbing headache. Her throat was parched, and her stomach felt empty. With considerable effort, she managed to pry her eyes open, revealing a dimly lit, barely furnished room. It offered no decor save for two chairs: one directly in front of her, and the other, to which she was securely bound. Whoever had executed this binding had done so with meticulous expertise; the restraints were unforgiving, and even the slightest movement of her fingers was thwarted. She found herself lacking the strength required to deploy any clever tricks that might liberate her from the thick, unyielding rope encircling her torso, or even the handcuffs. Chopping off her hands to get rid of the shackles was no solution either, and besides, she didn't have a hatchet with her.

In any case, her PAC had evidently been confiscated, as it now lay discarded on the floor a few feet away, showing clear signs of abuse from a rough handling, likely involving attempts to access the ISA channels. Faris, of course, would have changed the frequencies and password encryption after she left the building on her last day, following her resignation and decision to work with the Faction. This didn't imply she was incapable of contacting him, a fact her exceedingly attentive captors were undoubtedly aware of. She couldn't help but ponder who among them had shown such exaggerated concern for her well-being, ensuring she remained upright in her chair during her unconscious state to prevent any injury. Additionally, they were thoughtful enough, having dressed her in a grey overall and sparing her a chill. Remarkably, apart from the persistent ache in her head, she felt no other pain, suggesting they had refrained from further harm until now.

Manley berated herself relentlessly. Why, oh why, had she insisted on taking a holiday before moving on to her new assignment? And what in the galaxy had possessed her to choose Nergal B as her destination? The signs of this trap were now as clear as a supernova, yet she had failed to see them until it was too late. The only plausible explanation was that one of Claver's men orchestrated this scheme, for the public had never linked her name with the events of the past few months involving Claver and Ortiz. Not that her name had ever graced the lips of the public.

From outside, indistinct noises wafted into the room. Unfortunately, the throbbing in her head, now steadily escalating towards outright unbearable, kept her from localising the source. Yet, someone must have noticed that she was awake, for the door on her right suddenly flew open. A black-clad figure appeared. The sudden influx of light momentarily blinded Manley, but she quickly discerned that it was a man—and a rather imposing one at that. The type of man Manley would prefer to avoid encountering alone, unarmed, and in the dark, unless absolutely necessary. He shut the door behind him and sat down on the chair opposite Manley.

"Ms. Manley, I'm glad to see you're awake again." His expression remained neutral.

Manley furrowed her brow. "Why am I not surprised?" Her tone dripped with sarcasm. Her mind began to race. She had never laid eyes on this man before; she couldn't make any connection to any of her cases lately.

"I see, still stubborn." The man exhaled deeply. "I take it you're not inclined to help me acquire classified information through the secret channels of ISA."

The audacity! True, she no longer worked for ISA, but that didn't mean she would betray her former employer, especially not to some runaway coward who had resorted to kidnapping. "Do I really have to answer that?" The disbelief showed in her wide-open eyes and her distinct pronunciation.

"No, you don't. But I thought you might make it a little easier for me. I don't like treating women with violence."

Manley almost had to bite her tongue to keep herself from laughing out loud. "And why don't I believe that?"

The man's expression now changed and hardened into one of severe grimness. "All right. But don't say I didn't warn you." He turned and left the room.

Yet, Manley felt far from safe. He was probably coming back, and he still wouldn't be willing to let her go. She had hardly finished this thought when the door opened again, and the grim man—whom she mentally dubbed Po-Face—re-entered. He swiftly cut the ropes binding her to the chair and yanked her upright, an action that did no favours to her compromised circulation. Evidently, she had been confined to that chair for quite some time, as her knees buckled, sending her sprawling to the floor.

Po-Face seemed unconcerned by her collapse; he simply picked up her PAC—or rather, what remained of it—before returning to her. Insisting roughly, he hauled her to her feet once more. Manley willed her legs to support her, allowing herself to be pushed out of the room. She found herself in a corridor that seemed to stretch endlessly in both directions, lined with doors. No other people could be seen. After a few steps, her captor opened another door and gestured for her to enter. Manley's instincts screamed that this was a bad idea, but Po-Face's demeanour left no room for negotiation.

The new room bore a stark resemblance to the one she had just left, except for the table covered with unfriendly instruments clearly designed for inflicting maximum pain to extract information. The sight did nothing to improve her confounded state of mind. She forced herself to remain calm, drawing on past experiences. She had faced situations like this before and lived to tell the tale; she could do it again. Drawing in a deep breath, Manley steadied herself. Her resolve hardened; whatever awaited her, she would face it. For a second, she pondered grabbing one of the instruments meant for torture and fighting her way out. Then again, there might be a different way. She didn't even know where she was, she needed to gather some more information first.

"Well, Ms. Manley, what do you say?" The man looked at her with an almost gleeful, expectant expression, evidently anticipating a reaction.

And, to be honest, yes, of course, she'd rather be at home in her flat, gazing over the city on a sunny day, but that wouldn't make her betray Faris to some unknown criminal. If only she knew how many men were in this complex, and how to escape unnoticed, or how to get her hands on something that resembled a weapon. She would probably have to take some risks to find out. "Go to hell!" Manley glared at him in anger. She could see that her defiance clearly infuriated him. His forehead changed into a frown, and his eyes narrowed a lot. The large vein at the side of his neck started bulging.

Out of nowhere, two more muscle-bound henchmen appeared—were these guys so scared of her that they needed two men to tie her to a chair?—and did just that. They tied her to the chair opposite the table. This time, however, the restraints were not quite so excessively applied, allowing them to tip her over with the chair and still hurt her in the process. Her mood was not exactly improved by this. The two silent brutes then left the room, but not before ensuring the chair could be easily tipped to her left side. Manley hit something the floor hard with her left shoulder and arm, gasping for air. The soft crack was probably heard only by her. Great. Now her shoulder hurt on top of her headache. She carefully turned her head. There was a curb in the room, and she had narrowly missed it with her head.

Her not-so lovable companion Po-Face stepped up beside her, his boot menacingly close to her face. "I hope that was a lesson to you."

Manley rolled her eyes and bit her tongue, fearing he might kick her in the face.

"Then let me give you a lesson." With a sinister grin, he lifted the chair she was still strapped to and slammed it back down with a violent jerk.

Agony exploded through her shoulder and arm, a fresh wave of searing pain that shot through her body. The force of the impact had wrenched her shoulder brutally, sending sharp, stabbing pains down her arm and causing a dull, throbbing ache to settle into her bones. Her head throbbed in tandem, a cruel pounding that blurred her vision momentarily.

Manley clenched her jaw so tightly it felt like her teeth might crack. She had to fight hard not to let the pain show, not to give him the satisfaction of seeing her break. The effort of maintaining her composure was almost as excruciating as the physical pain itself. Her shoulder felt as if it were on fire, each breath sending fresh jolts of agony through her body. The pain in her arm was a constant, gnawing presence. It was as if a vice was clamping down on her shoulder, squeezing relentlessly.

Manley was really getting fed up. Her patience was wearing thin, her endurance tested to its limits. Yet, beneath the pain and frustration, a she remained determined. She wouldn't break. Not now, not ever. Couldn't these guys just realize they weren't going to get any information from her? Probably not. As devoutly as she could, she listened to her captor.

"I know you were involved in the events surrounding the privateers and Mr. Harlow. You have information that is very valuable to me. If you do not give it to me willingly, I certainly have ways around that." He gestured at the neatly arranged utensils on the table behind him. "Think about it." Then he left, and Manley was alone in the room again.

In another place, at the same time.

Darra glanced down at her PAC, a frown knitting her brow. She turned to Owen. "Owen, did you see this message too?"

Owen looked up from his computer, his curiosity piqued. "What kind of message?"

"A news station is reporting a kidnapping on Nergal B. Seems like a big deal. A hotel guest disappeared overnight, there were signs of a struggle in the room, but no one saw anything."

Owen's frown deepened. "But what does any of this have to do with us?"

Darra's confusion mirrored his own. "I'm not sure", she admitted, her voice tinged with uncertainty. "It's just a feeling..."

"Darra, Angel, as much as I trust your instincts on other things, I don't think we have anything to do with this. This sort of thing happens all the time on Nergal B; people usually turn up sober after a few days... You can keep following it, but I think we should be on our way now." Owen's expression was a blend of reassurance and urgency.

Darra sighed, a hint of resignation in her tone. "You're probably right." She glanced at her instruments again. "I think we're ready." The jump buoy for the hyperspace link to Birdu had appeared on her monitor. She and Owen had some unfinished business with Mr. Faris; he had, after all, promised them regular reports in return for their help. Of course, he hadn't necessarily meant face-to-face reports, but they couldn't be sure who was listening in on the radio frequencies these days.

Owen nodded in agreement, his gaze fixed ahead through the cockpit glass. "Well, let's go. Maybe they've finally found some more of Claver's men."

Darra adjusted the controls, her mind still partially on the news report. The jump buoy's coordinates locked in, and with a final system check, she initiated the jump sequence. The stars outside the cockpit blurred as they entered hyperspace, the familiar hum of the engines a comforting backdrop to her thoughts. Despite Owen's reassurances, she couldn't shake the feeling that the kidnapping on Nergal B was somehow connected to them. The universe had a way of intertwining fates, and Darra had learned to never ignore her instincts, no matter how unlikely their hints seemed.

As the ship surged through hyperspace, she stole a glance at Owen, who was now engrossed in monitoring their trajectory. They had faced so many dangers together, navigated treacherous alliances, and outwitted enemies at every turn. Whatever lay ahead on Birdu, she was confident they would face it with the same persistence and resilience. For now, though, she couldn't help but wonder about the mysterious disappearance on Nergal B and its potential implications for their mission.

***

Blake's night, too, was far from restful. He found himself in a state of half-consciousness, repeatedly shifting from one side to the other. The soothing sound of the ocean waves outside his window offered some solace in the darkness, but he still couldn't sleep. As the first light of dawn filtered through the open balcony door, he finally gave up on the notion of rest. It was too early for breakfast, but he was unable to bear the confines of his room any longer. He swung his legs over the side of the bed, planted his feet on the ground, and quickly dressed for a run along the beach.

The cool morning air and the rhythmic pounding of his feet against the sand slowly helped to clear his mind. Yet, his thoughts kept circling back to the events of the previous day—Manley's nightmare, her shell-shocked behaviour, the trauma that had caused her to freeze. As he splashed through the surf, the water soaking his blue shirt and clinging to his body, he shook his head in frustration. He kept running, determined to work through the confusion. Manley had a past; that much was clear. But everyone did, he reminded himself. He just needed to find a way to connect with her again, to understand her history and help her through it.

Returning to his room, Blake stripped off his wet clothes and stepped into the shower. The same shower where they had shared a passionate moment just days before. He touched the spot on the wall where he had propped her up, feeling a pang of longing mixed with optimism for the day ahead. The warm water cascading over him was rejuvenating, washing away some of his anxiety. After dressing in fresh clothes, he decided to check on Manley. He headed downstairs to her room and knocked gently on the door. "Dana? Are you alright?"

There was no answer. He knocked a little louder. "Dana?" Still no response. "Dana, I've got breakfast," he called, thinking himself clever. But she still didn't answer. Growing concerned, Blake tried to push the door open, but it wouldn't budge. He tried again, harder this time, even throwing his shoulder against the door, which earned him a puzzled glance from an elderly couple passing by. Still, there was no sign of Manley.

Blake paused, anxiety creeping into his bones. Could she have decided to leave without telling him? He quickly dismissed the thought. No, Manley wasn't the type to disappear without a word. They had shared too much in the past few days—too much understanding, too much mutual attraction—for her to simply vanish.

Determined to find answers, Blake collected his thoughts and took the lift down to the lobby. He approached the first receptionist he saw. "Excuse me," he began, his voice tight with worry.

The woman looked up from her computer screen. "Just a moment, please. I'll be with you in a minute."

Blake's fingers drummed impatiently on the reception counter. "This is urgent. I need your help looking for my... friend."

The receptionist, a brunette in her fifties, shot him an irritated look. "I said I'll be with you in a minute."

Blake inhaled sharply, barely containing his frustration. "My friend has disappeared, and I'd like your help to open her room. We need to start looking for her!"

Rolling her eyes, the receptionist met his gaze with a dismissive air. "Wow. Do you have any idea how many times a week I hear this?"

"No, I don't. And I don't care. This isn't your typical drunk-and-asleep case. If you can't help me, please go get someone who can." Blake's voice was growing louder now, and he noticed curious stares from the lobby patrons. He couldn't have cared less.

The receptionist remained unfazed. "Even if you're right, I can't open the door for you. I don't even know if you really know her." She turned back to her screen. She tapped away at the keyboard and didn't look back at him.

Blake felt his patience fraying. He leant closer, his tone low and menacing. "Listen up, sweetheart. I'm going to explain this one more time." He tapped his PAC and wired her a few credits for her efforts. "You are going to hand me a key card that will open room 723, so I can look for my friend Dana Manley."

The receptionist gave him a puzzled look, incredulous. "Do you seriously think you can bribe me?" She paused, then turned and shouted over her shoulder, "Max! I need help!" Her raised voice amplified the scene, drawing even more attention.

Michael Blake would have liked to strangle her. On the spot and very much in opposition to his daily trade as a lawyer. Instead, he kept drumming his fingers on the counter. When said Max appeared, looking bored, he did not wait for the woman to start talking. He jumped right in. "I need a key card for room 723. My friend isn't answering, and she might need medical attention." Change of plans. Desperate circumstances called for desperate measures. "Your colleague here still seems indecisive about what to do." Max looked from Blake to his colleague and back, noticing the crowd in the lobby that was watching the spectacle with ever-growing interest, probably expecting a brawl or at least an arrest. And Max made the only possible decision. "Give it to him.

And send security up with him to have an eye on this." With these words, Max disappeared again, not paying any more attention to the dialogue that had disrupted his routine of checking security monitors in the back of the reception.

The female receptionist handed him the key card with a hostile look. A thin, stoic security guard materialized beside Blake, gesturing silently towards the lifts. They rode up in silence. Each step closer to room 723 feeling like an eternity.

They reached the door, and Blake knocked again, his voice tinged with concern. "Dana, it's me, Michael. Open up! Are you OK?" Still no response. He tried once more, exchanging a worried glance with the guard. "We're coming in." With a determined air, Michael swiped the door with the key card, the lock clicking open. He stepped back, motioning for the armed guard to enter first. "After you, please."

The guard drew his weapon with a practised ease, his movements fluid and precise as he scanned the room for any signs of danger. "Clear," he declared after a few tense moments.

"What do you mean, clear?" Blake inquired cautiously, his anxiety mounting.

The guard emerged from the room, his demeanour oddly casual. "It's empty. There's no one in there."

Empty? Blake peered inside, his heart sinking at the sight of the dishevelled room. The bed was rumpled but unoccupied, Dana's clothes strewn on the floor. He turned to the guard, a plea in his eyes. "Do you mind if I...?"

The guard shrugged indifferently. "I don't care."

"Fine. I need a few minutes." Blake didn't wait for a response, his mind already racing as he stepped into the room. As a seasoned lawyer, he knew he was treading on precarious ground. He scanned the space with a sense of urgency, every moment ticking away like grains of sand in an hourglass.

His eyes darted around the room, searching for any clue that might shed some light on Dana's disappearance. She hadn't eaten here, indicating she had likely retired to bed last night. He approached the wardrobe, noting the locked safe. If someone had come for something she possessed, surely the safe would have been tampered with. No, this was about Dana herself.

Turning his attention to the area around the bed, Blake's trained eye detected the telltale signs of a struggle. The disarray of the pillows and duvet, the overturned lamp on the nightstand—all pointed to a violent fight. He felt a knot of dread tightening in his stomach. Dana had fought someone here, of that there was no doubt. It was only the absence of blood stains that made him feel a little less panicked. If someone had taken her unharmed, she was probably alive.

He checked the bathroom. The towels hung neatly, the shower and basin were dry. Dana hadn't been in here for hours. Panic surged within him again. Something was undeniably wrong.

Turning back to the room, Blake felt a sense of helplessness wash over him. There were no more clues to be found, no answers lurking in the shadows. Dana was gone, and he feared he might be the last person to have seen her. He needed to talk to someone he could trust, someone who could help him make sense of this nightmare.

Chapter 4

In the meantime, Manley had pondered how to react to Po-Face's demands, but she remained resolute *Let him rot*, she thought defiantly. If there was a hell, he surely deserved a front-row seat. Perhaps by now, someone had realised she was missing. She couldn't help but feel a pang of hunger and thirst gnawing at her. Po-Face's tactics were evident—he wanted to weaken her resolve. Yet, she refused to play into his hands. If she were to die of thirst, so be it. But she wouldn't give him the satisfaction.

Her mind raced with thoughts of escape. First, she needed to free herself from the rope. Her left arm protested every movement, the pain radiating through her. The handcuffs presented a particular challenge. But where there's a will, there's a way. She took a chance, knowing she wouldn't be disturbed—there wasn't even a camera in the room, a detail her trained eye had quickly noticed.

With a determined effort, she attempted to shake off the ropes binding her upper body, holding her breath and wriggling against the constraints. After several futile attempts, the ropes finally loosened, albeit agonizingly slowly. It felt like an hour before she was able to free herself completely.

Once on her feet, she scanned the room for a

means to remove the handcuffs. Her gaze landed on a bolt cutter lying on the table—a tool overlooked by Po-Face in his arrogance. She couldn't help but scoff at his oversight. Did he truly believe she wouldn't try to escape?

With a mixture of relief and apprehension, she pondered how to wield the bolt cutter with her hands still restrained. An idea struck her, and she positioned the cutter on the floor, placing the cutting edge against the chain of the handcuffs. With a careful manoeuvre, she pressed down, the metal yielding under the force.

When the chain gave way, she rubbed her wrists, the lingering discomfort a small price to pay for freedom. Yet, she couldn't shake the feeling of unease. This was too easy. She knew the true test lay ahead—getting out of this hellhole unnoticed. The challenge ahead loomed large as Manley prepared to navigate the corridor without detection. Though lacking a blaster, she refused to stop, drawing upon her past experiences to bolster her resolve. She had managed to get out similar situations, she just needed some luck. With cautious determination, she cracked open the door, her senses on high alert. Peering into the dimly lit corridor, she found it empty, and it made her nervous. She knew all too well that danger could materialize from any direction at any moment. She ignored her fear and drew on her desire to escape.

Her longing to return home or resume her holiday fuelled her determination. She needed to find the right door—the one that would lead her to freedom. She set out to explore the corridor before seizing any opportunity or fighting her way out.

Without a moment's hesitation, she stepped into

the corridor, her movements purposeful and confident. As she walked, undisturbed for a few precious minutes, a corridor opening appeared to her left, beckoning like a glimmer of hope in the darkness.

The wall in front of her, however, had been painted with a very well-done image that corresponded very closely to the corridor behind her. Cleverly done, she had to say. She veered left, determined to press onward down the corridor, sparing no more time than necessary in front of the impressive mural. Suddenly, one of the doors right next to her opened. With lightning reflexes, Manley darted behind the door, her heart pounding in her chest, her shoulder flashing pain through her body. Her body stopped the door from banging into the wall. It was just too bad that the man who had been holding that door just a moment ago looked around again and saw a woman behind the door.

In the blink of an eye, Manley had rammed the flat of her right hand into his face quickly and brutally. He slumped to the floor quickly and quietly. Taking a moment to steady her breath, Manley surged forward, her shoulder ablaze with pain.

Then she started walking quickly, ignoring the pain in her shoulder and finally nearing the end of the corridor. She was just wondering how many more of those beautiful murals awaited her when another door opened behind her. This time, she was out of luck. A blaster shot narrowly missed her, the heat singeing her hair and sending her adrenaline into overdrive. She didn't look back and raced, down the corridor, but she didn't get far before the blaster beam hit her in the back. It wasn't particularly strong, but it was painful, so she stopped, posing as an even better target. The gunman behind her hit her a second time, this time on her lower right leg. Agony radiated through her body as she collapsed to the ground, her world spinning out of control. With each painful breath, she wished she had not left the safety of her flat a few days ago. The pain radiated from her lower leg up to her knee and Manley had no choice but to remain exactly where she had just collapsed.

As the gunman closed in, the door next to her opened, revealing a familiar figure looming over her. Po-Face, his presence an unpleasant reminder of her dire situation. His curled lips and his cocked head told her that he obviously found it immensely amusing that Manley was lying defenceless right at his feet.

"Ms. Manley. I should have known," he sneered, his voice dripping with contempt.

Manley's thoughts raced as she struggled to stay conscious despite the pain. Oh, how he should have known. Yet, she remained silent, allowing herself to be dragged to her feet. Manley saw the fist coming, but she had no time to dodge it. And then the world around her went black again, and rather quickly.

Michael Blake paced his room. The gravity of the situation was weighing heavily on his mind. He knew that involving the local authorities would likely lead to a dead end, their indifference a common response to cases like this. No, he needed a more strategic approach. Activating his PAC's private mode, he reached out to Lannister Brown, his trusted colleague and confidant. Lannister's face materialized on the screen, a familiar sight that eased Blake's tension.

"Mike! Back from your holiday so soon? Didn't think you'd abandon the celebration after the Merkin case," Lannister greeted him with a hint of jest, knowing that Blake was probably enjoying himself a lot on Nergal B.

Blake exhaled impatiently. "Nice to see you, too, Lannister. I don't have time for your banter. I need your help." He watched the expression in Lannister's face change from humour to concern. "I met someone and I think she's been kidnapped. Local authorities won't be of much help."

"You met someone?" Lannister echoed

"I met a woman and — it's complicated." Blake shrugged, not knowing where to start telling Lannister that he was in deeper than he had expected.

But Lannister wasn't going to let him off the hook that easily. "You mean you were trying to haggle on the price, and she left."

"It's not like that", Blake was starting to lose his patience. "Seriously, are you willing to help or not?"

Realizing the seriousness of the situation, Lannister nodded solemnly. This wasn't the Blake he knew, he seemed genuinely concerned. "Alright then, sorry. What can I do?"

Blake breathed a sigh of relief. "Thank you. I need everything you can find on a certain Dana Manley. She has ties to the privateers and ISA." As he spoke, he realized how little he actually knew about her.

Lannister frowned ever so slightly, pondering his friend's request. "I'll see what I can find. Do you have any additional information? Anything that might help narrow down the search?"

Blake shook his head, feeling a pang of frustration at his lack of knowledge when it came to Manley's background. "Not much, unfortunately. She's a mystery to me." He paused, catching the mischievous glint in Lannister's eye. "What?"

His friend frowned ever so slightly. "I'm not quite sure. Can you give me anything else? I mean, she must have said a little more than that. What did you-" He stopped and smirked, cutting himself short. "I see."

Shaking his head slightly, Blake breathed in deeply. "I know what you think. It's like that but it also isn't. You've known me long enough to know this can't just be some meaningless fling. If it was, we wouldn't be talking right now." He could certainly see Lannister's point here, and if he was being honest with himself, he would have made the same assumptions,. He knew his own history with women wasn't exactly that of the faithful husband of many years. He looked pleadingly at his friend. "Seriously, Lannister. Remember when you fell for Ayla? I didn't ask any questions and I didn't make fun of you. Please return the favour."

On the other end of the line, Lannister Brown was struck by this appeal. Blake was right. He shouldn't have teased him. That man had been his best friend for the latest part of his life, ever since they had studied law together. "Alright, I'll see what I can do." He paused for a moment. "Promise me one thing."

Blake nodded. "Sure."

"Don't get yourself into anything overly dangerous."

Michael Blake shook his head. "Not planning to. Thank you. Blake out." He pressed a button on his PAC and let out a sigh of relief. Lannister would try and move heaven and hell to help him out. But he'd need a bit of time for his research. And while he might have been a patient man, Michael Blake could not just sit around, doing nothing. He decided to go for a walk to clear his head. Maybe he would find some new angle in this affair.

In the meantime, a certain Bode Parker stood in his dimly lit bar, the Sundown, on the bustling planet Nergal B, watching the news of the day unfold on the flickering screen above the worn black counter. The mysterious case of the tourist who had vanished from her hotel in the dead of night continued to baffle authorities. No clues had yet surfaced. Disappearances like this one were rare, but not unheard of in these parts. Parker, a seasoned observer of the ebb and flow of planetary troubles, paid little heed to it.

The broadcast shifted, detailing a few more arrests linked to the notorious Claver-Ortiz affair, the scandal that had recently rocked the sector. Parker's eyes drifted from the screen, sweeping over his patrons. The last few days had seen a revival of the bar's usual buzz, mirroring the gradual return to normalcy on the planet. The public, it seemed, had begun to shrug off the shock waves of Claver's and Ortiz' treachery, going back into their routines. People wanted to go out for a drink again, and Parker couldn't help but let a faint grin play across his lips.

He recalled a time, mere months ago, when Owen Harlow had stood in this very spot, perhaps pondering his fate. Back then, neither of them could have foreseen the events that were to unfold. Parker's smile faded into a more sombre expression. Owen Harlow would never again grace the Sundown with his presence. His death, though not in vain, seemed a tragically pointless sacrifice in the grand scheme of things. Parker shook his head, shaking off the melancholy. There was no sense in dwelling on Harlow's death now; life, after all, went on. Nothing he said or did would undo the events of the past few months.

Chapter 5

Day 2

Darkness... More pain... Manley was trying to fight the agony when her consciousness returned, but resisting was hard. Her entire body screamed in protest. She lay sprawled on the icy floor, every fibre of her drained of strength. Her memories of the torment she had suffered were fragmented, blurred by waves of relentless pain. She remembered falling unconscious by the brutal force of a blow to her face. When she had first resurfaced to consciousness, her captors had attempted to pry information from her about the ISA channels she knew. Naturally, her responses had not exactly aligned with their expectations.

Thus, the beatings commenced. Initially, she had fought back with all the defiance she could muster, but they were too many, their strength overwhelming. And she had been injured before that. She had struggled to mask the pain shooting through her whole body from her shoulder, to hold onto her resolve. She had not broken, she had not betrayed Faris. Then another man had entered the scene. His face stirred a flicker of recognition within her, yet she couldn't pinpoint the memory.

Manley attempted to open her eyes but managed only to part them slightly, her vision obscured by the dancing black spots that marred her sight. She had certainly seen better days. A sudden recollection flickered to life — there had been someone she was involved not so long ago. If only she could remember who it was. She had lost track of time. She still believed that she was in an underground facility, but this realisation did little to ease her concern. Escape seemed an impossible plan right now, especially when she lacked even the most basic knowledge of her location. Strictly speaking, she didn't even know which planet she was on.

Perhaps that man she had been with, the one whose face and touch lingered on the edge of her memory, would notice her absence and realise she was no longer where she was supposed to be.

Haylen North was on approach, her ship descending through the atmosphere of Nergal B. It was a destination she had not expected to visit again so soon, especially not on her own. Her business partner Dixie had chosen to embark on a solo journey for a few weeks. Haylen understood. They had been inseparable these past few months, but even the closest of friends needed a break from each other every now and then. Dixie was seeking out new opportunities in the clean-up operations on Hadad, hoping to secure a few profitable jobs.

Meanwhile, Haylen had reluctantly agreed to meet Manley on Janus. The agent had evolved from a mere contact to a trusted acquaintance over time. Besides, Manley had made the rare offer of a shared meal, an opportunity Haylen couldn't pass up. Typically, the flow of resources, especially food, was in Manley's direction, not the other way around. This promised encounter was a nice diversion, and Haylen intended to make the most of it.

As her ship neared the bustling planet, Haylen's mind drifted to the events that had led her here lately. The chaos, the betrayals, the alliances forged and broken—all seemed to converge on Nergal B. She could still recall the last time she and Dixie had navigated its slippery underworld, their fates hanging by the thinnest of threads. The thought of Dixie's independent streak both amused and worried her, but she knew that if anyone could handle being on her own, it was Dixie.

The docking procedures initiated, and Haylen felt the familiar hum. The planet's surface came into view. She braced herself for what was about to come after this visit, drawing strength from the knowledge that she was never truly alone. Allies like Manley and the promise of new adventures kept her resolute, ready to face whatever Nergal B and the rest of the galaxy had in store.

The spaceport of Nergal B lay just outside the vibrant pleasure zone, a hub of activity and indulgence. Haylen left her ship in the capable hands of the technicians for refuelling and maintenance, then made her way towards the ferries that shuttled guests to the myriad hotels. Seeking out Manley's hotel, she approached one of the pilots and was redirected to the appropriate colleague with a hint of courtesy.

Boarding the shuttle, Haylen slipped a few extra credits to the pilot, hoping to sweeten his mood. "Will the flight take long?" she inquired.

The pilot cast a quick glance over his shoulder. "About fifteen minutes," he replied curtly before turning back to his instruments.

Moments later, the shuttle took off smoothly, flying gracefully over the sprawling spaceport before gliding across the city. Below, people roamed, seeking entertainment and pleasure, yet Haylen felt no pull to join the bustling crowds. Recent events, marked by several attempts on her life, had significantly dampened her enthusiasm towards people she didn't know.

As the shuttle flew onwards, the glittering hotel complexes by the ocean began to emerge on the horizon. The pilot adjusted course, steering towards one of the grandest structures, which proudly bore the name Seaside Excellence. Descending steadily, he brought the shuttle to a gentle landing at the hotel's entrance.

"We're here. I hope you'll have a pleasant stay," the pilot grumbled.

He was managing more words in a sentence than Haylen had expected. She responded with a grateful smile, appreciating the unexpected politeness, and disembarked, taking in the opulent surroundings of Seaside Excellence. The hotel's name seemed well-deserved, with its sleek architecture and luxurious ambiance promising a time-out from the turmoil she had endured. With a deep breath, she prepared herself for the meeting with Manley. The short walk to the hotel lobby was thankfully covered, as the midday sun was blazing down with a vengeance, scorching Haylen's fair skin. In the shade of the canopy, the temperature was bearable, allowing her to stroll in comfort. She entered the grand lobby of the Seaside Excellence feeling unexpectedly refreshed.

Approaching the reception desk, she encountered a handsome middle-aged man whose polished demeanour suggested professionalism. With a spontaneous smile, Haylen addressed him, "Good afternoon, would you please be so kind as to notify Ms. Manley that Haylen North has arrived?"

As the words left her lips, a whole cascade of expressions flickered across the man's face. His initial broad smile rapidly gave way to a look of horror at the mention of Manley's name, only to be replaced by astonishment and disbelief when he heard "North". This bizarre sequence left Haylen momentarily perplexed. Before the man could phrase a response, she pressed on. "Tell me, do you have a problem with that?"

The receptionist stammered, searching for words. "Well, I... It's... We haven't seen Ms. Manley since yesterday."

Haylen's heart skipped a beat. "Did I get that right? Manley has disappeared?"

The man shifted uncomfortably. "Well, disappeared sounds quite harsh. She just hasn't been seen since..."

Haylen could tell he was holding something back. Her gaze narrowed as she leaned in slightly. "And what else are you not telling me?"

"Not telling?" The man, whose name tag read John Panda, looked as though he wished the ground would swallow him whole.

Haylen's patience was wearing thin. "Listen, John, you can either tell me what you know right now, or I will start a riot the likes of which this hotel has never seen. If you insist, I'll gladly shoot a hole in that really pretty ceiling of yours." She pointed upwards, pushing her jacket slightly aside to reveal her blaster.

That, at last, seemed to make an impression. He motioned her closer. "We've been muzzled. In fact, I'm not supposed to tell anyone anything." He hesitated. "Ms. Manley disappeared on her third night here. In the morning, her room was empty and there were signs of a struggle. So she didn't disappear of her own free will." He looked at her pleadingly. "It would be good if you kept to yourself where you got this information."

Little did Haylen know that a resourceful team of reporters had already spread this across the news channels. "Can you let me into her room?"

John Panda didn't seem thrilled. Haylen pointed to her blaster again. With a resigned sigh, he slid her a coded access card. "Not a word."

Haylen nodded and wired him a small sum of credits for his troubles. Without another word, she turned and headed for the lift. On the seventh floor, she stepped out and walked down the corridor until she found Manley's room number. The door was locked, but the card granted her immediate access. She entered and closed the door quietly behind her.

The room was a chaotic disarray. Manley's bed was a tangled mess of sheets, suggesting she had either neglected to make it—a habit quite typical of her—or she had been taken straight from it. Most of her clothes remained in the wardrobe, while some were scattered across the floor. Haylen was certain that Manley would have taken at least a few essentials if she had left voluntarily.

The safe caught Haylen's eye. It was locked tight. Fortunately, she had come into possession of a useful, albeit illegal, program for her PAC that could decipher the code and open the safe. A few moments later, it yielded, revealing exactly what she had suspected—Manley's blasters. Only the bare essentials, of course, as Manley had planned to be on a holiday. Haylen put the weapons into her own back, intending to return them to her favourite agent when the time came. Surveying the room one last time, Haylen concluded there was nothing more to be done here. It was time to consult with someone who had expertise in this sort of situation, or at least someone with the right connections.

Her thoughts turned to the Sundown, the bar where she had last seen Manley. That previous meeting had been fraught with pain for all involved, the absence of two team members—Owen and Darra—particularly poignant. They had sacrificed their lives to secure a crucial victory, paving the way for the others to continue the fight. Their absence was a heavy burden, because they could not witness Claver's downfall.

Arriving at the Sundown, Haylen found Bode Parker behind the bar, methodically cleaning glasses in the dim light. His face lit up upon recognizing her. "Haylen!"

"Bode." Her tone was serious, not mirroring his enthusiasm. "We need to talk. Is there somewhere we can speak privately?"

Bode's expression shifted to mild puzzlement. "Sure, let's go to the back." He glanced around the empty bar, deciding to lock the front door for the duration of their conversation. "You want a beer?"

Haylen hesitated. It was still early, but after the shock of what she had just learned, she felt she had earned it. She nodded, and Bode drew two glasses, handing one to her. He gestured towards a door behind the bar. "We'll be safe in there."

He led the way through the opening, Haylen following close behind. Once they were both inside, Bode swung the heavy door shut and locked it, securing it with massive bolts to ensure they would not be interrupted.

Haylen gave him an admiring look. "Been in trouble before, haven't ya."

Parker nodded. "Yeah, I—"

"That wasn't a question." Haylen gave him a weak smile. "Let's get down to business. Manley's been kidnapped. Over at the Seaside Excellence." She watched his expression shift from curiosity to wide-eyed disbelief.

"Seaside Excellence, you say?" Parker's mind started racing. The news report about a tourist who had disappeared from a hotel flashed in his memory. He hadn't paid much attention at the time; incidents like that happened about three times a week on Nergal B. "When?" he asked breathlessly.

"Yesterday." Haylen eyed him closely, sensing there was more to this. "What—"

Parker jumped up. "It was on the news! Yesterday! If I had known it was Manley..." He downed his beer in one big gulp.

Haylen narrowed her eyes. "So you knew about this?" She put her blaster in plain sight, a subtle reminder of her seriousness. Either Parker was more foolish than she had thought, or there was much more to this story than she knew.

He looked at her in horror. "No, I didn't! There was a report about a missing tourist at the hotel, no names, no specifics. It happens all the time. How was I supposed to know this was about her?"

Haylen took a moment to think this through. Parker wasn't a traitor. He was a man with a bar who knew a lot of people, but he wasn't a criminal—at least not technically. Haylen inhaled sharply, putting her blaster back into its holster. "I guess you didn't. Now what do we do? We have to find her."

Bode scratched his chin. "Should we tell Faris?"

Faris! Of course! Why hadn't she thought of notifying him herself? Faris had been Manley's boss for a long time. If anyone knew anything that would help find her, it would be him. "Yes. He needs to know. I'm not sure what all of this is about, but he needs to know."

"I'll contact him," Parker said, already getting up from his chair to pick up a medium-sized handheld computer tablet. Faris wouldn't exactly be happy about this, and Parker was trying to figure out for himself what else he could do. He tapped in a contact frequency sequence to reach the head of ISA. This wasn't exactly an official channel, but it wasn't an official matter, either.

It took a couple of long minutes for Faris's face to appear on the screen. He looked just the way he had a few weeks back when they had last seen each other, and he sounded annoyed. "Miss North, Mr. Parker. I wasn't expecting you."

Haylen exchanged a quick glance with Parker. "Nice to see you, too," she shot at the screen, "I'd rather be somewhere else, too. No offence." She looked at Parker, who took half a step back, giving her the space to lead the conversation.

"None taken." Parker still stared at the screen. "Faris, Manley's in trouble."

Faris smirked. "What did she do? Eat a whole buffet on her own?"

Even though the situation was dire, Parker and Haylen found themselves smiling briefly before the weight of the situation settled back in. "No, she hasn't. Actually, we don't know, it's possible, but that isn't why we're contacting you." Haylen paused for a second. "She's been kidnapped from her hotel room here on Nergal B. She was taken by force, and there's no trace of her right now."

As Haylen North spoke, Faris's expression shifted from mild amusement to actual interest. "Has anyone been to her room?"

Haylen nodded. "I searched it. No valuable clues. Whoever took her was a pro. They didn't leave any traces, were probably masked. I don't think there's a point in looking at security footage. I took her blasters for safekeeping."

Faris nodded. "She'll appreciate that. Thank you." He bit his lip, deep in thought. "I'll get my people on this. Don't go out on your own. All of you might be in danger. Stay put until I contact you again." Then he deactivated the channel, and the screen went black.

"I don't think so. I'm not gonna sit here like a duck, waiting for someone to grab me, too. I'll go and try to find out more." Haylen grabbed her blaster from the table, stood, and moved towards Rendler's solid metal door.

Parker watched in amazement as she opened it with the ease of a heavy-duty bodybuilder. Those bolts were heavy, he thought. Even he needed to muster a bit of muscular strength to move them. "Are you sure?"

Haylen looked him in the eye with an expression that allowed no doubt. "I am. I'll find someone who knows at least something. I can't just sit around. I mean, come on, we're talking about Manley."

Bode heard the worry in her voice. During their first meeting, he would never have thought that Haylen North could actually care about anyone except herself. But he had learned that under that arrogant, superficial shell, there was a young woman who was constantly shielding herself from the possibility of being hurt. Deep inside, she cared a great deal about the people they had spent the last months with, investigating the Claver affair. Her unsaid "Manley would do the same for us" hung in the air.

"Alright then. If you need anything, I'll be right here." He wasn't a hero. He wasn't the kind of person who ran to the front lines in a bout of courage. He liked to think things through and provide support from the background. "Be careful. Please."

Haylen nodded. "I will." With that, she turned away from him, fully opened the door, and disappeared from Parker's bar. He walked after her and locked the door again when she was gone. He glanced through the window as far as he could see to both sides, but there was nothing unusual there. Parker sighed. He had the distinct feeling that he was heading directly towards trouble. Again.

Haylen North started walking back towards the shore in the meantime. She was wearing tight black pants and a fitting shirt, along with her loose-fitting grey jacket. She looked like about a hundred other tourists in this part of the planet, and yet she was so different from them. Despite her low-key attire, there was an air of quiet authority that set her apart from the crowds of tourists that populated the area.

As the sole heiress of the formidable North empire, she wielded the immeasurable wealth, influence, and connections that came with her lineage. She carried her responsibility with newfound and determination. For Manley, a trusted ally and friend, she would spare no efforts to make sure that she was safe again.

She pondered the circumstances that had led Manley into danger. The seasoned agent was known for her steely resolve, her unwavering composure in the face of danger. Haylen thought back to their encounters, recalling Manley's cool demeanour, her sharp intellect. Save for the occasional indulgence in culinary delights, Manley approached every situation with calculated precision. Despite the difference in age and experience, Manley had welcomed both Haylen and Dixie into her inner circle with open arms, treating them as equals in their hunt for justice.

As Haylen walked, the buildings grew a less shady and more impressive. Some even showed the wealth and prestige that the tourists had brought. A few minutes later, the Seaside Excellence loomed ahead. For a fleeting moment, she hesitated, her mind confused with questions about the mysteries that lay within its walls. What did Manley do? And what secrets awaited Haylen in her quest for the truth behind Manley's disappearance?

Summoning her resolve, Haylen entered the lobby, looking for anything suspicious. She searched the crowd for familiar faces, but only found people she had never seen before. There was a group of middle-aged women to the side who were dressed scantily, but expensively. Haylen recognised the designer brands. Three couples of different ages were walking in different directions, and she heard clinking glasses and hushed conversations. It could have been a normal day in an expensive hotel, except for the fact that Haylen's friend was missing. Something was very wrong here, and she was going to find out what that was.

As she made her way towards the rear of the lobby, her attention was drawn to a figure standing apart from the crowd, his demeanour in stark contrast to the chatty, happy people she had seen so far. He was dressed in dark attire that accentuated his muscles beneath, and he had an air of quiet intensity. He focused on a conversation over his PAC. Haylen approached cautiously, catching fragments of his murmured dialogue.

"What do you mean, you couldn't find anything on Manley, Lannister?"

Haylen strained to overhear the conversation, her curiosity piqued by the mention of Manley's name. The man with the attractive back spoke with a mix of frustration and urgency. She edged closer, intent on gathering any information that could lead her closer to finding Manley.

She couldn't hear what the other side was saying but the man with the beautiful back said a name she knew. "Yes, Manley. Dana Manley. What's so difficult about that?" He listened again. "I know she was with

ISA, she definitely said that. Did you look in all the sources?" He was silent again. Then his tone changed. "I'm sorry, I know you did. It's just — this is really getting to me, Lannister." He sounded sad suddenly, even a bit desperate.

Haylen kept her distance. She didn't need to know more for now. This guy was clearly involved into whatever happened to Manley. How else would he know her name and that she had been at ISA? Haylen's pulse quickened as she realized the man had to be closely acquainted with Manley, his familiarity raising suspicions about his involvement in her disappearance. She would never have told just anyone about where she worked; after all, didn't secret service agent live a secret life?

As he ended the call and made his way towards the exit, Haylen followed him carefully. She spotted him walking up the stairs — who did that, anyway? But if she wanted to keep up with him, she had no choice. Ascending the staircase in silence, Haylen struggled to keep pace with his brisk stride, her heart pounding in her chest. She made sure he did not notice her following him and walked up floor after floor with him, keeping a safe distance. From flight to flight, she could see his muscles move under his clothing, and she knew she had to be careful. She observed his every move, noting the flow of his motions and the subtle signs of his training. This was no ordinary man; he was disciplined, skilled, and potentially dangerous. Fortunately, he was busy enough with his own thoughts, so he did not notice her. Haylen silently thanked the interior architects for putting thick carpets on the stairs and corridors.

Finally reaching the eighth floor, Haylen watched as he turned the corner and disappeared from her sight. She walked faster, closing the gap between them. As he slowed to swipe his key card, she seized the opportunity to strike, delivering a swift kick to the back of his knees.

As he stumbled forward, Haylen sprang into action, dragging him with her. With a kick of her leg, she shut the door behind them, effectively isolating them from being spotted. She let go of him. Breathing heavily, Haylen faced him, her gaze piercing through him. "Alright, where is she?" Her voice resonated with authority.

Michael Blake met her gaze with a mixture of confusion and defiance, frowning at her. "Who?"

Haylen's brow furrowed in frustration. "Manley. I heard you talking about her. Where is she?" Her tone allowed no room for evasion.

As Blake scrutinized her with a critical eye, he couldn't help but admire the strength hidden beneath her seemingly unassuming figure. Despite her petite frame, he saw the kind of strength and confidence that was hard to ignore. He begrudgingly acknowledged her skill to overwhelm him.

"And who are you?" His voice dripped with scepticism, trying to regain control of the situation.

Haylen returned his scrutiny with a measured look. Her expression was guarded yet resolute. "None of your business." Her response was curt. He didn't need to know who she was.

Blake bristled at her retort, his frustration growing into impatience. "Are you kidding? You drag me in here and ask for her, not even telling me who you are? For all I know, you could be in with the kidnappers." He did nothing to mask his irritation. His patience was wearing thin.

Haylen's brows furrowed in frustration. She had not expected this kind of response. "So we finally have something in common," she remarked dryly, gesturing towards the table. "Let me get this straight. I have no idea who you are, what you want and where we're going from here."

Haylen took a seat, her movements deliberate as she placed her blaster on the table with a resolute thud. It was a silent assertion that she was willing and able to fight him, that she should not to be underestimated. Gathering her thoughts, she decided to take a risk, revealing her identity in a bid to get his cooperation. "I'm Manley's friend. My name's Haylen North. Manley and I had an appointment, and I found out she's missing. I heard you talking about her in the lobby and assumed you know something at least," she explained, her voice steady, yet tense.

Blake blinked in astonishment. "North? Haylen North?" he repeated, his mind racing to process her words. It was a name he had heard before, a name synonymous with power and influence.

"Yes. It's a long story," Haylen replied softly, her tone tinged with weariness as she recounted their shared history. "Manley and I have worked together during the Claver-Ortiz affair."

Blake suddenly felt like this was blowing way out of proportion. Just a minute ago, he had been a lovestruck lawyer in an expensive hotel with a woman missing. Now this apparently was North's daughter right in front of him, and she was telling him that Manley had had something to do with the gigantic mess named the Claver affair he had heard about on the news channels. His head spun with the implications of her words, the gravity of the situation weighing heavily upon him. He realized, with a sinking feeling, that he suddenly found himself entangled in a web of danger far beyond his usual circles. Maybe Manley's caution had been warranted, he mused, his thoughts torn between speculation and self-recrimination. He had taken her silence about her job for granted, dismissing it as typical behaviour in her line of work. Now it seemed that she was in a mess a lot deeper than he had thought.

Lost in his reverie, he glanced up to find Haylen regarding him with a mix of concern and curiosity. "Are you okay?" she inquired, her voice soft with genuine concern.

Her question pulled him back to the present, and he struggled to find the right words. Blake blinked, his mind racing to catch up with the conversation. "Yes. No. I'm not sure. She's missing. I went to her room and she was gone."

"I know," Haylen said, feeling a sudden surge of compassion. He really seemed to be affected by Manley's disappearance. Then she remembered that she still had no idea about his identity. "By the way, who are you?"

He winced, cursing himself for his lack of manners. "I'm sorry. My name is Michael Blake. I'm a lawyer."

This discovery sparked a glimmer of hope in Haylen's mind. A lawyer could be a valuable asset in their quest to find Manley. "What did she do to need a lawyer?" she asked, a hint of amusement curling the corners of her lips as she considered possibilities. The image of Manley single-handedly eating the contents an entire buffet briefly flashed in her mind.

Blake could sense Haylen's curiosity, her gaze searching for answers he wasn't sure he was ready to give. But she seemed genuinely concerned for the woman who had brought them together in this unexpected moment.

"We had a casual... involvement," Blake finally confessed, the muscles in his back and neck tensing. He met Haylen's gaze, silently pleading for understanding.

Haylen took his reply in, her mind racing to make sense of Blake's revelation. She had always viewed Manley as fiercely independent, only married to her work with little time for personal entanglements. The idea of the tough agent having a casual involvement seemed in conflict with the image Haylen had constructed in her mind. "How casual exactly?" Haylen cocked her head a bit and tried to imagine what he meant.

"Casual and not so casual. And before you ask — yes, it was physical and consensual," Blake continued. He frowned slightly. This conversation was some somehow turning into an interrogation, and he seemed to be on the wrong side of it.

Haylen watched Blake with a mixture of curiosity and admiration. His grey shirt was tucked into his pants not-so-neatly, and it was unbuttoned at the top, baring his neckline. Haylen guessed that his torso was just as beefy as his legs and back. She chuckled silently. Having a personal involvement with a man like Blake wasn't something she would decline herself. His tousled blond hair and dishevelled appearance hid a strength and confidence that she found intriguing. She couldn't help but envy Manley for her personal involvement with a man like Blake.

"I see," Haylen responded, her tone measured as she processed the information he had shared. Yet, his confession only served to raise more questions, each one more pressing than the last. "So why weren't you with her when she was kidnapped, considering all that wild, personal, physical involvement?" she asked, curiosity and concern lacing her words.

"Valid question," Blake acknowledged, sensing where her question was leading. He leaned back in his chair, contemplating his response carefully. "She had a nightmare the night before and was acting odd all day. She hardly spoke, she acted like a traumatized victim of a crime. I've seen enough people act like that to know not to push. I took her up to her room and told her to sleep it off. She agreed, that's how I left her."

Haylen nodded thoughtfully, agreeing with Blake's approach. "Sounds sensible so far," she conceded. Her curiosity was not quite satisfied, though. "What happened then?"

Blake's expression darkened. "I don't know. When I wanted to pick her up from her room for breakfast the next morning, she was gone. Have you been to her room? I found signs of a struggle. Probably at least two attackers, and she gave them a good fight. By the way, where did she learn that?"

Haylen furrowed her brow, sensing that she would have to tread with care now. "Learn what?"

"The fighting. She's trained. And not just your average office-lady-with-a-training-area-trained. Why?"

Haylen weighed her words carefully, deciding it might be best to enlist Blake's cooperation. "You're right. She's been working with the head of ISA.

Helped us a lot during the Claver affair. I'm sure you heard about that on the news."

Blake nodded. In his head, thoughts started swirling, but he knew better than to interrupt the woman opposite him.

"Well, I met her a few months ago, and she's been really resourceful. We thought she was an assistant who could just help to get us every piece of information and material that we needed. Turns out she was Faris's most valuable agent, probably even with a killer agent training. She was the one who actually found Claver dead. She headed the team." Haylen paused before admitting something else. "I don't know much more about her. Hell, I don't even know where she lived or what she wore outside work." She could not believe it. Apparently, they had overlooked so many things. "We could probably ask Faris."

Faris. Daxton Faris. He had heard that name before. "The head of ISA?" Blake heard an alarm sound in his head. Obviously, he was getting himself into something big he didn't fully comprehend.

Haylen nodded. "Yes. I've contacted him already, he knows she's disappeared. What he doesn't know is that you're the last one who saw her alive." She looked around. The room was nice, definitely one of the better rooms she had seen in a long time. The bed was neatly made, apparently the maids had been in today already. She found everything in place, even down to a delicate floral arrangement. "We don't know who else is watching. We can't stay here. We need a safe place. I know where we can go."

They had to return to the Sundown and seek refuge with Bode Parker for the time being. It was their best shot at safety. They could bide their time there, waiting for reinforcements to arrive. Haylen was uncertain who these reinforcements would be or from where they would come, but one thing was clear—if the individuals behind Manley's disappearance could locate a secret service agent on a well-deserved holiday, they would undoubtedly find Haylen North asking around the planet. "Let's go."

Blake hesitated, doubt etched on his face. He wasn't sure if he should go with her, but her tone left little room for argument. She was almost insisting nicely. "Where are we going?" he inquired, rising from the table and moving towards the wardrobe that was built into the wall seamlessly.

Haylen stood as well, her posture tense with urgency. "Leave your things. I'll get you new ones. We don't know if they put any tracking devices on yours, and we don't have time to check. We'll just leave as we are." She began to move, her footsteps silent on the thick carpet. Then, as if struck by a sudden thought, she paused and turned back to face Blake. "What were you talking about down in the lobby? And with whom? When I heard you mention Manley's name."

Her voice carried that familiar tone of cross-examination she was so good at. Blake felt a flicker of defensiveness but answered steadily, "I was talking to my friend Lannister. He's a lawyer, too, and he knows people. I had asked him to look her up. He found nothing."

Haylen's frown deepened, her head tilting slightly. She felt curiosity mixing with suspicion now. "What do you mean, nothing?"

"There's nothing on public record about her. No birth certificate, no CV, no nothing. And Lannister's really good at looking into things like this. He even used some... semi-legal channels with people I don't want to know about, but they turned up with nothing, either. It's like she doesn't exist."

His words hung in the air, casting a new problem on their situation. How would they find someone who wasn't supposed to be found? This couldn't be. Manley was a real person. She might have been an ISA agent, but a skilled lawyer not finding even the slightest hint? "So you're telling me we're hitting a dead end here? That's it?" Haylen's disbelief showed in her frown and she shook her head slightly. There had to be a way to find Manley's trail before it grew even colder than it already was. She refused to believe that Manley was lost forever.

Blake shook his head. "I don't think so. Apparently we both know her by the same name, that's gotta be good for something."

Hear, hear. The good-looking lawyer wasn't only trained physically; he was also clever. "That's right. Come on, we're leaving. We need to talk to Faris. But not from here; we need a safe place." Haylen motioned for him to follow her.

"Where are we going?" He walked up to her, concern etched into his features. "How do I know I'm not the next one to disappear?"

Haylen sighed. She couldn't even resent Blake's mistrust. "You don't. But believe me, if I had wanted you to disappear, you'd be gone by now. Remember? I'm a North."

Michael had to admit she was probably telling the truth. Her family name carried weight, and she likely had unlimited access to resources and people beyond his imagination. "Alright. Let's go. Where?"

Haylen cast one last glance around the room, her eyes sweeping over every corner as if committing it to memory. "Out of here. This isn't a safe place." She moved with quiet determination, her steps precise and purposeful. She turned and left the room, her movements fluid and silent. She carefully avoided the lifts in the corridor, knowing she and Blake could be watched or trapped in them. The stairs were hardly used in a hotel like this, and they managed to reach the ground floor without meeting anyone.

"Darra, my angel, you are right as usual." Owen activated the frequency to ISA and hoped that Daxton Faris was not on leave and had an uncomprehending representative. After a few seconds, Faris's face appeared on the PAC's small monitor. Owen greeted him like an old friend. "Mr. Faris, good to see you."

Faris seemed equally pleased, if a little surprised. "I'm happy to return that, Mr. Harlow, even though I wasn't expecting you yet."

"You know, I would have liked to spare you that as well, but we have a problem. Manley has disappeared. Her PAC isn't transmitting, and I'm really worried. Surely you haven't been able to catch all of Claver's men yet, have you?"

Faris's expression darkened, the frown on his face deepening with concern. "I know. Bode Parker and Haylen North have contacted me already. She's the most recent person missing from the hotel on Nergal B. Do you think it's possible that one of Claver's men is behind this?"

Faris had heard about this? And hadn't contacted him? Owen's head was spinning. The news report. Darra had been right. As always. Unbelievable. Owen shook his head, trying to clear his frustration. "I don't know, but it's possible. But that would also mean there's a leak somewhere that gave Manley away. The thing with Claver's men was just my first idea, too. Why else would anyone make Manley disappear?"

"That's true," Faris acknowledged, his voice tinged with concern. "I'm already looking for the leak. You go find Manley. And I'd appreciate it if we could keep this matter between us. The thing with Claver has raised enough questions already. We couldn't do with a repeat right now."

Owen nodded, feeling a weight settle down heavily on his shoulders. "I understand. Harlow out." He ended the connection and turned to Darra, who was just re-entering the room. "What does the hotel say?"

Darra shrugged her shoulders, a gesture of helpless frustration. "She hasn't been seen there for a whole day. The last time anyone noticed her she was at the beach with a Michael Blake. She hasn't been seen after that."

Owen frowned. Manley with a man? He had never seen her with a man. Not in private, anyway. All right, she had been on holiday. That could explain a lot but not that her PAC didn't even send a signal or confirm receipt of a message any more. He would probably have to talk to this Michael Blake she had been with. Maybe he had something to do with it, or maybe he had seen something that would help him and Darra find Manley. He refused to believe she was already dead. Whatever whoever wanted from her, they wouldn't get it from Manley without resistance.

Manley was tough; he had found that out, too. She would gamble that someone would miss her.

Owen shook his head, feeling his emotions running high. Though he was madly in love with Darra, he felt strangely protective of Manley. He had put her in danger more than once during their joint investigation. He could neither name nor place the feelings he had for the tall redhead, but he knew they were totally different from the ones he had for Darra. He felt responsible for Manley, though in a different way than he felt for the woman by his side.

It was time to leave for Nergal B. Owen packed up the essentials for his search: blaster, PAC, some clothes, the analyser Manley had gifted him, the list of key ISA frequencies, another blaster, and, not forgetting, a spare blaster in case the other two gave out. As he prepared to depart, he picked up Darra, who had already packed without a word. Together, they walked the short distance to the spaceport where Owen's hunter was stationed. After the usual formalities, they boarded and took off, setting their course for Nergal B, leaving Birdu behind in their urgent quest to find Manley.

Just a few minutes into their journey, Darra and Owen were en route to the next jumping point to get to Nergal B from there. During the Claver affair, Manley had initially been an extremely helpful ally, simplifying so many aspects of their mission. There was no piece of vital information she couldn't find, no piece of equipment she didn't turn up with. But over the months, a real bond of trust and friendship had grown between them. Neither Owen nor Darra were remotely willing to give her up until they had seen her dead body. Manley was resilient; she would find a way to muddle through.

The jumping point slowly came into view. Owen glanced briefly over at Darra, who sat silently at her controls, her eyes fixed on the monitors. When she felt his gaze, she looked up briefly and nodded at him. "All clear, Owen. Ready for hyperspace." The jump buoy was a few hundred meters away.

Owen took a deep breath, the weight of their mission pressing down on him. "Initiate," he said, his voice steady. Darra's fingers danced over the controls, and the ship hummed in response. The stars outside the viewport stretched into silent streaks of light as they entered hyperspace.

As the ship settled into the smooth rhythm of hyperspace travel, Owen allowed himself a moment of reflection. The events of the past days had been a whirlwind, but now they had a clear objective. They had been busy cleaning up silently after themselves, making everyone believing that they were dead. But now, they were going to search for Manley, and they wouldn't stop until they had her back safe and sound. He turned to Darra, who was monitoring the systems with quiet ease. "We'll find her," he mutter, more to himself than to her.

Darra looked up, her eyes meeting his with unwavering determination. "We will," she said, her voice tinged with quiet determination. "Manley is strong. She'll pull through."

Owen nodded, feeling a renewed sense of purpose. A few minutes later, they dropped out of hyperspace. Ahead of them, Nergal B spun lazily in the vast expanse of space. Owen quickly picked up their landing clearance before they started their descent into the atmosphere. As the hunter touched down on the floor of the spaceport, Owen and Darra jumped up and grabbed their gear. Owen confirmed the landing and instructed the spaceport boy to take a look at the hyperspace drive. They left the hangar and headed for the transit ferry into town, where they intended to pay a visit to Bode Parker, a dear old friend, and probably rent a room there while they were at it. Then they would make their way to Manley's hotel and have a conversation with said Michael Blake.

"Owen?" Darra looked at him questioningly.

"Yes?" Owen looked back.

"Bode knows we're coming, doesn't he?"

Owen nodded. "I've sent him a message. Unless his PAC is also out of business, he should have it."

Darra frowned at him. "That's not funny, Owen."

Owen's dire expression mirrored her concern. "I know, Darra. I'm just trying to deal with the situation."

The Sundown still looked as hopeless as the last time Owen had been there. Fortunately, it was still early, so there were only a few remnants of the previous night outside the door—in other words: four drunks who probably wouldn't make it home on their own feet before mid-afternoon. The front door was still locked, and Owen knocked loudly. After a small share of an eternity, or so it seemed, Darra heard footsteps approaching the door from inside. Intuitively, she reached for her gun, but let it go again when a man she knew opened the door. It really was Bode Parker. Darra relaxed again.

"Owen!" Parker seemed genuinely pleased. Well, that would possibly change soon.

"Bode, we haven't got much time. Let's go in," Owen urged.

Bode looked from Owen to Darra—she nodded—and back again. "Well," he said. He stepped aside, closed the door behind them and dove behind the bar to whip out one of his well-known bottles for celebrating "good old days." He gave Owen a conspiratorial look. "I have a hunch why you're here. Let's go to the back." Bode motioned towards the room where Haylen North and Michael Blake were waiting.

Owen whistled. "Well, let's hear it, old chap."

Bode grabbed the bottle from the counter and added five glasses. "It's about Manley, isn't it?"

Owen and Darra exchanged puzzled glances. "How do you know?"

Bode had stepped into the back room by now, revealing Haylen North and Michael Blake. Parker filled the glasses with an indefinable liquid before answering. "Well, you're not the first people to look for her. We haven't been able to get anything more out of the hotel. Either they really don't know anything, or a lot of money was involved."

Darra and Owen were torn between the joy of seeing Haylen and Bode alive and disbelief that they, too, were looking for Manley. Owen's eyes narrowed as he took in the room. "And who's this?" he pointed at Blake before anyone could ask any questions as to how he was still alive.

Blake didn't wait for anyone else to introduce him. He remained seated but looked sternly at Owen and Darra. "I'm the one who saw her last. We had some... involvements. Michael Blake."

Owen raised an eyebrow. "Involvements?" he repeated, his voice edged with scepticism. "Care to elaborate?"

Blake's jaw tightened, and he took a deep breath before speaking. "Manley and I were... close. We spent a lot of time together."

Haylen stepped forward, her eyes sharp with determination. "We've been trying to piece together her movements, but everything's been a dead end. The hotel staff either know nothing or are being paid to keep quiet. We need to figure out who's behind this."

This was getting more intriguing by the minute for Owen. "So you're the last one who saw her alive." He straightened his shoulders, appearing a bit taller, and challenged Blake with his gaze.

"Yes, I am." Blake did not blink. He knew where this was leading. "And no, I have nothing to do with her disappearance."

Owen didn't buy it. "Easy for you to say. For all I know, you might as well be in with the kidnappers." He watched Blake closely, his eyes looking for signs of uncertainty.

Michael shrugged. "Sure. That's why I've been sitting in this hellhole waiting for people to throw inappropriate questions at me in a really impolite way. Just to keep my cover intact, when I could have just left the planet." He was growing a little tired of all this mistrust. The only crime he could admit to was having left her alone in her room, something he could hardly have seen as a danger. He looked at Bode Parker. "No offence meant."

"None taken." The lawyer was feisty, Parker had to give him that. Blake stood up to Owen without even standing.

But Blake wasn't finished. "God forbid I might actually care about the woman." He took up Owen's stare, his eyes blazing with intensity. "I don't know who you are, either. Hell, for all I know, you might as well be in with the kidnappers."

Silence fell like a heavy curtain, stopping any movement. Haylen watched the scene with a mixture of awe and apprehension. The lawyer had some nerve. She hadn't seen anyone lately who had confronted Owen like that and lived to tell the tale. Tension crackled in the air, thickening with each passing moment. The two men staring at each other could not have been more different right now. Owen, with his black hair pulled back into a long, carefully bound ponytail, exuded a quiet intensity, his black leather jacket adding to his air of mystery. He might not have had the bulging muscles of a typical brawler, but there was a coiled strength in his stance that spoke volumes.

Opposite him, Blake still sat at the table, his short blond hair catching the faint light filtering through the dusty windows. His bare arms rested casually on the table, revealing the wiry muscles beneath his expensive shirt. Despite his relaxed stance, there was an unmistakable air of confidence about him, a silent challenge in his body. She knew Blake was about a head taller than Owen. With the expensive shirt he was wearing, he didn't look like he would usually be seen around the Sundown. His bare arms rested on the table, and his look was defiant.

Neither Haylen nor Darra dared to break the silence, their eyes darting between the two men. Bode Parker, wise enough to recognize the brewing storm, chose to stay out of the conversation. He had no doubt that in a physical confrontation, the lawyer would emerge victorious. The way Blake had moved when he came into the bar showed that his body had been trained for years.

As Darra silently observed Blake, she couldn't help but notice his undeniable attractiveness. There was something magnetic about him, something that drew her gaze despite the tension in the room. She was starting to understand what had drawn Manley to him, aside from his striking good looks. But now was not the time for this trail of thought.

Michael Blake had finally had enough. With a decisive push of his chair, he crossed the room to confront Owen head-on. Standing toe-to-toe with the seasoned buccaneer, he held his ground, his voice determined, yet tinged with frustration. "I don't care what you think about me. If you think you can do this without me, go ahead. Go find someone else who saw her here and who can actually tell you something."

His words hung in the air, supporting his defiance. Owen felt a surge of adrenaline course through him, his heart quickening at the challenge. Manley had been more than just a colleague; she had been a friend, a trusted ally. Memories flooded Owen's mind—of late nights spent searching for information in old files, of Manley's stubborn determination in the face of danger. Manley was a friend. She had been there for him when he needed her most, her resourcefulness and quick thinking often saving the day. Despite their age difference, Owen had grown fond of her, a paternal instinct driving him to shield her from harm. He glanced at Darra, silently acknowledging the unspoken bond they shared over their concern for Manley's well-being.

Some women he had known in the course of his life would have been wild with jealousy. He felt the need to protect Manley from harm, and he knew he had failed her. And he felt he was about to fail her again if he didn't start giving this lawyer guy at least a chance. As Michael's glare bore into him, Owen realised that he couldn't let his personal feelings cloud his judgment. Manley's fate hung in the balance, and he needed to put aside his disbelief and focus on the task at hand. With a short, resigned snort, Owen gestured for Michael to take a seat. "Alright. Sit. Talk me through it. What happened?"

Blake decided not to push his luck with Owen. The guy seemed to have a genuine concern for Manley. As he broke the stare and returned to his seat at the table, he couldn't shake the feeling of being the outsider in this gathering. The others seemed to regard Owen with a mixture of respect and deference, leaving Blake feeling like an intruder in their midst.

Reaching for one of the glasses Parker had filled with the mysterious dark liquid, Blake slid it across the table to Owen. He then grabbed another glass for himself and downed its contents in one swift gulp, the liquid burning a fiery trail down his throat. Slamming the glass back onto the table, he steeled himself to recount his version of events. "I met Manley the day she arrived," he began, his voice tinged with a hint of nostalgia. "We had a chance encounter at a corner. We felt attracted to each other. I invited her to dinner, and she accepted."

Owen nodded, his expression unreadable. "She always did have a weakness for good food. What did she eat?"

Blake frowned slightly at the question, but he chose to humour Owen for the sake of the conversation. "She ordered some kind of pasta with mushrooms and cream sauce."

"Sounds just like her," Owen remarked with a faint smile. "Continue."

Feeling a mixture of frustration and resignation, Blake went ahead with his narrative. "After dinner, I walked her back to her door. We shared a kiss, and I left her, thinking we had all the time in the world. But later that night, she sought me out."

There was tension in the air as Blake hesitated, unsure of how much detail to disclose. He felt the weight of everyone's gaze upon him, their silent question making him squirm uncomfortably. "We spent the night together and the following day. The night after that, she had a nightmare. She only woke up when I shook her not so carefully. She was very different after that," he admitted reluctantly.

"Different how?" Owen's voice resonated with concern, his gaze piercing the lawyer decidedly.

Michael Blake carefully chose his next words, acutely aware of the weight they carried. "When I first met her, she was vivacious, cocky, funny—full of life. But after the nightmare, she hardly spoke, didn't comment on the food I brought her. It was like she was a different person altogether. I've seen this happen to people before, usually in the aftermath of trauma. Or renewed trauma. Since we never really got to discuss what happened in her life—what happened to her? What do you know about her?"

There was a moment of silence as Owen pondered Blake's words, his brow furrowing in deep thought. "I'm not sure," he admitted. "We've worked together for several months, but we always saw her at ISA. She was always on duty—I'm not even sure she left the agency to sleep. We never talked about her private life, if she had one." Owen paused, then added with a note of determination, "If she has one. But there's gotta be something we're missing here. I can't imagine her being anything but strong and confident. She's always been like that with us."

Blake let out a heavy sigh, the weight of the situation pressing down on him. "Believe me, she wasn't any of that when I last saw her," he confessed quietly. "I spent a day sitting beside her not saying a word. She just sat there and stared at the ocean. She didn't even register the food I brought her."

At Blake's revelation, Owen lifted his gaze from the table, his eyes showing a mix of concern and confusion. "She didn't eat?" he repeated, deep disbelief colouring his tone.

Blake couldn't help but feel a bit of annoyance at the obsession with Manley's eating habits. "Now what's with her and food?" he asked, a touch of frustration in his voice. "Everyone seems to feel the need to comment on her eating—or lack thereof."

Haylen and Darra exchanged amused glances, a shared understanding passing between them. It was Darra who spoke up first, her voice laced with subtle humour. "Well, to us, it seemed as if eating was her only passion. Besides her work," she remarked with a mischievous twinkle in her eye. Pausing for effect, she fixed Blake with a pointed look, her lips curling into a teasing grin. "Which now doesn't seem to be true."

Blake couldn't help but chuckle at Darra's playful jab, a cheeky smile playing at the corners of his lips. "No, it isn't," he conceded, deciding not to press further on the matter.

Meanwhile, Owen repeated his earlier question, his brow furrowing with concern. "She didn't eat?"

"That's not it. She ate," Blake clarified, his tone sombre. "She just didn't seem to enjoy it. And she made no sounds while eating. It was strange—considering our first dinner together, she was making cute, content, little noises. After the nightmare, it was as if she had lost all pleasure in the simple act of eating."

Blake continued to recount the events leading up to Manley's disappearance. He described how he had offered to escort her back to her room, his concern evident in his every word. He spoke of his reluctance to take advantage of her vulnerable state. As he delved deeper into the story, Blake talked about his efforts to locate Manley, from his inconclusive search of her room to his desperate plea for assistance from Lannister. He even recounted the confrontation with Haylen.

Owen listened in silence, his mind racing with questions and uncertainties. Despite his initial scepticism, he couldn't shake the feeling that Blake's concern for Manley was genuine. There was something about the lawyer's demeanour that resonated with him. In that moment, Owen couldn't help but feel a pang of sorrow, a fatherly instinct stirring within him. He was scrutinizing Blake not as a suspect, but as a potential ally in their quest to uncover the mystery of Manley's disappearance. As he pondered the great amount of unanswered questions swirling around them, Owen couldn't shake the gnawing sense of unease that gripped him. What had happened to Manley? And who was responsible for her sudden disappearance?

Blake directed his gaze at the black-haired man on the other side of the table. "Owen?"

Owen met his gaze, his expression attentive. "Yes?"

"What is this about? Does it have to do with the Claver Ortiz affair?" Blake's patience was wearing thin, his fingers tapping impatiently on the table surface. He hadn't anticipated having to plead his case to win over the trust of the group. He had assumed it would be simpler to join their search efforts.

Owen shook his head, frowning in contemplation. "I'm not sure. It's possible, but we'll need to find the connection first. You mentioned your friend..."

"Lannister. Lannister Brown," Blake threw in, eager to assist in any way he could.

"Yes, Lannister," Owen continued. "You mentioned he didn't find anything about her. Not even a birth certificate."

Blake nodded solemnly. "That's correct. There was no trace of her existence—no birth certificate, no official records. It's highly unusual. There must be something in her past that we aren't aware of. She said something like that after the nightmare. She mentioned that there was a lot I didn't know about her yet."

Silence fell for a few breath as everyone was pondering what the redhead might have meant by that. Blake pre-empted any further questions from Owen. "No, she didn't elaborate. That was the last thing she said before she asked me to pick her up for breakfast that evening. She remained silent for the rest of the day. I have no clue what she meant by that."

A collective frown settled on the faces of those gathered around the table. This was going to be difficult. Haylen was the first to break the silence. "It seems we have one more mystery to solve. We thought we knew her, but it turns out there's much more to Manley than meets the eye."

Owen, Darra, Haylen, Bode Parker, and Michael Blake exchanged meaningful glances, each processing the situation in their own way. Owen broke the tense silence, voicing everyone's concern. "Wouldn't Faris know? I mean, she's been with ISA for ages. If anyone has insight, it's him."

Blake re-entered the conversation, eager to get this investigation going. "The head of ISA? So Manley was like his assistant or something?" He struggled to reconcile the image of Manley as an administrative figure; she seemed far more suited for action than paperwork.

Everyone shaking head was the answer. "No, I don't think so", Darra said. "I had the impression she's a top agent in the disguise of an office leader. She was very adept at gathering intelligence and leading critical missions. She could find any kind of information, get us any equipment we needed. That makes her way more than a simple assistant. She was the one leading the team that found Claver dead in his office. I don't think a simple office assistant would be allowed to do that."

"Yeah, I've heard about that", Blake said.

"From whom?" Owen looked inquiringly.

Blake's gaze wandered towards Haylen.

"I see." Owen looked at her too, his gaze lightly irritated.

Haylen suddenly felt uneasy, though she didn't quite know why. "We were talking. I had to give him something. Come on, I brought you the guy who last saw her alive. Apart from the kidnappers, I mean. That's gotta count for something here."

"I know, it's fine." Owen rubbed his forehead and looked back to Blake. "We need to talk to Faris. He has to know something about her past that might shed some light on this." He looked towards Bode Parker. "Can we use your screen?"

Parker shrugged. "Sure. Feel free. But I suggest we seal off the room before you get started. You never know who else might be listening." With a swift motion, he moved to secure the door and activated his privacy protocols.

Owen nodded in agreement. "Good call, Bode." He stood and helped him close the door and shield the room. Then he sat and took the screen Bode handed him. He tapped a few commands and called Faris on a channel that wasn't exactly listed on the official charts. It took Faris a while to reply. When he logged on, he looked over his shoulder like he was checking on someone or something. "Owen. What did you find?"

"Are you alone?"

Faris frowned. "Yes, I am. I've just locked my door so no one can disturb us."

Owen nodded. "Good. I'm here with Darra, Haylen, Bode Parker and a lawyer named Michael Blake. He's the last one to see Manley alive."

"Interesting enough. What does he know?" Faris was speaking about Blake.

"He sure doesn't know where she is. But he tells us she had a nightmare and that she said there were a lot of things he didn't know about her yet. So what is it that she wasn't telling him?" Owen felt apprehensive. They were closing in on what this was about, he was sure. If anyone knew, it was Faris.

Faris shook his head. "I wouldn't know where to start." Then he fell silent.

Owen wasn't sure he had understood correctly. "What are you saying?"

"I'm saying that 17 years is a long time."

"17 years?" Owen asked back.

Faris's gaze was unmoved. "She's worked for me for 17 years, until a few weeks ago. She left. She's joining the Faction."

Faris's revelation sent a ripple of astonishment through the room. Owen exchanged a glance with Darra, his mind racing to process the implications of Faris's words. "She's worked for you for 17 years? And she's joining the Faction?" His voice sounded strong with disbelief.

Faris's expression remained unreadable. "You heard me. She left my employ a few weeks ago."

Owen's mind burned with questions. "But why? What prompted her to leave ISA after all this time?" His voice now betrayed a mixture of concern and confusion. He could not believe that the red-headed agent would just up and leave her agency after all that he'd been through with her.

Faris's response was cryptic. "I wish I could hand you a clear answer, Owen."

Owen felt that Faris was stalling. "Did anything happen in that time that would have caused her to be traumatised?"

"Traumatised?" Faris looked puzzled, glancing over his shoulder again for a second. "Traumatised how?"

This was going in a direction Owen didn't like. Faris wasn't really answering questions. "She acted traumatised according to the lawyer. Didn't speak, hardly ate. Just sat there for a day, staring at the ocean. Does that sound like something Manley would do?" Owen was feeling impatience rise in himself.

Shaking his bare head, Faris answered, "No, that doesn't sound like her at all." And then he left it at that. He was doing something with his hands, but Owen couldn't see them, he only saw the movement of Faris's muscles in his arms.

"So you have no idea what might have triggered that sort of behaviour?" Owen slowly but surely felt his blood pressure rise when Faris shook his head. "Listen, I need the whole story. We can't find her without knowing her history. We can't turn every piece of rock in the galaxy." Owen's jaw clenched as he struggled to contain his mounting frustration. "Faris, we're talking about a woman's life here. If you know anything—anything at all—that could help us find her, you have to tell us."

Owen watched Faris breathe in and out a few times. His opposite seemed to struggle with something without wanting to share was it was. Then the man on the other side of the screen straightened his shoulders and said, "She was quite young when she joined us, 17 years old. That was 17 years ago. I'm not sure what she did before that. There's nothing in her file. And we've never talked about it."

Owen frowned. "So you're saying you know nothing about her from before her time in ISA?" He couldn't believe what Faris said. He could have sworn that Faris knew something. After all, Manley had been working for him for so long. Usually, with that kind of time, people talked about more that just the weather and yesterday's meals. Even considering that yesterday's meals meant a great deal to Manley.

Faris shrugged. "I know that she'd been placed in a witness protection programme, but I don't have the details. And I didn't ask questions. Witness protection isn't something that's triggered easily. She wasn't in good shape when she started working for us, but with time, she became one of our best assets, if not the best."

"Assets? Really? You're calling her an asset?" Owen felt like the man he was talking to was a different one than a few weeks ago, even yesterday.

"Yes, I'm calling her an asset. Boy, Owen, you don't even know half of her. She killed people for a living, she's a trained agent, one of the best. You never saw most of what she's really capable of. She's made so many enemies over the years, you'll need some time to figure out which one's after her now." Faris looked annoyed that he had to give Owen this speech. "Listen, I'm grateful you're out looking for her but technically, this isn't even my problem. She doesn't work for me any more."

Owen couldn't believe what he had just heard. "Come on, Faris, don't you tell me she doesn't mean anything to you. I know that technically you're not supposed to care." He paused. "I'm not buying it. I know you care." From all he had seen a few weeks ago, Manley had been his personal protégée, more than just a simple employee. There had been a connection between them, a tie that went far beyond their work relationship. He didn't know what it was, but he knew he could trust his knowledge of human nature.

Faris shook his head slightly but otherwise did not let anything on. His expression had gone back to neutral. "That's not it. I can't justify sacrificing time and people to go out looking for her. We're sort of busy wrapping up the Claver thing. Still. You stirred up quite a lot of things and people there."

Owen exhaled through his teeth, the tension gripping his gut. The uneasiness crawled up his legs, refusing to let go. "There's gotta be something you can do. We'll scour the sector for her, dig for any scrap of information about where she might be and who could have taken her. Please, have someone delve into her past. We need to understand what she was talking about after that nightmare."

"I'll see what I can do." Faris paused, his expression tense, as if on the brink of revealing something monumental. Instead, he simply added, "Go find her. Faris out."

With that, Faris vanished, and the screen went black, leaving the room shrouded in a silence. Blake stood motionless, replaying the conversation in his head. He had witnessed countless cross-examinations and inquiries in his time; something about this didn't sit right. Faris was hiding something—Blake could feel it in his bones. The way Faris had spoken made him question if this was the same man the others had described. They had painted Faris as a paternal figure who would move heaven and earth to find Manley. Yet here he was, unsure if he could even spare the time to look into her disappearance. The difference in behaviour was unfathomable, casting Faris in a far different light than the gracious godfather figure he had expected. Blake hesitated, unsure if it was his place to voice his suspicions. Fortunately, someone else did.

"Is it just me, or did Faris just act differently?" Haylen's voice was sharp with irritation. She had anticipated Faris diving in head first, mobilizing every resource at his disposal. At the very least, she had expected him to care about his "valuable asset." This wasn't the man she remembered.

"Indifferently. Isn't that what you're trying to say?" Darra interjected, her voice a bit shriller than before. "I can't believe he doesn't care what happens to her. I don't get it."

Owen remained seated in front of the blank screen, his mind racing with a storm of questions. This didn't make sense. Why was Faris behaving so uncharacteristically? There had to be something Owen was missing, something Faris was deliberately withholding. Was it possible that other senators were entangled in the Claver affair, demanding his attention? Or perhaps there were threats lurking in this corner of the galaxy that Faris knew about, but Owen did not. His thoughts spiralled, each new possibility growing more troubling. He abruptly stopped himself—this line of thinking was getting him nowhere. "So we're on our own here," he stated, saying what everyone probably thought. His eyes fell on Darra, who seemed unwavering, his pillar of strength. He knew she would back him up on whatever course of action he proposed next, even though he wasn't sure what that would be.

Blake broke the silence, shifting his chair with an eerie scrape against the floor. "Faris is hiding something." His voice carried a careful accusation, aware that the others might see it as an affront. "I've seen a lot of people act like that—usually when they're concealing something personal or something critical to the case, protecting themselves."

Haylen agreed. "This wasn't the Faris I know. There has to be more to this story than what he just told us." She jumped up from her chair, her impatience making her pace the room with restless energy. "I can't believe he isn't telling us the truth."

The air seemed to sizzle with their shared suspicions. Owen felt a resolve harden within him. The mission to find Manley had just taken on a new dimension. Not only did they have to locate her, but they also needed to uncover whatever secrets Faris was keeping. His gaze swept over his companions, reading the determination in their eyes.

Darra clicked her tongue and crossed her legs the other way, the leather of her pants making a slight sound. "Seems like we can't rely on his help right now."

Blake exhaled with relief. At least he wasn't alone in sensing the betrayal. Faris knew something crucial, and he had chosen to keep it from them. They would have to find the truth themselves. Together. He glanced at Owen, who was still looking at the now-dark screen. "We need to start digging. Fast. We still have no idea where she is or who has her."

Finally, Owen broke his gaze from the screen and addressed the room. "Yes. Yes, we need to. Haylen, you go with Blake. I don't care what you have to do or who you have to bribe, find out how she left the planet. I'll go back to Enkil and hunt through the archives with Darra. Bode."

Parker snapped back to reality. "Yes."

"Keep your eyes and ears open. I know you don't like going off the grid, but maybe you can find out more from the underworld here," Owen said.

Parker nodded. "Will do. I have a few contacts I'll try to activate for some old favours."

"That's what I'm talking about, Bode. Thanks." He turned back to the others. "We need to move fast. I suggest we head straight for the spaceport, Darra. Haylen, Blake, I'll keep you posted. Let me know when you find something."

Haylen and Blake nodded in unison. "Of course."

With that, Owen rose from his chair. "Ladies and gentlemen, it's been good to see you. Let's get going." Darra stood and joined him while Bode Parker shut down the seal and opened the room door. Darra and Owen left without another word, knowing they had a long trip ahead.

Blake and Haylen left the Sundown, too, but not without thanking Parker for the sanctuary. "We'll be in touch. Thanks for the safe place."

Parker shrugged. "You're welcome. Go find her."

Haylen squeezed his shoulder slightly as she passed. "We will, Parker. We will." She only wished she felt as optimistic as she sounded.

Chapter 6

Day 3

Manley woke up with a jolt. She could hardly feel her fingers any more; the rope binding her hands behind her back was slowly, but surely cutting off the blood flow. Whoever had tied her up had made sure she wasn't going anywhere this time. The man with the high voice was still lurking in the shadows, just beyond the harsh glare of the lamp that was directed at her. Summoning what little strength she had, she spoke up. "So, is there anything I can do for you? I mean, as long as it doesn't involve moving around too much."

The man chuckled, a chilling sound that echoed in the dimly lit room. "You're truly unbelievable, Dana. You know very well what I want."

She nodded, her voice steady despite the fear gnawing at her insides. "I do. And still, I can't help you. All the information I have is outdated. In case no one has told you, I quit ISA weeks ago. They must've changed the frequencies about a dozen times since then. Don't tell me you think they left them open just for me." She glared into the darkness, trying to project more confidence than she felt. If she had to die here, she might as well go down fighting. Right now, the odds of escaping on her own seemed grim.

She was far too weak and injured to put up much of a fight. And given the meticulous precautions her captors had taken, it was clear they had no intention of letting her walk away.

"I see." The high-pitched voice behind the lamp remained unmoved. The man it belonged to stepped out of the darkness, and Manley finally saw his face. It was a face she had seen before, a long time ago, on another planet, in not-so-different circumstances. But it couldn't be. Claver was dead; she was the one who had found his body. This was impossible.

Apparently, he could see the turmoil in her eyes. "You're wondering how I can be here. Well, I'm not. Or at least, not the one you think I am. My father is dead, as you well know. I'm Landon Claver. It's so good to see you again." His voice was dripping with sarcasm as the corners of his lips curled into a cruel smile.

Manley closed her eyes as images flashed before her mind's eye. Claver, Darren, the gun—17 years ago. She felt herself being sucked into a vortex of memories. She was 17 years younger, feeling 17 years more helpless. She had made mistakes back then, seen crimes she should not have witnessed. Together with Darren, she had seen Claver kill two men, and Darren had paid for that knowledge with his life while she had managed to escape. She blinked furiously, dragging herself back to the present. This would not be dragging her down right now. Everything clicked into place. "You're the little brat Darren doted on. You're his friend." How had she not seen this? How could she have been so careless? "You're the one who shot Darren. You let me run and hide in the ISA, so you could have a sleeper when you needed one. And all this time, I thought I managed to get away."

She closed her eyes and took a shallow breath. A single tear slid silently down her cheek. Her ribs ached from the kicks she had endured earlier. Apparently, she had misjudged the situation 17 years ago—thoroughly misjudged it. She had thought she could forget what had happened. She had wanted to forget—the death, the pain, all that she had endured in the aftermath of Darren's murder. But it seemed she wasn't allowed to forget. She could only hope someone like Faris or Blake, the man from the hotel, was on the right track by now, out there looking for her. She knew he was. He had to be.

Claver Jr. smiled and twirled his blaster playfully. "Now we're on the same side." He seemed to revel a lot in the power he held over a woman who was cuffed and bound to a chair, injured, and in no condition to fight back.

"I seriously doubt that," Manley spat. "So you're going to kill me. That isn't going to help you. And it won't bring your father back."

Claver's smile grew wider, and Manley didn't like it at all. "No, it won't. But when your friends get here for your rescue, I can kill them all one by one and save you for last. And no one will ever know. It's almost a pity." He paused, savouring the moment. "You know, Amy, you're as beautiful a bait as you were 17 years ago."

Manley closed her eyes, overwhelmed by a crashing wave of emotion she couldn't name. She hadn't heard that name from anyone alive in a very long time. Hearing it now almost caused her physical pain, amplifying the agony already coursing through her body. Darren had been one of the last to use her childhood name, shouting it as he urged her frantically to run. She decided not to react to Claver's deliberate provocation. She opened her eyes again and stared at Claver, hatred burning brightly in her gaze. "You were a spoiled brat back then, and you haven't grown a bit. You're not getting away with this. They'll find out."

Claver chuckled. "Oh, I'm counting on that. I'm also counting on them rushing in here. I mean, who wouldn't come and save you after all that you've done for them in the past months?" He smiled sardonically. "It's taking them long enough to add one and one. I mean, come on. How difficult can it be to find that picture from that reception 17 years ago?"

Manley was trying really hard not to give away what went on in her head. So Claver had placed clues for her friends to find. Someone would eventually make the connection. The vital question was whether they could physically locate her, given the scant information. She assumed she wasn't on Nergal B any more. There were no underground structures on that planet. She knew some from her investigations and missions on Enkil, Birdu, Ashur, and Hadad. That didn't exactly narrow things down. This place didn't look familiar. Or did it? It was probably a location she hadn't worked in before; she usually remembered those.

Her thoughts drifted back to the tumultuous events of seventeen years ago. So much had happened since then, time and experience gradually clouding those distant memories. She could scarcely recall the reception—after all, she had been only sixteen or seventeen at the time. Receptions had hardly been a priority. Back then, her world had revolved around Darren, the boy from school with whom she had been madly in love. She had dreamed of marriage, a notion her parents had vehemently opposed. She had been so young, so naïve, knowing little of the world's complexities. Now, despite all she had learned, she wasn't sure she understood much more than she had as a teenager.

"Speechless, Amy?" Claver's sardonic grin remained fixed. He seemed to celebrate his apparent upper hand, lounging casually on the edge of the table, his eyes glinting with amusement.

Manley met his gaze with unwavering determination. "Amy has been dead for seventeen years. You killed her that day." She paused, letting the words settle. "Tell me, how did you get me into ISA? I'm curious. Witness protection for someone you placed there after you were done committing the crimes? It's an intriguing concept."

Claver looked down at her, his grin never faltering. "At first, it was a stroke of luck that you ran into Faris in the woods. It made things a lot easier. Later, we had help from the senate."

The senate. A dark realization began to take shape in her mind, an uncanny truth she knew she wouldn't like. Yet, she needed to hear it from him. She needed to understand fully. "Come on, you can tell me. It's not like I'm getting out of here alive, is it?" She held his gaze, her determination challenging him.

Claver's eyes flickered with something unspoken, a momentary shadow crossing his facial expression before his composure returned. "No, it isn't," he admitted, his voice a cold whisper that sent shivers down her spine. And then he took the bait she had laid out for him to swallow. "You see, Senator Ortiz hasn't only recently started to expand his business on the semi-legal side."

For the first time in this conversation, Manley was grateful that her face was somewhat contorted from the pain her injuries gave anyway. Otherwise, her shock might have shown in her face. What Claver proposed bordered on the realm of madness. Ortiz must have had some other help. He had hardly been older than Manley himself, and he hadn't survived his recent involvement in the affair around Claver's father. Did Claver really think she would believe this? A teenager couldn't have pulled off a stunt like killing Darren and placing her in witness protections with the Secret Service. Yet, she maintained her composure, veiling her disbelief behind a facade of collectedness. "I see," she murmured, a single phrase that masked the scepticism brewing within her. It was miracle enough that he had told her.

Claver seemed content with her obvious puzzlement. "Well, I'll leave you to ponder this for a while. I have a couple of business meetings in my office. I'll be back." And with that, he turned and left the room without further ado. As the weighty door thudded shut behind him, the chamber was plunged into darkness, save for the feeble glow from the lamp in the corner. Before Manley could decide which side of her neck muscles she was going to overstretch falling asleep this time, three men entered the room. With swift efficiency, they dismantled the threatening array of tools and replaced them with more benign furnishings — a mattress, a blanket, and a tray laden with a bit of food and drink. Manley's confusion was complete. Were they preparing to make camp alongside her in this room? Were they setting up camp with her? "So guys, what's it gonna be? Are we sharing lodgings tonight? Double twin room for four?" she asked in a desperate attempt to prove some humour.

No one answered. The men exchanged amused looks. The tallest among them, an impressive figure wielding a knife, approached her swiftly. Despite being a decade her junior, his physical presence loomed large. She wouldn't want to be in a fight with him right now. Actually, she wouldn't want to be in a fight with anyone just now, considering the injuries she had sustained over the past few days. How many? She had even lost count of the days, and injuries. She had no idea how much time had passed since she had been knocked out on Nergal B. Clearly, it had been a while. But she didn't know if it was a couple of days or two weeks. The young brute came closer with the knife and while Manley expected it at her throat any second, he simply cut the ropes and took them with him. Then he left, followed by the others, locking her up on her own without any other intervention.

Manley exhaled audibly. She had not even noticed that she held her breath. She had to fight with all her willpower not to fall off the chair she was no longer bound to. Her muscles were too weak to support her body weight right now, and slowly she slid off the chair, collapsing onto the floor in slow-motion, thankfully landing on her right side. She lay there resting for a while before the pain ebbed away, knowing that she couldn't stay on the cold floor. She would succumb to hypothermia in no time, given her present state of injury.

She decided to take the chance and crawl towards the mattress that had been placed about six feet away from her. Each inch of that distance felt like a marathon right now. Manley pulled her legs under her torso, wincing as she tried to push herself onto all fours. The broken bones in her left shoulder protested wildly, sending sharp jolts of pain with every movement. She lifted her left hand off the floor again and held it close to her torso, breathing in and out to steady herself against the blackness wavering at the edge of her sight.

With her legs and one arm, she somehow made it to the mattress. The soft fabric felt like it was literally from the other end of the galaxy, and she let her body melt right into it, savouring the massive relief it offered. With her good right hand and arm, she managed to pull the blanket around herself. It almost felt like an embrace, a small comfort in her desperate situation.

She wondered if she would ever see Michael Blake again. Right, that was his name. She had expected a fun holiday, and for the first two days, he had certainly delivered that. What had he done when he noticed her missing? Had he noticed? She shook her head inwardly. He must have noticed. He would have wanted to pick her up for breakfast, just as he had promised. And he would have noticed that she wasn't answering the door. But then? The images in her head didn't get any clearer. She had no idea what he would have done next. He was a lawyer, alright, so he knew something about law enforcement. But—law and enforcement on a planet like Nergal B were things that didn't go together naturally.

Manley sighed carefully, wincing at the sharp pain

that followed. She couldn't breathe in too deeply without aggravating her injuries. She felt a slight shiver run down her back, unsure whether it came from the cold of the room, her memories of Michael Blake and all the things they had done together, or the simple fact that she couldn't remember when she had eaten last. Food! They had left food on the tray. Manley opened her eyes again, looking longingly at the tray just out of reach of her outstretched arm. She couldn't get there; it was just too hard right now. She closed her eyes again, surrendering to the darkness that quickly approached, hoping against hope that someone would find her before it was too late.

Chapter 7

Darra projected the images onto the massive screen. "Take a look," she instructed, her tone urgent.

Owen stared at the display, bewildered. The screen depicted two scenes from an opulent social event. Attendees were adorned in formal attire; the women in resplendent gowns that shimmered under the lights. His eyes wandered over the familiar faces: Claver, three women, and four other men, all beaming towards the camera, champagne glasses raised in celebration. The photographs were clearly a decade old, annotated with coordinates pinpointing a location somewhere in the Northern Hemisphere of Enkil. Owen squinted, still at a loss. "What exactly am I supposed to be seeing?"

"The girl on the far right," Darra prompted, her patience wearing thin.

Owen's gaze darted back to the images, then to the coordinates, and back again. He couldn't piece it together. He fiddled absently with the trigger of his blaster. "I'm not seeing the connection. How does this fit into our narrative?"

Darra stepped closer, her finger jabbing at the smaller image. "Focus on her. Look closely." She wondered what was clouding his judgment today. Normally, he would have realised long ago. Clearly, today was far from normal. "It's Manley. On the far right. Younger, with longer hair, different colour. But unmistakably her."

Owen rubbed his eyes and leaned in, scrutinizing the image. "Damn, you're right. It really is her. But what's she doing in a picture with Claver?"

Darra's exhale was heavy with exasperation, nearly a sigh. "Let me spell it out for you, since you're clearly off your game. Dana Manley isn't who we thought she was. Her real name is Amy Carter, and she has a history with Claver that's been kept from us until now. Claver's family found her, and they're exacting their revenge on her. Do you understand now? We need to move quickly if we're going to save her. I'd rather not have to return her remains to Blake and face his wrath."

Oh, for heaven's sake. This was it. This was what he had not seen. Owen felt a sudden clarity, as if a fog had lifted. Manley had mostly been a means to an end in his eyes, a useful help in his mission to take down Claver and his organization. He had never considered her as a person with a past, with her own battles to fight. "I never realized… I just thought she was…" He trailed off, shaking his head. "We need to go. Now."

"Now you're talking, sweetheart," Darra almost sang, her voice dripping with a mix of urgency and allure. "I'm warming up the engines. We need to get back to Nergal B, and fast. Tell Haylen we're en route."

Owen shook his head slightly, a smirk playing on his lips as he glanced at her. "Tell me, who made you the boss around here?"

Darra's smile was deep and sensuous, a smile that never failed to touch his heart and stir something primal within him. "Oh honey, I've been the boss for a long time." She touched a few buttons with clear precision. "Want to call Faris now?"

Owen hesitated. Daxton Faris had been increasingly unpredictable of late. When they had expected the ISA commander to leap to their aid in locating Manley, Faris had inexplicably declined. Owen wasn't confident that he would be any more cooperative now. "I'm not sure. But we need to find out if he knows more than he's letting on about this."

Darra nodded, arranging the connection. She agreed that they needed to pry whatever secrets Faris was hiding from them. When Faris appeared on the small screen, at least he didn't look as irritated as the last time they spoke. "Owen. Darra. What've you got?"

Owen and Darra exchanged a quick, meaningful glance. Darra nodded slightly, encouraging him to proceed. Owen took a deep breath. "We found something. Something curious."

Faris's interest piqued visibly. "What is it?"

Owen exhaled slowly, steadying himself. "Manley and Claver knew each other before all of this began."

Faris's expression shifted, but Owen couldn't quite decipher the emotion behind it. "They knew each other?"

It took every ounce of Owen's self-control not to scream at the man on the other side of the screen. Faris was lucky that Owen couldn't punch him now, because that was exactly what was going through Owen's mind. "Yes, they knew each other. And you knew." He paused as Faris opened his mouth to respond, cutting him off sharply. "Don't you dare say you didn't know. It's a disgrace." Owen stopped, his heart pounding. He needed to see what Faris would do next. He needed to know if Faris was still the man he thought he was.

Faris felt trapped between a rock and a hard place. Owen and Darra had likely uncovered the missing piece of the puzzle, the piece he had desperately hoped would remain hidden. The cover story about the witness protection program hadn't fooled Owen's crew, and there was no point in pretending he didn't understand what Owen was talking about.

"I know," he admitted, pausing to summon the courage to tell the necessary story. "Manley is actually Amy Carter. She witnessed Claver kill two men seventeen years ago. Those men were part of my first command, and that mission ended in complete disaster. Manley's family was close with Claver, and she had been watching from outside a window with her boyfriend. She screamed, they got caught, and Claver executed the boyfriend but let her run. His plan was to plant her in the ISA as a sleeper agent, to be activated when he needed her. But before he could, you appeared, and Claver ended his own life. Now, it seems someone from her past is out for revenge."

Owen was impressed. It looked like Faris had actually come clean. "Then why didn't you tell us before? That could've saved us a lot of trouble." His disappointment was audible. "Honestly, Faris."

Faris's expression shifted to one of embarrassment. "This isn't something I'm particularly proud of. We were both young, and we made mistakes. People died because of those mistakes."

Darra needed to set something straight. "Just for the record: have you and Manley ever been involved as a couple? This might be important."

Faris shook his head, his expression serious. "No, we haven't. We've worked together for ages, our paths crossing time and time again. But we've never been romantically involved. I don't think she's ever been seriously involved with anyone since her boyfriend was killed."

"You might be wrong about that," Darra interjected, a knowing look in her eyes. Faris understood immediately who she was referring to.

Faris nodded, acknowledging the unspoken name. "But only recently. How's he coming along? Is he for real?"

Owen thought he saw a flicker of something in Faris's expression, something that bordered on jealousy. But it was fleeting, vanishing almost as quickly as it appeared. Owen wasn't even sure if he had really seen it. "Oh, he's coming along alright. He's a handful, feisty, but he helps. He knows people. And he knows people who know even more people." He paused for a moment, choosing his words carefully. "Faris, we'll find her. If she's still alive, we'll find her."

Faris blinked, his gaze intense. "She is alive. That hint you found wasn't a coincidence, nor was it just good luck. What exactly was it?"

"It's a picture from a reception," Owen explained. "There's no date, but Manley looks much younger than she does now, and she's standing beside Claver in a way that indicates familiarity. They definitely knew each other. There are also a couple of other people in the picture that I assume are her parents and friends. We'll send you the picture. Who do you think placed it for us to find?" Owen's curiosity was wide open, wondering if Faris would lead them to more answers.

"I'm certain it's the kidnappers," Faris replied, his voice unwavering. "They want us to find her. Why do you think you haven't found a body yet?" Faris seemed confident in his assumption.

Owen and Darra pondered this idea for a moment. Faris was probably right. Considering that nothing about Manley was officially on file, finding this photo had to be more than just a convenient coincidence. "Right," Owen admitted, his mind racing. "So why would anyone do that? What's the plan?"

For that, Faris had little to offer. "I'm not sure. But we need to be careful how we proceed. I'll have someone look into this quietly. It seems like someone wants us to be in a specific place, probably where they're keeping Manley." He paused, the weight of the situation hanging in the air. "Is there anything else? Have Haylen and the lawyer found anything?"

"His name's Michael Blake," Darra interjected. "They're investigating the route Manley might have taken. We haven't heard from them today, but I'm guessing they'd have called with new information."

Faris nodded, the lines of concern now etched deeply into his face. "Please keep me posted. I can't be involved officially, but I can keep an eye out for you."

"We appreciate that. You'll know what we find," Owen said, though a flicker of doubt crossed his mind. He wasn't entirely sure how much he would share with Faris, considering the erratic behaviour the head of ISA had displayed during their past conversations.

As Faris's image faded from the screen, Owen and Darra exchanged a glance. "Do you think he's hiding more from us?" Darra asked, her voice barely above a whisper.

Owen shrugged, a mix of frustration and determination in his eyes. "It's possible. But right now, we need all the help we can get, even if it's from Faris."

Darra nodded, her mind already racing ahead to the next steps. "We should check in with Blake and Haylen. If they've found anything, we need to know now."

Owen agreed. "Let's get moving. The longer we wait, the more danger Manley's in. And if someone's playing a game with us, we need to be ready to turn the tables."

As they prepared to leave, Owen couldn't shake the feeling that they were walking into a carefully laid trap. But if it meant saving Manley, they would have to navigate it with all the cunning and precision they could muster. The hunt was on, and failure was not an option.

In the meantime, Haylen and Blake had gone back to the hotel and escorted the manager on a rather unpleasant trip to the basement. They had been quite persuasive in ensuring that he understood the consequences of denying Haylen North a private conversation. Blake's imposing physical presence and his thorough knowledge of law enforcement had significantly aided their cause. Now, they were seated in a sparsely furnished basement room with harsh artificial lighting, hoping to exchange money for information. At least, that was the plan. At the moment, the hotel manager seemed far too terrified to spit out anything useful.

"Let me say this one more time," Haylen said, her tone icy and controlled. "Our friend's life depends on your cooperation. We need to see the security tapes from two days ago—all entrances, stairs, seventh floor. If I don't get those videos, you'll never set foot in a hotel again. Did I mention I'm a North?"

The hotel manager, whose name was Quincy Murkle, according to his name tag, was visibly trembling in his chair. "I can't give you those tapes," he stammered.

"Why not?" Haylen's patience was wearing thin. This was the third time they had circled back to this point. Also, considering all the whimpering the manager was obviously prone to, she couldn't believe that he actually headed this establishment. She desperately hoped that he had staff who actually knew what they were doing.

"They said they'd kill me if I do." Quincy Murkle's eyes were wide with genuine terror.

"Who? And what makes you think I'll let you live?" Haylen pressed, her voice rising with frustration.

Murkle shook his head vigorously, ignoring the not so subtle threat. "I can't say."

In a flash, Haylen leapt from her chair, her blaster drawn and aimed directly at Murkle's head. "Tell me," she demanded, her voice cold and unyielding.

"Haylen, stop." Michael Blake's voice sounded relaxed, even amused.

"What?" she snapped, her eyes never leaving Murkle.

"I don't think this is helping," he said calmly, crossing his legs the other way as if he were reading the weather report. "I think you need to shoot his leg first. If you take the head first, this game's over." He looked at Murkle apologetically. "Sorry, man. But she's asked you nicely three times now, and I think this isn't leading anywhere."

Quincy Murkle's complexion had shifted from a stressed, blotchy red to a shocked white that nicely blended with the colour of the concrete wall behind him. He couldn't manage to utter complete sentences now. "Oh no, please... this is... I can't..."

Blake raised his hands in a gesture of seeming helplessness. "Man, if you keep making her angry, I can't help you." He leaned back in his chair, exuding a casual menace.

Haylen decided to raise the stakes a bit more. "Blake, take the table."

Blake did as he was told, effortlessly moving the table to the other side of the room, barely straining his muscles.

Haylen aimed her blaster at Murkle's leg, just above the knee. She didn't want to inflict maximum damage, just a decent amount of pain. "Start talking."

Murkle remained silent, though his laboured, stressed breathing filled the room.

Blake raised his eyebrows. "Man, this isn't going to pay off for you."

"Last warning." Haylen's finger tightened on the trigger, her eyes cold and unyielding. The hotel manager said no word and looked down. Without hesitation, Haylen pulled the trigger. Murkle screamed, collapsing into a whimpering heap, clutching his leg. The smell of burnt flesh wafted through the room. "Who paid you?"

Blake was impressed. He hadn't been sure if she had it in her to actually shoot him, but she did. For a split second, he hoped none of this would ever reach the lawyers and judges he worked with. Active collaboration in something like this could be the end of his career if anyone ever found out. On the other hand, Manley's life was at stake, and he was willing to take that risk. He leaned down to the whimpering heap. "You wanna talk now?"

Murkle didn't reply. He kept holding his bleeding knee, emitting sounds that were unworthy of his position, or any position for that matter. Haylen wasn't planning on waiting for him to recover his strength. She placed the blaster against the wound, provoking a suppressed howl from Murkle. "I can do this again. I will. Talk to me."

Blake had to admit this might have been slightly amusing if no one's life were at stake. He briefly wondered whether he was in the right line of work. "Man, you better talk. I have no idea what else she's capable of."

Haylen emphasized her words with another push at the blaster wound. Before she could say anything else, Murkle moaned. "Wait!"

His voice was strained and barely audible, but it was enough to make Haylen pause. She didn't remove the blaster, keeping the threat imminent. "We're listening," she said, her tone laced with menace. She wasn't scared he would attack her. If he could, he would have done so by now. Besides, she had Michael Blake behind her, whose skills were not to be underestimated. He probably knew several ways to disarm and incapacitate people without any weapons. "Talk to me."

Murkle whimpered once more, the pain evident in his eyes. "I don't know their names, but they... they had a ship at the spaceport and paid me a lot of money to look the other way. I'll get you those tapes, but I'm not sure how they will help. The guys are all dressed in black, and you can't see any faces."

"So you've seen the tapes." Blake's interest was piqued. What else had this guy seen? And who had paid him?

Haylen had picked up on that detail too. "If you've seen the tapes, I'll need to see them. Now. Who knows what part of your body I might shoot off in my growing impatience." She pointed the blaster a little higher up his body, more toward the middle.

The whimpering manager stopped whimpering for a moment, his eyes widening in fear. "I can play the tapes down here, just don't..." He cut himself off, his gaze fixated on her blaster.

Haylen inhaled sharply through her teeth. "Do it. And do it fast." She retreated from the injured manager and took a seat opposite the screen mounted on the wall. Michael Blake joined her, his expression tense with anticipation. Murkle pushed himself up on his good leg and tapped the screen a few times in different places, his hands trembling, and started the tapes from the video cameras across the hotel from the time Manley had been taken.

The men with the black masks didn't even try to avoid the cameras. They moved with purpose, as if they were on a mission regardless of who saw them. There were four of them, all of roughly equal height and build, making them difficult to distinguish.

Haylen and Michael exchanged looks of recognition; they had both seen this type of calculated efficiency before, on either side of the law.

They watched intently as two of the masked figures disappeared into the back office for about a minute while the others stood guard. Then, as a cohesive unit, they walked the back stairs to the seventh floor—the same stairs Haylen had used on her second trip to the hotel. The masked men halted on the seventh floor and headed directly for Manley's room, which lay to the left of the stairs.

Haylen and Blake switched to the camera focused on Manley's door. They couldn't see inside the room, but they could discern the shapes of two men cautiously entering, while the other two remained in the corridor, standing watch. The timestamp indicated it was two hours past midnight on Nergal B. About half a minute later, the other two masked men entered the room. Then, for approximately five tense minutes, nothing happened—until the men emerged, one of them carrying the unconscious Manley over his shoulder. She was clad in a dark overall.

"I'm guessing this isn't her usual wardrobe," Haylen remarked dryly, breaking the silence that had settled over the room. Her eyes remained fixed on the screen, her mind racing with possibilities.

Blake shook his head, his expression grim. "Looks like nothing she wore during our time here. Too much fabric."

Haylen raised her eyebrows in a curious look.

"What?" Blake raised his hands a little apologetically. "Just saying. Please don't tell me you know her in that kind of clothes."

Shaking her head, Haylen guided their gazes back to the screen. "No, I don't. But I've only ever seen her in office uniform, and a few times in pilot gear. So they took the time to dress her. Which means she was still alive when they brought her out of here."

Blake squeezed his eyes shut in a moment of realisation. He was trying very hard to ignore the possibility that someone might actually want to kill the funny redhead. "Right." On the screen, he watched as four men dressed in black carried Manley out the back door of the hotel. They were just walking away, not even a vehicle in sight. "Don't you think it's weird they don't have a ship or anything parked nearby?"

Haylen nodded. "Definitely. But there has to be something. They wouldn't have carried her all the way to the spaceport. I mean, I know this is Nergal B, and you can get away with a hell of a lot here, but that would be too much even for this hellhole."

They both turned their attention back to Murkle, who felt visibly uneasy under their renewed scrutiny. Haylen fumbled with her blaster. "I have a question. If you were paid to look the other way, why did you keep the tapes?"

Murkle looked embarrassed, his eyes darting around the room. "I thought... I thought I might need them again for something else."

"Like getting money from someone else who asked for them?" Haylen forced him to meet her gaze.

"Like getting money from someone else who asked for them," Murkle admitted, his voice barely more than a whisper.

"I see." Haylen tapped a few buttons on her PAC. "Your efforts won't go unnoticed. Blake, secure the files to your device. Delete them from the hotel system."

Blake hesitated for a moment, contemplating whether he should follow the orders she was giving. They were sensible orders, and he would have given the same. But he had little to no experience in this whole freelancing affair, and he was glad that at least Haylen clearly knew what to do. "Yes, Ma'am," he replied with a cheeky smile and got to work.

Haylen suddenly found herself appreciating Blake's wit and competence. She realised what Manley might have liked about him initially, apart from his obvious physical attributes. He had a good sense of humour, and he knew when to shut up. He also knew when to argue and when to act. In a different context, she might have asked him if he had a twin brother she could borrow for her own amusement. She couldn't help but let her gaze linger on his muscular arms and body. He was a nice package, and she admired the fact that he wasn't just a good-looking playboy but also a lawyer with a wealth of knowledge, and she had only seen hints of what his brain could do even under pressure. Manley was indeed a lucky woman—if they could find her. Shaking herself from her reverie, Haylen refocused on the task at hand in the hotel basement where she had just shot the manager. "We'll be out of here now. We can take you upstairs, if you'd like," she addressed Murkle.

The manager violently shook his head. "No, thanks, I'll be fine."

Blake and Haylen exchanged shrugs. "Fine. See ya." With that, they turned and left, locking the room from the outside. They didn't need anyone following them now. In the corridor, Haylen glanced at Blake. "I'm impressed."

"By what?" He didn't even break his stride.

"By the fact that you didn't interfere. I'd have expected you to say something about the shooting."

Blake gave her a curious look. "Right. I'm not a fan of torture. Never have been. But we have a goal, and that guy had tapes we needed to look at." He paused for a moment as they headed up the stairs to the ground floor. "But honestly? I'm really grateful that you shot him. That I didn't have to do it."

Haylen nodded. "You're welcome. You can have the next one, if you'd like."

"The next one?" Blake frowned. He had a hunch about what she was going to say next, but he was hoping he was wrong.

"Do you really think that guy was the last one we're going to force? I've been at this for a while now, and believe me, there's gonna be more," Haylen smirked. She found the lawyer's openly displayed innocence quite amusing. It was probably difficult for him to navigate the murky waters between right and wrong.

Blake exhaled audibly. "I guess I'll have to take your word for it. Let's hope there won't be too many. We might be running out of time." He glanced around. "We need to get out of here. Maybe someone at the spaceport remembers four black-clad men carrying an unconscious redhead."

"Now you're talking," Haylen smiled. "Let's go." She led the way out and to the shuttle port in front of the hotel. Walking all that distance wasn't an option now; they needed every shortcut they could find. With Michael Blake in tow, she entered the shuttle at the front of the line, ignoring the indignant utterances behind them. There were only two seats left, so they sat side by side—close. Closer than Haylen felt comfortable with. She liked Michael Blake. He was decent, honest, good-looking—and so off-limits. She would never try to hit on someone who was with Manley; she respected the agent too much. Also, she was a little afraid of how Manley would react. Haylen's arms touched Blake's as the seats were designed quite small. Blake did his best not to take up too much space, but there was only so much he could do. He smiled apologetically. "Sorry, it's a bit tight."

Haylen smiled back. "Don't sweat it. Can I ask you a question?"

Blake smiled in a slightly puzzled way. "Another one?" he teased, with a wink.

Haylen gave him a grin. "Alright, I deserved that. Yes, another one."

"Fire away."

She scratched her nose, feeling slightly embarrassed. "How was she? I mean Manley. What was she like when you met? I've only ever seen her in duty mode, I have no idea what she might do or say without her work."

Blake fell silent for a while as the shuttle took off, heading for the spaceport. When he finally spoke, his voice sounded heavy with emotion. "Haylen, she's more to me than just a holiday fling. I've never believed in love at first sight, but this is pretty damn close. I've only shared two days with her, and I can't wait to spend more time with that funny, kind, passionate woman. I can't really tell you who she is and what she's been through to become who she is, but I sure know I want to find out."

"Wow." Haylen didn't know what else to say. She wasn't sure what she had expected as a reply, but it certainly wasn't this kind of epic love story.

Blake gave her a curious look. "Surprised?"

"Not quite. And yes. I mean, it's obvious you care, but I had no idea how much. I can totally see why she chose you," Haylen said. She swallowed back a sudden wave of emotion that she didn't want to show right now. They had to find her. They just had to. Even if it was just for the sake of her being able to spend time with this gorgeous man who seemed to be one of the very few decent ones left in this part of the galaxy. Haylen looked at the floor until the shuttle touched ground.

Michael Blake was relieved that he didn't have to talk about Manley any more right now. He was going crazy with worry, and he didn't want to imagine what would happen if they didn't find her alive. He refused to accept that possibility. From all he had heard in the past hours, Manley wasn't one to give up easily. And maybe, just maybe, all they had to do was find her and pay someone to let her go.

The spaceport was buzzed with energy, when Haylen and Michael left the shuttle. They paused, their eyes scanning the buildings nearby for any sign that would point them in the right direction. Their mission was clear: speak to someone from security about the tapes from the night Manley vanished from the hotel.

Haylen's fingers danced across her PAC, her focus undisturbed. After a moment, she gestured to the left. "That way."

Blake remained silent, his stride matching hers. He knew his way around the courtrooms and judges but

Haylen knew a lot about how to get her way in the world of honest and not-so-honest people. The likelihood of bribery within the spaceport was high, and he steeled himself for the potential ordeal of interrogation and not-so-subtle coercion. Following Haylen, he entered a nearby building marked "Security." She moved with a natural instinct, heading straight for the correct office, though he knew her PAC was likely guiding her with precise schematics. Without hesitation, she knocked and then boldly stepped through the door before any response could come. Michael noted the plaque that read "Chief of Security" as he locked the door behind them, earning an amused glance from Haylen. She mouthed a silent "Thanks" and advanced toward the man behind the desk, who was still staring at his screen, seemingly oblivious to their presence.

Haylen positioned herself resolutely in front of the desk, her posture exuding quiet confidence. Michael observed her with a growing sense of admiration. She was employing a different strategy with this individual, opting for patience and an unspoken challenge. She stood motionless, her gaze fixed on the man, the silence stretching into what felt like an endless amount of time. After several minutes, she tapped a series of commands into her PAC. He could only guess what she was doing, and to be honest, he had no idea. But whatever she did, it had an immediate effect on the man behind the desk.

He abruptly swivelled toward her, rising from his chair with an air of forced authority. He wasn't exactly of the tall kind and had a rounded middle. What remained of his hair was a scant, patchy mixture of grey and dark, framing a face that had seen more years than he'd likely admit. His attire was an assembly of black: slacks, an indistinguishable shirt, and a scarf loosely draped around his neck. "Miss North, what can I do for you?"

Haylen's smile was a practised blend of charm and resolve. "You have information I need, Mr. Walker."

Walker eased himself into a comfortable position at the desk. "And what kind of information would that be, Miss North?"

"Mr. Walker, there were four men carrying an unconscious woman with red hair into your spaceport two nights ago, well past midnight. They paid you to look the other way." Haylen's tone allowed no argument, the statement hanging in the air. Walker remained still, his gaze fixed on her, unreadable.

"I need to know what they paid you, so I can raise the stakes. I need to know which ship they left on and where they were heading." Her hands, now folded neatly on the table, were a picture of composed determination as she waited for his response.

Michael Blake continued to observe from his silent post by the door, his presence a subtle reminder of the stakes. Walker leaned forward on the desk, his eyes appraising Haylen with a mixture of curiosity and caution. "Miss North, I'm going to need twice the sum you've wired me."

"Consider it done." Haylen's fingers moved swiftly over her PAC, the transaction completed in moments. She resumed her calm demeanour, her voice steady but laced with an undercurrent of menace. "Now, what I didn't mention before is that I might be really, really pissed if you decide to lie to me or withhold any of the information I'm asking for. I also know very well what my friend over there"—she gestured towards Blake with a casual thumb, weaving him seamlessly into her narrative—"is capable of. Is that understood?"

Walker's gaze shifted to Blake, assessing the silent, imposing figure. The combination of Blake's apparent determination and his physical presence seemed to be enough to convince him. "That is very well understood."

Haylen nodded, a signal for him to proceed. "I'm listening."

The security chief exhaled deeply, his gaze shifting from Haylen to Blake and back again before he began speaking. "They arrived here at 4:30 in the morning, under cover of darkness. The woman was unconscious but appeared unharmed—I didn't see any blood on her. Their ship was parked behind the building next to this one. The registration numbers were removed, and the digital registration they provided was clearly fake. Before they left, I overheard them mention something about a flight to Hani."

Hani. The place that made Nergal B look like a lawful children's playground. It was a world where carrying an arsenal of different weapons was a necessity, unless one fancied being stabbed, robbed, or otherwise brutally mishandled. Michael Blake had suspected their next move might lead them there. Haylen appeared momentarily satisfied. "I see, Mr. Walker. What type of ship were they using?" She was intent on extracting every ounce of information from this man, whose idea of integrity was faint at best.

"A Sloop Hunter."

A traditional Laster clan ship. Haylen's heart started beating faster. This revelation suggested a probable connection to the Claver affair. Claver and Ortiz had notoriously recruited former Laster pirates into their ranks. "You're being very helpful, Mr. Walker. Would you mind sending a copy of their registration to my PAC? I have associates who might be able to dig deeper into this."

"Not at all." Walker tapped a few commands into his screen, then returned his gaze to her. "I hope you'll find what you're looking for."

Haylen stood and gave a curt nod. "Thank you. I trust you'll know how to find me if anything else regarding this matter comes up."

"Of course, Miss North." Walker returned the nod, his attention already drifting back to his screen. "As far as everyone else is concerned, I haven't seen you."

"We understand each other perfectly." With that, Haylen turned, heading for the door, which Michael Blake unlocked for them. He had felt like little more than a piece of furniture throughout the exchange. Once they were outside the building, he pulled Haylen around the corner, his face a mask of confusion. "What was that?"

Haylen's smile was enigmatic. "I don't know what you mean."

"Are you kidding? What did I miss? Why did he just talk? Shouldn't we have shot him like that hotel guy?"

Haylen shook her head, a hint of amusement in her eyes. "No, we shouldn't have. That would've drawn too much attention to ourselves. There's a big difference between a whiny hotel manager in a quiet basement and the spaceport security chief. Walker knows people who could complicate our investigation. He had a price, he named it, and I paid him."

"Without thinking twice?"

"Yes, without thinking twice. We want to find Manley, and that man had valid information. We know we're looking for a Sloop Hunter, and we know our next stop is Hani. That's a lot more than we knew half an hour ago. Plus, we know she was still alive when they arrived here. They wouldn't have hauled a dead body all the way to the port if they didn't plan to take her away. Happy?" She looked at him as if his comprehension was questionable right now.

As he listened to her, Michael realized she was right. They had gathered significant intel from the brief interaction, and money seemed to be of no importance in their quest. "Not in the literal sense. But you win. Where's your ship? We need to move quickly. If they're heading to Hani, we haven't got much time."

Haylen's eyes sparkled with determination. "Dock 14, that way." She started walking briskly, her mind already focused on the next steps. "We need to move quickly. If they're heading to Hani, we don't have much time." Blake's urgency sped her on. She didn't want to waste any more time, either. "We'll leave right now, in my ship. That way, we can be around Hani within five hours. We can sleep on the flight."

Michael Blake nodded, though a part of him wasn't thrilled about leaving his own ship behind. Still, travelling together in a single ship would attract less attention from the unsavoury elements lurking on Hani—and elsewhere. "There's still the matter of clothes."

Haylen couldn't resist a playful jab. "You think you'll need any?" She saw the seriousness beginning to cloud his face and quickly added, "Just kidding. I ordered some earlier today and had them delivered to my ship."

Blake grinned despite himself. "You almost had me there. Thanks, Haylen."

"No, thank you. If you hadn't posed as the silent thug, I'm not sure Mr. Walker would've complied so easily." She nodded towards the other end of the spaceport. "Let's go. We have someone to find."

As they walked, Haylen sent a quick message to Dixie. "Need help with digital registration. Please find someone who can decipher something from this." She attached the file, hoping Dixie knew someone who could take care of this. When she looked up, Michael Blake had vanished from her view. She stopped, searching the surroundings, and then spotted him thirty feet behind, seated in a cargo cart. He had his hands on the steering wheel, looking at her expectantly. "You coming?" He patted the empty passenger seat beside him, urging her to jump in. They would save at least a few precious minutes this way.

Haylen smiled in mild amusement. "Are you switching over to the dark side?" She hadn't expected the lawyer to do anything unlawful today, yet he kept impressing her. She turned back and joined him in the cart, not minding the shortcut to her ship.

Blake hit the accelerator, sending the cart speeding along fast enough to tip over. The early hour meant minimal traffic on Nergal B's ground; this wasn't a morning planet. Haylen pointed out the directions until they finally skidded to a stop in front of her Drekar.

Blake whistled through his teeth, eyebrows raised in admiration. "Only the best will do, won't it? This is the most expensive Drekar model I've ever seen. And I've seen a few."

She shrugged with nonchalance. "Being a North has its advantages." She unlocked the ship with a tap on her PAC and moved towards the hatch door on the left side, motioning for him to follow. Right beside the door lay a package. "Ah, your clothes. Would you mind?"

Blake didn't mind. He picked up the package, surprised by its weight, and followed her into the Drekar. The interior was state-of-the-art, an opulent display of flat black fittings that made the ship look even more expensive. He trailed Haylen through the narrow corridor to the cockpit, curious about the sleeping arrangements simmering in the back of his mind. After a day filled with intense interrogations and making plans with strangers, the thought of rest was tempting.

In the cockpit, he set down the package and waited for Haylen to settle in. She moved efficiently, initiating pre-flight sequences and ensuring everything was in order. The sleek control panels and advanced navigational systems responded to her touch, coming to life with a series of soft hums and beeps.

The heiress of the North funds and empire settled into the pilot seat with a grace befitting her lineage. She motioned for Blake to take the co-pilot's seat and began working on the controls. What had she got herself into? All she had wanted was to have a drink or two with Manley, for old times' sake. Instead, she found herself on a desperate hunt for the cunning agent who seemed to have vanished into thin air. True, she knew a ship carrying Manley had flown to Hani, but that didn't guarantee she was there. Worse still, it didn't even fully guarantee she was alive. But that uncertainty wouldn't keep Haylen from doing what was right.

Reluctant to join Owen's crew at first, she had quickly realised the importance of uncovering the truth about the villainous entanglements of Claver and her father. Yet, she hadn't expected to be thrown into another adventure quite so quickly. At least she had competent help in Blake. She glanced at him and caught him looking at her. With a quick smile, she said, "You might want to unpack the clothes. There's a fresh PAC for you, one that can't be traced easily. I took the liberty of connecting it to your ship, so you can lock it up from here." She saw his expression change to one of genuine surprise.

"Thank you." He looked around, taking in the sleek, high-tech surroundings. "Do you need any help taking off?"

Haylen couldn't resist a playful jab. "Again with the clothes," she said, grinning.

Blake realised his slip and blushed for a split second. "I meant the ship. Take-off. Leaving the bloody planet."

"Sorry," she smirked, enjoying the momentary fluster she caused. She knew she was keeping him on edge while he was obviously searching the sector for the love of his life. She nodded towards the back of the ship. "Once we've entered hyperspace, we can retire to the rooms in the back. There's one on each side of the corridor. It isn't much, but it's better than sleeping in the cockpit." With that, she resumed tapping the controls and fastened her seatbelt. Blake did the same. "We need to send a message to Owen," she murmured, more to herself than to Blake.

He still heard her and nodded. "Do that, I've got this. You know how much Owen needs to know right now." He transferred the flight controls to his side of the cockpit and fired up the Drekar engines. Though he had never flown one before, the controls were surprisingly intuitive. After all, this was a state-of-the-art ship equipped with the latest technology, designed to make piloting as easy as possible.

Haylen nodded and started tapping on her keyboard. She kept the message short. "Found trail. Following to Hani." Owen would know what to make of this. She leaned back in her seat, watching Blake deftly handle the Drekar. For once, things felt almost easy. Blake piloted the ship with natural ease, the controls responding to his touch as if they were an extension of him.

As the jump buoy loomed ahead, Blake glanced at her, a silent question in his eyes: did she want to take over? Haylen shook her head and motioned for him to continue. When the streaks of hyperspace appeared on the screen, she rose from her seat. "Put the ship on auto-pilot. It'll take us to Hani from here. We need to get some sleep."

Blake nodded. "Agreed. I'll hit the controls with my head if I don't." He activated the autopilot and grabbed his package. "You mentioned rooms."

Haylen led the way down the narrow corridor, stopping near the end to press two invisible buttons on either side. Two doors hissed open, revealing compact but comfortable rooms, each with a bed and a tiny bathroom corner. There was even a shower. While the space was limited, it was more than adequate, especially compared to the accommodations on Blake's own ship. He set his package on the floor. "Nice. Alright, sleep tight."

Haylen yawned, the tension of the past few days suddenly weighing heavily on her. They were far from the end of this mission, but for now, she could rest. "Good night." With that, she turned, and the door closed behind her.

Blake stepped into his room, the door sealing him in. It felt like a wardrobe with just enough space for a bed and the bathroom. He tested the mattress, which yielded slightly to his touch. It promised a good night's sleep, a luxury he hadn't indulged in for days.

He stripped off his clothes, dropping them in a heap on the floor. Weariness descended on him like a heavy coat. His muscles felt strained despite the lack of recent physical exertion. The thought of a shower seemed almost too much, but he knew he needed it. He couldn't remember the last time he'd had the chance. He forced himself to his feet, sighing as he turned on the water. It was surprisingly hot, enveloping him in warmth. Showers with Manley had been a lot more fun. This one was merely functional, rinsing away sweat and the lingering sense of dread.

What had he got himself into? The mission, the stakes, the uncertainty—it was all overwhelming. He wasn't quite sure why he had set off to find his holiday fling, except that it was starting to dawn on him that Manley was much, much more than just a woman he had been with on a holiday.

He had the distinct feeling that there was no turning back. As the hot water soothed his tired muscles, he allowed himself a moment of vulnerability, a brief pause before plunging back into the chaos. A few minutes later, he stepped out of the shower and dried himself off. He let himself sink onto the bed, too exhausted to bother with clothes. He was way too tired now to care about that. He was even too tired to consider venting out all the emotions Manley's disappearance had caused him to feel. It was almost surreal to think he had finally found someone he could imagine spending more than just fleeting nights with, and now he had lost her again so soon.

Hell, there was a whole crew of peculiar characters on the lookout for her. People he had never seen before, and people he wouldn't trust under normal circumstances. But since he wasn't in normal circumstances, he was going with the flow. Maybe he could learn a thing or two from Owen, Darra, and Haylen. And maybe, just maybe, they would get lucky and find Manley. He found himself struggling to recall small details about her appearance. Her eyes had been blue, hadn't they? He closed his own eyes, which burned from the water and the long hours spent navigating Nergal B and its underworld.

What was he doing out here? Risking his career, and possibly his life, for a woman he hardly knew? Rolling with the flow of a crew that orbited around a mysterious man who clearly didn't have much regard for law and order? He was acting totally out of character. Where was the cool, determined lawyer he used to be? The man he liked to see in the mirror? The man who had a way with the ladies yet never stayed with one for too long? Now he was sanctioning, even aiding, torture to gain information.

He was running with a pack of wolves he had never met before, acting on pure instinct. This wasn't him. He had always prided himself on his rationality, his ability to weigh the pros and cons, to calculate every risk. But now, driven by desperation and hope, he was throwing caution to the wind.

He sighed, the weight of his romantic history and career choices bearing down on him. Trisha had been a whirlwind—a colleague's sister he'd met at an office party. She possessed a charm that went beyond her beauty; she was clever, challenging him in debates that sparked both intellectual fire and passionate nights. The chemistry between them had been electric, the intimacy unforgettable. Yet, as swiftly as it had begun, his interest had waned after a few months. It wasn't her fault; he simply hadn't been ready to commit to anything. He saw himself as unfit for the dedication and consistency required in long-term relationships.

That kind of life demanded devotion, constant work, organisational skills and will. It was hard to maintain a working relationship for years. Reflecting on his own choices and those of Lannister and Ayla, he couldn't ignore the contrasts. Lannister juggled his career and family life, perpetually weighing the demands of his firm against the stability of his home. Blake knew first-hand the toll these decisions could take on personal life; he saw Lannister contemplating selling his firm, planning for a path that wouldn't consume him with late nights and overtime. Unlike Lannister, Blake couldn't envision abandoning the career he had diligently built. He had sacrificed sleep and social outings to excel in his studies, striving to stand out among his peers. While others seemed to breeze through the theoretical aspects of their studies,

Blake thrived in the practical application of law—defending and prosecuting, negotiating the intricate details of high-stakes divorces.

Initially, he had entered the legal field as a criminal law expert, navigating the adrenaline-fuelled world of courtroom dramas. However, the allure of divorce law soon drew him in with its promise of substantial financial rewards without the physical risks inherent in criminal cases. He specialized in cases where substantial assets needed to be divided strategically, ensuring favourable outcomes for his clients. His success was built on meticulous preparation and exploiting the weaknesses of opponents unearthed by his team of investigators. He had people working for him digging up dirt on the opposite party, but he had never done the dirty work himself. Until now. And his motivation had never been this infused by feelings. Until today.

When he had met Manley for the first time, when she had almost hit him in the face on the hotel corridor, he had found her appealing, a blend of attractiveness and wit that intrigued him. Initially, he had expected nothing more than a few enjoyable nights together before parting ways. Yet, their dinner that night had shifted something within him. Accustomed to women who typically lavished attention on him, he found himself drawn to Manley's independence and the subtle aloofness she displayed.

The way she immersed herself in her meal, seemingly oblivious to his attempts at conversation, only heightened his determination to win her over. When she casually mentioned feeling tired, he had hoped it was a tactic to make herself more enigmatic, less readily available to his advances. It had thrown him off at first, questioning if he had misread her signals up to that point. However, when he finally kissed her, any doubts evaporated. The response was immediate and electric, her body pushing against his with an intensity that left him breathless. He had wagered she wouldn't simply retire to her room and leave it at that. And he had been right.

When she sat there opposite him on the balcony, the champagne glass poised at her lips, her demeanour effortlessly alluring. She seemed oblivious to the magnetic pull she had on him, but his body spoke volumes, urging him toward a night that promised to be unforgettable. He struggled to maintain his composure, attempting to prolong the moment before inevitably leading her inside, yet his desires threatened to overwhelm him.

In a sudden rush, he dashed to the bathroom to compose himself, the cold surface of the wall a temporary anchor against the desire rising within him. Every second felt like longer than usual as he strained his ears to catch any sound that might indicate her departure. When minutes passed without a hint of movement, he cautiously emerged, hoping she had stayed.

And she had. Seeing her there meant that she wanted the same thing he had been thinking about the whole night. The crackling between, almost audible, them felt unbearable to him. He grabbed her hips before he bent down to meet her lips. With an expert move, she had thrown off her dress, turning him on even more. Their bodies met and started something that he still didn't fully understand.

He grasped the physicality of their encounter—two strangers finding joy in each other during a holiday break, seeking a break from their respective burdens. Understanding Manley's ordeal in the wake of the Claver affair, he wouldn't have been surprised if she had simply slept through her entire three-week stay at the hotel. Dealing with what she had gone through must have felt utterly devastating.

Comparatively, his own professional struggles, like navigating the contentious divorce of Dorothy and Peter Merkin, felt trivial enough, though demanding. The Merkins' battle over every possession and investment, worsened by Dorothy's provocative advances toward him, had tested his resolve. But none of that compared to meeting Manley.

He couldn't pinpoint why, but he felt an inexplicable need to delve deeper into who she was, to uncover the layers of her being, and simply to be in her presence. This was uncharted territory for him. He missed her fiercely, yearning to have her by his side, to reveal her past, to understand what shaped her into the person she was now. Equally, he wanted to share his own story with her, to connect on a level that went beyond their initial encounter. He wanted to believe that he could still do all these things when he had found her. After all, he was Michael Blake, and he did not fail. He just wasn't so sure if he could live up to his own reputation on this particular mission.

What he didn't understand was the mental connection he felt. Sitting on a sun lounger, gazing at her, he found himself completely content. He liked bringing her food for joy. He also liked bringing her all kinds of other joy. But even now, with all that he knew about her past, he felt like he just knew her, even without knowing it all. It was as if he already knew her deeply, far beyond what their shared moments had revealed. He could envision a future with her, something far beyond his usual fleeting encounters with women. He had always prided himself on keeping things light, avoiding anything too deep or serious. But with Manley, it was different. He could almost sense her presence, as if her fragrance lingered in the air, and the memory of her touch made his skin tingle. He heard her voice in his mind, whispering about possibilities and a shared future, stirring emotions he wasn't sure he had ever felt before. He could almost smell her hair even though she was nowhere near. He almost heard her voice whispering in his ear, talking to him about promise and future.

When Blake finally stirred awake from dreaming about her, he disoriented in the darkness. It took him a few moments to remember that he had fallen asleep aboard Haylen's Drekar, bound for Hani in pursuit of Manley's kidnappers. Taking a deep breath, he sat up, triggering the motion-activated lamps that flooded the cramped room with light. The technology impressed him. His own ship didn't have this kind of technology.

He rummaged through the package Haylen had ordered for him—clothes, all in black and fitted snugly. It seemed she intended him to blend seamlessly into their surroundings, even among the shady characters they were likely to meet soon enough. With a resigned shrug, he dressed quickly. Clothes this tight weren't his usual style, but practicality outweighed fashion when tracking down a missing person. He chuckled wryly to himself at the thought of wandering Hani in clothes less suited to his task. A half-naked lawyer asking about a kidnapped woman would draw all the wrong kinds of attention, especially on a planet where his reputation preceded him in certain circles. Being on Hani, where his law firm had its office, was feeling entirely too close for comfort. If any of his clients recognised him, his cover might blow in an instant.

Once he laced up the sturdy boots included in the package, he ventured out of his room. To his surprise, Haylen was already up and about, piloting the ship through Hani's orbit after dropping out of hyperspace. Her determination was palpable, and Blake couldn't help but feel a surge of admiration mixed with a tinge of apprehension.

When Haylen caught Blake's eye, she offered a knowing smile. "Looks like I nailed the sizing," she remarked casually.

Blake nodded. "I wouldn't have been surprised if they were just a little too tight", he said with a grin and went for his seat. "What's new?"

"Owen replied to our message. He says that Manley and Claver knew each other before the stuff we went through during the past few months. She knew him 17 years ago and went into witness protection with ISA after seeing Claver kill two agents. Owen thinks it's all connected to her kidnapping." Haylen eyed Blake carefully from the side. She knew that he couldn't quite judge the scale of this piece of information yet, but he kept his composure well.

Blake frowned. His mind started racing. So Manley knew Claver. The Claver family had been based on Enkil for generations, not on Hani. So probably Manley had met him there. 17 years ago, she had been what? 15 years old? And her family was from Enkil, too. "What else?" he asked urgently, sensing there was something else. There had to be some other piece of information he was missing.

Haylen raised an eyebrow, impressed by Blake's quick grasp of the situation. "Her real name hasn't always been Dana Manley. Before witness protection, she was Amy Carter. Faris confirmed it."

Amy Carter. Amy Carter. Where had he heard that name before? And was this what she had said he didn't know? Was this was she had not been able to tell him? How did this connect? What came about to make her take that new identity and become an ISA agent? Pieces of this puzzle were starting to fit together, but the picture remained unclear. Oh, how he would like to have his connections digging into this. But he knew this would attract too much attention right now. Keeping a low profile for the moment was key.

"That's interesting." Blake looked down at the controls below his fingertips. He was going to have to ask Lannister again. He couldn't go investigating this himself. As soon as his name popped up, he might put the whole mission in danger. His right hand moved towards his PAC on his left hand.

"What are you doing?" Haylen's voice interrupted his concentration.

"I need to reach out to a friend," Blake explained without looking up, still focused on establishing contact with Lannister. "Someone who can dig into Amy Carter's past. We need a better chance of understanding what's going on now", he said.

Haylen nodded thoughtfully. "Smart move," she acknowledged, leaning back in her seat. Blake was still tapping, trying to establish a connection with

Lannister. His friend finally answered, sounding drowsy.

Finally, Lannister's tired voice crackled through the PAC. "Blake. Do you have any idea what time it is?" There was a hint of annoyance in his tone, tempered by the need for discretion. He was speaking quietly, probably trying to not wake up his wife Ayla.

Blake exhaled softly. "Sorry to wake you, old friend. We just dropped out of hyperspace; I've lost track of time."

"We? Who's we?" Lannister sounded careful and curious.

"Someone who's helping me find Manley." Blake glanced at Haylen, silently reassuring her of his discretion. Haylen shrugged nonchalantly, giving him the go-ahead.

"Who, Blake?" Lannister pressed, his tone becoming more serious.

Blake sighed again, deciding to disclose the truth. "Haylen North."

There was a brief pause on the other end of the line, followed by a quiet whistle from Lannister. "Alright, Blake. Really, who is it?"

"Lannister, I'm serious," Blake insisted, ignoring the scepticism in his friend's voice. "She knows Manley. She convinced me that working together might speed up the process. She's part of the crew Manley worked with during the Claver affair." Silence hung heavily for a moment. "Lannister, are you still there?"

"Yes, I'm still here," Lannister finally replied. "Blake, are you drunk?"

Blake rolled his eyes. "I know how this sounds, but I need your help. Look into someone named Amy Carter from Enkil. She disappeared 17 years ago."

"Blake…" Lannister hesitated, clearly unsure about the situation.

"Lannister, this is serious," Blake urged urgently. "It's all connected to Manley's kidnapping. She went by a different name 17 years ago—Amy Carter. Please, look her up. Her life might depend on it." Blake was hoping that this would be enough to make his friend get out of bed in the middle of the night and look up someone he had never heard of just because Blake asked him to.

"And why can't you do this yourself? You know how to do it," Lannister countered, sounding more annoyed by the minute.

Blake acknowledged Lannister's valid point. "I can't have my name associated with this. It could jeopardize everything. I'm asking a lot, but please…"

Lannister remained silent a little longer than Blake liked. But when he spoke, he was back to his usual self. "Alright, Blake. I'll start digging. But this better not come back to bite me. Where are you?"

"In orbit around Hani. But I'd rather not come home right now."

Lannister chuckled knowingly. "Yeah, I can imagine that. And here I was about to ask you to explain all of this to Ayla."

"I swear I will, once this is over," Blake promised, knowing he was pushing boundaries.

"Alright. I'll look into it."

There was a rustling of sheets on the other end, and Blake imagined his friend getting out of bed. "Thank you. I owe you one," Blake said gratefully.

"No, you don't. Actually, you owe me two by now. Remember? I already did some digging for Manley," Lannister reminded him matter-of-factly. Before Blake could muster a witty retort, Lannister continued in a more serious tone, "If you don't marry that woman and live the rest of your life having the time of your life, I'll make Ayla think of ways to torture you. You know that, right?"

"Absolutely," Blake chuckled softly. "Thanks again, Lannister."

"Thank me when I'm done. Talk to you soon."

With that, Lannister ended the call, leaving Blake to ponder his friend's words. Suddenly, the smart lawyer was wondering if Lannister had already understood something that he still wasn't ready to admit. Was he truly prepared to spend the rest of his life with Manley, assuming they both survived this mission? Did Lannister know that Blake would have run if he weren't serious about her? Taking a deep breath, Blake turned to Haylen, who had quietly observed the entire conversation without uttering a word.

"Are all of your friends this feisty?" she asked.

Blake chuckled softly, a hint of amusement in his eyes. "I wouldn't call it feisty, but yes, we tend to question everything and doubt the first version of events we hear. Comes with the job," he explained, flashing her a wry smile.

"I see," Haylen replied. Before she could delve further into their banter, a new message flashed on her screen. It was just plain text, and it was from Dixie. The message read, "Found original signature within fake registration. Ship intended for Hani, but never docked there. Tracked it to Enkil using false credentials. No sign of the crew. Good luck finding Manley. I'll update you if I uncover more."

Haylen read through the message quickly, processing what it meant. She glanced over at Blake. "She's not here."

"What do you mean, she's not here?" Blake frowned.

Haylen projected the message onto the main screen for Blake to see. "This just came in from Dixie. The kidnappers' ship never made it to Hani. They ended up on Enkil. Looks like that's our next destination," she explained, watching him closely for his reaction.

"Apparently so," Blake replied absently, his gaze fixed on the screen. The text blurred before his eyes, morphing into enigmatic patterns. He felt a surge of frustration, unable to focus. He sat zoomed out until Haylen talked to him again.

"Blake, are you alright?" Haylen's voice pulled him back to the present.

He blinked, refocusing on her concerned expression. "Yes. No. Yes. I'd rather wait to hear from Lannister. The less distance this information travels, the better."

"I agree," Haylen nodded thoughtfully. "I'm starting to think that someone wants us to find her. And they want her alive. If they wanted her dead, we'd have found a body on Nergal B." She winced slightly. "Sorry."

Blake shook his head resolutely. "No, you're right. If someone just wanted her out of the way, she'd be dead by now. The fact that there's no body means she's still alive. We'll wait for Lannister's intel and then head over to Enkil." His tone left no room for an argument.

"It's a plan, Blake." Haylen activated the ship's autopilot and rose from her seat. "Let's eat."

The mention of food made Blake suddenly aware of his own hunger. "Agreed. What's on the menu?" He watched as Haylen quickly manipulated controls on the cabin wall. A concealed panel slid open, revealing a compact kitchen. She retrieved two packages from a cabinet. "Looks like something with steak," she remarked as she placed them in the oven without waiting for his input. From the fridge, she produced two bottles, tossing one to him.

He caught it effortlessly. "Thanks." He popped the top and had a mouthful. "What made you think I'd catch that?"

Haylen flashed a knowing smile. "You're well-trained. I figured you could handle it. And I was right. So what else can you do? In terms of training and combat, I mean."

Setting his bottle down, Blake considered her question. "I'm not exactly adept at combat. I own a blaster, but it's more for show. Never been in a real fight, though I could probably handle myself in a brawl. In a firefight? No clue. I'm a lawyer, not a soldier."

"Duly noted," Haylen replied, her attention briefly diverted as the oven dinged softly. "Dinner's ready."

This time it was Blake cocking an eyebrow. "Dinner? I don't even know what time it is."

Haylen deftly opened the oven, releasing an unexpectedly delightful aroma into the cockpit. The packages had self-opened, revealing fries paired with some sort of steak. Its exact origin was ambiguous, but Blake wasn't concerned; their primary focus was feeding their bodies to maintain their edge.

Meanwhile, the urgency to reach Enkil lingered in his mind. When he looked up to address Haylen, she was already tapping commands into the cockpit console, swiftly plotting the course for Enkil. Catching his gaze, she winked. "All set. Now we just wait for Lannister. Once we're done eating, we can jump into hyperspace," she remarked, already digging into her meal.

Blake nodded in agreement, savouring a few fries. "He won't take long. Lannister's quick and thorough. He'll find what we need in no time."

True to Blake's confidence, within the hour, Lannister called back. He forwarded a series of newspaper clippings. "Local girl disappeared – parents plead for help," one headline read. Each article centred on the same event: the sudden disappearance of 17-year-old Amy Carter from a mansion she had visited with her boyfriend. Tragically, her boyfriend Darren Halloway had been found dead near the same mansion owned by the prominent Claver family, though they claimed not to know anything. Landon Claver, who attended school with Amy and Darren, had stated he left them briefly to fetch food, only to return and find them gone. Despite investigations by local authorities, no conclusive evidence had emerged, but the air of secrecy surrounding the Claver family hinted at deeper complications.

Blake pored over the clippings, sensing there was more to find, linking Amy Carter's mysterious past to Manley's current predicament.

Lannister had managed to get into an ISA databank he shouldn't have had access to, extracting a fragmentary file that shed light on Amy Carter's disappearance and Dana Manley's subsequent identity. According to the hacked data, Daxton Faris had stumbled upon Amy, traumatized and injured, near the Claver mansion. He had brought her to ISA, where she remained under their protection until her official death declaration six months later, which coincided with Dana Manley's emergence as a new ISA recruit. Considering Lannister's limited time, he hadn't uncovered photographs, but Blake was convinced they were dealing with the same person. Everything aligned with what they had learnt so far—except for the one startling revelation Lannister had scrawled in a note: "She isn't just an ordinary agent. She's listed as second-in-command at ISA." Lannister had just sent the files, with a short "See you soon", and Blake knew better than to call him up now. He glanced up at Haylen, who had finished reviewing the files next to him. "Owen. He needs to know", she said.

Blake nodded in agreement. "But we can't broadcast this across the sector. Tell him to rendezvous with us on Enkil. I'm almost certain that's where we'll find her. If they still want her found, she'll be there."

Haylen had already called Owen's ship. Owen had apparently been asleep. His hair looked tousled as he appeared on the cockpit screen. "Owen, we need to talk. In person. We have information we can't send. We meet on Enkil. We don't have time to explain. Please trust me", Haylen shot at him.

Owen just glanced at her and Blake and nodded. "We'll head there right away. Whoever gets there first waits in orbit."

Owen's brisk acknowledgment and directive to rendezvous immediately on Enkil set the tone for urgency. Haylen closed the channel and turned to Blake, her usual confident demeanour giving way to a rare moment of nervousness. Blake couldn't shake the feeling that they were diving deeper into a plot with unknown twists and turns, unsure of where it would lead. "Go get some sleep, Blake," Haylen finally said, her voice tinged with concern. "I'll set the ship on auto-pilot. We need to be sharp when we arrive at Enkil."

Michael Blake couldn't agree more. The news from Lannister's file had shed some new light on the dimension of the case. The fact that Manley held such a high-ranking position in ISA, one she hadn't disclosed, both impressed and puzzled him. What else had she kept hidden? And what crucial pieces of the puzzle were they still missing? He still couldn't put the pieces together. As he settled into his bunk, Blake mulled over the implications. The link to Claver felt increasingly significant—perhaps it held the key to understanding why Amy Carter had vanished and resurfaced as Dana Manley. His mind raced through scenarios, trying to piece together the motives and connections that had led them to this point, until his body surrendered to sleep finally.

Chapter 8

Day 5

Manley drifted in and out of sleep for a while. She had no idea how much time passed, and right now, she truly didn't care. She was so tired from the ordeal Claver and his henchmen had put her through, she didn't mind being only half awake for now. At least she didn't feel any pain as long as she lay still. So much and yet so little was going through her head. It was almost spinning from the absurdity of the events since she had woken up in her hotel in the middle of the night.

Why had Claver gone to such lengths to bring her here, to this forsaken place? He had gloated about using her as bait, to draw her friends into his trap, make her watch them die and kill her last. But surely, he underestimated them. Did he really expect her friends to walk blindly into this trap? Should he not see that this wouldn't happen? That they were too clever to not see the trap they'd be walking into? She shook her head ever so slightly. Owen wouldn't, if he was still out there. Haylen would have noticed by now that Manley wasn't where she was supposed to be. She would undoubtedly be aware by now that something was amiss, would be on high alert. She would never allow anyone to stumble into a trap.

So why was she still alive? Right now and in her current state, she was of no use to anyone. Yet, Claver wasn't getting rid of her because he was using her as bait. She opened her eyes just a fraction, her gaze falling upon a tray of food placed just out of reach. There was a hunk of dark bread, a slice of yellow cheese, and a cup of what she hoped was clean water. To reach it, she would have to move out of her comfortable fetal position and risk the agonizing flare-up of pain from her battered ribs and shoulder. Despite dreading the impending pain, she knew she had to eat and drink. Her body needed food and drink to heal, to survive. And with a sudden clarity, she realised she didn't want to die in this place.

She knew she had to cling to whatever strength still lingered within her if she ever hoped to see the light of day again. She knew that she had it in her. She had done it before, and she could do it again. She had fled from Claver Senior's clutches once, when she had been unguarded for a moment. That night was seared into her memory—a night of fear, despair, and sheer willpower. She ran into the shrubs behind the house that she knew so well and somehow found her way out a small security gate nestled in the tall wall around the estate. Without a backward glance, she fled down the hill, her legs moving with frantic energy, ignoring the branches that whipped at her face and the rocks that threatened to trip her.

Looking back on those harrowing days, she marvelled at her own survival now. It was nothing short of a miracle that she hadn't broken her neck in a fall. For hours she ran, and for days she hid in the dense, silent woods. By the third night, she was lost, her surroundings an unfamiliar tangle of trees and underbrush. Yet she pressed on, driven by the horror she had witnessed, the memory of the deaths that had shattered her world.

The scene replayed in her mind with brutal clarity now. She had seen Landon's father, Kirk Claver, execute two men in cold blood. She had peeked into a window, looking for Landon who had gone into the house. She had not expected to see two men on their knees with weapons at their heads. Before she could process the scene, Claver Senior fired his blaster, and the men crumpled to the floor. She screamed in horror, a sound of terror and disbelief that still echoed in her own ears from time to time. Darren had pulled her away, his hand clamping over her mouth, but it was too late. The men inside had heard her. They ran out, finding the two terrified teenagers huddled just outside the mansion's doors. Darren and Amy were holding on to each other, scared to death. Two men with big blaster rifles motioned them into the great hall, where the bodies lay cooling on the polished floor.

Claver Senior had grinned at them, a wolfish smile that still sent shivers down her spine. He had shoved them into a room next door without a word, leaving them to their fear. Amy and Darren clung to each other in the corner, paralysed by terror. When Claver returned, he took Darren, leaving Amy alone in a silence that was soon broken by screams and laughter from the other room. Amy stood alone, unable to move, unable to process what her 17-year-old mind was experiencing. She had to escape, to run, to flee the nightmare. The window was open, and she didn't hesitate. She heard Darren's voice, a desperate, urgent shout: "Run, Amy, RUN!" She scrambled out the ground floor window, her heart pounding in her chest. A blaster sound rang out, followed by a muffled scream. In that moment, she knew Darren was gone, another victim of Claver's cruelty. Claver had killed him because of what they had seen. She would be next. And Amy kept running until she didn't know where she was.

When the third night was nearly over, she stumbled upon a small ship at the edge of a clearing in the woods. Every step was a painful reminder of her desperate flight—her body was wracked with hunger, fatigue, and a thirst that seemed unquenchable. Her vision blurred, and she barely registered the young man who suddenly stood before her, gripping her shoulders to stop her. His mouth moved rapidly, but she heard nothing. Silence enveloped her as she stared blankly at him, resigned to whatever fate awaited her. She fully expected to be killed.

That man was Daxton Faris, whose team members Claver killed. In her shock and exhaustion, Amy was unresponsive, a shell of the vibrant girl she had been mere days before. She was not reacting to anything Faris did, but he took her in and brought her to ISA. Even without her recounting the horrors she had witnessed, Faris pieced together her story from his own sources. ISA declared Amy Carter dead, and Faris watched from a distance as her parents mourned at a funeral for the daughter they believed they had lost forever. He made sure that no one saw her outside the secure confines of the ISA complex for several years.

Faris made it his personal mission to rehabilitate her, to redeem himself for the losses he had suffered.

He made her eat, drink, and clothe herself, lending a hand whenever she was unable to complete a task on her own. He made her breathe and walk and work through the barriers the trauma had built. He gave her a purpose within ISA, assigning her tasks and missions that restored her sense of self-worth. Their partnership was unbreakable, a bond forged in shared pain and determination with no regrets about their history together. Yet, what Faris couldn't give her finally was hope.

That spark only ignited when Owen appeared, taking on the criminals who shared Claver's dark world. For weeks and months, Dana had dreaded the possibility of confronting Claver face-to-face. Faris had done everything in his power to shield her from that confrontation. But eventually, she found the courage to volunteer for the mission to hunt Claver down. The team she led finally breached his office, only to find him dead. His suicide felt like a betrayal, a cruel twist in her long-simmering desire for vengeance. For years, she had fantasized about what she might do if she ever got her hands on him. But his death also meant that the secret connection between her, Amy Carter, and Claver would stay hidden forever.

And now, all she could do was hope that Haylen would uncover the secrets she had kept from her and the others, not mentioning with a single word that she had a history with that man. But there was another hope, a more personal one, intertwined with the memory of Michael Blake. It scared her to admit it, even to herself, but he was more than a fleeting romance. He had touched a part of her that had remained unreachable for the past seventeen years.

His understanding was almost uncanny, a silent communication that made her feel safe, a feeling she had only known with Faris.

She had never been intimate with Faris, but she trusted him implicitly. Michael, however, had ignited something deeper within her. Their connection surpassed the physical side that both enjoyed, even though they just knew a few snippets out of each other's lives due to the short amount of time they had together. Manley sighed deeply. She would have to get out here if Michael Blake was supposed to remain more than a pleasant memory she could resort to in her sleep. If she wanted to spend more time with him, she needed to get herself up and out of his complex. She still wasn't sure how she was supposed to do this, but she knew that at least she had to get started.

She willed her left eye to open again. The tray with the food was still there, but it seemed light years away. She was afraid of the pain she would inflict on herself trying to get there. Breathing deeply, she propped herself up on her right arm. Waves of pain crashed through her left side, but she gritted her teeth and waited for them to subside, her right arm trembling under the strain. Closing her eyes again, she pushed her arm forward a few inches, dragging her body across the floor toward the tray.

The pain was relentless, stabbing through her with every inch she moved. She stopped, breathed. In and out. Breathe in, breathe out a little longer. Repeat. She pushed her arm forward again, pulled her body towards the tray. She pushed forward again, each movement an exercise in sheer willpower. It felt like hours to cover the mere four feet separating her from the food. When she finally reached the tray, she collapsed onto the floor, panting heavily. Her heartbeat thundered in her ears, and each laboured breath sent fresh waves of pain through her injured side. She lay there for a few moments, gathering her strength, willing her pulse to slow. Carefully, she pushed herself up into a sitting position, using only her right arm. The effort was excruciating, but she needed to eat and drink. She reached for the water first.

She couldn't recall the last time she'd had a proper drink of water. Truthfully, she couldn't remember when she had last eaten, either. It must have been that day on the beach with Blake, after waking from a nightmare. How many days ago was that? The passage of time had become a blur, but she knew she had to keep her body and mind busy if she wanted to survive. She took a cautious bite of the soft bread, chewing on the right side of her mouth, where the pain was less intense. She swallowed each bite with a sip of water. It wasn't much of a meal, and certainly not one she would have chosen under normal circumstances. But right now, it meant she could sustain her body for another while and survive until she found a way out of this hellhole.

When she had finished her meagre meal, she crawled back to the mattress, allowing her battered body some rest. She knew she had to immobilize her left arm and shoulder to manage the pain better. She needed a makeshift splint. Glancing around the room, she saw the same bare, desolate space as the last time she had been awake. Claver's henchmen hadn't left her a first-aid kit, of course. She moved her right hand, touching the coarse blanket beside her. She would have to tear it into strips to make a sling. The prospect didn't thrill her, especially since she lacked the tools to cut the fabric. There was no cutlery on the tray, and the henchmen had removed all potential tools before they left her alone. The tumbler and plate were made of sturdy plastic, so she couldn't hope to break them into pieces that could serve as cutting knives. She needed a more subtle approach.

She pulled the blanket closer to her face and inspected the stitching closely. The thick, grey thread holding the edges of the blanket wasn't in perfect condition. If she could fray the edges enough, perhaps she could rip it by hand. Manley carefully pulled it out on one side and found it easy enough to undo the stitching. She took her time carefully taking out the threading. She used both hands, even though she had to find a comfortable position first. She held her left arm close by her side, being careful to only move her left hand. From time to time, she squinted her eyes, struggling to concentrate. Her vision blurred, making it almost impossible to focus on the thread she was unravelling. She wasn't sure if it was a lingering effect of the head injury or the sheer exhaustion that had settled deep within her bones. Every few minutes, she had to take longer breaks, her body demanding rest. Pain radiated through her, intensifying with each small movement.

She sat hunched over, her hands in her lap, her head bowed low to see her work. The position was torturous. Her neck started aching from the unusual position, and the head trauma from a few days back didn't much help in the process. Instead, it produced a growing headache that slowly moved from the back of her neck to front of her head. Yet, Manley kept working. She knew that the moment she stopped, she would pass out, and she didn't know for how long. She needed to complete this first step before she gave in to her weakness.

She hated that she couldn't fully control of what her body was capable of right now, a bitter reminder of the trauma that still haunted her from her youth. After Faris had taken her in and stabilized her, she had vowed never to be vulnerable again. She had trained relentlessly, honing her body into a finely tuned instrument of survival. She prided herself on always being in control, always having a plan, and knowing precisely how to improvise her way out of any plan gone haywire. She never ventured anywhere without a blaster, even though she rarely needed it. The combat training at ISA enabled her to fight her way out of almost any situation unarmed.

The situation she was in right now wasn't exactly something she was very good at accepting. This sense of helplessness gnawed at her, an unfamiliar and unwelcome sensation. She felt wounded, not just physically but deep within her spirit. The four men who had ambushed her in the hotel room had caught her off guard, right after the nightmare that had shaken her. She hadn't been able to fully use her training, to respond as she had been conditioned to. There was no one to blame but herself for that lapse, a simple human mistake. Now she needed to forgive herself and focus on escaping this dire situation.

She blinked, her vision blurring at the edges again. The strain of her efforts was taking its toll. Manley sighed heavily. This was going to be a lot harder than she had thought. Pulling out the last bit of the thread, she closed her eyes and took slow, deliberate breaths, each inhale and exhale an effort to calm her frazzled nerves and prepare her body for the prospect of actual sleep. She needed rest to heal, to gather her strength, and to think clearly. When she felt she had steeled herself enough against the impending pain, she let herself sink sideways onto the mattress, moving with cautious deliberation.

She lowered herself gently onto her right side, careful not to put any strain her injured left side. The movement was agonizing, each shift of her body sending sharp jolts of pain through her. Using her right arm, she pulled the rough blanket up, cocooning herself in its minimal warmth. She closed her eyes, her body trembling with the effort and pain. The darkness enveloped her, and she passed out almost instantly.

Chapter 9

Day 6

When Haylen's ship finally emerged from the starlit depths of hyperspace, gliding into the orbit of Enkil, both Haylen and Blake woke from their sleep. They met in the cockpit after a few minutes of slowly sitting up, remembering where they were and why. They straightened their appearances as best as they could, smoothing hair and aligning facial expressions into something presentable. Blake slumped into his seat, letting out a contented sigh, while Haylen was already engaged, her fingers dancing over the control panels with practised precision. She glanced his way with a fleeting, reassuring smile. As their ship settled into orbit around Enkil, Darra and Owen were already anticipating their arrival. The two groups decided to rendezvous at a discreet bar nestled within a narrow back alley of Packet, the bustling capital city of Enkil. Arriving in pairs made them less suspicious than as half an army, but they knew they were probably being watched anyway.

Darra and Owen secured a table near the back door, positioning themselves to have an eye on new arrivals and make sure they could exit quickly. Haylen and Blake entered the bar only moments later. Haylen's attire—a short, black dress that clung to her form—was as audacious as it was provocative, undoubtedly something that would have elicited disapproval from any traditional mother figure. Blake, on the other hand, was dressed in black pants and a fitted shirt that bore no insignia, a minimalist ensemble that Owen suspected had Haylen's influence written all over it. Owen gestured for them to join at the table and swiftly ordered four drinks, in an attempt to blend in and avoid curiosity.

"So, what've you got? What's in her past that none of us knew about?" Owen inquired, his tone low.

Haylen inhaled deeply, a silent exchange of meaningful glances with Blake hinting at the intimate and intense discussions they had shared during the journey. Owen leaned in closer. With a solemn expression, Haylen broke the silence.

"Manley isn't who we thought she is."

"I'm gonna need a little more than that, Haylen." Owen's gaze was sharp and unwavering, one of the kind that made very clear that messing around and stalling were not appreciated.

"I know," Haylen responded, meeting his stare with equal intensity. "Manley has been Manley for about seventeen years now. Before that, she went by the name Amy Carter. The Carters were business partners and close friends with the Claver family. Seventeen years ago, Amy Carter witnessed Claver senior murder two ISA agents. Her boyfriend, Darren Halloway, was killed too. She managed to escape, and by sheer luck, she ran into Faris in the woods. He brought her to ISA, and she was placed in the witness protection program, declared dead, and given a new identity. That's when she became the agent we know today. But she's been more than just an agent; she's been Faris's second-in-command for the past ten years. I'm convinced all of this is connected." She paused, her eyebrows raised meaningfully. "And I'm also convinced that Faris knows a lot more about this than he's letting on."

Owen exhaled audibly. "Now that's a lot." His head started spinning with all the questions this new information raised.

Haylen nodded. "And we couldn't tell you this over the comm system."

"No, you couldn't. That would have been stupid." Owen turned his attention to Blake. "So what do we do next?"

Blake shrugged, a gesture of both resignation and determination. "We go find her, save her, put the guy into prison." The simplicity of his words belied the complexity of their taske.

"Agreed." Darra set her empty glass on the table with a decisive thunk. "Should we ask Faris again what he knows?"

Blake and Owen shook their heads in perfect unison. "No," Blake said firmly. "I'm not sure what's going on, but I'd rather leave him out of the picture for now. I'm not sure we can trust him. He's kept things from us before, hasn't he?"

Owen pondered this for a minute, the weight of Haylen's words settling in his mind like a heavy fog. It was true, Faris hadn't been very forthcoming with the knowledge he had about Manley's past. If they had known about her history with Claver, they might be closer to finding her by now. Owen's thoughts churned with questions—why hadn't she said anything? Manley had never mentioned her past encounter with Claver, not even when it became clear that he was entangled with Ortiz. It seemed their camaraderie had not been as unshakeable as he had assumed. Or perhaps she had her reasons, deeply personal ones, for keeping this part of her life concealed. From what he'd just learned, those past events must have been traumatic. Maybe that was why she had often remained in the office, avoiding the risk of running into Claver on their missions. Whatever her reasons, Owen hoped for a chance to discuss it with her soon.

"I say we keep this to ourselves for now," he decided aloud. Then a new realisation struck him. He turned his gaze back to Haylen. "You mentioned Claver senior. I take it he has a son." He almost scolded himself for not looking into family ties before today.

Haylen nodded. "He does."

"What do we know about him? Where is he? What does he do?"

Blake shrugged, a gesture tinged with the frustration of insufficient information. "We haven't had the time to investigate him. We left Birdu right after Lannister sent us the file on Manley, and we came here straight away."

"We'll handle it," Darra interjected decisively. "You two look like you could use some sleep."

"Oh, we've slept," Blake said, but his words were met with amused glances from Darra, Owen, and Haylen. Realizing the implication, he hastily added, feeling a warm blush creep up his neck. "I mean, we've slept in our separate beds in separate rooms."

"I see." Owen's smirk persisted, a mixture of amusement and something more contemplative. If Blake was out for just the fun and a good time, he would have left already. "Anyway, we'll look into Claver junior. We'll call you when we find something relevant. We'll meet here again."

He gestured for Darra to go ahead. "I'll be right with you." Owen's mind continued to race as he watched the others leave, each to their tasks. He leaned back in his chair, the dim, flickering light of the bar casting long shadows over his face. Manley had hidden so much from him, from all of them. The revelation of her past identity and connection to Claver senior was something he had to digest.

Why hadn't she trusted him with this information? Owen replayed countless conversations in his mind, searching for any hint or clue she might have dropped, any sign of the huge burden she had been carrying. But he couldn't remember anything that might have been connected to her past. He felt a pang of betrayal mingled with understanding. She must have had her reasons. The trauma of witnessing such violence, of losing someone she loved, going through this so young, was likely a wound that never fully healed. Did she fear judgment? Did she think they'd see her differently if they knew she had once been Amy Carter, a girl whose life had been torn apart by Claver's brutality?

And then there was the matter of his own disappearance during the space fight when he and Darra had seemingly died. They had faked their own deaths, so they could go and investigate without being bothered to watch their backs constantly. Manley was unaware of this. They had decided not to tell her, so she wouldn't have to keep a secret that went so deep. Back then, they had had no idea about the secrets she was keeping already. And as far as Manley was concerned, they were dead, and she would certainly not expect them to come to her rescue any time soon.

Owen sighed, running a hand over his hair. Manley had always been the fierce, dedicated agent, and now he understood there was a depth to her resolve that he hadn't fully appreciated. The office-bound duties she often volunteered for now seemed less like a preference and more like a necessity—a way to avoid crossing paths with ghosts from her past.

Yet, there was something else gnawing at him. Faris. He had always seemed to know more than he let on. How deeply was he involved in all of this? His role as Manley's protector and mentor now seemed more complex. What other secrets was he keeping, and why? Owen felt a surge of frustration at the thought of Faris manipulating them, controlling the flow of information to suit some hidden agenda.

He glanced around the bar, its patrons oblivious to the gravity of his thoughts. This place, this mission, felt more dangerous now than before. Manley's secret history, Faris's hidden knowledge, Claver's shadow still looming over them—it was all interconnected, forming a web of intrigue and danger.

As he watched Darra leave the bar, Owen stood and walked to the window, looking out at the bustling city of Packet. The neon lights reflected in his eyes as he vowed silently to find his favourite agent.

When Manley started feeling the sleep fade, she kept her eyes closed and concentrated on her surroundings. The silence was almost suffocating; she was still alone in her prison room. She willed her mind to become more aware of her body. The pain, though dulled, lingered in the background, a reminder of the beating she had endured. She suspected it would flare up once she began to move. At least one bone in her shoulder was definitely broken, and her ribs—she didn't even want to think about them. The physical distress was overwhelming, but she couldn't afford to succumb to it.

After what felt like an eternity, Manley slowly opened her eyes. The room was shrouded in shadows, the only light coming from the dim lamp in the corner, casting eerie shapes on the walls. She realised she was still lying on her right side. Holding her breath, she carefully rolled onto her back, bracing herself for the inevitable surge of pain. It didn't come. She exhaled slowly. Apparently, her body had begun to heal, ever so slightly.

Manley turned her head to the left. During her unconsciousness, someone had entered her room. The tray with the empty plate and tumbler had been replaced with a fresh one, even holding a sealed bottle of water. She sighed, understanding Claver's intent. He wanted to keep her alive, at least until Owen and her friends showed up. Her escape plan needed to be foolproof and swift.

Maybe taking the blanket apart wasn't the best idea. Without it, she risked hypothermia during sleep or unconsciousness. She couldn't afford that. However, she still needed to immobilize her left arm and shoulder. The makeshift sling would have to do for now. And she needed to stay awake, alert enough to engage whoever came to exchange the food tray. Any interaction could provide a clue or an opportunity for escape.

But first, she needed to eat. Manley struggled to sit up, biting back a groan as her body protested. She reached for the tray, her hands trembling slightly. With the experience she had gathered these past few days, she expertly moved herself in the direction of the tray and carefully pulled it towards her mattress when she could reach it with her hand. The bottle of water was a small mercy. She twisted the cap off, carefully using her left hand to steady the bottle, and took a long drink, the cool liquid soothing her parched throat. She needed to save all the strength she could. There was fresh bread on the plate, a piece of some dark cake, an egg, and even an apple. Apparently someone had noticed that she might need a little more than dry bread if she was supposed to live—even for whatever little time it took for her friends to come to her rescue. Manley slowly ate what was on the tray. She saved the apple for last, savouring its fresh taste. The meal was simple, but it was enough to raise her strength. When she had finished, she drank another sip from the water bottle, saving some for later.

Then she took the blanket in her hands again, looking for a weak spot where she could begin to pull a long piece free that was enough to tie her left arm securely to her torso. The only method she could think of was to bite a dent into the fabric. Placing the blanket between her teeth, she pulled with all her remaining strength. Fluff lodged between her teeth and stuck to her tongue, but the dent was still too small to start tearing. She repeated the process, again and again, her frustration growing each time. Eventually, the dent was large enough to attempt ripping the fabric.

Manley's plan, crude as it was, started to work. Clamping down on the blanket with her teeth, she used her right hand to tear the fabric. Her jaws ached, and her right arm trembled uncontrollably from the exertion. When she finally managed to free a suitable strip of fabric, she collapsed back onto the mattress, sobbing from sheer exhaustion. The pain flared up again, but she was too drained to care. She knew she couldn't afford to stay down for long, though. Her survival depended on her ability to move, to keep her muscles from wasting away any further. She had already lost too much strength, and any more could mean the difference between life and death.

For now, she allowed herself a brief respite. It took all of her self-control to chase away sleep. Her eyes fluttered open and closed, each blink threatening to drag her into unconsciousness. Minutes, or perhaps only seconds, ticked by. Slowly, the overwhelming fatigue ebbed, and her body began to respond to her commands again.

She sat up again, eyeing the strap of fabric she had produced with her hand. Now all she had to do was tie it around herself to hold her left arm close to her torso. With one hand, preferably. Easy. Manley inhaled sharply, steeling herself for the task, and swung the strap around her back, angling it, so it would come down near her torso where she could grab it again with her right hand. The manoeuvre was awkward and painful, but she managed to catch the end of the fabric.

She found herself grudgingly grateful that someone had taken the time and effort to exchange her black overall for a pair of black pants and a shirt while she had been unconscious. The change of clothes made her current task easier and allowed for better personal hygiene. Though she couldn't ignore the unapproved touches that must have occurred during the switch, she chose to push those thoughts aside for now.

Manley sighed. She needed a plan. She needed to get out of here, and she would probably need help from Claver. Help he wouldn't be willing to give her just because she asked. She was too weak and too injured to find a way out of this complex on her own. She would have to wait for someone to come, as apparently no one reacted to the things she did in her chamber. She had to talk to someone, she had to demand to speak to Claver and convince him that she was a better bait somewhere else. She still had no idea where she was, what planet he had dragged her to. But she was in no condition to fight her way out of this, she needed all the help she could get. And she needed time so Haylen or Michael or whoever was out looking for her could actually find her.

She sighed. She forced herself to tie the fabric into a knotted loop that she painfully put her injured arm into. She tightened the knot, so her arm was pressed up against her torso, practically disabling it.

Manley wondered how on earth she was supposed to start a new job after this. The thought of returning to normalcy felt impossible. Manley knew she was going to need a lot of time to heal from this ordeal, not just physically. She was staying away from the emotional pain that she was gathering. Her brain knew that she would probably be suffering from some sort of post-traumatic stress disorder in addition to the physical injuries. The broken bone in her shoulder would need to heal before she could start thinking about anything else than light exertion again. If she found herself on the wrong side of good luck, she would even need surgery for her shoulder, pushing back healing for several weeks. Given that she found a way out of here and back to people who would be willing to lend her a helping hand in getting back home. Which brought her back to depending on Claver's help.

If Claver junior was anything like his late father, he was a narcissist. Which made him a willing target for flattery. *Think, Manley*, she told herself. There had to be something she could do. She couldn't just stay put in this hellhole and simply wait like the literal damsel in distress, hoping for her knight in shining armour. Well, she didn't have anything against a knight in shining armour lending her a helping hand, considering that she had only one good arm right now. She just didn't want to be the helpless victim who couldn't help herself. She needed to convince Claver that she didn't find him so terrible. That was going to be hard enough, given the pure contempt she felt and had already expressed towards him.

Back when they had all been so much younger, she hadn't felt particularly interested in him. He had been a friend of Darren's, with rich, influential parents. Her own father had worked together with Claver on many occasions, and they were familiar. She had never cared to ask what they were working on, but she had been a teenager wrapped up in herself and being in love for the first time. It was only natural that she never knew what her father was working on.

But by now, she was wondering what kind of enterprises her father and Claver had been involved in together. Had they engaged in criminal arrangements? Or had it all been innocent trading of actual things?

Would her mother know? Oh, her mother. From time to time, Manley had wondered how she was. Faris had told her after attending Amy's make-believe funeral that her parents were heartbroken, that they mourned their loss deeply. Manley had never dared to venture near them again, for fear of being dragged back down into the abyss she had worked herself out of. She had never asked about them again after the funeral, and she had never ventured back into that part of the world she knew. She had known that she needed to burn all bridges in order to protect herself and her family from further damage.

Manley sighed. She had no idea whether or not her parents were still alive after all this time. Feeling her well of emotion stirring, she wasn't sure what she should do. Allow the feelings to vent? Hold them back until she had time and space to live them? She pressed her hand against her chest, feeling the dull ache that wasn't just from her injuries. The emotional scars, the loss, the memories she had buried so deep they were almost forgotten—they were all bubbling to the surface now, threatening to overwhelm her.

She thought for a second too long as a first teardrop formed in the corner of her eye. Before she could do anything about it, the tears started falling. Manley started sobbing, gasping for breath. The emotional pain that seemed to work itself out of her felt almost physical, adding to her torment. She allowed herself to sink down onto her mattress and curl up into a ball. *A box of tissues would come in handy right now*, the sarcastic entity at the back of her mind thought. She had been in trouble before but never before had it felt this hopeless — at least for the past 17 years. No one knew where she was, and there was no guarantee anyone would come and get her. She was injured, and badly enough so. And she was well aware that she wasn't going to get out of here all by herself.

Manley could see her parents standing by a headstone saying "Amy Carter. Beloved daughter, taken too soon". She could hear her mother sob uncontrollably, she could see her father supporting her silently, muffling his own crying. She had never been at the cemetery herself, but Faris had described it to her. He had had someone go by after a year or so, just to be sure everything was looking the way it was supposed to. The headstone was perfect, and Faris had made sure the planting was paid for in advance. Manley could not imagine the pain her parents were probably feeling back then, and she had been in a haze herself, barely having made it out of her dangerous road of self-endangerment during recovery. She had been in no condition to take care of anyone or anything besides herself. She wasn't even sure she could do this now. And yet she longed to be held by her mother, to have her father pick her up and carry her to her bed on the first floor of their house on Enkil. If her parents knew that she had been so close and alive when they believed she was dead...

Manley forced herself to breathe in and out, trying to steady her ragged breaths. She felt a little dizzy, the result of crying so hard that she had deprived herself of much-needed oxygen. It wasn't the first time tears had overwhelmed her. She vividly remembered the night she fled from Claver's mansion, blinded by tears that blurred her vision as she ran desperately. She had narrowly dodged several obstacles that could have injured her before she reached the security gate in the high walls. The tears had turned into gasps for air as she ran. Right now, there was nowhere to run. She was locked up in this room, which was probably underground somewhere in the part of the galaxy she knew. Her demons kept her company, though. And they didn't seem to be willing to leave.

Also, there was the complication of Michael Blake. Manley was certain now that by letting him into her life, she had unwittingly unlocked Pandora's literal box of her troubled past. He had stirred emotions she had long believed conquered and buried. Her assumption of having moved on had been naive. Yet, she felt no regret for letting him in. Being with him had brought her joy. Images of the things they had done flashed before her eyes. With no distraction in this godforsaken dungeon, it would have been so easy to get lost in them. In this bunker, with no distractions, it would have been all too easy to lose herself in those memories.

He was different from Darren in many ways. Darren had been gentle, shy, hanging on her every word and smile, as she had done with him. Blake, on the other hand, exuded confidence and directness. He conveyed his affection through subtle yet meaningful gestures, which had touched her deeply during their brief time together. And who knew what grand gestures he was capable of, given the chance?

Manley sighed once more, releasing some of the tension within her. She made a decision: sleep first, then exercise. It was a basic principle ingrained in her from years of training. Resting adequately before exerting herself, especially in her current weakened state, was essential. She settled back onto the mattress, adjusting the makeshift sling around her injured arm with a wince.

Closing her eyes, she focused on relaxing each muscle she could consciously control. Slowly, deliberately, she regulated her breathing, allowing her body to sink into a state of calm. Her mind wandered away from the harsh reality of her captivity.

In her mind's eye, she conjured a forest unlike any she had ever known in her troubled past. This was a place of refuge, where trees as old as time stood sentinel and a gentle breeze whispered through the leaves overhead. The path she imagined herself walking was soft underfoot, winding through thick brushwood that seemed to part at her approach.

For a while, she allowed herself to lose track of time, allowing imagined serenity envelop her. The darkness of the forest welcomed her, its soothing embrace lulling her into a state where reality and dream blurred together. Gradually, exhaustion pulled her deeper into the realm of sleep.

When her unconsciousness receded, Manley felt a sense of refreshment washing over her. It was a feeling she hadn't experienced for too long. She surveyed her surroundings, noting that nothing had changed during her brief respite. The empty tray remained untouched, a sign that no one had entered her room since she had drifted off.

Slowly, she sat up, bracing herself for the expected surge of pain. It hit her like a tsunami, fierce and unforgiving, but it subsided quicker than before. A hopeful smile tugged at her lips. Perhaps her body was finally responding to the rest and the makeshift sling she had managed to create. Maybe, just maybe, escape was within reach.

Taking a moment to assess her situation, Manley observed the small, windowless room bathed in the dim glow of the solitary lamp in the corner. It confirmed her suspicion that she was likely underground, isolated from any natural light or sense of time.

Summoning every bit of determination, she pushed herself backward until she felt the cool concrete against her back. Leaning her head against the wall, she allowed herself a moment to gather her strength. This was progress, she assured herself. Now came the next challenge: standing.

With her injured arm securely bound to her torso, Manley drew her knees and feet closer, using her good arm to steady herself against the wall. The effort was excruciating, but she knew it was a necessary step if she wanted to find a way out of here.

Standing upright, Manley leaned heavily against the wall, feeling the cold seep into her back, draining the warmth from her weary body. She couldn't afford to linger. Taking a deep breath, she focused her mind and summoned all of her resolve. With a small step forward on her right leg, she tested her balance and the strength of her legs. Her lower leg quivered slightly when she shifted her weight onto it. She held her breath, willing the trembling to subside before daring to move her other foot forward. Seconds stretched into agonizing minutes as she fought the fear of losing her balance. She desperately tried not to imagine the pain that would shoot through her if she fell. She took another step, and then another, until she reached the opposite wall of her prison.

Turning and leaning against the wall, Manley felt a rush of relief flood through her. It felt almost like breaking the surface after being submerged underwater. Her head swam, whether from exertion or the dark, unwelcoming environment, she couldn't tell. Closing her eyes, she focused on regulating her breathing, inhaling deeply and exhaling slowly to calm her racing heart. In and out, in a steady rhythm. The exertion of just crossing the room after several days of almost no movement at all blew her away. Her throat felt dry, and she could hear her breath going through her larynx, making a wheezing noise. Breathing this hard made her injured shoulder move a bit, too. The pain, though dulled compared to before, still flared with each movement. At least, it was ebbing away quite quickly, compared to the past few days. She had to keep going. She had to. She needed every bit of exercise and strength to get out of here.

Manley took one more deep breath and started walking back to the wall she had come from. The path seemed a little easier, her legs protesting less vehemently with each crossing. She could almost ignore the pain coming from her shoulder when she crossed the room for the sixth time. By then, sweat was forming decidedly on her forehead, and her back was definitely wet, too. And not the nice kind of wet. Since she couldn't just take off the shirt to dry it, she decided to be sensible this once and take a break from her exercise. Resigned to her situation, she leaned back against the wall, allowing herself to sink down onto the floor. At least getting down was a lot easier than standing up. Then she worked her way back to the mattress. She closed her eyes, focusing on the sensation of her body meeting the soft surface beneath her. For a moment, she allowed herself to be weak, the rhythm of her breath gradually returning to normal.

The next time Owen, Darra, Haylen, and Blake gathered in the dimly lit bar, there was a sense of urgency and determination in the air. Owen's confidence radiated as he took his seat, and without wasting any time, he placed his sleek tablet computer on the table amidst their drinks. His eyes, sharp and focused, met those of his companions.

"We've done some research on Claver junior," he began, his voice steady and assured. "His name's Landon, and it turns out Manley went to school with him and that boyfriend Darren. From what we've gathered, he inherited his father's companies, and there are quite a lot of them. Not all are under his name; he uses a few aliases. Interestingly, one of those aliases owns the ship that transported Manley."

Blake's eyes narrowed, the glint of resolve in his eyes reminiscent of a bloodhound catching a fresh scent. As the group absorbed the information in silence, Owen pressed on, his tone growing more resolute. "I say we head for his mansion. I know it's risky, and it's just a hunch, but I have a strong feeling he's hiding her on his own premises."

"Good. When are we leaving?" Blake asked.

"We can't go there unprepared. We have one shot, the way I see it. I've got a friend looking into the building plans of the mansion, so we don't get lost in a maze. These plans aren't in the public files, so it might take a few hours to find and access them." He paused, letting the gravity of their mission sink in. "If we get those plans today, I wanna go out there tomorrow morning. I don't wanna do this in the dark. We have no idea how we'll find Manley, and we might be there for a while." He took a deep breath before speaking on. "We have no idea what condition Manley is in. We should expect her to be injured, and it will be easier to navigate our way out if we can see where we're going."

Haylen, ready for action, drummed her fingers on the table. "Agreed. Is Dixie looking into this?"

Owen nodded. "Yes, she is." Just as he was about to elaborate, his PAC beeped with an incoming message. Swiftly, he read the contents and transferred the files to his tablet. A satisfied smile tugged at the corner of his lips. "She's good. She found the files. The mansion itself won't really be a problem. We have to find one of the gates in the perimeter wall to get in. And we have the codes."

Blake nodded approvingly. Dixie had assisted them before, and though the others weren't openly discussing her, and though he sensed some unspoken tension between her and Haylen, she still felt like an integral part of this group. "You mentioned the mansion isn't the main issue. What's the real problem, aside from the fact that we need to get in, find her, and get out? Unharmed and unseen, preferably."

"Yeah..." Owen searched for the right words, knowing there was no easy way to deliver the news. "There's a seven-story bunker beneath the house."

Darra's and Haylen's eyes widened in unison. "Seven stories? Underground?" Darra repeated.

Owen nodded solemnly.

Blake was silent at first, running both hands through his hair in a gesture of mounting frustration. "Boy, that *is* going to be a problem. We'll never get through seven stories unnoticed."

Darra, always the one to add a bit of levity, chimed in with a mischievous grin, "What would Manley say? We'll just have to bring enough blasters and charges."

Blake frowned, his expression stern. He knew Darra was taking the mission seriously; she probably just wanted to lighten the mood. Yet, he could find nothing amusing about the prospect of navigating seven subterranean levels, not to mention the two above ground, in a desperate bid to find Manley. All the while, they had to contend with Claver's undoubtedly well-armed staff, who wouldn't simply allow them to wander freely through the mansion and bunker. This was shaping up to be a kamikaze mission, and Blake was beginning to think that not all of them would come out of it unscathed. The others thought it, too, he could see it on their faces.

Owen tapped a few rapid commands into his tablet computer, the device's screen casting a faint glow on his determined face. "I'm sending you the plans. Memorize them, save them on your PACs. We rendezvous at the spaceport tomorrow morning, just before sunrise. 5:30 a.m. sharp. We'll use my ship; that way, we only need to conceal one vehicle."

Everyone nodded in silent agreement They downed their drinks in a unified, solemn toast to the task ahead and left the bar, heading back to the various hotels they had checked into under assumed names. Night grew into a blanket of quiet anticipation, each member retreating to their room, knowing that a good night's sleep was essential if they wanted to move this mission to a happy ending tomorrow.

Chapter 10

Daxton Faris sat brooding in his dimly lit office, deep within the fortified bunker of the ISA headquarters on Enkil. He was meant to be in a crucial meeting with high-ranking officials from the other end of the sector, but today, politics felt like an insubstantial distraction. His mind was distracted by the remnants of his last conversation with Owen. Faris still grappled with the aftermath of his decision to reveal the dealings between Manley and Claver from so many years ago. The revelation gnawed at him, especially because he had disclosed only a fraction of the truth. He had carefully omitted his own entanglement and the reality of what had happened to lead up to Amy's escape from the mansion.

Now, the shadow of doubt loomed over him. He was acutely aware that Owen and his entourage, including the lawyer Manley had met on Nergal B, were likely to unearth the full extent of their shared past. The sense of relief he had felt when Manley informed him that Claver had taken his own life in his office chair was short-lived. Faris had believed that the darkest chapter of their history had been buried with the man responsible for ending Manley's young love half her life ago.

Yet, the circumstances surrounding Manley's disappearance seemed disturbingly inconsistent. Why now? Certainly, Manley had collected so many enemies during her time at ISA, though few knew her by her name. In fact, almost no one did. Daxton could understand why some of her adversaries might want her gone, but the majority of those she had crossed paths with were either imprisoned or dead. She had a reputation for leaving no loose ends when tasked with eliminating a target. It was doubtful that more than a handful of her former targets were still alive.

Still, someone had taken her and meticulously left clues for those close to her to follow. The information Haylen and Michael Blake had been gathering felt like a scavenger hunt, each fragment slowly revealing the events of that fateful night when Manley vanished from her hotel on Nergal B. It seemed inevitable that they would soon locate her. The photograph Owen and Darra had discovered was no coincidence. Its appearance unnerved him more than he cared to admit. He had believed they had eradicated every trace of Amy Carter from existence. Months had been spent tracking down files and pictures, ensuring that nothing could be inadvertently uncovered. He had scrutinized every scrap of information about her, deciding what to erase and what to retain.

By now, only the barest remnants of her existence should have been left, and that photograph certainly wasn't supposed to be among them. He would have deleted it immediately due to the glaring link between Manley and Claver. So why had Owen and Darra found it? Who had planted it for them to discover? And where had it been hiding all these years?

The unease gnawed at Faris. The photograph's sudden appearance suggested someone orchestrating things from the shadows. It implied that someone knew far more than they should, someone who had managed to outmanoeuvre his careful clean-up. He was trying to piece together who could be behind this. The implications were serious. If someone had access to that photograph, what else might they have? The thought that there might be more evidence, more links to the past he had tried so desperately to bury, was scaring him.

Faris sighed. He knew he was about to cross a line he shouldn't, mixing his professional duties with personal matters. As head of ISA, he shouldn't be diverting resources or staff to investigate issues of a personal nature. Yet, this special situation was different. With a firm press of a button on his desk, he spoke into the intercom. "Jennings, I need to talk to Henders. Get him right now." He didn't wait for a reply; he trusted that his personal assistant, Henry Jennings, would carry out the order promptly. Agent Mark Henders would be in his office within minutes. Until then, Faris could only hope that the rescue mission Owen and Darra were spearheading would succeed and save Manley from whatever peril she was in.

The door to his office hissed open, pulling Faris from his troubled reverie. Agent Mark Henders entered, his demeanour sharp and professional. He stood before Faris's desk and said, "You wanted to see me, Sir?"

Faris nodded, gesturing for Henders to take a seat. "Please, sit. I have a problem that needs to be handled very discreetly."

Henders sat down, his expression attentive. "I see. What is it about?"

Faris hesitated for a moment, then straightened his shoulders. "It's about Manley."

Henders' brow furrowed in confusion. "What about her, Sir? I thought she left ISA."

"She did," Faris confirmed, nodding slowly. "Which technically makes all of this none of our business." He paused, choosing his next words carefully. "But it is. She's still one of us. I'm not sure if you've heard about a tourist who disappeared without a trace on Nergal B. That was Manley. As far as the rest of the world knows, her trail has gone cold. Some people are already out to find her—"

Henders interrupted, a note of urgency in his voice. "What people, Sir?"

This wasn't easy to confess. "Not our people, Henders. Owen Harlow and his entourage, including Haylen North, are trying to find her, along with a lawyer named Michael Blake. Manley met him on Nergal B. They're piecing together what happened and making progress. I want you to assist them. Under the radar. I'm pulling you from all other assignments—this is your sole priority from now on. Find Manley and bring her back alive." Faris watched the subtle changes in Henders' expression. He understood the confusion Henders felt, but the agent was seasoned enough to know that this wasn't the moment to question Faris's directive.

"I see. What do we know? What should I keep in mind?"

Faris sighed deeply. "Have you ever worked with Manley?" He knew the answer. Manley had almost always operated solo. She didn't play well with others, her mind constantly racing ahead, her instincts rarely failing her. She was faster and more precise than most agents, and since she consistently delivered results, Faris had let her work in her preferred manner—alone.

Henders shook his head. "Never, Sir. I've just heard she was an exceptional agent."

"Is," Faris corrected him firmly.

Henders frowned momentarily, then nodded. "Is."

"Manley was kidnapped from her room. There were signs of a struggle. She's been taken somewhere unknown. She might be injured, but as long as she's alive, she's a capable agent who will fight to her last breath. You'll keep this operation quiet. I'll compile everything I know, and you'll start digging. Do whatever it takes to recover her. This is an ultimate authorization. If you need to kill to save her, do it." He knew Henders wouldn't doubt his orders.

Henders simply nodded, signalling he understood. "I'll get started right away. Anything else?"

Faris shook his head with determination. "You only report to me. Nobody else." Henders gave a curt nod, then turned and left without another word.

As the door closed behind him, Faris felt a wave of relief wash over him. At least now he was taking steps to correct the situation. Manley had been a significant part of his life for so long; this couldn't be the end, not on someone else's terms. Henders was a good agent, one of the best. Not quite as extraordinary as Manley, but then again, few ever were. Henders was capable enough to track her down, assuming she wanted to be found.

Faris leaned back in his chair, his thoughts drifting. Was there more behind his actions than just seventeen years of professional camaraderie? He had always maintained that his relationship with Manley was purely professional. Yet, there had been a moment—a fleeting, delicate moment—that had almost changed everything. That day, their relationship could have steered this way or that. It had been about two years after their first encounter, after a long and exhausting day. Manley had popped her head into his office to check if he was still there. He had motioned her in, offering her a drink. They had started talking about their respective days, sharing laughter and stories. She was particularly animated, excited about the progress she was making in her investigation of some Faction lord. Faris couldn't even recall which one he had assigned her to dig up dirt on. They found themselves sitting on the edge of his desk, side by side, conversing as if they had never done anything else.

Despite her evident exhaustion, she was brimming with life, happier than he had ever seen her. Faris must have been looking at her in some peculiar way because she suddenly stopped mid-sentence and locked eyes with him. She didn't say a word, but she didn't need to. He felt it too—the electric undercurrent of excitement that could so easily shift into something more intimate. In that silent exchange, there was a flicker of hope, a sense that she could still have a happy life despite everything that had happened.

Everything seemed to be on fire in that one, precious moment. He could see her sheer need to feel physical touch when she felt so disconnected from the life she once had. Warm sunlight framed her now red hair, a few strands rebelliously hanging loose from her bun. Before he could decide how to respond, she broke eye contact, shyly smiled, and gathered up her purse and glass in one smooth movement. She downed her drink and placed the glass back on the desk. "I'll head over to the gym. See you at home," she said quietly, leaving without waiting for his reaction. She had made the decision for both of them, choosing to step away from the dangerous edge of excitement.

When he returned home later that night, she wasn't there. A few months ago, this would have worried him, but he knew better now. She always told him where she went. She had said she was headed to the gym, and that was where she would be. She spent countless hours there, rebuilding her body from the trauma she had endured. She rarely spoke about it, but he guessed she never wanted to feel that helpless again. She was meticulous, ensuring her muscles complemented her slender figure without drawing unnecessary attention. But he knew her well enough to notice the subtle changes. He had seen a lot more in the years they had worked together.

Yet, there were moments, like the one earlier, where her vulnerability peeked through the cracks in her hardened exterior. He could still see the young woman she once was, filled with hope and dreams, now shaped into a formidable agent by the harsh realities of their world. He admired her resilience, her ability to adapt and excel in their dangerous line of work. But he also felt a pang of sadness, knowing the price she had paid.

He had watched her transformation into a professional operative, capable of killing when ordered. She could take on men in combat that he himself would have hesitated to face. Her skill with blasters and other weapons was unrivalled among the ISA agents he led. She had never looked back after requesting to see her parents one final time, at least not openly. She had embraced her new role as his assistant fully, covering her past with layers of duty and skill. Together, they maintained the facade, even as she evolved into his most valuable asset for tackling issues across the sector. When a problem needed swift resolution, he entrusted it to her, confident she would return with the outcomes he sought. Some tasks were straightforward, like recovering stolen Faction cargo. Others, involving elusive serial criminals and their intricate networks, required more time and finesse. Yet, Dana Manley never failed Faris, even when she returned home bearing battle scars.

Comparing Dana Manley now to the girl named Amy Carter he had unexpectedly encountered in the woods, Faris struggled to figure out how they could be the same person. Deep down, he knew traces of the young, innocent girl who had witnessed Claver's brutality must still linger within her. But Manley had become adept at keeping Amy buried beneath layers of steeled resolve and professional detachment. Usually. Now, however, Faris sensed a shift—a glimpse of the past that threatened to unearth Amy from the shadows.

Faris shook his head, trying to clear the swirl of thoughts that threatened to overwhelm him. He needed focus. Sending Agent Henders the gathered files from the past few days was his top priority now. With swift precision, he tapped commands on his keyboard, compiled the dossier and transmitted it. As the files transferred, he exhaled deeply and sank back into his chair.

Mark Henders quickly left Faris's office, his mind already racing. As he made his way to his own office, he gathered his gear, preparing himself mentally for the task that lay ahead. Waiting for Faris's detailed mission statement would guide his initial steps, but he knew deep down he couldn't afford to rely solely on instructions. This mission demanded his utmost resourcefulness and determination.

Everyone within ISA knew that Dana Manley held a special place in Faris's heart, and perhaps vice versa. The rumours about their connection were still wafting through the halls—stories of shared secrets, an unspoken bond that went far beyond their professional roles. There were whispers of them living together for a time, though details were scarce. Whatever the truth, it was undeniable that their relationship was profound.

Henders felt apprehensive. If he failed, it might not look good for him in ISA. He would forever be the one who didn't manage to bring back Manley, even if it happened through no fault of his own.

When the notification pinged on his PAC, confirming the transmission of the Manley dossier from Faris, Henders sat down at his desk. His office was a stark contrast to Faris's spacious quarters—compact, functional, focused solely on the essentials: a chair, a desk, and a cabinet housing his arsenal of weapons and equipment. It took him the better part of an hour to digest the information laid out before him. Dana Manley's history unfolded like a complex puzzle.

Rescued by Faris seventeen years ago from Claver senior's clutches, she had been thrust into witness protection, becoming Faris' personal project. Involved in the complex web of the Claver affair, she had accepted a new role within the Faction, her reasons known only to a select few.

He was in the agency long enough not to wonder why she had chosen to change sides. She probably had her reasons. And now she had been kidnapped from Nergal B after meeting a lawyer named Michael Blake. Faris had cleared him, he was who he said he was and didn't seem to have a hand in the kidnapping. Information from Owen Harlow's network indicated Manley's last known location at Enkil spaceport, suggesting she was nearby.

Henders's fingers flew over his keyboard, a masterful hacker in his element. He pushed through the spaceport's security system with ease, tracing the breadcrumbs left by the ship that had carried Manley. Despite recent attempts to erase data trails, Henders identified a crucial lead—a camera image of the ship's parking space. To others, it might have seemed a dead end, but to Henders, it was a pivotal clue. With swift manoeuvres and clever re-routings, he uncovered the ship's owner. And while many wouldn't have known what to do with the name he found, he knew it was an alias. An assumed name for a dangerous criminal posing as a hard-working member of society. Henders grabbed a bag and a few blasters, not forgetting extra charges for them. He had an idea where he was going to start his hunt for Manley.

A few minutes later, he found himself in a district of the city he usually took great pains to avoid. Before him loomed an imposing, seemingly deserted warehouse, its weathered facade climbing several stories high. The rusted plates at the entrance offered no assurance of safety or legitimacy. His gaze zeroed in on the plaque at the far right, the one for the top floor, bearing the inscription "Ratched Enterprises." The name had caught his attention before, linking the enigmatic company to the ship in question. It was also the name of the company that owned the ship Manley was transported in. His prior investigations had revealed that "Ratched" was the alias employed by the Claver family whenever they needed to obscure their involvement in questionable ventures.

He was convinced that the Claver family had their hands deep in this murky affair. Though the exact nature and purpose of their involvement remained vague, his instincts nudged him toward the truth. He knew he had to return to his office. There, he could delve deeper into the myriad of hideouts the Claver family maintained. And then he would figure out which one to go to, and he would get Manley out of there.

It didn't take Henders long to deduce that the Claver family's most fortified refuge was the seven-story bunker beneath their sprawling mansion just outside the city limits. This was the very mansion Manley had fled from seventeen years ago, according to the detailed files Faris had provided. With a keen understanding of the psychological profile common to criminal narcissists like Claver, Henders felt a grim certainty that she would be found there. Claver's sadistic tendencies would drive him to ensnare Manley's allies, drawing them into his web only to eliminate them.

For the next hour, Henders committed the layout of the mansion and the bunker to memory. The underground labyrinth of rooms and tunnels presented an intimidating challenge, but there was no alternative. If necessary, he was prepared to take hostages, turning Claver's own ruthless tactics against him. With a weary sigh, Henders acknowledged the grim nature of his mission. No agent was looking forward to the task of rescuing one of their own.

Resolved to face the challenge ahead, he decided to head home. A good night's sleep would be essential for the next day. Tomorrow, he would pilot his ship to the Claver mansion and execute his plan to rescue his colleague. With a final glance around his office, he switched off the lights and stepped into the cool night air, leaving the building behind.

Early next morning, Henders picked up his ship from the small, discreet spaceport ISA owned. Under the cloak of pre-dawn darkness, he piloted his craft northwards, heading for the secluded hills where the Claver mansion was nestled. He knew the cover of night was his ally, but he also understood the limits of his technological camouflage; while he could scramble search signals and evade electronic surveillance, he could not obscure his presence from vigilant human eyes. Navigating low over the treetops, Henders expertly manoeuvred his ship to a concealed position just two hundred yards from the mansion's formidable security wall. He landed in a small clearing, hidden from view, and waited for the first light of dawn. Charging in under the cover of darkness was too risky. He had no idea what condition Manley was in, and a daylight rescue would reduce the chances of a dangerous, blind escape through unfamiliar terrain.

As the sun began to climb into the sky, casting long shadows across the forest floor, Henders exited his ship and made his way stealthily towards the mansion's security perimeter. With precision and skill, he temporarily disabled key components of the security system, granting him a brief window to slip through a small, seldom-used gate undetected. Moving swiftly but cautiously, he utilized the cover of the dense greenery surrounding the mansion to avoid detection.

Approaching the mansion itself, Henders kept to the shadows, his movements fluid and silent. As he neared a pathway, he paused, scanning the area for any sign of guards or surveillance. His heart pounded in his chest as he listened for the faintest sound of movement. Suddenly he froze.

Henders could see a group of four inching toward the back entrance from where he was concealed. From Faris' dossier, he recognized Owen Harlow and his entourage—Haylen North, Michael Blake, and Darra Finn. They had picked up Manley's trail as well. It was unfortunate that he couldn't join forces with them; his orders were clear, and time was of the essence.

With expert precision, Henders breached the small service door on his right. The dimly lit corridor beyond stretched out, ending in a larger one a few yards ahead. Pressing himself against the wall, he paused, listening intently to the surrounding silence. As his eyes adjusted to the murky light, he noticed another corridor branching off parallel to the first one, just two yards ahead. Faint noises came from this secondary passage.

Tightening his grip on his blaster, Henders prepared himself for whatever lay ahead. The sounds were subtle but unmistakable—someone, or something, was there. Silently, he inhaled, steeling his nerves. With a swift, fluid motion, he rounded the corner, his blaster leading the way, ready to confront any threat that awaited him.

Chapter 11

Day 7

When one of Claver's henchmen came back to deliver fresh food, Manley knew it was now or never. She had waited patiently, biding her time, and now an opportunity presented itself. The guard was alone, though armed, but she had resolved that this might be her only chance for escape. Sitting beside the tray she had emptied of all food, she remained still, feigning compliance as he approached to retrieve it.

The guard's face registered a flicker of surprise; she was awake and appeared in better condition than before. His blaster dangled carelessly at his side, and with a swift, practised motion, she seized it with her uninjured hand. In an instant, the weapon was aimed directly at his face, her finger hovering over the trigger. The guard's eyes widened in shock as she simultaneously disengaged the safety. "Shhhhh," she commanded softly, motioning for him to back away and circle around to the far end of the room. Rising slowly, she kept the blaster trained on him, every sense heightened. There were no cameras in the room—Claver, in his arrogance, hadn't deemed them necessary—but it wouldn't be long before the guard's absence raised alarms.

She advanced, her eyes fixed on him, allowing no room for error. She had no interest in his name; he was merely a tool. The fear in his eyes became evident as she closed the distance between them. Clearly, he knew exactly who he was dealing with. If she had been at full strength, she would have incapacitated him effortlessly. However, given her current state, a more direct approach was necessary.

Pointing the blaster down at his crotch, she smirked. "Now, I think the two of us could have had such fun with each other if we had only met in a different place. And under different circumstances." She watched a shy grin creep onto his face, making him appear younger and more innocent than he likely was. And before he knew what happened, she struck, bringing the handle of the blaster down hard on his temple. He slumped with a surprised little noise, and it took Manley all but a few seconds to get out of the room, lock the door, put the keys in her pocket and started out. She slid down the corridor to her left silently, noting that this passageway was rougher and more primitive than the one she had memorized. She must have been on a different level by now.

Directionless but undeterred, she picked a path and committed to it, her senses on high alert. The absence of nearby guards was a stroke of luck she couldn't afford to spend any thought on. A few yards ahead, another corridor branched off from the one she was traversing. She halted, her surroundings eerily silent. Moving with the utmost caution, she crept to the corner, ears straining for any sound beyond her own too-loud breathing. She dared to inch her head forward, peeking around the corner. To her surprise, the corridor was empty. No guards, no signs of life. It was strange, almost unnerving, but she couldn't afford to ponder the reasons for her good fortune. She needed to put as much distance as possible between herself and the room she had escaped from. She needed to get away from the corridor she had been in as quickly as possible, so she wouldn't arouse suspicion if she ran into someone.

Manley seized the moment, moving leisurely yet purposefully around the corner into the new corridor, her movements swift and silent. This corridor was empty too, a seemingly endless stretch of dimly lit passage. A few yards in, she heard a noise from above—a noise that spoke of impending trouble. It was a faint, almost imperceptible sound, yet it sent a shiver down her spine, signifying danger.

Quickening her pace, she moved on. Wherever she was, she needed to get out. And fast. Recognizing that she was likely deep underground, her eyes darted around for any sign of an upward route. Lifts were out of the question; they were too obvious and too dangerous. But then she spotted a door on the opposite side of the corridor. A small sign with a ladder icon hinted at an emergency staircase.

She approached the door, unlocked it, and slipped inside. Her suspicion was confirmed: a narrow ladder was bolted to the wall, leading upward. The climb looked long and arduous, several floors separating her from potential safety. The tight vertical shaft offered the advantage of easy enough ascent with only one good arm. She sighed, making a mental note to treat herself to a well-deserved holiday if she survived this ordeal. Certainly not on Nergal B, though—anywhere but that hellhole.

Securing the stolen blaster to her pants, she clenched her fist and took a deep breath. Determination hardened her resolve as she grasped the ladder and began the climb. The ascent was gruelling, each step a test of her persistence. She paused occasionally, leaning her back against the shaft to catch her breath, counting the doors as she passed them. The higher she climbed, the more noises she heard—muffled voices, distant footsteps, the hum of machinery.

There were definitely people behind those doors going about their business. What she also noticed was that the noises she heard were becoming a little more hectic every time she heard some. She took that as a bad sign. Many hectic noises during a mission where usually happening when something went wrong. After passing five doors, she noticed that the sixth one seemed to mark the end of her ascent. She paused, clinging to the ladder, and pondered how to open the door without drawing attention. Minutes ticked by, each one filled with the anticipation of being discovered.

Suddenly, she heard a crescendo of noises from below, from where she had climbed. She pressed the red button beside the ladder, opening the shaft to another corridor. She hesitated, listening intently. Footsteps echoed through the corridor, but they were leading away from her. Manley closed her eyes briefly, summoning her courage, and then propelled herself into the corridor. It was narrow and poorly lit, shadows dancing ominously along the walls. She glanced in both directions and felt a strange sense of déjà vu, as though she had been in this very passage before. Just a few steps to her left, another corridor intersected hers. Someone was approaching.

Frantically, Manley searched for a hiding spot. The only option was the shaft she had just exited. Before she could act, a man in grey clothing rounded the corner cautiously, a blaster in hand, aimed directly at her. She recognized him instantly. His expression shifted from determination to shock as their eyes met. "Manley!" he mouthed silently, not without a good bit of surprise. She desperately tried to remember his name. Mark. Mark something. She had been on the same floor with him at ISA. He was a colleague. He was probably here to find her. Faris must have sent him. She nodded silently and motioned him to get out of here with a tilt of her head.

Mark Henders handed her a blaster without uttering a word, his gaze lingering on her for a moment as he took in the extent of her injuries. Her face was swollen, marred by large bruises of black and blue, and her left arm was supported by an improvised sling, clearly necessitated by some injury. She appeared much thinner than he remembered, her once vibrant red hair now unkempt, and her complexion pale. Her eyes were sunken, betraying the toll of her ordeal, and she was far from her best shape. Naturally, Mark Henders would never mention any of this aloud. He silently gestured for her to follow.

Manley didn't hesitate. His presence here was no accident. Henders—yes, that was his name—was here to rescue her. Together, they edged into the adjoining corridor. Her heart pounded loudly in her chest, and she feared someone might hear it. She was so close to escaping. With Henders at her side, her chances of survival had significantly improved. Suddenly, recognition dawned on her. This was the Claver mansion. She had been here before, so long ago. That explained why the corridor felt so familiar; it led along the back of the house towards the kitchen. She paused briefly as memories of her last visit here flooded her mind. It was long enough for someone to aim a shot and barely miss her. She darted after Handers, who was running towards the back of the house, with someone hot on their trail. Manley lost her step and fell, again narrowly avoiding another blaster shot. She struck her head on the corner she had tried to navigate. Dazed, she felt someone grab her arm and haul her up. Her ears rang from the impact, and as she staggered along, she noticed blood dripping from her forehead. Not good. They rounded another corner, then another, and suddenly Henders halted.

Manley looked up, her breath catching in her throat. She couldn't believe what she saw. They were both staring into blaster barrels. Four of them. All aiming at them. She blinked, her mind racing. In a split-second, she thought that it would have been too nice to get out there and back to her life. That she would like to give Claver a little speech about the things she would like to do to him without anybody else watching. That she shouldn't say any of those things as she was being threatened by his men. She blinked. Those weren't Claver's men.

In front of her were Owen and Darra, and Haylen and Michael Blake. Owen and Darra were dead. Supposedly. Apparently, they weren't as dead as she had thought. Haylen North was there. Haylen had come to her rescue. And Blake. Wonderful, crazy, reliable Blake who looked even more daunting in the black, tight enough clothing he was wearing now, as he was pointing a blaster in her direction. Manley couldn't believe it. She had fantasised about this moment for days, and now that it was here, she was at a loss for words. She didn't trust her voice, so she said nothing at all.

For a few seconds, she looked from one to the next, holding eye contact with Blake a little longer than with the others. She could see his concern — and he was probably noticing the extent of her injuries. She felt memories, thoughts, events rush past her in a whirlwind, everything mixing up to a volume she could hardly bear. It was too much to process now.

Owen asked quietly, "Manley, who's that?"

She didn't react. Henders answered for her, "I'm a colleague of hers. Mark Henders. Faris sends me to get her home."

Owen assessed the situation quickly, realising he had no other option but to trust the man who was helping Manley. Apparently, Faris had come to his senses. He motioned to Henders, "Take her out of here. Get her somewhere safe. We have some business to attend to."

Henders nodded, his expression grim and determined. Blake knew better than to contradict now. He had faith that Henders would be able to get Manley out of here alive single-handedly, if he was a trained agent. And Manley needed to get out of here. She didn't look like she could take any more strain than she had on her already. He would stay with Owen and make sure that Claver did not live to tell the tale of how he grabbed the best agent ISA had.

He could reunite with Manley later; her rescue was only minutes away now.

Henders knew he was only supposed to follow Faris's orders right now. But that didn't mean other orders weren't just as sensible as the ones his boss gave him. His mission was to bring Manley home alive, and he intended to see this mission through. He knew Owen was one of the good guys and Henders gave him enough grace to know that this course of action was the right one. Grabbing Manley's right arm again, he pulled her along with him. She followed willingly, suddenly weary of always being the strong agent she had been for so long. She just wanted to get out of here, and quickly, before her body gave in to the trauma and the stress. She stumbled along with him as quickly as possible, ignoring the pain, and suddenly found herself blinded by the light of day. They had reached the back door, seemingly unseen, unheard, unbothered. After so much time underground, the light was overwhelming for Manley. "I can't see," she whispered, covering her eyes with her good hand. "I need a moment!"

"We don't have a moment, Manley. Claver might notice that you're gone any moment, and I don't wanna be here when he does. We need to get to the trees, I have a ship outside the premises", Henders hissed urgently.

Manley suddenly found herself transported back in time, seventeen years. The trees. The running. The ship. Her legs buckled, and she sank to her knees, still covering her eyes, unable to stand. She sensed Henders' growing impatience, understood it, but she couldn't move. She couldn't. Her legs wouldn't respond, and the pain from the blinding light was excruciating, piercing her temples. Her head spun, and all she wanted was to lie down and escape this nightmare. Sleep off this nightmare that she had found herself in. The agent in her knew this wasn't possible. And for all things, it wasn't possible now.

Before she could react, Henders scooped her up. He still clutched his blaster in one hand. Her own weapon had fallen when she sank down, but there was no time to retrieve it. He slid his arms under her legs and hoisted her over his shoulder, her head dangling down unceremoniously. Dignity was a luxury she could afford again once they were home, safe and sound.

For Manley, the world turned upside down. The ground now hung above her head, and she bobbed along with Henders' quick strides toward the trees. The light, while still intense, was less blinding from this angle. Why couldn't it have been the middle of the night when she finally escaped this hellhole? She would have preferred moonlight to the full sun exposing them to every pair of eyes that might look their way. She was grateful, at least, that Henders' shoulder pressed into her right side, sparing her bound-up left arm, which was supposed to remain immobile.

Henders moved with determination, his steps sure and swift. Every step sent a wave of pain through her body, but she bit back any sound. Suddenly, the world around her changed again. It turned green as the trees loomed above, and her perspective shifted once more. Henders was setting her back on her feet. Her legs, unused to bearing her weight after being carried, immediately buckled. Henders caught her, his arm grabbing her waist before she could fall. He steadied her against his body, holding her firmly until she regained her balance. And even though she wasn't sure how many seconds they had gained on the people who were probably following them, Manley was glad they had them. A moment later, she slowly raised her eyes to meet Henders' gaze. "How did you find me?"

Henders shrugged, his expression a mixture of indifference and urgency. "Wasn't so difficult after all the work that crew put into the search. Faris gave me their research, and I took it from there." He paused for a few seconds, then motioned to the dense woods in front of them. "We should go. Before someone catches up with us."

Manley nodded. She wasn't sure at all how far she could go, but she completely agreed that they needed to get out of here. "Lead the way", she said, forcing a wry smile. "I'll be right behind you. As long as we're not making this a marathon."

Henders allowed himself a brief, appreciative smile. So she hadn't lost her humour, Henders thought. That was probably the best he could have hoped for, given the circumstances. She certainly looked like she had been through an ordeal since she had been kidnapped on Nergal B. He motioned a little to their left, indicating a path through the thick greenery. "My ship's over there, behind the wall," he pointed down the hill they were still standing on.

Wall? Manley couldn't see a wall. There were only tall trees, their crowns barely touching each other. The wall must have been a low one, or else it should have been visible somehow. She glanced to her left, then to her right, trying to make sense of it. And then it dawned on her. Of course. The trees had grown.

She had been right here seventeen years ago, and the trees had been much smaller then. Her heart pounded faster with resurfacing fear, and she heard phantom shouts of people who weren't there. With great effort, she pulled herself out of the memory trap, knowing that both their lives depended on it. She nodded firmly and motioned for Henders to move.

Henders didn't need any further encouragement. He started walking toward the invisible wall, glancing back every few seconds to make sure Manley was still with him. Barely two minutes later, he stopped abruptly. Manley, not quick enough to react, bumped into him. "Sorry," she whispered, wincing as a sharp pain shot through her left arm and shoulder. Henders shushed her, quickly working on his PAC. He was probably disabling the security in a very clever way, making sure their escape would go unnoticed.

She knew he was adept with electronics. She eyed the wall, recognizing it as the same one she had passed through seventeen years ago. Judging by the short distance from the house, it was likely the same gate door she had used back then. Suddenly, the door sprang open with a low "bang," revealing her way to safety once again. For a split second, Manley wondered how many times in her life she would walk, run, or crawl through that door.

"Just two hundred yards," she heard Henders say as he began to move forward. She followed him, her steps unsteady but determined. They didn't bother to close the door behind them; whoever was pursuing them would disable security just as easily as Henders had. They had to get to his ship as quickly as possible. Manley's breath came in hard gasps, blackness wavering at the edges of her vision. She knew she was pushing her healing body dangerously. But there was no other way. Medical could probably get her back on her feet in no time—well, maybe a little time, considering the broken shoulder and whatever other injuries they might find.

As these thoughts swirled in her mind, she reached Henders' ship, standing at the tree line of a small clearing. It reminded her of the one where she had once met Faris, though it was too close to the wall to be the same. Henders opened the door via remote and motioned for her to climb inside. She complied, and he quickly followed, slamming the door shut and locking it up. He enabled the automatic defence system before turning around to face her. For a moment, Henders and Manley stared at each other, the weight of their escape hanging in the air. Then he spoke, his voice a mixture of relief and reproach. "You had a lot of people very worried out there."

Manley tried very hard not to shrug. She remembered the pain from minutes before when she had run into him. "It's not like I had a fun time out, you know." She gave him a hard look, trying not to let show how much she wanted to curl up, cry, and sleep for at least two weeks.

Henders raised his hands in apology. "I'm sorry, I know." He didn't know what else to say and pointed to the small private chamber his ship had. "If you want to get a bit of sleep…" His voice trailed off.

Manley looked from Henders to the small door and back. She was considering turning the offer down. After all, she was on her feet now and doing okay, wasn't she? And then she heard the nagging voice at the back of her mind. *If you sleep now, you could be wide awake when you get to meet Blake the next time. You could have healed some more and forget about all that happened for a while.* She looked back to the door and said, "Okay. I'll take a nap. But you'll wake me when we get to — where are we going?"

It hit Henders that his offer of sleep wasn't going to be a long-term one. "Faris told me to bring you to him. He's at HQ here on Enkil."

Silence hung between them for a moment. Enkil. It fully hit her that she had been home all this time. They had brought her home and hid her where no one would be looking. She couldn't get her head around that she had been in Claver's mansion all along. She hadn't known he had a bunker below it, but it suited his personality. For all she knew, that bunker had been there 17 years ago, and she could have ended up down there, even back then.

Manley also knew what Henders' words meant. If this was Claver's mansion, they would barely be in the air for more than twenty minutes. Not enough time to fall asleep and gain some actual refreshment. Not in the current state of injury she was in. Chances were she'd slip into some sort of unconsciousness as soon as her head hit the pillow. Manley sighed audibly. "Alright, no sleep."

She looked around, her eyes searching for a medical kit to get some painkillers. Apparently, Henders kept it in a different place than she did on her ship, where hers was always accessible right next to the door in her Packet. Her ship. It was still back on Nergal B. Probably. She decided to not mention this for now — Henders would probably think she was even crazier than he had heard. She raised her voice again. "Can I borrow your medical kit for some painkillers? My shoulder's in pretty bad shape." Along with the other injuries, but she didn't insist.

Henders nodded and gestured towards the cockpit. "Have a seat. I'll get it." Of course, agents at their level were educated in first aid to they could handle their own injuries. Except that he wasn't going to let her do that. He opened the door to his sleeping cot and dropped to his knees. He had stowed away the medical kit under the bed, right beside the tools for his ship. When turning back to her a few seconds later, he wondered how she could still be conscious, walking and talking. He had hardly ever seen anyone this exhausted, and he was sure it wasn't just from lack of sleep. He knew first-hand how agents were trained to mask pain, so her request for painkillers and describing her shoulder as "pretty bad" signalled a serious injury. He would have to be on the brink of breaking down to admit anything like that himself.

Manley had settled into the co-pilot's chair, but she was clearly trying not to relax. Her whole body was tense, and he had an idea of how much pain she was in. He remembered that one time, about two years ago, when he had taken a blaster hit to his back. At first, he thought it wasn't so bad but boy, he was wrong. The resulting haematoma had compressed down on his spine, nearly crippling him. He had spent for days after emergency surgery in a hospital bed, lying very still. The medical team told him he was lucky it had happened so close to home rather than in a remote sector where the outcome would have been far worse. He might never have walked on his own feet again.

Henders walked over to Manley and sank into his seat, contemplating their next moves. He knew they needed to depart quickly, but starting the ship and ascending into the atmosphere would put more pressure on her body than she could likely handle. Getting those painkillers into her system was crucial if he wanted her to remain conscious. Opening the case in his lap, he carefully prepared a syringe with a clear, potent liquid—a strong painkiller meant for serious injuries, judging her weight with his eyes.

When Manley held out her good hand for the syringe, Henders shook his head firmly. "I know you can, but I'm not letting you do this right now. Let me handle it. I'm uninjured, it'll be quicker and easier," he insisted, his tone gentle yet authoritative. He saw her struggle, between her strong-willed, independent nature and the necessity to trust someone else in this moment of vulnerability. He wasn't sure if she couldn't tune down her composure right now or if she just didn't care any more to let him see what she thought right now.

For a few tense seconds, Manley hesitated. Normally, she wouldn't easily yield to another's help, not in work or personal matters. Her reputation for feistiness preceded her, and Henders respected that about her. Yet now, under the weight of exhaustion and pain, she seemed to recognize the practicality of his offer. Finally, she nodded quietly and extended her arm, relinquishing a bit of control without actual contradiction—an action that spoke volumes about her current condition.

As he prepared to administer the injection, Henders couldn't shake the unease he felt seeing Manley in this state. Her usual defiance and self-assured demeanour were gone. On any other mission, he might have lightened the moment with a playful remark, teasing her about putting the injection in a more unconventional place. She was undeniably attractive, and she knew it, and under different circumstances, he might have relished the opportunity to banter with her. But now was not the time for jests or flirtation. Manley hadn't uttered a word about the horrors she had faced, but Henders could read the signs. It was written all over her body that she hadn't been in a self-decisive situation these past few days. It wasn't his place, nor anyone else's, to add to the burdens she already carried.

Setting the syringe down for a moment, Henders retrieved his medical scissors and carefully cut through the sleeve of her shirt. His gaze fell on the darkened bruises marring her arm, a silent testament to the violence she had endured. He knew better than to mention them; she didn't need reminders of what she had been through. Instead, he focused on finding a suitable vein for the injection, gently probing the crook of her arm.

After a moment's search, he found a small, unbruised area between the contusions—a narrow window where he could administer the painkillers without causing her further discomfort. It had to be this spot; moving the other arm, visibly injured, would be too much for her without the numbing effect of the medication. Henders thanked his luck for finding a vein so quickly.

Henders acted swiftly. Disinfecting the injection site was a luxury they couldn't afford; medical facilities at HQ would take care of any infection later. She would receive a high dose of antibiotics, anyway and just in case. His focus was on administering the painkillers efficiently.

Also, they had no more time to lose. It was still hard to believe no one had followed them or was aiming some bad-ass weapon at the ship. Biting off the syringe cap with a practised motion, he discarded it without a second thought. Every moment counted now. He tapped her vein a few times to be sure he wouldn't have to do this twice, then he inhaled and pinched her.

Manley flinched and held her breath violently as the needle entered her skin, a visible reaction that betrayed her pain. He could feel the muscles in her arm tense a lot. He pushed the plunger steadily, making sure the painkillers took effect swiftly without overwhelming her system. As the medication flowed into her bloodstream, he observed her body language, noting the gradual relaxation in her posture. Henders took that as a good sign, knowing that the drug was working and that she was feeling less pain.

"Feeling better?" he asked quietly, his voice a soothing contrast to the urgency that had filled the cockpit moments ago. He watched as Manley nodded faintly, a hint of relief crossing her features.

He took some sterile pads from the case and gently wiped away the blood from her forehead. The cut stretched from her eyebrow to her hairline, a jagged crimson path, though mercifully it had already ceased to bleed. She'd need stitches, of course—provided he could get her to medical in a timely manner. He allowed her a few moments of peace, letting her collect herself before quietly stowing the medical kit away. "You'll need to buckle up. I can do it for you," he said softly. Manley nodded, her eyes heavy with fatigue and pain. She lifted her uninjured arm, allowing him to fasten the safety belt securely around her. She couldn't find the right words.

He swivelled her seat to face the front of the ship, giving her a clear view of the cockpit's screen. He began tapping control panels, discreetly firing up the jets. As the ship lifted off, he heard Manley sigh. He dared not glance at her, knowing that the ascent would inevitably strain her injuries despite the painkillers. Instead, he kept his focus sharp, his fingers dancing over the controls, guiding the ship to skim low over the treetops. He was acutely aware of the audacity—escaping with Claver's personal nemesis from the very heart of his palace.

A private message to Faris confirmed he was en route with his "package." He knew Faris would order a medical team to wait for them on the roof of ISA headquarters, ready to take Manley to safety. Once there, his plan was simple: drop her off and vanish. He intended to leave the planet and lie low for a few days until any potential pursuit went cold. Within a week, he would be back in business, the incident nothing more than a fading memory.

Manley sat motionless in her chair, her gaze fixed on the screen displaying the feed from the front cameras of Henders' ship. They were gliding over the dense woodland, the lush green canopy blending into a seamless carpet beneath them. The details blurred together, and her vision wavered, teetering on the brink of a physical collapse. She could sense Henders' furtive glances, his careful effort not to look at her so often. She couldn't blame him. She had never been tasked with retrieving a colleague from the field, but she could imagine how had that was. Undoubtedly, Faris would hold Henders accountable if anything more happened to her under his watch. Nobody wanted to be on the bad side of Faris and Manley.

She observed Henders carefully from the corner of her eye. He was wearing a grey military outfit, the kind they used for unofficial missions. There were no logos or insignia to identify him as a member of ISA. Black attire had proven too conspicuous of late, unsuitable for urban combat or forest pursuits. It was clear Faris was keeping this mission under wraps, trying to maintain a low profile. She could easily understand why. Even though he was leading this agency, she wasn't his employee any more. In fact, she was on the verge of switching sides, aligning herself with those branded as the "bad guys." If anyone outside ISA's inner circle got wind of this, Faris would face a barrage of questions from a host of overconfident politicians. She wasn't eager to see interrogations about her involvement either. There would be too many probing questions about her connections to Claver, and she couldn't blame anyone for suspecting her of being a double agent, even though those accusations couldn't be further from the truth.

She glanced at Henders once more. His short, black hair was neatly clipped, a stark contrast to the dishevelled state she found herself in. He seemed unmoved by the physical ordeal they had just endured. She envied his resilience. Had she been in full health, she wouldn't have been bothered either. But she wasn't. She was hanging on by a thread, regulating her breath with precise counts to stall hyperventilation, her eyes fixed on the horizon, willing the trees to give way to the familiar silhouette of the city's skyscrapers. She knew this skyline by heart, each building a landmark in her mind. Henders was piloting them straight towards the centre now. As they approached, the distinctive structure of ISA headquarters loomed into view. On hovering just above the roof, she saw the medical team waiting for her, and Faris unmistakable among them. Of course, he was there.

Henders brought the ship down with an unusual gentleness. Before she could muster the strength to move, he was already unbuckling his harness and then hers, helping her rise to her feet. His hands were steady as he supported her, guiding her towards the exit. The bright sunlight enveloped her as she stepped out, her fragile frame casting a thin shadow on the rooftop. She managed a few steps before her legs gave in. The medical team and Faris, anticipating this, had already closed the gap. One of the doctors caught her just in time, his arms firm yet careful as he eased her onto the stretcher they had brought. She raised her head once more and looked directly at Henders. "If you tell anyone about this, I'll find you next week…" she murmured, a faint smile playing on her lips. The words were a weak attempt at humour, but they carried the weight of her gratitude and trust. Henders nodded, understanding the unspoken bond forged by their shared ordeal.

Henders winked. "Understood, Ma'am. Over my dead body." With a brisk nod to Faris, he placed two fingers to his forehead in a casual salute, then turned back into his ship. He sealed the door without a backward glance, fired up the engines, and took off swiftly. He knew he would return in a few days, once the dust from this harrowing mission had settled.

Manley let herself sink back onto the stretcher, barely registering the medical team's efforts. Closing her eyes, she felt the gentle support of the mattress beneath her, a relief from the tension and discomfort she had endured. Safety enveloped her like a warm blanket, quite literally, as someone had thoughtfully draped one over her. For the first time in days, she felt a semblance of comfort. And apparently someone had already hit her with the good painkillers because she noticed that all of the pain was gone. The pain that had been her constant, unwelcome companion for the last few days, at least while she had been awake, it was finally gone.

Summoning the last of her strength, she forced her eyes open again and sought out Faris's gaze. When their eyes met, she whispered, "Faris, he knows. Landon Claver knows." An involuntary quiver of fear laced her words. She knew that he wouldn't ask questions when the name came up. He knew just as well as she did that there was a clear connection to their common past, going back 17 years in time. He would know that Claver had seen through her alias as the red-headed agent. He would know that Manley's cover was blown.

Faris, who had taken his place by her right side, nodded, his fingers softly caressing her uninjured shoulder. "I know. He's been taken care of. He'll never hurt you again. You need to get to the hospital. You're injured, and you don't look too good," he said gently, yet with enough determination to quell any protest from her. The two doctors and two nurses nodded in agreement. Working on her to stabilize her for transport, they had deftly managed to insert an IV into her hand, allowing them to administer a cocktail of drugs and liquids. And liquid drugs. Manley felt a warmth spreading through her, a nice contrast to the cold that had seeped into her bones during her time in the dungeon. She felt her muscles relax, easing some of the tension that had gripped her. Faris gently moved a stray strand of hair from her face. "Try to get some sleep, my dear. Right now, you're not missing out on anything. It's all taken care of. I've got you covered," he reassured her.

What Manley didn't see was that the doctor was discreetly injecting a reliable dose of narcotic into her IV. She dozed right off when Faris said it. If she had known, she would probably have had something to say about it. Or maybe not. The combined weight of the physical and psychological strain of the past few days bore down on her, and she simply couldn't take it any longer. She closed her eyes and welcomed the blackness that surrounded her.

The medical team took the cue, swiftly securing Manley to the stretcher and moving her towards the lift that led down from the rooftop. Prior to Henders' landing, Faris had instructed them to conduct all necessary tests while she slept, even if it meant prolonging her sedation. From the deep gash on her forehead, he knew she'd need stitches. He had seen enough agents wounded in action to make a superficial assessment of the situation, and this was serious. Beyond the visible injuries, there were concerns about dehydration, internal damage, and other hidden troubles. Manley would never willingly submit to hours of scans and blood tests, so it was imperative to complete them while she was unconscious. Moreover, from the brief glimpse he had got, she desperately needed rest, regardless of what she might have had to say about it.

As the medical team whisked her away, Faris remained on the rooftop of ISA headquarters for a few moments longer, taking count of the day so far. Henders had managed to bring Manley back alive. She had been conscious, able to walk mostly on her own, and she had recognized everyone around her. That was a good sign. Faris felt relieved; she would pull through, she would heal, and she would live to tell the tale, should she choose to. Her physical condition was dire, but not beyond the reach of medical intervention. The psychological scars, however, would take much longer to mend. He felt an unexpected sense of responsibility for her suffering, even though he knew, logically, that no one—least of all Manley—could have foreseen this outcome.

He decided to bring Megan Miller into Manley's recovery process. Megan was ISA's finest trauma counsellor, and only the best would suffice for Manley. She could guide Manley through the emotional aftermath, helping her navigate the hard truths and lingering fears. Faris could only hope that Manley would recognize the necessity of this process. From what he had witnessed today, he believed it had to be possible to bring these two together. He had failed Manley once, when he hadn't insisted on counselling 17 years ago. He wasn't going to fail her again.

Chapter 12

Behind Manley and Henders on their hurried exit, Owen, Darra, Haylen, and Blake provided critical cover, firing a few blind shots into the corridor from which the pair had just emerged. Blake had to utilise immense self-control to restrain himself from chasing after the two agents as they left the mansion. He knew there would be time to reconnect with Manley later, especially now that he knew she was alive. He clung to the belief that she would stay alive, even after she left his sight. He tried to ignore the nagging voice in the back of his mind that replayed the image of her battered state. Her black-and-blue, swollen face and the sling on her left arm would likely haunt his dreams for a long time.

He fired his blaster at a shadowy figure attempting to peek around the far corner of the corridor. Though he missed, the hand and the weapon it held retreated, buying them a few precious moments. The team took turns, a coordinated dance of firing and ducking behind cover, maintaining a relentless barrage to keep their enemies at bay.

The general plan now wasn't to penetrate deeper into the mansion but to create enough chaos and confusion to facilitate Manley and Henders' getaway. It was a matter of time before they could retreat to safety. Blake fired another shot, then ducked behind the imposing marble statue he was using for cover. He glanced over at Haylen, who was hunkered down behind a column on the opposite side of the corridor. Something gnawed at Blake, a bitter realization that Claver, with his wealth and connections, would likely slip through the fingers of justice again.

Blake didn't want this to happen. In a brief pause between volleys, Blake hissed across the corridor to Haylen, "You wanna go find the bastard?" His voice was laced with a mixture of frustration and determination, well aware that he was ignoring the plan they had made.

As if she had been waiting for him to say that, Haylen grinned and fired a couple of well-aimed shots from her blaster, providing Blake with the cover he needed. She motioned for him to go, and Blake, casting off his lawyer's restraint, surged forward. Landon Claver would not escape unpunished. The memory of Manley's bruised and battered face fuelled his determination, overriding the cautious voice at the back of his head that typically guided his actions. The man who had fallen madly in love with the woman who had just left the mansion found it all too easy to embrace the hunt.

Blake moved with purpose, remembering the layout of the mansion. It wasn't difficult to see that they needed to enter deeper into the building, probably upstairs to the less accessible rooms, if they wanted to find Claver. He cast a glance towards Darra and Owen, who looked puzzled but resolute. He pointed towards the grand staircase at the mansion's centre. With Haylen covering him, Blake and the team advanced, swiftly neutralizing the shooter at the far end of the corridor. He signalled Darra and Owen to take the stairwell quickly. For now, no other threats were in sight.

Haylen and Blake followed close behind, covering their teammates as they walked up. At the top of the stairs, they paused, surveying their surroundings. The corridor lay silent, but several side passages branched off unpredictably. They were heading towards Claver's office at the end of the hall, a room marked on the building plans with an anteroom and a secret staircase leading out to the back. With Manley safely on her way out, their focus shifted to Claver. They intended to extract a few answers before any officials arrived and took over.

Darra led the way, each step deliberate and silent as they crept over the thick, red carpet that lined the corridor. They hoped that Claver remained unaware of the unfolding situation. The office branched off a side hall, and Darra motioned for Haylen to grab the door handle with a finger pressed to her lips, signalling for absolute silence. They had planned this meticulously during their flight. Speed and surprise were their allies, and they needed the secretary's cooperation, even if it had to be coerced. Darra counted down silently with her fingers—*three, two, one*—then everything happened in a blur of coordinated action.

Haylen tore the door open, and Owen and Blake rushed in, training their blasters on the secretary. Darra swiftly approached the woman, whispering urgently, "I know he's inside. We need to talk to him, and you are going to let us in." Haylen followed them in, locking the door behind her to prevent any unannounced interruptions.

The secretary, a chubby woman in her fifties with blonde hair dressed in a green costume, looked terrified. Her wide eyes darted between the four people in her room, but she found a sliver of courage to say, "You're not the first to try. I can't do it."

Darra moved closer, her lips almost brushing the secretary's ear. "What's your name, dear?" Her tone was soft but carried an unmistakable edge of authority. Meanwhile, Owen and Blake kept their blasters trained on the woman from different angles, ensuring she felt the full weight of the situation.

The woman whispered back, her voice trembling. "Edith."

"Edith, listen, dear," Darra said with a measured calmness, her eyes locked onto Edith's. "We don't want to hurt you. We have no business with you. Our business is with him, because he hurt one of our friends. You will stay here, and I'll tie you to the chair, and I'll gag you very carefully. These two," and she gestured towards Blake and Owen, who stood like sentinels with their blasters, "will make sure you don't get hurt. Do we have an understanding?"

Edith, her face pale but composed, nodded and carefully moved towards her desk chair.

"Hands where I can see them," Darra hissed, her voice low but commanding. She moved behind the chair, deliberately placing her own blaster just out of Edith's reach. With swift movements, she grabbed Edith's hands and secured them behind the backrest using the cable straps she had brought. She then pulled out a cloth from the back of her pants and, with a mix of firmness and gentleness, tied it around Edith's head, ensuring it tightly covered her mouth. Darra pushed the chair into the desk opening, blocking it with another chair that had previously stood by the wall. Leaning close to Edith's ear, she whispered, "Thank you, Edith. I'm really sorry for the inconvenience." Darra joined Blake, Owen and Haylen at Claver' door. They repeated the door procedure. *Three, two, one, go.*

Haylen ripped the door open with a forceful yank, and Owen and Blake practically leaped into the spacious room. They trained their blasters on Claver before he could so much as flinch. Darra rushed in next, with Haylen following close behind, locking the door with a swift motion before both aimed their blasters at the man behind the desk. "Hold it," Owen hollered, his voice echoing off the walls.

Claver's expression remained infuriatingly smug, a mirror of his self-assured arrogance. "Look who we have here," he drawled, his tone dripping with mockery. "It's Owen Harlow and his entourage. You're really making my day. What took you so long? Did I place the hints too far away from each other?"

An uncomfortable silence hung in the air as Owen, Darra, Haylen, and Blake exchanged slow, uneasy glances. Realisation seeped into their minds like a cold, creeping dread. Claver had been playing them all along. He knew exactly how they had found him. It was no coincidence that Dixie had stumbled upon the building plans and security codes. Their unimpeded journey from the city wasn't a stroke of luck; it was part of his plan. He had wanted them to come here. This was a trap they had blindly walked into.

Darra finally took the lead, her voice steady and authoritative. "We're not here to talk about the clues, Claver. We're here to talk about Manley and why you took her."

Claver's smile widened, his smugness radiating from every pore as he leaned back in his chair. "Oh, so you still haven't found her."

A smirk tugged at the corner of Owen's mouth. "Oh, we've found her. And by the looks of it, she got away."

Apparently, this caught Claver off-guard. For a fleeting moment, his confidence wavered, his eyes widening in surprise. "She got away? How?" But he quickly masked his surprise with a dismissive laugh. "Nah, that's impossible. You don't even know where she is."

"Was," Blake interjected, his voice cutting through the tension like a knife. He stood in line with the others, about twelve feet from Claver's desk, his blaster held steady.

Claver folded his hands on the desk, his smile never faltering. "If that's what you say. Like she could've left in the shape she's in."

Blake fought the urge to leap across the room and punch Claver in the face. His empty fist closed tightly. He clenched his jaw and looked Claver in the eye. "You're underestimating her. Again."

"Impossible," Claver replied, still exuding an unsettling calmness as he sat behind his desk.

Owen stepped forward, his eyes boring into Claver's. "Oh, believe me, she left your dungeon. A few minutes ago. We saw her walking out. But we needed to talk to you, that's why we're here." He left out the detail that she had been accompanied by an ISA agent, keeping that piece of information close to his chest.

Claver looked down at the desk top, then back up, his eyes narrowing with a calculated menace. "You're just messing with me. You're trying to get me to tell you where she is. But that isn't the plan."

Owen eyed him carefully, his gaze steady and unflinching. "So what's the plan?"

"The plan is that I kill all of you. And then her," Claver replied with chilling nonchalance.

Haylen almost lost it. "Not happening." The tension in the room was wearing her thin. Her muscles felt as if she were running a marathon, the grip on her blaster tightening until her knuckles turned white. Claver remained seated in his chair serenely, clad in a dark grey suit. To a casual observer, he might have seemed an affable, charming man. But Owen, Darra, Haylen, and Blake knew better. This was the man who had kidnapped their friend, beaten her, and locked her away in his underground bunker. Forgive and forgot was a long way from here.

Darra wasn't quite sure where this was leading. "Is it really just revenge for your father's death?"

For a brief moment, Claver's composure slipped, a flicker of genuine emotion crossing his face. "Just?" He scoffed, then shook his head. "No, it isn't just that." He offered no further explanation. Instead, with a movement so swift it was almost imperceptible, he produced a blaster.

None of them could later recall where it had come from; his hand had moved like lightning. In an instant, the rescue party of four found themselves in a tense stand-off with the man they had been trying to corner. Owen's voice dropped to a dangerous whisper, "Put it away. It's four against one. You don't stand the slightest chance."

Claver refused to obey, answering with a shot that narrowly missed Blake. Before Blake could react,

Darra fired back, her shot grazing Claver's right shoulder. He let out a muffled cry, the blaster slipping from his hand and clattering onto the desk. Owen, Haylen, Darra, and Blake tightened their grips on their own blasters, ready for anything. "Told you to put it away," Owen said quietly, his voice a cold warning.

Claver glared at him, his eyes burning with defiance. "You're not the one giving orders around here." He clutched his injured shoulder with his left hand, his right arm hanging limp and useless.

"I beg to differ," Owen replied, his tone steely. "Right now, you're in no position to hand out any orders. This is over."

A flicker of desperation crossed Claver's face as he made a small, almost imperceptible movement towards his blaster with his left hand. Blake saw it, his rage flaring to an intensity he had never known. In a split-second decision, he roared, "Hold it!" and charged towards Claver. Claver didn't stop. Driven by instinct, Blake pulled the trigger and shot him. He didn't think—he acted, and it felt disturbingly satisfying.

Owen, Darra, and Haylen watched in stunned silence, the realisation that Blake was capable of killing someone sinking in. Relief mingled with shock as they recognised that the ordeal seemed to be over. Claver toppled forward without a sound, collapsing face-first onto his desk. The room fell into an eerie stillness, the air thick with the aftermath of violence. Blake stood there, his blaster still raised, aimed at the now-empty space where Claver had stood.

No one moved. Haylen felt paralysed, unsure of what to do next. She looked at Owen, whose eyes met

Darra's. Both of them mirrored her uncertainty, caught in the surreal moment. Blake, breathing heavily, remained rooted to the spot, his body rigid with the adrenaline of what he had just done. The silence stretched on, each of them processing the gravity of their situation.

"Blake?" Haylen's voice was soft, tentative, as if she wasn't sure he could hear her. Blake stood motionless, his eyes fixed on the empty space where Claver had been moments ago.

She tried again, a little louder, "Blake!"

He blinked, a puzzled look crossing his face, but he still didn't reply. Haylen approached him slowly, gently touching his hands that were still gripping his blaster. She pressed down on his hands, softly wrestling the weapon from his grasp. She threw the blaster towards Owen, who caught it with his free hand. "Blake, it's OK. Take a seat. We're all good," she said, her voice soothing. She stood in front of him, her hands resting on his chest, applying gentle pressure to guide him backwards toward a chair against the wall. "Sit," she instructed.

Blake moved mechanically, his eyes never leaving Claver, even as Haylen stepped into his line of sight. She frowned with worry, stepping aside, but Blake's gaze remained locked on the lifeless body on the desk. Owen approached the desk, checking Claver's pulse at his neck and wrist. When he shook his head, confirming what they knew already, Blake exhaled loudly, his head falling into his hands. Manley was safe, and Claver was dead. This wasn't how Blake had imagined it. He had envisioned Claver answering for his crimes in court, rotting in prison for the rest of his life. The reality of a dead Claver hadn't crossed his mind. He half-expected someone to deliver a speech about the necessity—or lack thereof—of Claver's death, but the speech didn't come.

Owen felt a curious blend of satisfaction and emptiness. He would have liked to pay Claver Junior back personally, especially after seeing what Manley had endured. That wasn't going to happen now. But at least Claver would never harm Manley—or anyone else—again. It was also slightly ironic that Landon Claver died at the same desk where his father took his own life. Before anyone else could react, he spoke to Blake, his voice firm and decisive. "We all saw that he was threatening you. You acted in self-defence."

Neither Haylen nor Darra contradicted him. They knew it was only half true, that Owen was bending the truth in Blake's favour. They understood why he did it. Without Blake, they wouldn't be here at all, and Manley would still be in captivity—or worse, dead. They weren't entirely sure why the lawyer had snapped, but they had a strong suspicion it had to do with his feelings for Manley.

Haylen found her composure first. "We need to tell Faris." She saw nodding heads. "Owen, I think you should talk to him. Blake definitely shouldn't, and I don't want to." She looked at Darra, who shook her head in agreement.

Owen sighed. He had suspected that he would be the one who had to break the news to the head of ISA. "Alright, then let's get this over with." He tapped buttons on his PAC, instructing the device to open an audio channel to Faris.

Faris answered immediately, his voice sharp and direct. "What is it, Owen?"

"You know Manley's out, right?"

"Yes. Agent Henders is on approach, they both got to the ship alive." Faris sounded content enough.

"Good." Owen paused for a moment, gathering his thoughts and taking a deep breath. "We took out Claver."

Faris hesitated for a second, the line crackling with tension. "Is he dead or captive?"

"Dead." The word hung in the air for several seconds, each one stretching out like an eternity.

"Good." Faris's voice carried a note of satisfaction, though he quickly tempered it. "I mean... I see. Get out of there right now. I'll have ISA take over."

Owen nodded, even though Faris couldn't see it. "Consider it done." He cut off the connection and glanced at Darra and Haylen, their faces reflecting a mixture of relief and lingering tension. "We're out of here. Right now. Quietly." He pointed to the not-so-secret staircase near the window. Maybe they could even get out unnoticed.

Chapter 13

Day 8
When the heavy darkness around Manley's head slowly began to dissolve, she remained motionless, trying to assess her surroundings. It was dark. She was half expecting to be back in the dungeon, but the room she was in felt different. She was lying on her back, feeling something soft beneath her, and a heavy duvet covering her body. She listened intently, tuning into the faint sounds around her. The steady, rhythmic beeping of medical equipment filled the air, signalling life and continuity. She had been trained to mask her recovery, to keep her heart rate steady and not reveal her consciousness. Today, this required immense effort, proving how badly she was hurt. Apparently she hadn't slept long enough to fully heal. She suspected Faris hadn't allowed her to be put in a coma, fearing what she might do when she awoke. A faint, inward smile tugged at her lips as she strained her ears once more. Someone was there, sitting quietly. She could hear their steady breathing to her right. She opened her eyelids just a fraction, enough to see Blake.

Reliable, attractive, exhausted Blake. His head rested on the side of her bed, and he was breathing deeply and evenly. He had fallen asleep while watching over her. Manley's eyes welled with tears. He had come for her. Blake had come, along with Owen, Darra, and Haylen. Her friends had found her, together with Henders. She was alive and she had escaped Claver's clutches. Again. A sharp intake of breath escaped her as the tears began to flow freely, her nose swelling shut from the crying.

The sudden sound jolted Blake awake. He looked at her with utter shock and disbelief. "You're awake!"

"Apparently," she croaked, her voice barely audible, a mere whisper of its usual vibrant timbre. Blake met her gaze, and in that exchange, a flood of unspoken emotions surged between them. Neither knew where to begin nor how to break the intensity of the moment.

Silence enveloped them like a heavy fog. Blake's trembling hand found hers delicately, mindful of the IV line tethered to her, the lifeline of drugs that supported her fragile state. He exhaled deeply, overwhelmed by a mixture of relief, anguish, and admiration for her resilience.

He looked at her in sheer amazement and didn't know what his puzzlement meant. He knew that she had got him involved in something way bigger than himself, and he knew he didn't care as long as she was here with him. Tears streamed down his cheeks unchecked, mirroring her own silent anguish. He wanted to wipe away her tears, to offer solace in the face of her suffering, but held back, respecting the rawness of her emotions. After everything he had learnt from Faris and the medical team, she was entitled to a good bout of crying, even if they didn't know the full story yet.

She had several broken bones in her left shoulder and arm, three broken ribs, and she had suffered internal injuries from someone beating and kicking her, which thankfully weren't too serious and healing already. He hadn't been able to listen to the full report. The mere thought of what she had endured made his stomach churn with helplessness and rage.

They had meticulously stitched up the deep cut she had incurred during her daring escape. The medical team murmured about possible facial surgeries for a complete recovery, though definitive plans were still pending. What was certain, however, was the prospect of Manley needing potent painkillers for weeks, possibly months, to ease her excruciating recovery process. To those who knew her well, the idea of her spending extended periods on bed rest was unthinkable, so she would need the drugs for moving around.

In the confines of the ISA medical facility, where few were granted access, Blake found himself in a surreal limbo. While Faris conferred with the medical staff, making decisions that would shape Manley's path to recovery, Blake stood watch over her. He felt simultaneously grateful for the opportunity to be by her side and disheartened by the feeling of being excluded from the important discussions and medical decisions.

On the other side, he was being left alone with her in the heart of ISA medical, a place that most people never even set foot into. So things could have been a lot worse from his side of the table, though Blake cringed inwardly when he started to think about how someone had injured her this way. Yes, he had played it a bit rough from time to time with her a few days ago but never violently and never with the intention to hurt her. Whoever had treated her like this clearly deserved a long bit of time in some sort of detention centre.

Manley felt the tears welling in her eyes, tracing paths down her cheeks, mirroring the tracks of emotion on Blake's face. She watched as he hesitated, his thumbs poised to brush away her tears before he restrained himself. It was a small gesture, but it spoke volumes—a silent acknowledgment of the overwhelming torrent of feelings coursing through her. At least he wasn't trying to minimise what she felt right now. She wasn't sure what that was, but it was a lot. Relief surged through her veins, knowing she had escaped Claver's clutches yet again. But relief was swiftly overtaken by an overpowering wave of exhaustion that threatened to pull her under. Rage simmered just beneath the surface, a righteous anger at the injustice she had endured. And woven through it all was an immense gratitude for Blake's presence by her side.

She wasn't sure which of those emotions would break her first. She wanted to scream, to release the pent-up fury and fear that had gripped her during her captivity. But her voice failed her, weakened by strain and trauma. Her breath hitched, lungs labouring against the range of emotions too vast to contain. She knew she was going to cry long and hard, and she wasn't sure she wanted it to happen while Blake was here. Thankfully, she still didn't feel any pain, which was probably because some transparent liquid kept dripping into her veins slowly but steadily through the IV access on the back of her left hand. That shoulder and arm were bandaged and immobilized in a plastic splint, so she couldn't use them anyway. She sobbed once, twice, trying to hold it in when the dam broke.

Before she could even attempt to reign herself in, she extended her good arm toward Blake in a desperate plea for solace, and he responded without hesitation, enveloping her in his embrace. He leaned down to her, his movements gentle yet resolute, and carefully wrapped his arms around her, holding her tightly as if to fuse his strength with hers. She could feel him sobbing, too, with all the feelings they had bottled up during the past few days. She tried to form words, to express the tumult within her, but her voice failed her once more. Blake, sensing her struggle, shushed her softly and lifted her into a sitting position, never breaking his hold, a silent promise that he would not leave her side.

They didn't remember for how long they had been sitting this way. When Manley's sobs subsided, she was left drained, her body sore not with pain but with the profound exhaustion that comes from too much of everything—too much fear, too much relief, too much grief. Blake gently released her only to fetch a handful of tissues thoughtfully placed on the nightstand by the nurses. As he handed them to her, Manley took in her surroundings for the first time.

The room was painted in calming shades of green, the blinds drawn against the darkness outside. Hours must have passed since she had lost consciousness on the roof. Gratitude washed over her as she realised she wasn't confined to one of the smaller, more austere hospital rooms. This was one of the premium rooms, reserved for senior agents and select individuals outside the agency. Despite the presence of a functional hospital bed, the room had been designed to resemble a small, comfortable apartment, complete with a couch, a table, and a second bed tucked behind a partition. To her right, a compact kitchen offered a semblance of normalcy, and to her left, an adjoining bathroom promised the luxury of a shower. A shower—she suddenly became acutely aware of how long it had been since she had felt the cleansing touch of water. Nearly a week had passed since her last shower, and the thought of one, even a utilitarian rinse, was profoundly appealing. Though the memory of a more intimate shower with Blake flickered in her mind, she knew she would welcome any semblance of cleanliness at this moment.

Blake noticed that something was going through her mind. "What is it?" he asked softly, his voice a gentle caress.

Manley cast a glance toward the bathroom. "I need a shower," she whispered, the words barely escaping her lips.

Blake hesitated, uncertainty clouding his thoughts. "Are you sure this is a good idea?"

She shook her head slowly, the movement accentuating her weariness. "I don't know. But I also have to use the..." Her voice faltered, trailing off into silence.

Understanding dawned on Blake. This decision wasn't his to make. He stood up and popped his head out the door. The first nurse to meet his gaze was a young woman with calm demeanour. "I could use some help in here. Agent Manley needs to get to the bathroom."

"She's awake? Already?" The nurse's eyes widened in surprise before she shook her head, a bemused smile playing on her lips. "Unbelievable. We'll be right there."

Blake couldn't help but chuckle softly to himself. It seemed they were now approaching her care in teams, likely a precaution orchestrated by Faris, anticipating that Manley wouldn't be the type to remain docile and compliant for long. As he pondered this, two female nurses entered the room, moving to Manley's left side.

"Can you put your legs down and out?" one of the nurses asked, her tone professional yet kind.

Manley complied, though it took considerable effort. One of the nurses, with a determined expression, motioned for Blake to step aside. "We've got this, sir. We'll take care of her," she said firmly. They carefully disconnected Manley from the IV drip. Blake hesitated, torn between wanting to assist and respecting Manley's dignity. He knew she might feel embarrassed if he were the one to help her with the intimate tasks she needed to perform. Silently, he nodded and walked over to the couch, picking up a magazine. He pretended to read, though he held it upside-down accidentally, his thoughts far from the glossy pages.

The nurses supported Manley on either side, guiding her with gentle precision. She looked so frail in the oversized hospital gown they had dressed her in while she was unconscious. The sound of running water echoed softly from the bathroom, and Blake imagined the nurses helping her under the shower, their voices muted to whispers. He couldn't make out their words, but he sensed the tenderness and care in their tones.

After a while, one of the nurses emerged from the bathroom and briefly left the room, returning with a fresh hospital gown. It was likely more for Manley's psychological comfort than necessity, as the gown she wore had been on her for less than six hours. But whatever made Manley feel better, except leaving the hospital, he remembered Faris's orders for the medical staff. He had told them to comply with Manley's every wish (well, almost) so she could feel okay. If anyone could ever feel okay after a week like the one she had in captivity in Claver' mansion. After a week of torment in Claver's mansion, the road to feeling "okay" was long and treacherous.

Blake also recalled Faris's specific dietary directive: only serve her soup due to the injuries on her face, sparing her the pain of chewing. He sighed, knowing Manley wouldn't appreciate this restriction. She valued her food, and this limitation would chafe at her spirit.

It turned out that Manley also didn't like being dependent on other people when it came to personal hygiene. She looked stressed when the two nurses accompanied her from the bathroom back to her bed. "I can walk, you know?" she said, her tone laced with irritation.

The nurses nodded, their expressions calm and unruffled. "We know," one of them replied, her voice steady. They still supported her, unaffected by the sharpness in her voice. Handling injured senior ISA agents with an attitude was part of their job, and Manley was far from the first. And it wasn't the first time she was here. When they had carefully settled her back onto the bed, they gave a nod to Blake and left without another word, their professionalism evident in their silent departure.

Manley remained sitting on the edge of the bed, her body tense, as if any movement might shatter her fragile balance. Her head hung low, resting against her chest, and she took deep, measured breaths, trying to recover from the exertion of the shower. Despite sitting on a stool and the nurses manoeuvring the shower head over her body, the ordeal had left her drained. They had meticulously washed her, their gentle reassurances a soft background to her insistence on cleanliness. "We've washed you before while you were asleep," they had told her, but she had insisted on doing it again. The nurses had dried her with careful precision and wrapped her in a fresh hospital gown, accommodating the splint on her injured arm and shoulder. The injury rendered her arm useless, so the effort of dressing her was more about maintaining her dignity than her ability to move. Now, back on the bed, she felt the overwhelming exhaustion seeping into her bones.

Blake saw her sitting on the bed, unmoving, and he could imagine how spent she must be after the effort of leaving it. He wasn't certain about the exact effects of the painkillers the doctors had administered, but he knew enough to recognise that whatever medication she was on could cause extreme fatigue. Coupled with the trauma of the past week, it was no wonder she seemed utterly exhausted. He cleared his throat softly. "May I help?" he asked gently.

There was no reaction from her. He couldn't tell if she hadn't heard him or if she simply couldn't muster the strength to respond. Regardless, he decided to take the initiative. Rising from the sofa, he approached her bed and leaned over, wrapping his arms around her from behind with tender care. She didn't resist. Gently, he guided her to lie back down on the mattress, and she allowed him to help her, her body too worn to do it on her own. She looked so tired, her weariness etched into every line of her face. Blake breathed a soft kiss to her forehead, a gesture filled with both love and sorrow. He pulled up the duvet, tucking it around her with meticulous care. She closed her eyes gratefully, too drained to speak. She wished he wouldn't just kiss her on her forehead, but she also knew that this would only be wishful thinking for a while.

Blake still stood next to the bed, unsure about what to do now. She would have to sleep some more. He would have to eat. Though he had had the occasional meal with Haylen, his body was complaining about the strains he had put on it during the last week, too. He had had too little to eat, too little rest, and way too much stress for a single week. "I'll be right back", he whispered softly into her ear, his voice a gentle caress. "Sleep tight." She responded with a faint nod, the movement so subtle it seemed more imagined than real. With a final, lingering look, Blake turned away, his footsteps muffled against the sterile floor as slipped out of the room. He walked purposefully, the fluorescent lights casting a harsh, clinical glow on the hallway as he made his way to the nurses' station at the entrance to the ward. "Is there a way to order any decent food?" he asked, his voice sounding with a blend of hope and weariness.

One of the nurses, who had been attending to Manley earlier, glanced up from her computer screen.

"Sure. Faris told us you might ask for some. What do you want?"

Blake hesitated, caught off guard by the straightforward question. "Oh, er... I guess a burger and fries will do. As long as it's hot and tasty," he replied, a hint of embarrassment colouring his tone.

The nurse nodded, her face softened by a touch of empathy. "I'll bring it when it gets here. I'll order this from the outside. The canteen is closed at this time of day."

Blake acknowledged her help with a grateful nod. "I'll be back in there," he said, gesturing towards Manley's room.

She smiled warmly. "Faris said you might not be willing to leave. Don't worry, you're all safe here with us."

And while Blake was having doubts right now that anywhere in this universe was a safe place, he knew that the ISA hospital wing was as close to a sanctuary as it was going to get. "Faris may be right", he replied, returning her smile with a weary one of his own.

It took a little more than a decent meal to lift his spirits. Being stuck in a hospital room for hours was far from his idea of a good time, though, truth be told, he was truly spent on the notion of real adventures after the past week. If anyone had told him a week ago that he would go on a search for the pretty lady he met in a hotel, he would have laughed it off as a really good joke. Now the joke was on him, and during that search, he had done things he had never thought possible. He helped blackmail several people with his words and his sheer physical presence. He condoned physical violence. He shot a man. And all of this while he still held himself to be a good lawyer.

As he savoured the last bite of his meal, Blake set the plate in the sink, debating whether to wash it. The clatter might rouse Manley from her much-needed slumber, and he decided against it. He looked at his PAC. It was 3.30 in the morning. Manley remained still, enveloped in deep sleep. He could use some rest himself. He recalled Faris mentioning there would be no standard hospital procedures with Manley, so they wouldn't be disturbed in a few hours by morning rounds. The bed behind the table beckoned him with the promise of comfort, yet so did the thought of spending the remainder of the night beside Manley. The decision was easy. He slipped into bed with her, enveloping her in his arms. The warmth of her presence soothed him, and within minutes, he drifted into a deep, untroubled sleep, finding solace in the shared quiet of the night.

Manley could feel his strong arms enveloping her, the familiar embrace bringing a rush of warmth to her heart. She didn't need to open her eyes to know who it was; Blake holding her as she slept was enough to quicken her heartbeat. For a fleeting moment, she yearned to turn around and draw him into something more intimate. But then, like a wave crashing down, memories of the kidnapping and the injuries she had endured came back. The mere thought of straining the shoulder that had been mercifully pain-free since waking in medical brought tears to her eyes. It had only been days since she was plagued by relentless pain with every movement in her underground prison. She would not revisit that agony, not willingly.

She kept her eyes closed, her breathing steady and deliberate, savouring this serene moment. She dared not move and risk shattering the fragile beauty of it. Gradually, sleep reclaimed her, and she drifted off once more. When she awoke again, Blake was still there, though he had shifted slightly, creating a small but significant space between them. His right hand still rested gently on her waist, and she could tell from his breathing that he was awake. She couldn't see him, but she pictured him staring at the ceiling, counting the minutes or hours that stretched before them.

Drawing a deep breath, she signalled her return to consciousness. She shifted onto her back, inching closer to him, offering a tentative, yet genuine smile. "You're still here," she whispered, her voice barely more than a breath.

"I'm still here," he whispered back. His hand moved from her waist, gliding with deliberate care up her body, until it hovered just below her face, the warmth of his presence lingering without yet touching her skin. He leant closer and kissed her softly. Manley closed her eyes and felt herself melting against him, her thoughts drifting back to the two magical nights they had shared before the nightmare began. Only she was in no condition to take on any of that now. Blake was mindful of her injuries, ensuring he placed no weight on her left side, but the need to kiss her was too urgent, almost desperate. He needed to be with her, far away from the chaos that had enveloped their lives. It would happen, he told himself. Later. With a gentle sigh, he broke the kiss, his forehead resting against hers. "I'm not going anywhere," he said.

Manley smiled. She didn't know what to say. Maybe there was nothing to be said right now, maybe she just needed to take this as what it was — a sign of his affection, if she still needed any. He had proven it ten times over by helping to find her and coming to her rescue. She moved her right hand up to his face, touching his face carefully, and kissed him with all her heart. She closed her eyes. She felt his hand grip her waist with a new determination, a promise of protection and unwavering support. The familiar tingling sensation he could so effortlessly evoke began to stir just below her stomach, a reminder of the life and passion that still pulsed within her, hidden below her injuries. For now, this was enough—a quiet, tender connection that spoke of resilience and the promise of brighter days ahead.

Before either of them could think or say or do anything else, the door hissed open, and in came Daxton Faris, head of ISA. He hadn't knocked, evidently not anticipating any situation in this particular hospital room that might have warranted such a courtesy. Given what Haylen and Owen had shared with him, he should have known better. Faris' eyes fell upon Manley and Blake, entwined on the hospital bed, clearly absorbed in something far from a professional encounter. He opened his mouth to speak, but words failed him, and he closed it again.

He had known, of course, about their romantic involvement; the files had made that much clear. But seeing Manley nestled in Blake's arms, serene and secure, was another matter entirely. Memories flooded back of the countless times he had held her himself, years ago. She had never looked so at peace in his embrace. Instead, those times had been marked by her silent, desperate tears, her body shaking with muffled sobs. A pang of possessive jealousy tightened in his chest. His favourite agent, Manley, in the arms of another man—a man she was so clearly drawn to, who held her with such tenderness after everything she had endured. This man had risked everything, including his own life, to find her, confronting her friends and foes alike, driven by a profound care that Faris had rarely seen.

Faris inhaled sharply, then exhaled quietly, collecting his thoughts. "Manley," he finally said, his voice a blend of authority and an unspoken, lingering affection. He looked to Blake and offered a nod, accompanied by the faintest hint of a smile. Blake, to his credit, didn't even look embarrassed by the situation.

Neither did Manley. If anything, she might have felt a flicker of annoyance at the interruption, but the expression vanished almost instantly. "Faris," she said smiling. She recalled seeing him upon her arrival here, on the roof after Henders had flown her in, but this was the first time she had actually laid eyes on him since then. She blinked and carefully sat up, pulling her shoulders back in an instinctive attempt to find some semblance of dignity, then thought better of it and let herself sink back into the pillows. There was so much she needed to say, but she didn't know where to start.

Blake looked from Faris to Manley and back again. Something was happening here, and he wasn't quite sure what it was. He had seen a puzzled expression flash across Faris's face, and he noticed the way Manley looked at Faris with more affection than one would normally bestow upon a superior. Clearing his throat, Blake said awkwardly, "I'll give you two some space," starting to retreat, preparing to leave the room. He knew Faris needed to talk to her, to question her about what had happened. He wasn't sure if she wanted him there for that. He only knew fragments of what she had suffered; perhaps she needed to recount it to Faris first, on her own terms.

"No." Manley and Faris spoke in unison.

Blake stopped, looking from her to Faris and back until Faris his gaze. This was unexpected.

Faris motioned for Blake to come back. "I need to talk to both of you. I probably owe at least one of you an explanation," he said and turned towards the couch at the other end of the room. "Blake, can you bring the bed over here? So we can all talk comfortably? I don't want her to walk. No offence." He looked at Manley with a trace of regret. She nodded in understanding.

Blake knew this wasn't the time to argue with the head of the ISA. Faris was a powerful man, and Blake might cross paths with him again in his line of work. So, he nodded. Manley wasn't connected to any IV drips at the moment, making it easier to move the bed. He carefully manoeuvred it across the room to a suitable spot near the couch. Once he had positioned the bed, Blake climbed back in with Manley. He wanted Faris to have to look up to him, a small gesture of reclaiming some power in the situation.

Manley lay quietly, anticipating what was to come. Blake adjusted the bed-head, raising it to help her into a more comfortable position.

"Dana, what happened? Can you talk me through it?" Faris asked carefully, his voice gentle but insistent.

Manley nodded but didn't reply right away. She had known that she would have to tell him at some point.

It was standard procedure when an agent was injured in action. They had done this before. She remembered the time she had been in a brutal fight with a couple of pirates who were none too keen on her arresting them. She had fought her way out without any weapons, relying solely on her combat skills, but she had ended up with a few broken bones and had needed to spend time in medical until she had healed enough to return to duty. Then there was the time she had barely escaped with her life from a confrontation with some Faction members. Her ship had been badly damaged, and she had needed every ounce of her flying skills to get back to base with just enough oxygen to stay conscious. It had taken her a few days to get cleared for duty again. But this time was different. Never before had the events leading up to her injuries been this personal, not in the past seventeen years.

Blake watched her closely, his heart aching with every moment as she steeled herself for what was about to come. That was probably some technique she had learnt as an agent. She breathed in and out a few times, closed her eyes for a few heartbeats, gathering all the strength she had left. Then she began speaking quietly, looking Faris directly in the eye. "I woke up in the middle of the night. My room door was open, light was coming in. I heard someone behind me, I jumped up and tried to fight them. There were two men in the room, and I think two more in the corridor. They were too strong, and they hit me on the head with something. I blacked out."

Manley paused, clearly needing a break. She closed her eyes and concentrated on her breathing, keeping it steady and strong. When she started to speak again, her voice sounded a little shaky to Blake, but Faris still seemed unimpressed. "I woke up in a locked room, tightly bound to a chair. They were trying to make me give up the secure channels to you at first." She fell silent again, taking a few breaths. "They weren't successful. I tried to get away at the first opportunity, but they caught me and weren't too happy about it. They asked again for the frequencies a couple of times, I said no just as many times." Blake knew this was when she had received the injuries on her shoulder and her face. He had to restrain himself from jumping in to protect her from the emotions welling up inside her. He could see the muscles at the back of her neck tense, and she clenched her jaw and bit her lip repeatedly as she spoke. Yet she kept on talking. He could only guess how much strength it cost her to exercise this much control over herself. He didn't care about interfering any more; he softly put his hand on the small of her back, supporting her, keeping her grounded.

She spoke on, violently pushing back the images and memories forming in her mind. "Claver gave up his cover and finally confronted me. He said me he was leading my friends my way, so he could kill them first, one by one, before getting to me last. Then he gave me food and water and had someone cut the ropes. He was waiting for you. Several days must have passed, I lost track of time. I bound up my arm to protect the shoulder to prepare for escape. One day, I managed to get away. When I was already on my way out of the mansion, I ran into Henders first, then into Owen and the others. Henders took me here and handed me over to you. You know the rest better than I do." She looked at Faris defiantly, tears in her eyes, and waited for his reaction.

Blake was stunned by what she had said. She had probably left out a lot, and he didn't dare to ask her about it. He watched Faris, really interested in how this conversation would continue.

Faris, who had been looking at Manley unwaveringly the whole time she was talking, suddenly hung his head. He rubbed his eyes with the fingers of his left hand and breathed deeply. He knew how much she wasn't telling them—about her injuries, about the way they had beaten and kicked her until she passed out from the pain. About how they had been too many for her to take on. He had talked to the doctors and knew how seriously she had been injured in those few days. It was nothing short of a miracle that everything was starting to heal, and that she probably wouldn't need surgery. And he knew how long it would take to heal just from the physical pain, let alone the scars he couldn't see — getting caught up again in the net the Claver family had spun so many years ago, living through the memories again that she had so kept hidden for so many years. She might have been a well-trained agent, but this was so much all at once.

When he looked up again, he looked defeated. "Dana, I'm sorry. I'm so sorry this is happening again."

She blinked, a single tear tracing a path down her cheek. She made no sound, but Blake felt her shaking all over now. Without hesitation, Blake wrapped his arm around her back and drew her close into his protective embrace. He could feel her trembling. Her breathing was ragged, each inhale a struggle against the memories threatening to overwhelm her. He held her tightly in his arms, looking at Faris steadily over the crown of her head. Faris held his gaze, not looking away, signalling him that it was okay, that he could take the silence.

Blake had never heard this full account from her before; she had shielded him from the darkest details, and he had respected her need for that distance. He could only guess what had happened in the bits she had left out in her re-telling of events. He cursed himself silently for not having heard the hustle in the room below in the hotel back on Nergal B. It wasn't that he thought he might have stood a chance against four huge, brawny kidnappers. But he might have found her missing earlier, and authorities might have reacted differently when an actual witness to the crime would speak.

That hotel seemed like a lifetime ago, a whole different world they had met in. A world where there was so much more fun than in the one he found himself in right now. Now, in the hospital room at ISA headquarters, he cradled the woman he loved as she grappled with the aftermath of unfathomable trauma. Her grief, her pain, her physical and psychological wounds—all were evident, etched into every line of her face, every quiver of her body. She sobbed silently.

Faris had seen this all before, each poignant moment carved into his memory. He had been there most of the time that Manley, or Amy, had been feeling this bad. At least 17 years ago. Faris understood the toll it took on her to weep without sound. Her pain resonated within him as if they were bound by some unseen connection. He kept his visual connection with Blake. That man had gone to lengths he had not thought possible, for a woman whom many would have dismissed as a fleeting encounter, not worth the effort. But what existed between Manley and Blake was profound, a bond that surpasses any superficial fling. Faris was acutely aware that his role in her life was nearing its end. For the sake of both their futures, he needed to retreat, to allow Manley to embrace the chance for a life unburdened by those shadows of the past. Even if she chose to take that job with the Faction, he sensed that Blake would be a part of her new reality.

It took Manley a while to come back to the real world, to the world where she was in Blake's arms and nothing could happen to her right now. Minutes passed, each one marked by the ebbing of her distress. Her heart rate slowed, her breaths became less laboured, and she consciously unclenched the muscles that had tightened around her chest. Leaning into Blake, she felt the silent, unwavering support he was granting her. She needed to breathe freely, and yet, she wasn't willing to break away from Blake who still held her steadily.

The door hissed open once more, a sound that sliced through the heavy silence of the room. Blake and Faris turned their heads in unison, their gazes locking with Owen's. They hadn't expected him now, and his timing wasn't exactly impeccable.

Owen's eyes flicked between them, rapidly assessing the scene. He seemed to have come at an exceptionally inconvenient time. All he could see of Manley was the crown of her head, her tousled, unkempt red hair peeking out from where she was ensconced in Blake's arms. Faris, sitting opposite them on the couch, observed in silence. Owen's entrance had clearly disrupted something delicate. He hesitated, poised to leave as quickly as he had come, but before he could retreat, Manley looked up, freezing him in place with a gaze that stole his breath away.

Her usually vibrant blue eyes were hollowed out, encircled by dark shadows. She was very pale, her skin looking ashen and pallid. Beneath the hospital gown, her left arm and shoulder were hidden, but he knew they were encased in a splint, shielding them from further harm. Bruises mottled her face and arms. He had never seen her so fragile, so diminished. This sight of her, battered and broken, clashed violently with his memories of the spirited, quick-witted woman who had been his steadfast ally. The image of her now, as a mere shadow of her former self, inflicted him physical pain.

Instinctively, he wanted to sweep her into a fierce embrace, to shield her from this tense atmosphere. He knew better than that, of course. Faris' presence signalled that this was no casual visit; it was an interrogation, however unofficial, conducted by the head of ISA himself. Owen forced himself to approach Blake and Manley. She had seen him already; retreat was no longer an option. Not again. Not after she had believed him dead. He fumbled for words, but they eluded him, so he opted instead for a brief, gentle hug, hoping it conveyed the depth of his concern and the promise of his support and knowing that it couldn't deliver any of that.

Manley let it happen, remaining silent for now. She didn't hug him back, her arms limp at her sides. She just gazed at him, her eyes lingering on his face, the room's tension amplified by the watchful eyes of the three men surrounding her. After a moment that stretched unbearably, she finally spoke, her voice trembling, "You look good for a dead guy."

"You don't look too good for a living chick," Owen replied instinctively, slipping into their familiar, quick-witted banter without thinking. Immediately, he regretted his words, realizing the insensitivity of referring to her appearance. Yet, she didn't react. The Manley he remembered would have had a sharp retort ready, or she would simply have hit him in the face with the palm of her hand before he knew it. Her silence, her lack of any response, drove home how deeply she was affected, how far she had fallen from her usual self.

A weak smile tugged at her lips, a ghost of her former self. "Sit," she said, nodding towards the table.

Owen moved to the other end of the sofa where Faris was seated, the space between them filled with unspoken words. He still didn't know what to say, each word he thought of seeming inadequate. He settled on something he hoped would resonate with her, something to bridge the gap between their shared past and this fractured present. "Listen, I know what we did wasn't exactly what you expected."

Manley fixed her gaze on him again, her brow furrowing as she carefully chose her words. "That is nicely put. You made me think you were dead. After all that we've gone through. I thought you were dead."

Her voice trembled with restrained emotion. It took every ounce of her strength not to yell at him. She knew she couldn't take him on in a fight now, but had she been in better shape, she might have tried.

The truth was, she couldn't engage in any fight at the moment, and she knew Owen was painfully aware of this. She had seen the look on his face, the brief, unguarded expression of shock, guilt, and pity before he managed to compose himself. He knew what her injuries signified, and she silently prayed he wouldn't bring it up.

Her expression shifted, morphing into something Owen couldn't quite read. Was it anger? Sadness? Disappointment? He sighed, his shoulders sagging slightly as he dropped his gaze to the floor, then slowly raised it to meet her relentless stare once more. "I'm sorry. It seemed like a good idea at the time."

"Well, it wasn't," she stated flatly. She bit her tongue, fighting the urge to lash out. She knew that venting her anger at him wouldn't improve the situation.

Blake and Faris watched the dialogue unfold in silence, their expressions curios and concerned. Blake felt a sense of deceit hanging in the air, unsure of the dynamic between Manley and Owen. It was apparent that, much like with Faris, this wasn't a simple, distanced work relationship. There was a deeper connection, but Blake wasn't sure he wanted to delve into it. This woman seemed to have a knack for forming bonds with men that went beyond the obvious.

Faris, on the other hand, understood the depths of what Manley, Owen, and the others had gone through together, the losses they had suffered in those few months. He knew why Manley felt betrayed. She had intertwined her personal vendetta with Owen's mission, only for him to seemingly die on her. Now that she knew he hadn't, Faris believed she had every right to be furious. There were battles they could have faced together, burdens they could have shared, but instead, Manley had been left to fend for herself after Owen and Darra's apparent demise.

Manley, in the meantime, was wishing for a blaster or two, or at least the physical ability to hit Owen hard. But he was too far away, and she wasn't about to leap out of her bed, risking further injury. Her mind churned with names to call him and unfair accusations to hurl. Yet, she restrained herself, knowing better than to give voice to the torrent of thoughts raging within her. Finally, Manley found the strength to say what was going through her mind in a very civilised manner. Her tone, though, betrayed her. Her voice sounded disappointed, aggressive, even dangerous. "I thought we were friends, Owen. You kept your plan from me. You kept secrets. Friends don't keep secrets. And then you ran away, letting me believe you were dead." Her words hung in the air.

Owen's face tightened with regret and guilt, each syllable cutting deeper than any physical wound. He looked as if he were being hit by a round of old-fashioned bullets.

Blake marvelled at how this fierce fighter, a man of unyielding strength, could look so utterly defeated in mere seconds. Something profoundly serious must have happened between them.

Owen broke eye contact with Manley, his gaze dropping momentarily before he looked back up at her. "I know. I'm sorry."

Blake's mind raced with questions about the history shared between Owen and Manley. What bond had they forged before Owen decided to fake his death? And how did Darra fit into this tangled web? Blake was certain that whatever existed between Manley and Owen was different from what he and Manley shared. If there had been any romantic involvement, someone would have hinted at it—Haylen would have told him. So, what exactly was the nature of their connection?

"Don't you ever do that again", Manley whispered, her voice carrying a determined, almost threatening edge.

Owen shook his head. "I won't." Now this was a lot closer to the Manley he knew. He saw in her eyes that she had wanted to say more, to unleash a torrent of words she was holding back. He understood where that came from. He preferred the happy, chatty version of her, but any display of emotion was more bearable than her silent disappointment. He was acutely aware that he had shattered the trust she had placed in him. He had spent weeks agonizing over his actions, berating himself for the pain he had caused. Yet, there was nothing he could do to undo the past. He resisted the urge to point out that she had kept secrets too—secrets from her past that had nearly cost her life.

"Good," Manley said, pushing herself into a sitting position with her good right arm. She turned her gaze to Faris. "You were saying?" She knew exactly that he had wanted to ask her more questions about her time in Claver's mansion. But right now, she had nothing more to say about that. She needed time to sift through the mental notes she had painstakingly collected. There were so many details she needed to document, or at least have someone document for her. These notes were crucial for whatever legal proceedings would follow once she left the hospital.

An official investigation loomed on the horizon, possibly even charges of kidnapping and physical abuse. She was determined not to let Claver escape unpunished again, but she needed more time to prepare.

Also, she couldn't bear to discuss it with Blake and Owen in the room. It was bad enough that Blake was probably already imagining in his head all the things that she had obviously left out in her re-telling of events. She couldn't stand Owen's shock and pity, either. He would blame himself, though there was nothing he could have done to prevent Claver from kidnapping her.

Faris cleared his throat, understanding her unspoken request for a break. His interrogation was over for today. He would return tomorrow to continue. He didn't mind; he had known that this would be challenging for her. Manley was accustomed to asking questions, not answering them. Besides, Owen and Blake's presence hindered any smooth investigative interrogation.

Faris decided to pivot to something that might offer her a glimmer of hope. "I was about to say that I'm having a safehouse prepared for you at the beach," he said, a hint of a smile softening his features. "The one on the west coast. You can go there as soon as the doctors release you. Maybe I can arrange for you to be taken there earlier than planned, so you don't have to stay here as long." He knew she would want to be out of the hospital as soon as possible.

Manley nodded approvingly, her mind already drifting to the serene location. She knew the house he was referring too well; she had accompanied a couple of crime victims there in the past. It was a beautiful place, perched on the beach with no direct neighbours, so surveillance would be easy enough, and a stunning view of the sunset. "That sounds like an immensely good idea to me. Can you arrange for medical staff to keep an eye on me there? Can we leave today?"

Faris shook his head, a sympathetic look in his eyes. "Not today. I know you want to get out of here, and I promise you will soon enough. Medical will come along, as will protection agents. But not today."

Manley sank back into the pillows, leaning on Blake's unwavering arm. She understood that even the head of ISA needed more than a few minutes to make such arrangements. Faris would likely handle the preparations personally, keeping the circle of those informed small—a course of action she decidedly agreed with. The fewer people knew what had happened for now, the better. "Alright," she conceded. After a brief pause, she added, "So, what's for dinner?"

Her unexpected question broke the tension, and everyone burst into laughter. It felt surreal, sitting in a hospital room and laughing heartily after everything that had happened, but none of them could help it.

"No, seriously, I'm starving. I'm guessing it's soup again, so I don't have to chew?" She looked at Faris, who nodded apologetically. Manley sighed. She knew medical likely meant well, allowing her facial muscles and tissues to heal properly. She wasn't sure if surgery would be necessary and didn't want to ask, not wanting to give anyone ideas. She figured if anything urgent had been found, she would already have been on an operating table. After all, they had stitched the cut on her forehead while she was unconscious. She looked around at the three men gathered around here. "So is this some sort of dinner party?"

Owen, Blake, and Faris exchanged amused glances. Blake, always quick with a quip, grinned. "Well, if it is, it's the worst one I've ever attended. The menu's pretty limited."

Faris smiled, noticing Manley's use of humour. Good. Progress. He turned to the others, "Seriously. Who wants some dinner? I'll have something delivered. I figure you're not exactly vegetarians?" Owen and Blake shook their heads. "I see. I'll figure something out. Make yourselves comfortable."

Manley chuckled quietly. "I don't seem to have a say in this." Her smile was weak but genuine.

Faris paused, halfway off the couch. "If you want us to leave..." He let his voice trail off.

She shook her head instantly. "No, please stay. I was just trying to be funny."

Faris stood and walked towards the door. "I'll be back in a while. I need some fresh air."

Blake scrambled after him. "Me too. You two look like you need some time." He didn't want to be in the way when they started to unpack their baggage. It wasn't like Manley was going anywhere.

Manley and Owen found themselves alone within seconds. She sank back into her pillows, trying to pull up her duvet with her right hand. Owen saw her struggle and quickly walked over to lend a hand. When he grabbed the duvet, he accidentally touched her hand. He pulled back immediately, half-expecting her to hit him. He deserved a good punch, after all. She met his gaze, and he saw her eyes brimming with tears. Unsure of what to do, he hesitated for a moment. For a couple of seconds, he just stood there. When her tears began to fall, he cast all doubts aside. Whatever Blake might think, he quickly sat on Manley's bed and took her in his arms.

"I thought you were dead," she sobbed quietly. "And then I might have been dead, and we might never have seen each other again," she continued before her voice broke.

Owen held her tightly, his own eyes stinging with tears. "I'm so sorry. I'm so, so sorry." Manley rested her head on his shoulder, and he would have held her tighter, if he weren't afraid of causing her more pain. He closed his eyes, hugging her as firmly as he dared. She had wrapped her good arm around his waist, turning her face away from him. The sight of her like this, so vulnerable and broken, made him feel utterly helpless. If he could have taken on her pain, shouldered her suffering, he would have done it in a heartbeat. Probably, Blake and Faris would join him in this endeavour. If Claver wasn't already dead, Owen would make sure he paid for every bruise, every tear.

His thoughts drifted back to the man they had left dead in his office. The scene replayed in his mind: Claver slumped over, lifeless, the room still echoing with the finality of the blaster shot. Owen was impressed with Blake; he hadn't thought the lawyer had it in him to pull the trigger. He wondered if anyone had told Manley that it had been Blake who ended Claver's life. He wondered if anyone had had the time to tell her anything at all. Gently, he moved his thumb over her back in slow, comforting circles. "Your lawyer's got some nerve, you know that?" he said softly, trying to distract her from her tears.

She looked up at him, her eyes red and swollen, the bruises on her face casting dark shadows beneath them. She frowned. "Like how?" she asked, her voice strained and still plagued by sobs.

Owen chuckled softly, "He searched the whole sector for you, and he did a whole lot of things his lawyer friends probably wouldn't be too happy about." He chose not to elaborate; Blake should have the chance to share his story when they had time. But Manley needed to know that Blake had moved heaven and hell for her. She needed to know that he was real. She deserved that. "Also, he stood up to me in a pretty impressive way. Though I'd never tell him that. He's one of the very few who live to tell the tale."

Manley wasn't sure where this conversation was leading. She swallowed hard and hung her head again. "What are you telling me?" she whispered.

Owen continued to stroke Manley's red hair gently, his touch tender and reassuring. "Blake's a good guy. He's very much in love with you, even if he hasn't said it. There can't be any other explanation for what he did."

He felt her relax against him, a small smile playing on her lips. She shifted slightly, resting her head more comfortably against his chest. If it had been any other woman, Owen might have felt a pang of discomfort, knowing he would have to explain this closeness to Darra. But with Manley, there was no room for jealousy; their bond was built on trust and understanding, something Darra knew well.

Manley pondered Owen's words for a moment, silently agreeing with him not just matter-of-factly, but with all her heart. He had put into words what she felt deep inside. Despite the short time they had known each other, the connection between her and Blake was undeniable. She took a deep breath, gathering her courage to ask the question that had been weighing on her mind. She hadn't dared to bring it up while Blake was in the room; she needed to know, but she also feared the answer and didn't want Blake to witness her distress. "What... What about Claver? Is he..." Her voice trailed off, uncertainty and unease evident in her tone.

"He's dead. I checked on him myself. He's never going to hurt you again, I promise", Owen reassured her, his voice firm and resolute. And before he could stop himself, he added, "It was Blake who shot him. Darra had wounded him before, but Blake got to him first and shot him at point-blank. We couldn't have stopped him." There was a brief pause, heavy with the weight of their shared actions and the consequences that followed. "Nor had we tried."

Manley's head slowly rose from Owen's chest, her gaze locking onto him with wide, disbelieving blue eyes. "He's gone?"

"He's gone," Owen confirmed with a solemn nod.

"He's gone," she repeated in a whisper, sinking back against him. A wave of relief swept over her, draining the last bits of tension from her body. She suddenly felt exhausted, her limbs heavy and her mind finally able to rest. Claver was gone. For a fleeting moment, regret flared up in her—she wished she could have been the one to deliver justice with her own hands.

But then she exhaled deeply, closing her eyes, allowing herself to simply be. Owen held her close. They sat in silence, the only sound the soft rhythm of their breathing. Gradually, Manley felt life seeping back into her limbs, a gentle return to the present moment. She lifted her head to meet Owen's gaze once more. "Does he have a son? Who might be coming for revenge?"

Her voice held a trace of concern, a learned wariness born from past betrayals. She had misjudged a man named Claver once before; she wouldn't make the same mistake again.

Owen shook his head, understanding the source of her question. "No children. No partners who could come after you. This ends here."

His words hung in the air, and while he pondered that, he also wondered where Faris and Blake had gone. He knew Manley could use the comfort of Blake's sturdy presence and Faris' calm reassurance just as much as his own. He knew that Manley had cried on Faris' shoulder a lot so many years ago, she probably wouldn't feel uncomfortable doing it now. But he couldn't bring himself to break the embrace; she needed his support now. He owed her that much. He had left her unprotected weeks ago when he and Darra had gone into hiding. Memories of their abrupt departure and the agonizing uncertainty it had caused flashed through Owen's mind. He wanted to explain everything—why he and Darra had vanished, the weight of the decisions they had made to protect those they cared about—but now wasn't the time. Manley needed support, not explanations. This visit wasn't about him; it was about her, and he would do whatever it took to be there for her.

When the door finally hissed back open and Blake and Faris returned from the corridor, Manley didn't stir from Owen's chest at first. She took a few laboured breaths, then slowly lifted her head, each movement seemingly requiring immense effort. Blake tried to mask his confusion as he climbed into the bed from the other side, his hand gently stroking her back. Without looking at him, she shifted into his embrace. Faris handed her a glass of water in silence, and she clutched it with a trembling hand, gulping it down in big, desperate swallows. Blake took the empty glass from her and passed it to Owen, who was rising from the bed. The man with the long, black ponytail set the glass on the table and glanced back at his friend, now enveloped in Blake's arms once more. According to his watch, he had only been alone with her for a little over ten minutes, but it felt much longer. Manley seemed to have aged within that brief span, and suddenly, the notion of a dinner party in her hospital room seemed ludicrous to him. He turned to Faris. "Is there another place we could eat? I think our favourite patient here needs a break from all of this."

Faris nodded. "I know. I've had the meeting room across the hall prepared." He paused, heading for the door. "Whenever you're ready, Blake. We'll be over there." With that, he departed, and Owen followed, realising he wasn't needed here right now.

Blake and Manley were alone a few moments later. He commanded the computer system to dim the lights, knowing she would fall asleep, or pass out, within minutes. The events of the last hour had taken a toll on her, no matter how resilient she had seemed to them before this past week's ordeals. He had talked about his outside with Faris, but he also understood that Manley needed to see Owen and convince herself that he was alive and well. Now, she needed at least one good night's rest before he would allow any other visitors beside himself. He pondered why he had taken it upon himself to act as her advocate. Being a lawyer suited him, but never before had he stood up for someone he loved like this. Perhaps it was because he had never been in love like this before.

Manley's head rested gently against his chest, her breath now softer and more even. He held her, waiting patiently until she slipped into sleep. Once he was sure that he wasn't going to wake her up, he carefully disentangled himself from her embrace, tenderly laying her head onto the pillow. She remained motionless. Taking a moment, Blake adjusted the bed-head to lower it, making sure she could sleep more comfortably. Satisfied that she was settled, he tiptoed out of the room. His stomach rumbled. Manley, sustained by the IV drips, could afford to sleep most of the day away, but he needed food, and the idea of a proper meal was tempting.

In the meeting room Faris had mentioned, Blake was greeted by an impressive spread. Faris had selected an array of fine meats and vegetables, complemented by an assortment of side dishes, enough for half a dozen people. Blake couldn't help but quip, "Oh, is Manley coming after all?"

Faris and Owen looked up from their plates, grins spreading across their faces. Owen was quick with a retort, "Shouldn't you know?"

Blake chuckled, curious what they had been discussing before his arrival. "Well played, Mr.," he said, unbothered by the innuendo. They were all adults here, and the camaraderie was comforting. He settled into a seat and began to dig in. It had been ages since he last enjoyed a proper meal in an actual room, at a table, with other people. This was a welcome change. Manley would have savoured this, too, he thought. And she would, soon enough, once her recovery progressed a bit further.

The three men ate voraciously, as if they hadn't seen food in quite some time. Their bond was their shared concern for Manley, though each cared for her in his own distinct way. All three, however, were equally horrified by the condition in which Manley had returned. Faris had witnessed her injured before, but never this gravely. He trusted in the capabilities of ISA's medical team and knew she would recover physically. The psychological scars, however, were another matter entirely, and only time would reveal how she would rebound.

Owen struggled to reconcile the reality that even his favourite agent, Manley, was merely a human being. The thought of what Claver had done to her infuriated him, with her injuries suggesting only the worst. He shuddered at the speculations swirling in his mind, imagining the violent treatment she had received from Claver and his minions. Claver himself probably hadn't dirtied his own hands, but that didn't lessen the brutality inflicted on Manley. The hospital gown concealed some of her visible injuries, but it did little to flatter her appearance. He suspected she would prefer to be anywhere other than this sterile hospital wing.

Blake, on the other hand, was wondering how long they would be confined to the hospital wing, especially after Faris had mentioned the possibility of a beach house. There was no doubt he would remain by Manley's side, and he certainly didn't mind being at her side on the patio of a beach house. What he did mind was if she was going to be safe on the patio of said beach house, because he sure wasn't longing to go on another scavenger hunt across this side of the galaxy. Between bites, he glanced at Faris and asked, "What kind of security does that beach house have?"

Faris quickly swallowed and took a sip of water before replying. "I'll have a pair of security personnel in the house working three shifts, anti-aircraft defences, electronic shielding—every high-level measure we can implement. A nurse will be stationed there around the clock, and a doctor will be on standby, ready to arrive within minutes. Does that sound good?" He looked at Blake, confident that the lawyer would approve.

Blake agreed, silently. But he wasn't ready to let that show yet; he still had questions. "Who else knows about this? How many people are involved? How can you be sure she'll be safe?"

Faris should have anticipated that Blake wouldn't stop asking question quickly. "Three shifts of security pairs that I coordinate personally, three nurses, the doctor, the pilot for the two of you and the doctor. Me. You. Owen. Let me be honest—even I cannot guarantee 100 percent security. It's impossible. But I'm confident we have a solid plan here."

Blake thought about this for a moment. Faris was likely right; after all, this was his domain, and he managed situations like this daily. But Blake wasn't willing to let the head of ISA off the hook so easily. "She thought she was safe before. What's different now?" He took another bite and chewed thoughtfully.

Faris had to admit, Blake was persistent. "Claver is dead. You killed him. There's no one left to seek revenge; everyone from the mansion has been accounted for and is off-planet in holding cells." He paused, then spoke again with a touch more emphasis. "And then there's you. From what I see, she trusts you. For all the right reasons. She'll be okay eventually if you're with her."

Owen joined the conversation, his tone earnest. "Blake, I understand why you're suspicious. I really do. But it doesn't get any better than this. I can't think of a safer place for her in the galaxy than that beach house with Faris' security measures. Well, maybe in Rendler's back room, but who would possibly want to stay there for more than a few hours? She didn't have that kind of security in the hotel room. And it wasn't your fault that she got kidnapped." He smiled, asking the lawyer to drop his charges.

Blake smiled back, remembering their first meeting in the back room of the Sunset, which Owen had just referenced. That encounter hadn't exactly gone smoothly. They had clashed, albeit in a civilized manner, with a lot of tension hanging in the air. "Alright, alright. I hear you. And I know you understand why I needed to ask."

He fell silent, focusing on his food. He started to wonder why he hadn't seen Haylen or Darra in the hospital wing. After tracking Manley down through the sector, he would have expected them to want to see her too. After all, Haylen and Manley had planned to hang out on Nergal B. His ship was still on that desolate rock, as was Manley's.

"Faris?" Blake's voice broke the silence.

The head of ISA looked up from his plate. "Yeah?"

"My ship is still back on Nergal B. Manley's is, too. Is there any way you can get them for us?"

Faris nodded, his eyes steady. "Consider it done. Send me their registration, and I'll dispatch someone to retrieve them right now. I'll also arrange for someone to pick up your belongings and hers from the hotel."

Blake acknowledged with a curt nod. "Thank you." Relief coursed through him at the thought, for he had a particular fondness for that black dress she had worn. The one that had cascaded sensuously from her body on their first night together, its low-cut back leaving little to the imagination. But this was a sentiment he had no intention of sharing with Faris. Besides, Manley probably wouldn't be wearing it anytime soon, given the cumbersome splint encasing her arm and shoulder. It was likely best if she refrained from wearing that dress for a while, considering the doctors had prescribed weeks of meticulous recovery, insisting on her taking everything very slow. And he needed to know about her injuries. Until now, Faris had handled the doctors alone. It was high time Blake put himself into that narrative. "What about her injuries, Faris? How bad are they?" He raised his eyes from his plate, his expression resolute.

Faris held his gaze with a grave intensity. "Do you really want to know? Now?"

Blake exhaled a long sigh. "Faris, if I'm to stay with her at the beach house, I need to understand the full extent of what she's up against."

"Alright, you have a point. But brace yourself, this isn't going to be pleasant."

"I wasn't expecting it to be," Blake retorted, his voice edged with determination.

Faris chewed thoughtfully and swallowed a bite. "Minor burns on her left leg from a blaster hit. Head trauma from kicks and punches, concussion, the cut on her forehead. Three broken ribs, three broken bones in her shoulder and arm. Internal injuries to her liver, diaphragm, spleen, both kidneys. Bruises all over. It's nothing short of a miracle none of that is life-threatening." He watched as Blake's expression subtly shifted, likely imagining the brutal ordeal she had been through.

Blake hung his head. It was more, and worse, than he had anticipated. "Boy. And she walked out of that mansion on her own feet. I wouldn't believe it if I hadn't been there."

"Not for long," Faris interjected. "Henders told me he had to pick her up outside and carry her for a while. She was on the brink of a breakdown during the flight. She walked out of his ship on her own but almost passed out, so we had to catch her. She was with medical within twenty-five minutes of your meeting, and Henders had given her some painkillers before he took off." He took another bite, chewing heartily before continuing. "I know this sounds grave. And it is. But she'll be okay eventually. Doctors say the injuries are healing already."

Blake nodded, feeling slightly relieved. "That's a good thing." Yet uncertainty gnawed at him. She was in no shape to handle anything on her own. That was likely why Faris had planned for a nurse and a doctor to be on standby at the beach house. But something else troubled him, something he wasn't keen on discussing in the presence of others, though he needed to know. "Faris... Have the doctors... I mean, did they…" He fumbled for the right words, his voice trailing off.

"You mean if she was assaulted sexually?" Faris met his gaze directly. There was no point in sugar-coating this part of the conversation.

Blake nodded, thankful Faris had found the appropriate phrasing.

"According to the doctors, she hasn't been. There are no injuries of that nature, and I'm certain she would have fought tooth and nail if they had tried."

Blake's eyes closed, and he breathed heavily a few times, allowing the wave of relief to wash over him. "Good." The possibility had been unnerving. Men trying to teach women a lesson often resorted to despicable behaviour. He had seen it all too often in his line of work. Usually, there were no witnesses, and the violated women often shied away from prosecution, dreading the ordeal of reliving the trauma. It was a genuine relief that at least this wouldn't haunt her.

"One more thing." This time, it was Owen who needed clarification. He directed his gaze at Faris, his voice carrying a hint of accusation. "Second in command? Really? You led us to believe she was your assistant, not your deputy. If we had known we were dealing with your representative, and if we had known about her position, we might have handled things a bit differently."

"Actually…" Faris grinned, a mischievous glint in his eyes. He didn't need to know how they had unearthed the truth; it was obvious that Blake and Owen, when working together, could uncover all sorts of information that wasn't meant to be found. "We never explicitly discussed positions. I referred to her as an assistant. Assistant director, to be precise. It's been both convenient and quite amusing for us when outsiders underestimated her on a regular basis." He turned back to Owen. "We didn't mislead you intentionally. It just happened. We didn't state her full title, and you made assumptions."

Owen nodded. "Point taken. But boy, you two've been some duo."

"I know." Faris wondered if he should share what was swirling in his mind. *Oh what the hell*, he thought. "We were really good at this together. She took to the agent's training like her life depended on it, and looking back, maybe it really did. She needed something to live for, and she turned out to be exceptionally talented in this line of work. I've never seen anyone else so comfortable with weapons. She could handle them all in her sleep. Hell, she could probably shoot us with a blaster from her hospital bed."

He allowed himself another bite, savouring the taste as he continued. "Two years into her training, she was ready for missions that others would have tackled only after three years or more. She's highly intelligent, unbelievably determined, and, let's not forget, very good-looking. That isn't a prerequisite, but it certainly helped her many times."

He was determined, however, not to delve into the details of how she had used her looks to seduce targets, only to either kill them or have them arrested. She knew precisely how to use her body to her advantage. He also refrained from mentioning how ruthlessly she operated from time to time. A few times over the years, he had been genuinely glad to be on her good side rather than her target. He remembered one particular instance when she had executed a Faction lord with an almost frightening efficiency—knives, blaster, her bare hands. She must have been exceptionally furious that day; there had been blood everywhere. He had read the grim report from the clean-up team.

He simply concluded, "She also had the necessary cruelty for the job. Seven years into her time here, my assistant director was killed on a mission. We needed to fill his position quickly, as the sector was teeming with criminals back then. Several colleagues asked me why I didn't offer the job to her. So I did, and she accepted—but only if she could continue working as a field agent as well. So that's what we've been doing for ten years, until she quit now."

Well, that explained the shape she had been in when they met, Blake thought. And by now, he wasn't surprised that she hadn't revealed her real job to him. Assistant Director of ISA. That wasn't something you'd put on a badge, unless you were in a room filled with very old and very conservative men. Her position alone would have made her a target in countless ways. The fact that it didn't even play a role in the kidnapping added a certain irony to the whole situation. Claver probably hadn't even realized that she was co-heading the agency, just as none of them had. He quietly returned to his meal, but his mind kept wandering off towards the things she might have done as an agent.

When Blake left after tucking her in carefully, Manley lay in the darkness, unable to find sleep. She felt so exhausted, but her eyes kept fluttering open, her mind too restless to succumb to sleep. Owen had been there. She had thought that she would never see him again after running into him in Claver's mansion. The friend she thought she had lost weeks ago, the one who had unwittingly entangled her in Claver's sinister business. She had mourned him deeply, his memory haunting her thoughts in painful reminiscence and quiet contemplation. The revelation that he had faked his death left her reeling. She understood why he did it—he needed to operate in the shadows in order to keep her and the others out of greater danger. He had to convince their enemies that he no longer posed a threat, making them careless. Yet, even when the immediate danger had passed, he had remained in hiding, not sending her the smallest message.

His behaviour felt like a profound betrayal. He hadn't even let Manley in on his plan. She didn't care if anyone else knew; it was his exclusion of her that hurt. The chaos of believing him dead, only to see him alive while she was fleeing from Claver, created a mix of emotions she was struggling to process.

A new thought crossed her mind, one that twisted her heart with fresh anguish. What about her parents? How would they feel? How were they feeling? She hadn't dared to think about them for years, each attempt forcibly pushed aside. She knew she had caused them unbearable pain when she got herself into trouble and was declared dead. Back then, she had been a teenager, not fully comprehending the scope of her actions. She had only grieved for her own loss, the fact that she had to navigate the world alone now. It had never occurred to her that her parents were suffering too, that they had to endure a funeral service and watch her empty coffin being lowered into the ground. Faris had kept the details of the service from her, knowing she would likely run away and attempt to attend.

Manley felt a tear roll down her cheek. If she could, she would undo the pain she had caused her parents. As a sassy teenager before her disappearance and supposed death, she had fought with them daily over trivial matters—homework, curfews, and Darren. None of it had been worth the fights, she knew now. None of it had been worth the heartbreak she had inflicted. If only she could take it all back—but, could she? Was there a way? What if she could go back and tell them why Faris had made them believe she was dead?

He probably wouldn't allow it. He would find numerous reasons to explain why they couldn't simply reverse a witness protection placement. And he would likely argue that they couldn't go around revealing that she was a top-secret government agent, tasked with eliminating dangerous individuals in the name of the greater good.

Manley took a deep breath, trying to fill her lungs with oxygen. A wave of grief washed over her—grief for the family she had once had. She barely remembered her mother's face. She wasn't even sure if she could recognize her in a photograph. Her mother had once had dark brown, almost black hair, and she had always been slim. Her eyes had usually been kind, though sometimes they had looked sad, especially during their arguments.

And her dad. Quiet, yet resolute, with short, blond hair. He loved his garden and spent way too much time working, often leaving his wife and daughter alone. When he was home, he tried to fulfil Amy's every wish, attempting not to get between her and her mother. Her parents were affectionate with each other, except when her mother was really furious about something. In the months leading up to the events at the Claver mansion, the cause of fury in the Carter household had usually been Amy's stubbornness. Much like her mother, she wasn't very good at complying with things she didn't want to do.

Manley's chest tightened with the weight of her memories. She remembered the warmth of family dinners, the comfort of her father's quiet presence, and her mother's occasional soft laughter. She remembered the love that had been there, even amidst the conflicts. The realisation of how much she had lost, and how much she had taken from her parents, was almost unbearable now. If only she could see them again, explain everything, make amends. But even as the thought crossed her mind, she knew it was impossible. Her life had changed irrevocably. The girl her parents had known was gone, replaced by someone who lived in shadows and secrets. Someone who could never truly go home again.

Manley didn't know if she would ever have another family, if she would find someone who would take her in and be her person. The future loomed uncertainly, a vast expanse of unknowns. She didn't know if things would work out with Blake once the initial thrill of physical attraction faded. Could she enjoy mundane everyday life with him, or would it eventually bore her? To find out, she would have to take a chance and stay, or she could choose to disappear from the hospital and vanish into the night. But she had a hunch that Faris wouldn't agree to her vanishing act, and deep down, she knew it wasn't what a responsible adult should do. Being a grown-up meant working through the hard stuff, staying when things got tough, and remaining truthful despite the difficulties. It meant confronting her fears and insecurities head-on instead of running from them.

She sighed deeply. Being a grown-up suddenly didn't seem so attractive any more. From where she was now, being a carefree teenager again, with no burdens and no responsibilities, seemed infinitely easier. Back then, life had been simpler, her biggest worries revolving around trivial matters that seemed laughably insignificant now.

As Manley lay there, wrestling with her thoughts, exhaustion finally claimed her. Her eyelids grew heavy, and despite the turmoil within her, sleep began to pull her under. In the moments before she slipped into a well-deserved slumber, she felt utterly drained, her body and mind worn out from the emotional roller-coaster of the past weeks.

When Faris returned the next day, he came prepared to deliver the sombre speech about all the injuries she had sustained. He didn't want the doctors to do it; she needed to hear it from someone she knew and trusted. The doctors on duty today hadn't seen Manley before this visit. He carried a small box of chocolates, hoping that her injured face would allow her to enjoy them, even if just a little. Manley was sitting in her bed, leaning against the propped-up headboard. Blake wasn't around, but he would probably return soon. He never left her alone for long. Faris entered quietly, his expression serious yet gentle. "Hey there," he said.

She looked at him with an expression that said she knew what was coming. "Hey there", she replied.

Faris placed the chocolates on the nightstand. "For later." Then he pulled up a chair to her bed and took off his black jacket, draping it over the back of the chair before sitting down. "You know we need to talk about what happened."

She closed her eyes for a moment, steeling herself. "I know."

"Prepare for this. I'll tell you about your injuries, so you know what to be careful about." She nodded, bracing for the details. "You've noticed you feel foggy. That's because of head trauma and a minor concussion. They stitched up the cut on your forehead. You've got three broken ribs. You haven't felt them because you're on heavy painkillers for three broken bones in your shoulder and arm. There's a minor burn on your left leg. And internal injuries—liver, diaphragm, spleen, both kidneys. None of it is life-threatening."

He let that sink in, watching her reaction. Her expression didn't change, she was staring through him, apparently. "You've been very lucky so far, considering the circumstances. You need to be very careful when you're released to the beach house. If any of those injuries suffers any more trauma from stress or too much movement, you'll be back here in no time, and you'll have to stay for weeks. Am I making myself clear?"

Manley was only half-hearing what he said as she counted her injuries. It was worse than she had expected. The moments she had sustained those injuries flashed before her eyes, catching her off guard. She closed them reflexively, trying to chase the images away. She could see the fist coming for her head and vividly remembered being kicked to her torso by several of Claver's henchmen. Breathing became a struggle, and she needed all her strength to keep herself from plunging into a full-blown panic attack.

Faris saw her struggling with the weight of his words. He knew he couldn't spare her this; she needed to understand what she was up against, no matter how hard it would be. He moved his chair closer to the edge of her bed and reached for her hand. He half-expected her to pull away or hit him, but she didn't. "Breathe," he said softly. "You need to breathe." He watched her fight through it, battling the panic. He had seen her do this before, though mostly many years ago.

It took Manley a few minutes to return from the edge of panic. Too many scenes flashed before her eyes, each one bringing back the pain and the feeling of helplessness. She wasn't good at handling that right now. Seventeen years ago, she had sworn to herself that she would never again be as helpless as she had been the day Darren was killed. She had sworn to always be in control. And she had been, mostly, until she found herself in Claver's underground prison. She focused on her breathing, each breath becoming a little calmer, a little steadier, until she could finally breathe without gasping for air.

"Clear," she managed to say after a while, not looking at Faris. He was still holding her hand, providing a physical connection she could cling to. "Perfectly clear." Her voice shook violently when she continued. "How much detail do you need about my captivity?"

Faris did not release her hand. "I understand you can't provide names now. Tomorrow, I will return with some photographs, and I need you to identify who did what, if you can recall."

Oh, she could recall. The faces of the men who had assaulted her after her escape attempt were etched into her memory. Especially the po-faced one. And the one she had locked in when she escaped. And the others who had held her captive in that dungeon. She nodded solemnly. "What else?"

"Can you recount what Claver said to you?" Faris asked, still not meeting Manley's eyes but maintaining his grip on her hand.

She nodded again. "I can write it down for you, if you provide me with a tablet."

"Do that," he agreed. Both of them were acutely aware that there would be no official prosecution of her captor, as the main suspect and known criminal was dead, though neither of them insisted on it. But documenting it would help her process and ultimately come to terms with the ordeal. "I'll have someone bring you tablet. You should rest now", Faris said. He stood up and headed out of the room, pausing at the door. He looked back at her. "You did a very good job today. It will get easier."

She didn't react, but he knew she had heard him. Faris sighed and walked out. He had other business to attend to.

Haylen tiptoed towards the door Blake had indicated for Manley's room. She wasn't sure what to expect. What should she say? Blake had briefed her on Manley's injuries and hinted that Manley might try to escape with her. She cast a glance back down the corridor before quietly entering the room. Manley lay on the bed, her back turned to Haylen, seemingly asleep. The duvet was pulled up to her shoulder, concealing most of her body. Her breaths were shallow, and an IV drip was attached to her arm. Haylen noticed the edge of the splint Blake had mentioned. She considered retreating when a weak voice broke the silence.

"I'm awake, you know?" There was a pause. "I just can't lie on my back any more right now. Can you please come over here?"

Haylen smiled softly. This was unmistakably Manley's voice, though it sounded a lot more fragile than she remembered. She walked around the bed, fetching a chair from the set around the table on the other side of the room. As she approached and saw her friend's face, she froze momentarily. Manley's eyes were still closed. The bruises Haylen had seen at the mansion had darkened and deepened, painting her face black and blue. Yet, through the hurt, a small smile emerged, and Haylen couldn't help but smile back as she sat down. "Girl, you had me worried there."

"Haylen!" Manley opened her eyes, revealing a glimmer of her old, cheerful self. She attempted to prop herself up on her good arm but failed, collapsing back onto the pillow.

Haylen leaned in, giving her a careful half-hug, mindful of not causing more pain. "I want to say I'm so glad you're okay, but I'm not sure that's the appropriate greeting right now," she said.

Manley smiled again weakly. "Compared to last week, I'm excellent. They give me painkillers and food in a drip—what more could you possibly ask for?" she joked, her voice lighter than her exhausted appearance suggested. The late afternoon sun filtered weakly through the curtains, casting long shadows. Manley had fought to stay awake all day, resisting the urge to nap, but the fresh dose of painkillers added to her fatigue.

Haylen sat with her arms resting on her knees, her head sinking to her chest for a moment. "This isn't funny, Manley. I was worried about you. We were all worried about you. And rightfully so, if I might say."

Manley's gaze softened. "What do you want me to say? I know you had a hard time finding me. But you did. I had a hard time, too." Her tone held a trace of reproach, though she knew Haylen wasn't trying to make her feel guilty. Yet, the constant reminders of the trouble she had caused, through no fault of her own, were beginning to wear on her. She had done nothing, in the grand scheme of things, to deserve to be knocked out, kidnapped, and hidden away in an underground dungeon. Or to be reminded of this constantly.

Haylen North, sole and mighty head of the North imperium, suddenly appeared far less aloof. "I'm sorry, I didn't mean it like that." Her voice faltered, unsure how to express her regret. She paused, searching for the right words before changing the subject. "When can you leave?"

Manley closed her eyes briefly, looking for some inner strength. "I'd rather get out of here sooner than later. Apparently, this time it's really up to the doctors, Faris has me convinced."

Haylen nodded. She refrained from saying that Manley didn't look ready to leave the hospital, or capable of taking on any fight—verbal or physical. She was certain that in any current confrontation, Manley wouldn't be on the winning side. "Might be sensible", she said instead. The Manley she knew would have snorted in irritation, rolling her eyes. Now, her friend merely exhaled a little louder, a shadow of her former self.

Manley observed Haylen. She looked like she needed a holiday herself. Dark shadows lay under her eyes, and she seemed haunted. Manley considered advising against a stay on Nergal B, but stopped herself. Haylen could make her own decisions, and after days of searching for Manley, she might need something other than a planet overrun with tourists seeking fun. Instead of offering advice, she simply said, "Thank you."

Haylen looked up, surprised. "For what?"

"For taking on the search. For finding me." Manley held her gaze, conveying the depth of her gratitude without additional words.

The North heir blinked, momentarily taken aback. "What else would I have done? And by the way—you still owe me that drink. I suppose you don't keep a little stash of booze in that cupboard over there, do you?" She smiled, clearly joking.

Manley playfully rolled her eyes and shook her head. "Doctor's orders. Something about the painkillers." She giggled softly. "Who knows what kind of funny trips those might cause?"

Haylen grinned, her smile broad and genuine. "Nah, we'll save that for some other time. What are you gonna do when you get out of here?"

"Faris mentioned something about a beach house where I might spend a few weeks to heal. He knows I'll be a pain in the ass here in no time." She closed her eyes briefly, as if savouring the thought. "I can't tell you how much I'm looking forward to that house.

No dark walls, no closed doors. I'm not good with confined spaces right now."

"I can imagine." Haylen paused, then asked the question that had been gnawing at her. "Manley, what did they do to you? And I don't want the white-washed version. I can take it. I shot a man in the leg looking for you."

Manley's eyes widened in surprise. Sweet, composed, yet passionate Haylen had finally shot someone. Despite the gravity of the situation, she almost smiled with a hint of pride. "I got a fist and several feet in my face, as you can see. Also in my torso. They bound me to a chair for a while and made a point of toppling it over. That's when my shoulder and arm broke. When I tried to run for the first time, they beat me until I passed out. That's probably when I got the broken ribs."

She watched as Haylen's expression shifted from prepared calm to shock and rage. "I hit my head on the run with Henders, they stitched me up. But I'm not in pain now, just constantly tired from the drugs." She gestured to the transparent bag of liquid connected to the IV in her arm. "At least I can move around a bit. Sitting still in that room in the underground mansion drove me nuts."

Haylen could see that Manley wasn't revealing the full extent of her ordeal. She decided not to press her friend. Manley probably had her reasons for holding back. Instead, Haylen offered an easy distraction. Stressing Manley out now would be pointless. "We'll have that drink some other day. You're not getting out of that. When I couldn't find you at the hotel, I had to drink at the Sunset."

"Oh my. I'm so sorry." Manley grinned. She knew what that meant. The Sunset wasn't exactly known for high-quality beverages with fancy garnishes. But the booze was strong and clean, at least. "You'll have your drink, I promise. We might even get seriously drunk. Not in here, of course. But we'll get there. Maybe in a few weeks."

"In a few weeks." Haylen nodded, a reassuring smile on her lips.

Manley turned on her back, wincing slightly. "You might have to coordinate with Blake, though."

"So you're keeping him." It wasn't a question but a statement. Haylen was glad to hear her friend mention the man who had set the entire search in motion. It would have been a shame to waste a perfectly good lawyer after a chase through the sector without seeing what else he could do.

"I think I'm keeping him, yes. At least for now. He's helpful enough in here." Manley smiled, a hint of mischief in her eyes. "He's been quite helpful with the search, too, I hear."

Haylen nodded. "A couple of things he found out with his friend helped put us on the right track. Also, he's really nice to look at." She grinned, her eyes twinkling with amusement.

Manley grinned back. "I know. He's also very clever with his hands. And he's got a couple of other qualities that I won't go into detail about."

"So it's all about the sex?" Haylen asked, her tone teasing. It was a trick question. She knew it wasn't true, at least not solely from what she had heard from Blake. And she knew she could ask without serious repercussions. Manley wouldn't bite her head off.

Manley's expression sobered, her eyes taking on a faraway look. "It was. And it wasn't. You know, this has never happened to me before. Yes, the sex was great, and honestly? I haven't enjoyed it this much for a while. But there was something else, something I can't really explain. There's a connection between us, he just gets me."

Haylen noticed how Manley's eyes sparkled with an emotion that went beyond mere attraction. It was clear that what had started as a seemingly superficial fling between Manley and Blake had evolved into something much deeper. "You know, he said something very similar about you." She smiled at Manley, offering her reassurance.

"So you've been talking about me," Manley stated, her tone tinged with curiosity.

"Apparently. After all, we were looking for you and needed to pass a lot of time waiting for information or in hyperspace jumping queues." Haylen grinned. "But believe me, I have no details of what you two did with each other. I asked him why he went out looking for you when he could have just shrugged it off as a one-night stand. And at first, he couldn't really explain it because something like that had never happened to him before. I think he only understood it himself a couple of days later. Something his friend said to him."

"What did he say?" Manley's curiosity deepened, her eyes locked onto Haylen's.

Haylen frowned for a moment, trying to recollect the exact words she had overheard Lannister say to Blake. Then, with a playful smirk, she disguised her voice and quoted, "If you don't marry that woman and have the time of your life for the rest of your life,

I'll make Ayla think of ways to torture you, you know that, right?"

Now it was Manley's turn to furrow her brow, a delicate crease forming between her eyes. "Who's Ayla?" Could this friend's mention of marriage really be about her and Blake? Were they supposed to commit to each other forever? The thought tugged at her mind, weaving a web of what-ifs and doubts. After Darren, the idea of tying herself to one person had felt foreign, almost intimidating. And now, here she was, confronted with the possibility that someone else saw a future for her long before she did.

"I'm not sure. I guess his wife. But he seemed to know that Blake wasn't just going to let you go", Haylen replied casually, watching Manley closely. She noticed a subtle shift in Manley's expression. She couldn't quite say what happened in Manley's mind at the moment, but something seemed to settle with her. Her frown relaxed, and the little happy wrinkles around her eyes re-appeared.

Manley mulled over the information, fitting it into the mosaic of thoughts she had about Blake. Each piece seemed to click into place, forming a clearer image of who he was. But how did this image align with her life now? She shook her head slightly, about to speak, when Blake re-entered the room, followed by a nurse who quietly tended to her IV. She asked, "Are you free of pain?"

Manley nodded, "Just tired. You know."

The nurse, whose name was Rhonda, according to her name tag, nodded back, "That's completely normal. Maybe you should take a nap?" She looked at Haylen in a way that could only be interpreted as a prompt to leave.

Haylen caught the hint and nodded to Rhonda and then to Blake. "I'll step out. I'll come back another time." She couldn't help but add, looking at Blake, "It's good to see you here, with her." With a brief hug, she departed. Rhonda ushered her out, leaving Manley and Blake alone.

Blake noticed the inscrutable expression on Manley's face, unsure of what had passed between the two women but sensing he had been part of the conversation. He settled on the edge of her bed, tenderly stroking her hand where the IV needle was placed. "How are you feeling?" His voice was soft, filled with unspoken concern and perhaps a trace of hope.

"Pretty much like an hour ago, when you left," she murmured, a soft smile gracing her lips. "I feel like I could sleep for days, but when I try, I just can't."

Blake understood her struggle all too well. He had noticed her restless nights, her attempts to hide her wakefulness. She was adept at pretending, yet her body betrayed her with every touch he dared to place upon her, even when she seemed lost in sleep. I

He chose, as he often did, not to press the issue. "Maybe things will improve once we're out of here," he offered gently, acknowledging the discomfort the splint caused her. Sleeping on her back or right side must have been gruelling, despite her efforts to endure silently. He hated his inability to ease her suffering. All he could do was wait, wait until they were discharged, until her bones healed, until she could feel the warmth of the sun on her skin once more. From what Faris had shared, Blake harboured no doubt that she would recover fully in time. She had the resilience and determination needed to heal, fortified by the support he was committed to providing. Leaning down, he brushed a tender kiss upon her forehead. "I'll go talk to Faris. You need to get out of here." With that, Blake quietly slipped out of the hospital room, heading purposefully towards the nurses' station. "I need to speak with Mr. Faris," he stated firmly, addressing the middle-aged nurse with blonde hair who was engrossed in digital paperwork.

Stephanie, as her tag indicated, glanced up, her expression neutral. "I can open a channel for you in the meeting room."

Blake shook his head, preferring a more direct approach. "I'd rather do this in person."

The nurse remained unmoved. "I can open a channel for you in the meeting room, so you can discuss scheduling a meeting."

"Alright," Blake relented with a sigh. "Please do. I'll be there." Gesturing towards the meeting room across the hall from Manley's room, he added, "Thanks."

A few moments later, Blake arrived at the meeting room where the channel was already open. Faris appeared on the screen, momentarily distracted but returning his attention when he noticed Blake's arrival. "Faris," Blake greeted, ready to delve into the necessary discussions ahead.

"Blake." Faris appeared harried.

Blake knew Faris was just a few floors down in his office, yet seemingly unable to spare the time to visit the hospital wing. "We need to discuss Manley being discharged," Blake pressed, his tone earnest.

"I know," Faris acknowledged without elaboration.

"You do?" Blake's surprise was evident, wondering how Faris had understood his intentions pre-emptively.

"Yes. I've reviewed the doctors' notes. Her lack of sleep is becoming problematic. It's affecting her blood work, though nothing critical yet," Faris explained, impressing Blake with his thoroughness. He hadn't realised her insomnia was already impacting her health metrics.

"That's exactly why I want to get her out of here. She's hardly sleeping. I think she'll fare much better at the beach house," Blake asserted confidently.

Faris's expression wasn't easily deciphered. "I'm almost with you. We both know she hates it in the hospital. But I need to be sure that she'll be able to handle the house and the increased level of movement she'll have there. We need to be sure we're not doing this too early. I don't want her to come back to the hospital in an emergency."

"I hear you, Faris. But haven't you arranged for a doctor to be on standby once she's there? And a nurse round the clock?" Blake countered, watching Faris nod in confirmation. "So what's the real risk? She's aware she'll need to dial it back if she overdoes it. She needs proper rest, and I don't see that happening here." He paused for a few seconds. "You know it, too."

Faris sighed, a gesture of conceding to Blake's logic. "I'll speak to the doctors. Let me see what can be arranged."

Blake felt a surge of impatience creeping up within him. "Faris, honestly? You're the head of ISA. You could just give the order to release her," he urged, pushing a bit further. "I know you've done it before."

Faris exhaled audibly through the feed. "Alright. I'll arrange for a transport to take you to the house later. I'll send you the details of the agents who will pick you up. Expect them in about two hours. The ship will be waiting on the roof. Pack your things. Faris out." With a decisive click, he ended the conversation, the screen going dark.

A satisfied smile played on Blake's lips as he exited the meeting room, his mind already focused on the next steps. Finding Manley's room, he discovered her in fitful sleep, her expression troubled as if she wrestled with dreams that refused to let her rest fully. Quietly, he set about gathering their belongings, which amounted to little more than essentials. He resolved to ask Haylen for a favour—to fetch a change of clothes for Manley. Surely, she wouldn't want to arrive at the beach house in a hospital gown. Blake tapped out a quick message on his PAC, instructing Haylen to bring something comfortable and suitable for the journey ahead. He knew Haylen would welcome the opportunity to contribute in a meaningful way after days of worry and waiting. The end of their hospital ordeal was a relief they all shared, and Blake anticipated Manley's reaction when she woke to find herself en route to a place where she could see the sky and feel the breeze of the ocean.

Blake walked back to Manley's room with the good news.

Chapter 14

Day 15

Faris kept his promise about the beach house. Nestled on Enkil's tranquil northern mainland, it sat a mere hour's journey from the city, just thirty yards away from the gentle, lapping waves of the shore. Thankfully, there were no heady tides on Enkil.

As Manley disembarked from the unmarked ISA transport, her eyes were momentarily dazzled by the sunlight. She shielded them with a hand, taking in the familiar sight of the floor-length windows and open doors that allowed the ocean breeze to flow freely through the house. This house was exactly what she needed now.

Stepping cautiously onto the warm sand, Manley felt an instant urge to slip off her shoes, but with only one functional arm, she realized she would need Blake's help. The air was comfortably warm, the gentle wind stirring the trees and dancing on the waves. Positioned discreetly at the house entrance were two figures clad in dark attire, their presence a silent assurance of security. Manley inhaled deeply, savouring the salt-tinged air. Here, with the ocean in sight and the breeze in her ears, she sensed a place where her body could mend and her spirit could find peace.

Moving towards the house, she acknowledged the agents with a nod, recognizing their role in ensuring her safety and well-being over the coming weeks. They greeted her back with respectful nods, maintaining a professional distance that suited her current state of mind. She had no desire to know their names or feel the weight of responsibility for their presence; the less she knew, the easier it would be to focus on her own recovery. Manley trusted Faris enough to have selected the best people for her protection. Right now, all she wanted was to settle into this peaceful retreat, where the only sounds were the whispers of wind and sea, and where healing could begin.

Blake trailed behind Manley, carrying with their belongings alongside his own. With Haylen's credits, he had managed to assemble a modest collection of clothes and toiletries, confident they wouldn't require much else for their immediate stay. And by the looks of the house, and Manley's content face, and the images that were forming in his mind involving activities usually needing few to no clothes, he should be right about this. His persistence with Faris and the doctors had paid off. Despite the severity of her injuries from the underground prison ordeal, Manley had miraculously avoided the need for surgery. The medical team had stressed the importance of a cautious recovery, emphasizing rest and prohibiting any physical exertion. In the end, they had consented to her transfer to the beach house.

Blake wondered if Faris had pointed out the personal relationship. He couldn't help but wonder if their assurances to follow the doctors' instructions would hold true to the letter. He knew they had bent the rules discreetly before, recalling their secret escapades in the waters of Nergal B. No one had noticed. Maybe that would work again. He slightly shook his head, took a deep breath and followed Manley.

As Manley discovered the bedroom overlooking the sea, she paused in the doorway leading to the patio, turning to Blake with a smile. "Now this isn't too bad, is it?"

Blake shook his head playfully, a mischievous glint in his eyes as he set down the two grey canvas bags he had been lugging. "It's quite alright, I guess." With a gentle grin, he leaned in to kiss her softly on the lips, then gestured for her to turn around. Slipping his right arm around her waist from behind, he held her with tender care. He knew he had to proceed with caution, mindful of her injuries, yet he was keenly aware of the mutual desire between them. Trailing kisses along the side of her neck, Blake let his right hand move slowly down her body, applying just a hint of pressure. His left hand rested gently on her waist, just below the protective splint that shielded her injured arm. He could feel her lean into his touch, a silent plea in her response. Sensing her urge to turn towards him, he hushed her softly, holding her close and continuing to cherish the intimacy they shared.

His own body responded instinctively, a natural reaction to the closeness and their deep connection. In his desire, a rational voice cautioned him to tread carefully, minding of her recent trauma. Another voice, fuelled by compassion and a yearning to restore her sense of normalcy, urged him onward. She deserved this closeness, this affection. They both did. Aware that their security detail lingered nearby just out of sight, likely positioned in the hallway leading to the bedroom, Blake paid them little mind. They were professionals, dedicated to their duty. His current task was clear—to make sure that Manley felt safe, protected, and cherished enough to confront the shadows of her recent ordeal. He knew from the fragments she had shared that her journey toward healing would demand immense strength, likely more than she had let on so far.

It took Manley a lot of effort not to pull off the splint, wrapping her arms and legs around Blake and drag him to the bed. She could still hear the doctor's warnings echoing in her mind, cautioning her about the potential consequences for her shoulder if she pushed too hard. Recovery would take much longer after surgery, and that was something she wasn't willing to risk. They had all the time in the world now that they were here, they would probably find other ways to waste their time.

Pleasant shivers danced along her spine as Blake's touch caressed her, familiar yet charged with a depth of emotion they had only just begun to explore. She wished that they could keep on with this, that they didn't have to stop. Blake was holding her firmly and running his hand over her body, something he had done before. Back then, it had only been the beginning of something. Today, amidst the tranquil ambiance of their beach retreat, this would have to suffice.

She hung her head for a moment and breathed deeply while Blake slowly moved his hand over her arm, locking her in his embrace him behind. Blake breathed another tender kiss to her neck before resting his head on her right shoulder. Breathless from both desire and the overwhelming beauty of their surroundings, Manley gazed out at the sea, gathering her thoughts before speaking. The way he managed to drive her crazy with a simple touch was unbelievable. It took her a moment to find her voice, her words quiet and reflective. "You know," she began softly, "if we had met under different circumstances, I don't think we'd be here today."

Blake frowned in confusion, still looking out at the sea. "What do you mean?"

"I mean," she continued, her gaze fixed on the horizon, "if we had just passed each other on the street somewhere, I don't think we would have connected the way we did." Her voice carried a hint of melancholy. "I might not be alive now if it weren't for you. Claver would have lost patience eventually, and no one at the hotel would have noticed I was gone if it weren't for you."

Blake held her a little tighter, his embrace offering both reassurance and a silent vow of protection. "But I was there, and I noticed you were missing," he murmured. Here, surrounded by security and in the sanctuary of their beach retreat, Manley was gradually letting her guard down. He hadn't anticipated this happening so swiftly, but he welcomed it with a profound sense of gratitude. "You're right," he continued softly, his lips brushing against the nape of her neck as he spoke. "In another place, under different circumstances, we might not have started off the way we did. But we did, and I'm grateful for it. In fact, I don't think I've ever been more grateful for anything." He still held her close, cherishing the intimacy they shared in that moment.

Manley pondered his words, the promise they held stirring something deep within her. It was a promise of a future, something she hadn't dared to hope for in seventeen long years. The last time someone had promised her a future had been Darren, and she knew all too well how that had ended. In the past 17 years, though, she had grown up and knew that the chances of Blake getting killed, too, were slim. Statistically spoken. If he had survived the search for her, he was undoubtedly resilient. Maybe, just maybe, there was a chance for them. A soft smile played on her lips. "Tell me about yourself," she finally said, breaking the gentle embrace.

Blake lifted his head slightly, meeting her gaze with curiosity. "What?"

"Tell me about yourself," she repeated, her voice gentle yet firm. "I realise I know very little about you, other than you're a lawyer, a skilled swimmer, and apparently quite talented with your hands and other parts of your body. I want to hear your story."

Blake exhaled audibly, knowing this moment had been due to come. He hadn't expected it to come so soon, but he understood her need to bridge the gap in their knowledge of each other. "It's going to take some time," he cautioned softly.

"I'm aware," she replied with a slight chuckle. "I have nowhere else to be today. You've learned so much about me this past week, mostly without my consent. It's only fair I get to know a bit about you, too." She looked back out at the ocean and the waves.

Blake admitted that Manley had a valid point. The physical intimacy they both craved would have to wait for another time. He gently released her from their embrace and watched as she turned to face him, her expression expectant. "You're right," he began, contemplating her request. "What do you say we get some food and maybe a stiff drink?"

"A drink?" Manley raised a sceptical eyebrow. "That wouldn't be my first choice," she remarked dryly. Catching the amused glint in Blake's eyes, she added hastily, "Because of the painkillers, obviously."

"Obviously," Blake chuckled, his grin widening. "I'll rustle up something to eat. You find yourself a comfortable spot. We're gonna be here a while."

Manley returned his grin playfully. "You're that old?" she teased, settling down on the bed, attempting to ease her muscles. A short while later, Blake returned with a tray laden with sandwiches featuring soft bread from the refrigerator, a selection of fruits and vegetables, and various juices and lemonades. Setting the tray down carefully, he began to fill Manley in on his life story. He shared anecdotes from his childhood and upbringing on Gibil, where his parents managed a prosperous trading business similar to the enterprise Manley's family owned on Enkil. Unlike many in his position, Blake had chosen not to follow in his parents' footsteps, instead developing a passion for law. As he spoke, Blake recounted how he had met Lannister Brown during his time on Hani. Lannister was the man he would name as his best friend without a doubt, though he wasn't sure how Ayla, Lannister's wife, valued their friendship. After all, he had repeatedly disturbed his best friend in the middle of the night, asking for pieces of information, requiring said friend to get out of bed and spend some time on his computer.

He didn't shy away from discussing his past romantic encounters, from fleeting affairs to the few women he had genuinely cared for but had kept at arm's length. He told her about the jokes Haylen had kept making about his clothes and his muscles. He told her how her friends had banded together when they realized that the missing tourist was Manley. When he finished, providing a broad overview of who Michael Blake truly was and the twists and turns his life had taken, he fell silent, studying her with anticipation and vulnerability. "Is that okay for now?" he asked quietly, hoping his disclosure had deepened their connection rather than created distance.

Manley, who had remained silent apart from the occasional question, looked back at him. Her response was measured yet accepting, "For now." The room was bathed in the warm hues of the setting sun, casting a serene glow through the floor-length windows. Her head was swimming with all the pieces of information from his life that Blake had told her. She could see so many pictures and passages of the things he had gone through, and her mind was already mingling them with her own. Feeling a need to move, Manley gently pushed aside the blanket Blake had draped over her and made her way towards the bathroom. She sensed Blake's instinct to assist her, but she waved him off with a small shake of her head. "I've got this. I'll be right back," she assured him, her voice carrying a hint of determination mingled with gratitude for his consideration.

Left alone, Blake sank back into the pillows they had shared for the past few hours, reflecting on the depth of their conversation. He really needed to let her do things on her own again. And even if she needed help, there was a nurse somewhere who could do certain things for her. Things she might not have wanted Blake to help her with. And he understood that she might be needing a minute or two on her own after hearing about all of his life and the women and whatever else happened for him. He was wondering why he had told her about his history with the other women. He hadn't hesitated when the subject appeared but right now, he wasn't so sure that had been a good idea. He understood that learning about his past relationships might have stirred complex emotions in Manley, and he hoped he hadn't caused her distress. But soon, Manley returned from the bathroom, her weariness apparent as she settled back into bed beside him. Sensing her need for rest, Blake extended his arms, pulling her gently into his embrace. She nestled against him, seeking comfort and closeness.

"Thank you for letting me in on you," Manley murmured softly, her eyes drifting shut. Within moments, the rhythmic rise and fall of her breathing signalled that sleep had claimed her.

When Blake awoke the next morning, sunlight streamed through the open windows, casting a warm glow over the room. Manley lay beside him, her face turned away as she slept peacefully. He quietly slipped out of bed, mindful not to disturb her rest. Normally, he might have gone for an invigorating swim or a brisk run along the beach, but today he felt restless, a desire to be close when Manley woke after their intimate conversation the day before. Instead of diving into his usual routines, Blake decided against reading and instead focused on writing messages to Lannister. He updated his friend on their current situation, reassuring him that they were safe in a secluded beach house, still in the process of recovering. He praised once more how crucial Lannister had been in uncovering Manley's old identity as Amy Carter, the girl who had vanished 17 years ago.

As the morning light gently filled the room, Manley stirred, shifting onto her back with a soft moan. Blake abandoned the lounger where he had been sitting, observing her with a fond smile. "Mornin' sleepyhead," he greeted her warmly.

"Mornin'," she replied, her voice tinged with a deep yawn. "I still feel like I haven't slept at all."

Blake returned to the bed, leaning in to kiss her gently on the lips. "It'll get better in a few days, I promise."

"I'll take your word for it," Manley murmured, propping herself up with effort. She shifted uncomfortably, clearly annoyed by the splint restricting her movement. "This thing is driving me insane. I can't even move around on my own."

Blake moved closer to her and climbed on her lap, careful to support his own weight, so she wouldn't have to carry him. He cradled her face in his hands, tilting it upwards to kiss her forehead tenderly. When he pulled away, he stood up from the bed. "I'll go get your morning drugs."

"Thanks," she sighed, closing her eyes briefly. The feeling of dependency was bugging her, reminding her of her vulnerability. She longed to regain control over her body and her life, but she knew the road to recovery would be challenging. Weeks, maybe months, lay ahead before she could use her shoulder as she once did, and she was keenly aware that this journey would test not only her patience but also the patience and support of those around her.

Later that day, Blake looked up as Manley returned from her walk along the waterline with the security detail, visibly drained. She had taken up the walking to get back in shape, and Blake suspected that she was being too hard on herself. She muttered, "I need a shower. I'll be back," before disappearing into the bathroom.

Three messages to Lannister and his parents later, Blake started to wonder where she was. Just as the worry crept in, Nurse Callie appeared with a concerned frown. "Mr. Blake, I think you need to come with me."

Panic surged through Blake as he followed Callie's brisk pace. "What is it?"

"She's in the shower, and she isn't responding. I'm not sure what's happening," Callie explained urgently.

Blake's heart raced as he jumped up from his chair and darted to the bathroom. Callie remained outside, leaving him to enter alone. He could hear the steady flow of water, and when he peered around the corner into the shower, his heart sank. Manley sat huddled on the floor, her knees drawn to her chest, oblivious to the water cascading over her. She was naked except for the splint still secured around her shoulder with its familiar straps. Her wet, red hair clung to her back.

"Manley?" Blake's voice trembled with concern. There was no response. Blake noticed her breathing, and even though it was calm and regular, it was obvious that something was wrong here. He stepped up to the shower frame and tried again. "Dana?"

She didn't move. She seemed frozen, seeing something that clearly wasn't visible to anyone else. He approached cautiously, stepping into the shower without regard for his own clothes becoming soaked. Gently, he sat behind her, wrapping his arms around her, pulling her close. Still, she remained unresponsive, staring into a void only she could see. The warm water enveloped them both. He whispered softly into her ear, "Dana? Talk to me. What's going on?"

He guessed that she was probably having some sort of flashback, locking her in. "I'm right here." He softly started stroking her arms. "He's gone. We're all here to protect you. I'll stay with you whatever it takes."

Minutes ticked by as Blake stroked her arms tenderly, hoping his touch would lead her back to the present. Manley remained silent and unmoving, lost in whatever haunting memory gripped her. She just sat there, not even actively acknowledging his presence.

Finally, the sound of footsteps interrupted the quiet moment. Blake turned his head to see Callie cautiously entering the bathroom. "I've got this, we're ok."

Technically, that was a lie, and he guessed that Callie knew it. But there was nothing she could do right now if Manley didn't even react to Blake. With a nod of acknowledgment, she retreated, leaving Blake to comfort Manley. He just hoped she wouldn't call the doctor.

Manley heard him talking through the haze that enveloped her mind. She remained paralysed, trapped in a whirlpool of fear and memories. She felt the water on her back, and on her head, and she felt

Blake's embrace. She didn't care that she was naked, and she didn't mind him being there. Her whole body seemed unable to move, to do anything, invisible chains binding her. She told herself over and over again that she was safe now, but she didn't believe it. She had thought she was safe in her hotel room on Nergal B, and the dreams and Claver's henchmen had still found her there.

Safety had become an abstract concept, shattered by her harrowing ordeal in Claver's clutches. Right now, she wasn't sure she would ever be safe anywhere again. Yes, she had wanted to get out of the hospital because she felt like a caged animal in there. But at least she had been in ISA headquarters, her one and only safe place. Faris had been there and armed guards had been there, and she didn't have to deal with the outside world. Her room had been small enough to oversee, and she had been sure that no one could surprise her there. Here, in the beach house, she wasn't so sure.

The guards were here, yes, and they were armed, and there were all the measures she couldn't see and touch. Faris had handed her the dossier before they got here. But how could she know that there wasn't going to be a surprise? Blake's voice persisted, drawing nearer with each attempt to reach her. "Dana, talk to me. I'm here. You're safe."

His words pierced through the fog, and finally, after what seemed like an eternity, she managed a faint response. A slight shake of her head, a whispered admission of her inner turmoil. "I can't. I can't," she murmured.

"It's alright," Blake assured her gently, his arms still wrapped around her. "I'm here. I'll help you out of here, you can't stay here." His voice was steady, almost commanding.

She heard him, and intellectually, she agreed. But her legs were refusing obedience, and she couldn't move a muscle. "I can't," she whispered again, her voice barely audible above the sound of the water.

"I know." Blake sensed her distress and loosened his embrace. "I'll lift you up, dry you off, and then we'll get you back to bed, so you can rest," he offered calmly. There was no urgency to involve anyone else; this was a moment for him to support her quietly. This was no immediate medical emergency, and she was in no grave danger here, so there was no need to involve medical or security. Carefully, he knelt down, one arm securely around her waist while the other reached for a large towel. Thankfully, it was a really big one, one that he could just wrap her up in. He helped her up until she stood on her own feet again, but her posture spoke volumes—head bowed, shoulders slumped in defeat.

In many other situations, he might have felt very differently about what to do next. She was naked, and he wasn't exactly wearing formal attire either, and there was a shower, and they were still wildly attracted to each other. But this was not the moment for anything else beside giving her comfort and reassurance. His touch was tender and purposeful, lacking any sexual intent. There would be a time for that, but that time wasn't now.

Blake carefully dried her hair with a towel, making sure it was sufficiently dry before lifting her gently into his arms and carrying her back to the bed. Callie entered the room with a frown on her forehead, clearly concerned, but Blake pre-empted any questions with a reassuring shake of his head. "She's alright. She just needs some rest," he informed Callie softly. It was evident that someone had briefed the nurse not to question Blake's judgment, likely Faris, who understood better than most the bond between Blake and Manley. Callie nodded silently and left them to their privacy.

With meticulous care, Blake tucked Manley under the covers, arranging her onto her side to avoid any discomfort from lying on her back. He slid into bed behind her, drawing her close into his protective embrace. He could feel the steady rhythm of her breathing gradually calming, a small reassurance amidst the tumult of thoughts swirling in his mind. She would tell him tomorrow what happened, and even if she didn't, at least she would have had a good night's sleep. He could feel her breath grow calm and regular soon, but he couldn't sleep. The sun was still in the sky, though declining, casting a warm glow through the windows, and he wasn't really tired.

He wondered if he was doing the right thing. He had never once questioned that he wanted to see her again, and he hadn't doubted that finding her was what he wanted. What he hadn't thought about was what she wanted. Did she want him around? Was it appropriate to just assume that she would want him by her side? What if she just didn't have the strength to send him away? What if she did send him away when she felt better? Blake sighed. He had thought she was making progress. Yet seeing her like this, completely zoned out in the shower, made him wonder if she was really going to recover from this.

In his mind's eye, he tried to envision the horrors she had faced—the violence, the fear, the relentless captivity. He knew, intellectually, that she had been subject to violence for days, more than once, and in different ways. He knew her training had prepared her well, but no amount of preparation could shield anyone from the psychological toll of such trauma. He marvelled at her resilience, how she had managed to survive and emerge from that captivity, albeit scarred and wounded. These experiences had left scars way beyond what he could see on her body. And the visible scars and injuries were a lot already. He had no idea how she could have sustained all of those injuries and still walk out of there on her own feet. Adrenaline couldn't be the only reason.

What if Manley didn't want him around any more once she felt better? What if she was merely using his presence as a crutch to cope with her trauma? What if his desire to stay by her side was more about his own need than what she truly wanted? Blake sighed again. His thoughts were going around in circles. And he didn't really believe the nagging voice at the back of his mind, telling him that he should get away from her. His whole body and just about every waking thought told him differently. He had felt her clinging to him in the hospital, he had felt her fall asleep in his arms. That couldn't be a sign that she wanted to get rid of him. It just couldn't.

Restless and unable to quiet his mind, Blake knew he needed to talk to someone, to gain perspective beyond his own anxious thoughts. He carefully entangled himself from her and left the bedroom, instructing one of their security detail to keep an eye on her. "One of you needs to watch her. I need to make some calls." The man on the left nodded and headed for the bedroom, finding himself a chair and keeping an eye on Manley.

Blake got himself a glass of water from the kitchen and sat down outside, looking at the beach and the water. He knew he was far enough away from the bedroom window even if she woke up soon. With a few taps on his PAC, he initiated a call to Owen. "Hey man", he said when Owen's face appeared on the screen, concern etched across his features.

"Blake, what's going on? Is she okay?" Owen's voice carried a note of worry, immediately tuning into the seriousness of Blake's expression.

Blake shook his head, his gaze distant as he recounted the recent events. "I don't think so. She took a shower earlier, and something happened. She completely zoned out, didn't respond to anyone. I had to go in and bring her out."

Owen knew better than to tease Blake about the shower and what he had probably been thinking about. This wasn't the time. If Blake called him, it was about something serious. "That doesn't sound good. Was it similar to what happened back at the hotel?" Owen's question was measured, probing for details without pushing too hard.

"No, I think it was worse", he said quietly. Blake paused for a few seconds to find the right words. "She was completely unresponsive for a while. She came around after about twenty minutes that I spent hugging her and talking to her. She said she couldn't talk, and I put her to bed. She was out within seconds."

Owen's concern mirrored Blake's own. "Sounds like some kind of serious flashback."

"I agree. Owen, can you come? Maybe she'll find it easier to talk to you. You've gone through stuff together, I missed out on all of that. I was just there before and after." He was really hoping that Owen would agree.

"I can be there tomorrow. I still have some things to wrap up tonight, but I'll be there in the morning."

Blake was hoping his face didn't show too much of the relief he was feeling. "Thank you. I really appreciate that."

"Don't worry about it. See you in the morning."

With that, Owen closed the channel, and Blake's screen went black. He was considering talking to Faris, too. Faris would be here at any time of day, if Blake asked him to. But Manley probably wouldn't appreciate bringing even more people in on his.

When Owen arrived at the beach house in the early hours of the morning, the sky was just beginning to show the first hints of dawn. He wanted to be there when Manley woke up, to offer whatever comfort he could, even if it was simply his presence. Blake had evidently informed the security detail of his visit, for they merely nodded at him as he approached the entrance. The house was cloaked in a serene silence, the kind that preludes the stirrings of a new day. He made his way towards the kitchen, drawn by the muted clinks and clatters within. The nurse, Kendra, was busy preparing Manley's medications. "Morning," Owen greeted her quietly.

"Mornin'," Kendra replied, a soft smile playing on her lips. "You want some coffee?"

Owen declined with a shake of his head. "Nah, I don't wanna wake them. I take it they're still asleep?"

Kendra nodded. "Both are still sleeping soundly. But the coffee's ready; I made it a while ago. Let me get you a mug."

"Alright", he said. "By the way, I'm Owen."

Kendra turned, a steaming mug in her hand. "Oh, I know who you are. We've been briefed on who's allowed here. I'm Kendra, by the way." She smirked. "Director Faris has made it very clear that any unannounced visitors can be shot."

"Lucky me." Owen accepted the mug, intending to find a seat, when Blake entered the kitchen. Clad only in a pair of boxers, it was easy to see why Manley cherished his company. Any woman might have enjoyed time with a man that lean yet modest.

"Owen! You're here already!" Blake's voice sounded pleasantly surprised, opting for a firm handshake as a greeting. Then he addressed Kendra. "She's just waking up. I'll take the meds to her bedside, so she can take them right away."

Owen's brow furrowed with concern. "Is it still that bad?"

Blake's expression sobered. "It hasn't even been two weeks. We're not taking any risks. She needs to be moving if we don't want her to go crazy, and she can't do that with the pain those injuries would cause her."

That made sense, though the thought of his friend relying on heavy-duty painkillers to get through the day made Owen feel uneasy, especially knowing how she had sustained those injuries. "I see. Anyway, I'll be here all day. Maybe we can have breakfast together?"

Blake nodded from the corner, his expression thoughtful. "I'll ask her. I'm not sure if she's any better than last night." But as he walked back into the bedroom, he found Manley awake, her eyes open but shadowed with exhaustion. She sat up in bed, still naked but unbothered.

"Hey there," she greeted him softly.

He set the small tray with her medications on the nightstand. "Hey there. I brought you something." He handed her two small cups, which she downed without hesitation. She then took the glass of water with her good hand and chased the pills down. Only after this ritual did she allow herself to collapse back into the pillows. "What's for breakfast?"

Blake decided to reveal the surprise immediately. "How about an old friend?"

Manley frowned in puzzlement. "Is that some kind of speciality from Birdu?"

He shook his head with a gentle smile. "No, it isn't. I called Owen last night and asked him to come."

"I see." Her expression shifted from cheerful to confused. "I need to get dressed. Can you hand me something?" The splint on her arm made dressing a particularly challenging task. Haylen had found her a collection of wrap-dresses that Blake could easily tie around her. When they didn't expect any visitors, she usually lounged around in her underwear.

Blake handed her a shimmering, grey dress that made her hair shine even more brightly. He motioned for her to turn around after she had slid her right arm into the sleeve and expertly tied the dress behind her back. "Underwear?" he asked softly.

She nodded. Although she disliked the necessity of him dressing her, she preferred his intimate assistance over the impersonal help of the nurses. The usual dynamic involved him taking her clothes off or her getting of them herself, but at this moment, she required his help in so many ways. He knelt before her, holding the delicate piece of fabric close to the ground, so she could step into it easily. Pulling it up with him as he rose was the hardest part. He had to keep himself in check, so she didn't make this into something that it wasn't as his hands were gliding up her legs. He stood there for a moment, his hands resting gently on her hips. Their eyes locked, and for a fleeting moment, the air thickened with unspoken emotions. "I'm sorry about last night," she murmured.

Blake shook his head and pulled her closer, his voice a tender whisper. "Don't be. I'm right here. You were in a bad place, and right now, you aren't." He kissed her softly, a touch full of reassurance and affection, breaking away only after a few heartbeats. "I'll get us breakfast in here. You go to the bathroom, I'll bring the food and Owen."

Manley nodded, acknowledging his words. When she returned from getting herself ready, Blake and Owen had already arranged a breakfast tray by the side of her bed. She embraced Owen, holding him a moment longer than necessary, drawing strength from the familiar comfort of an old friend. Then she settled back onto the bed.

Blake gestured for her to tuck her legs in, positioning the tray over her lap. "There you go. Dig in."

Manley surveyed the tray before her, impressed. Despite the circumstances, Blake had somehow procured some exquisite kipper, accompanied by perfectly scrambled eggs. The portions were generous enough for all three of them. Though she wasn't one to easily comply with health directives, she appreciated a well-prepared breakfast. They ate in comfortable silence, savouring the meal. Once they were finished, Blake collected the plates and took them back to the kitchen, allowing Manley and Owen a moment alone.

Owen remained at the table, his eyes fixed on Manley. Despite the toll her experiences had taken, the essence of his friend was still there. Her eyes, though slightly dimmed, retained a spark of their former vivacity. When Manley didn't speak, Owen broke the silence. "What happened last night?"

Manley lowered her head, her voice subdued. "I don't know." She paused, then continued, "My head started swimming with all these thoughts and flashbacks, and I sat down, so I wouldn't fall. And then I couldn't get back up."

Owen moved his chair to the bed, sitting in front of it and looking up at her. He took her hand gently. "You were out for the better part of an hour. Blake was with you most of the time after the nurse found you like that."

Manley slowly met his gaze, her eyes reflecting the turmoil within. "I kept wondering if I was really safe here. And then I couldn't tear myself away from that train of thought."

Owen moved his thumb softly over the back of her hand. "I'm sorry this is so hard. I wish I had been there to keep an eye on you."

"This still would've happened, you know that, don't you?" Manley's voice was edged with a touch of bitterness.

Owen shook his head gently. "We don't know that."

"Exactly. We don't know. But it did happen, and we'll have to deal with it." Her voice came out sharper than she intended, but she let the moment pass without apology. After a brief silence, her tone softened. "Where's Darra?"

Owen smiled. "Off for some family business. She'll be back soon. She sends her regards." He hesitated, knowing he needed to broach a painful subject. "From what I know, you must have gone through hell in the mansion. How... How did you get out? That's nowhere in the books. I mean, I know Henders took you outside and to ISA and someone mentioned you met him only seconds before running into us."

Manley's face fell, the question coming unexpectedly. "You really wanna go there now?" When he remained silent, she took a few deep breaths, steeling herself. "I took a blaster from a guard, cornered him, knocked him unconscious. Then I found a ladder in a shaft and climbed. Upstairs, I met Henders." She rubbed the back of her nose with her fingers and closed her eyes for a moment, as if trying to erase the memories. "I can't really say how all of this worked out, considering I had no drugs back there."

Her eyes began to glisten, tears threatening to spill. "I... I knew I had this one chance. If Claver had caught me again that day, I would've been dead. He wouldn't have taken that a second time." Her voice broke into a sob, and she clung to Owen's hand as if it were her lifeline, tears streaming down her face.

"Shhhh." Owen climbed into bed beside her as she pulled away her hand. She rested her head on his shoulder, and he wrapped his arm around her back, holding her close. She needed this moment to calm down, to let the storm of emotions pass, and he was there, offering silent comfort. Blake would understand.

Blake stood around the corner, listening intently to Manley and Owen's conversation. He hadn't intended to eavesdrop, but he also didn't want to intrude. His curiosity about what Manley might confide in Owen, that she hadn't shared with him, had drawn him there. To his surprise, she had recounted the same harrowing story she had told him. She hadn't kept anything from him. Now, hearing her cry once more, it took all his self-discipline not to rush in and play the hero. Owen was with her, handling the situation with a reassuring competence that Blake could not deny. Quietly, he turned and retreated to the kitchen, stepping out onto the beach to soak in a few moments of the morning sun.

Still dressed only in the boxers he had slept in, Blake decided to take a swim, the cool water promising refreshment. He dove into the waves, the salty embrace of the sea revitalising him. After twenty minutes, he emerged from the water, feeling both exhausted and renewed. From his vantage point on the beach, he could see into the bedroom. Manley and Owen were still on the bed, her body nestled against his in a comforting embrace. They weren't talking; instead, they seemed to be sharing a silent, intimate moment.

Blake observed them, marvelling at the bond they shared. It puzzled him how two people who hadn't known each other for very long could be so comfortable and familiar. Initially, he had felt annoyed at the physical closeness of their friendship, but he had come to recognise the difference in their touches. Owen's interactions with Manley were tender, protective. His embraces were filled with a friendly care that was distinctly different from Blake's romantic and intimate touches. He touched her with tender care, much like a father would do with his beloved daughter. He put his arms around her and hugged her, but he never did any of that with more than friendly intentions.

Seeing Manley completely relaxed in Owen's arms could have sparked jealousy in Blake, but it didn't. Instead, he felt a sense of relief and gratitude. He was glad she had found comfort with Owen, understanding that she needed different kinds of support from each of them. He stood watching for a few minutes until they noticed him. They waved happily, breaking apart without a hint of embarrassment. Manley stood up from the bed with Owen and walked towards Blake. As she approached the waterline, she beamed at him, her smile radiating happiness. Blake moved to meet her, wrapping his left arm around her waist, pulling her close until their bodies were pressed together, skin on skin. His right hand gently traced her neckline. He kissed her softly and smiled, his voice tender. "Better?"
Manley nodded, her eyes bright with a mixture of relief and affection. "Much better."

He could also see it in her posture: she stood upright, her face relaxed, no longer burdened by the events of the previous night. "I'm really glad to hear that."

His gaze shifted to the house, where Owen had stayed behind, respecting their intimate moment. Though he still harboured silent questions about the bond between Manley and Owen, he couldn't deny the ex-privateer's decency. Owen had an impressive, almost formidable presence with his black clothes, black hair, and black eyes. Despite the weight of the universe's good and bad etched in his features, Owen always seemed to hold on to uncovering the truth. Blake had seen that determination in Owen's eyes when he had resolved to find Manley. It had always been only a matter of time. And it would only be a matter of time until Manley fully healed. "Do you wanna stay outside?" he asked her. When she nodded, he added, "I'll go get a towel we can sit on." She smiled at him and happily walked towards the water.

Manley greatly enjoyed the feeling of the cool water against her feet. The waves gently lapped at the beach, and the day was calm, with hardly a breeze. She squinted against the bright light and took a deep breath, grateful that she felt no pain from her shoulder and ribs. She was also thankful that Blake had called Owen. The memory of last night's despair still lingered, but it was a distant echo now. The cold, bland helplessness that had ambushed her in the shower seemed like a bad dream. Owen's presence had somehow banished that darkness, and she felt okay now.

Blake returned with three large towels, laying them out side by side about three feet from the waterline. Owen helped, then motioned for Manley to take the middle one. With Blake to her left and Owen to her right, she carefully lowered herself onto the towel and sighed contentedly. She closed her eyes and murmured, "Now this isn't so bad."

Opening her eyes slightly, she noticed Owen still dressed in his dark clothes. "Aren't you feeling hot in all those clothes?"

Owen shrugged, his casual demeanour not betraying the intensity of the thoughts running through his head. "I'm good," he repeated. Beaches were foreign to him; he was more at home navigating the concrete jungles of cities or the narrow passageways of starships. But here, on this serene beach, Manley seemed to thrive, perhaps enjoying the freedom from the ruthless demands of her past life as an agent. He offered her a reassuring smile. "Seriously, I'm good."

"Fine with me," she replied, closing her eyes again, basking in the sunshine. Blake, seated on the towel beside her, glanced back at the house. One of their security guards was stationed on the porch, eyes scanning the beach. The sight was a comfort. Blake wasn't overly concerned for his own safety—Claver was dead, after all—but the guards were crucial for Manley's peace of mind. She understood their importance better than anyone. Faris had mentioned her having the necessary cruelty for the job, a comment that Blake now pondered. The thought of Manley as a Secret Service agent, trained to kill if necessary, was unsettling. Yet, considering what she had endured on the other side of the law, it was no wonder she wished to leave that life behind. He wanted to ask her about her future plans with the Faction, but he couldn't imagine her confined to a simple office job. With much selfishness, he dreaded the idea of her undertaking dangerous missions for the syndicate.

Owen left later that day, several meals later, but still while the sun was in the sky. He wasn't sure if he would ever return or see Manley again. Yet, he had a strange premonition that their paths would cross, intentionally or not. He hugged Blake, silently acknowledging that he was the one she ran to every time. Holding on a bit longer to Manley than usual, he hugged her tightly, aware that she was embarking on a new chapter with the Faction. "Take good care of yourself," he said, fighting the urge to plead with her to be more cautious.

Owen would still be her friend, even if they wouldn't see each other for a while now. Manley looked incredibly sad, her eyes welling with tears as she clung to Owen. She seemed unable to speak, perhaps because she knew this goodbye might last longer than either of them wanted. She wiped away a couple of tears while still in Owen's embrace, her heart heavy with their impending goodbye. Finally, she stepped back, giving him a teary smile.

Manley tried to see him walking away through her tears. Each step Owen took seemed to pull at her heart, leaving her more exhausted with every passing second. She didn't want to say goodbye, but she understood that he needed to seek answers to the questions that still drove him onward. As Owen finally disappeared behind the trees where his ship was hidden in a small clearing, Manley felt an unexpected sense of calm. She stood there for a moment longer, staring at the spot where he had vanished, her thoughts a mix of sorrow and resignation. Blake moved up behind her and carefully wrapped his arms around her, offering silent support.

"Let's go back inside," she said finally, her voice steady but soft. "I'm starving."

Manley woke up later that week to the soft slapping of waves on the shore. The floor-length windows were wide open, as were the patio doors. A light breeze wafted through the room, carrying the salty tang of the air. Outside, it was still dark, with only the faintest hint of dawn creeping over the horizon. Her right shoulder ached from lying on it for too long, and she carefully rolled onto her back, trying to moderate the discomfort. As she shifted, she glanced to her left and saw Blake bathed in the silvery light of the moon streaming through the open windows. He was naked, and the soft moonlight danced on his body. She could see his abs and while they were relaxed right now, she knew what he could do with them and the other muscles he was so very smart in using.

Manley flinched slightly, reminded of her own limitations. She was dressed in a short pair of grey pyjamas made from the softest fabric, chosen solely for their comfort and practicality given her injuries. Blake had been adamant about not taking advantage of her vulnerability, refusing to let their physical relationship progress while she still struggled with the use of her left shoulder. All she could do was watch him as he slept, dreaming of all the things she would want to do with him when her body had healed.

Her mind briefly wandered to her security detail. She knew they were nearby, ever vigilant, their presence a silent reassurance. Their job was to remain unseen while keeping a close watch over her. High-level security measures, including electronic shields and anti-aircraft defences, almost guaranteed her safety. It would be next to impossible for anyone to breach these defences unnoticed. She smiled faintly, amused at the thought of the concealed budget Faris must have tapped into for this operation. Though no longer officially a member of ISA, she suspected some witness protection funds were being quietly repurposed for her safety. Again.

Manley closed her eyes, willing herself to rest. Her body needed all the healing it could get. Yet her thoughts kept drifting back to the man beside her. She shivered with anticipation, imagining the day when her injuries would no longer hold her back. Wrapping herself tighter in the sheets, she tried to mimic Blake's embrace, longing for the warmth and security it provided. She couldn't turn onto her left side to snuggle up to him because of the splint her shoulder and arm were in. Instead, she had to wait for him, hoping he would instinctively move closer to her in his sleep.

Manley was grateful that she didn't feel any pain at this moment. The injuries to her shoulder and arm—the broken clavicle, acromion, humerus, and three ribs—were severe enough that without the regular doses of strong painkillers, she would have been confined to bed, unable to do much more than count the passing hours. Yet here she was, walking on the beach with Blake, extending their strolls a little further every day. The exercise left her exhausted, often needing a nap afterward, but she welcomed the ability to move freely.

The beach offered a soothing setting, the rhythmic crash of waves a backdrop to her thoughts. She was only beginning to confront the horrors of her captivity. Megan, her therapist—a wise, white-haired woman twice her age—guided her through the painful memories, from the initial kidnapping to the agonising moments before her rescue and arrival at the beach house. Facing these memories was crucial for her recovery, Megan assured her, a path paved with tears and heavy breathing that seemed to intensify the physical strain on her fragile bones.

Despite understanding the therapeutic necessity, Manley couldn't help but feel a primal urge to run whenever Megan arrived. Her training as an agent insisted on confronting challenges with cold logic and resolute intellect, yet her instincts pleaded for escape, to bury the memories as she had once done seventeen years ago. The internal struggle cost her a lot of strength as she navigated the aftermath of her harrowing ordeal. She suspected the nurses of administering a slightly stronger dose of painkillers before each therapy session. The sessions inevitably led to prolonged crying spells and heavy breathing, woresening the strain on her mending bones in her shoulder and arm.

Manley sighed wearily. Perhaps she should return to sleep. With sheer determination, she adjusted herself into a position that eased the tension in her muscles and slowed her heart rate, preparing herself to drift back into slumber. She focused on each breath, inhaling deeply and exhaling slowly, until she felt the comforting embrace of sleep begin to envelop her once more.

Manley flinched as she caught sight of Megan approaching the beach house from the edge of the forest. The therapist emerged with deliberate steps, a reminder that it was time for another session. Despite her reservations, Manley understood the necessity of these meetings. Over the years, she had recommended similar therapy to countless individuals affected by the consequences of her actions or those of the people she had targeted.

Her sensible, intellectual side knew that she needed to work her way through the painful memories and own them and turn them around into something that wasn't going to define the rest of her live. Yet, emotionally, she recoiled every time Megan arrived with her gentle inquiries and empathetic demeanour. Deep down, Manley knew that mere sympathy wouldn't assist her recovery. The horrors she had lived through in Claver's captivity were horrifying, a fact she couldn't dispute. Intellectually, she understood that none of it was her fault—she hadn't provoked Claver's insane plan, nor had she personally driven his father to suicide. The blame lay squarely with their choices, not hers.

Yes, she had had a hand in cornering Kirk Claver down with actual proof of the secret dealings he had established with Ortiz. But he could have taken responsibility and countered the allegations in court. He would likely have walked out with probation, giving his connections. Instead, he had chosen to kill himself with a mix of alcohol, drugs, and a blaster.

But still, Manley had to wrap her mind around the fact that she had been beaten up repeatedly by a couple of Claver's minions, and she wasn't taking this lightly. She had been the best agent ISA had, and she had not been able to protect herself, as she should have been. She certainly blamed herself for that.

While all of that went through her head rapidly, Megan had crossed the sand and walked up to the house. The security detail remained motionless; they had already assessed her well before she arrived. Today, Megan carried a small, elegant purse, a stark contrast to her usual sessions when she produced a large, old-fashioned notepad brimming with meticulous notes penned by hand from a black leather briefcase. "Hey there," she greeted, her voice light yet tinged with purpose.

"Hey there," Manley replied, her tone reflecting curious anticipation.

"Are you up for a short walk?" Megan asked, revealing a small backpack slung over her shoulder that had escaped Manley's notice until now. She put down the purse.

"Sure," Manley responded, curious about the new approach

Blake, engrossed in the flickering messages on his screen, looked up briefly. "Do you want me to keep an eye on you?" he asked, his concern evident.

Manley shook her head gently. "You don't need to. We'll take security. We'll be fine." She had a feeling that she knew what Megan was doing. She was trying to get Manley to dis-associate the memories of being beaten up with closed rooms. She was trying to get her to move on, to move along with the memories, to physically move away from the trauma. Not to ignore it but to keep on living. The trauma would come along, anyway, if she didn't work through it. And she knew very well that there was no way around it. She had tried that 17 years ago, and it had seemed to work for a while until it backfired spectacularly on Nergal B. She would not repeat that mistake. She was going to do all the hard work, no matter what.

There was no need to grab a coat or handbag; there was nowhere special to go. The next house, as Manley had inquired from her security detail, was a secluded villa two miles away, hidden behind a bend. She didn't bother asking if it was another safe house for ISA. She didn't want to know. With resolute steps, Manley and Megan ventured out of the house, heading south towards the sun. Manley, barefoot, allowed the gentle waves to caress her feet as they walked along the waterline. Glancing to her left, she saw Megan treading on the firmer, dry sand. "So no ordinary session today?" she queried. The security guards trailed behind them, maintaining a discreet distance.

Megan's smile was warm and reassuring. "No ordinary session today. You deserve a little break from that." She gestured towards a cluster of trees on the edge of the forest their left. "Let's go sit over there." Finding a comfortable spot beneath the verdant canopy, Megan retrieved two bottles from her backpack and handed one to Manley. "I cleared this with the doctors. It won't interfere with your meds. Enjoy."

Manley frowned in puzzlement. "You're getting me drunk?"

"I'm getting you drunk. It's therapeutic," Megan replied with a mischievous smile, opening her bottle and taking a long, satisfying gulp. She exhaled loudly. "Man, that's what I call a stiff drink."

"You sure?" Manley eyed the bottle sceptically, unsure if this was some kind of test. She eyed the bottle closely. She had seen this before, and her memories of than encounter were a little sketchy. She remembered having one too many after an exceptionally gruelling day and waking up with a throbbing headache in her apartment.

Megan flashed her a mischievous smile. "Come on."

"Why?" Manley's scepticism was obvious. She was still suspecting a trap.

"You think I'm messing with you, don't you?" Megan's eyes sparkled with amusement. Manley simply raised her eyebrows in response, a silent challenge. Megan smirked. "I'm not messing with you. You could use a break from all the trauma stuff. I'm granting you one. Don't tell Faris."

"So Faris doesn't know?" This was actually getting interesting.

"Faris doesn't know. He told me to take the best care of you, and that's exactly what I'm doing. You've been incredibly brave, facing the trauma with me every single time I asked you to. Today, we're not going there." Megan clinked her bottle against Manley's. "Drink."

Manley glanced between the bottle and Megan, uncertainty showing on her face. "Well, if you call this therapeutic..." She opened the bottle and took a sip, only to start coughing. "Boy, this is as strong as I remember," she managed to say once she caught her breath.

"I know," Megan grinned, turning her gaze out to the vast expanse of the ocean. They sat in sociable silence for a few moments, savouring the gentle breeze and the serene view.

"This almost makes up for no sex," Manley suddenly blurted out, giggling like a teenager.

"Does it?" Megan glanced at her sideways, smirking, clearly fishing for a reaction.

Manley shook her head, a wistful smile playing on her lips. "No, not really." She gazed out at the sea, the bottle held loosely in her right hand. Her mind drifted to the days when she and Blake had been inseparable, their chemistry electric and undeniable. She sorely missed what she and Blake had had when they first met. When she closed her eyes, she could almost feel his arms around her, could feel him touching her everywhere.

Megan took another sip from her bottle, this time a smaller, more contemplative one. "He's still here; that's gotta count for something."

Manley nodded thoughtfully. "He's still here. And I don't think he'd leave even if I told him to."

"You've done this before, haven't you." Megan's tone wasn't questioning, merely stating a fact.

"I have." Manley fell silent, her thoughts drifting as she took small, measured sips. After a few minutes, she continued. "I've never had a real relationship since Darren got killed. Oh, I slept with men when I felt like it, and I can't say I was always sensible about it. There were a guy or two who tried to play games with me, and I only got out because they underestimated me. I never met the same guy more than twice, and none of them meant anything to me." She looked out at the rolling waves. "And then came Blake."

"And then came Blake," Megan echoed. "What's so different with him? It can't just be the sex, or he would have left already."

Manley chuckled softly, a hint of mischief in her eyes. "Who says—never mind. No, it can't just be the sex. Though it was really good." She avoided Megan's gaze, feeling a blush creep up her cheeks. She had nearly confessed that they hadn't adhered strictly to the doctors' orders regarding their "intimate exertions."

The therapist caught the almost-confession. "Manley, it's okay. You're two grown-ups apparently in love. There are more ways to please one another than in the strictest sense of the word. I'm a therapist, but I'm not stupid." Megan smiled gently. "Apparently you're careful enough, or your shoulder wouldn't be healing as well as it is. That's what counts. And I'm bound to professional discretion. No word from me."

She was pretty sure that this was the smallest problem anyone caught up in this mess could have — doctors included, as long as the patient was careful. Usually they said that whatever helped make the patients feel good couldn't do much harm. But counting in the different injuries that were listed in Manley's medical file, this case might have been an exception. Any other agent would have been confined to the hospital wing or at least their apartment for the time of healing. Manley was lucky enough to have the head of ISA backing her up, allowing her some special treatment, given the history she had with Faris. "That's good to know." Manley stared at the waves, still evading Megan's gaze. "I don't know, we just hit it off. I almost hit him in the face when he caught me off guard on Nergal B. If I had really hit him, I probably wouldn't be here today. He would've ended up in the hospital. We wouldn't have had what we had, and he wouldn't have come looking for me. Claver would have grown impatient eventually. I'd be dead by now." Her voice wavered, and she felt her eyes brimming with tears. An uncontrolled sob escaped her lips, followed by another, and another. It was getting harder to breathe, and she set the bottle down in the sand.

Megan slid closer until their legs were touching. She placed a comforting hand on Manley's back, softly stroking her. "You're not in his debt. He did all of that of his own free will. He's still here for you. If you ask me, there's nothing in this world that you could do to drive this man away." As Manley's sobs grew more intense, Megan wrapped her arms around her and held her close. She spoke softly, her voice a soothing balm. "You know, what happened to you wasn't your fault. It's the result of unprocessed trauma and grief, together with the crazy ideas of a maniac. The happiness you felt with Blake must have triggered the memories of seventeen years ago. When Darren was murdered and you ran away from it all. The kidnappers caught you off guard because you were distracted by your own memories, and they were too many for you to fight on your own."

Megan paused, giving Manley a moment to absorb her words. "They brought you here and beat you up, and you still managed to survive. Your friends, including Blake, made sure they found you in time and alive, and you got away to tell the tale. That is pretty impressive, if you ask me."

She knew that Manley would need time to fully process what she had just said. The wounds, both physical and psychological, were still too fresh and too deep for real healing. Manley's sobs began to subside, her desperate gasps for air becoming fewer and further between. She remained curled up, hugging her legs and crying, but the intensity was slowly ebbing away. Megan continued to hold her, her presence a steady anchor in the storm of emotions.

Megan was quite content with herself. Her plan had worked. She had finally managed to get her stubborn patient to release some of the tension she had built up over weeks. Until now, Manley had been almost too calm and collected during their meetings, as if she were striving for a gold star in therapy, much like she achieved gold-star standards in her daily work. But today, she had finally let down her guard, and the drink had certainly played its part. It was an unconventional approach, getting your patient drunk to provoke an emotional breakdown, but it had worked.

She knew this wasn't easy for Manley. Megan was well aware of her patient's reputation as Faris' right hand and top agent. Manley had never let on if a mission had put any strain on her; she was the one who headed out for a wild night alone and returned the next morning, punctual, even if she was still wearing the same clothes. No one had ever questioned her reputation. She got work done, and her colleagues respected her for that. But Manley had never been Meghan's patient before. She was usually the one bringing victims of crime to Megan, urging them to work through their trauma. Now, Manley found herself a victim of something entirely out of her control. Megan could only guess how much that tormented her. She spoke softly, her voice a gentle murmur against the backdrop of the rolling waves. "I know you understand all of this intellectually. But it's different when you're the victim suddenly. It's okay to question things. It's even okay to question the direction of your life."

Megan hadn't been around when Faris brought Manley into ISA seventeen years ago. However, from what she had heard and read in Manley's medical file, the girl had not been cooperating with anyone but

Faris. Several doctors and therapists had given up after months of trying. The only one who had managed to break through her walls was Faris. He hadn't kept a record of what he did, but he had at least brought Manley to the point where she could interact with others, even if she never let anyone truly close—until now.

Blake must have triggered a part of her that longed for connection, or maybe he was simply "the one" for her. Time would reveal the truth. For now, Megan was confident that Manley would eventually heal. Coming to terms with the violence and the loss of control would take time, but with Blake and Faris standing up for her and catching her when she fell, she had more support than most could claim in this part of the galaxy.

Manley's sobs had diminished to soft whimpers, and she remained hunched over her knees in the same sitting position. Megan carefully moved away an inch, keeping a hand on Manley's back to maintain the physical connection. Physical contact was crucial for Manley, whether she had recognized this pattern herself or not. The therapist in Megan certainly had. "Do you want me to go and get Blake?" she asked gently.

Manley shook her head violently, her red hair moving wildly. "No. I don't want him to see me like this." Her voice was shaky, her throat hoarse from crying.

"Why not?" Megan asked softly, her voice a gentle coaxing.

"I can't. I just can't." Manley's breath was coming in laborious gasps, her body trembling with the effort of releasing pent-up emotions.

"Mm." Megan persisted gently. "Why not? He's seen you in worse shape in the hospital wing, hasn't he?"

"Right. And it's not happening again. Not like this. He needs to know I'll be okay." Manley's sobs were finally ebbing away, leaving her exhausted but more coherent. "I can't stand him looking at me like I'm a wounded deer or something. This isn't me, this isn't how people know me."

Megan had anticipated Manley's resistance. "Thing is, Manley, this is you right now, even if it won't be like this forever. You're hurt, inside and out, and there's nothing unusual about that after what you've gone through. Blake has seen you as you were, and he fell in love with you. He'll help you become that person again." She watched as Manley took a deep breath, the tension slowly draining from her shoulders.

Manley couldn't help but wonder how drunk she would need to get before Megan stopped probing. "We'll see about that," she said, taking another sip from her bottle. "I mean, what am I supposed to do with him?"

"What do you want to do with him?" Megan countered, using the classic therapist's approach to get Manley to confront her own feelings.

"I don't know." Manley looked at Megan, in a mix of curiousity and despair. "I can't uproot my whole life again. Have you heard about agents with a partner for long? Or a family?"

Megan shook her head slowly, understanding where Manley was coming from.

"Because it doesn't work. You can't be an ISA agent and have some middle-class life in the suburbs,"

Manley continued, her voice sounding bitter and resigned.

"But you aren't an ISA agent any more," Megan pointed out gently, her expression soft with understanding.

Manley twisted her lips into a slight pout. "Like that's gonna make much of a difference. Being a Faction agent isn't gonna be a completely different line of work."

"Point taken." Megan set down her empty bottle, her gaze unwavering. "But what is it that you want? Do you want him to leave?"

Manley shook her head immediately, the answer instinctive. "No, I don't. I just don't know how all of this fits together, and it's driving me crazy."

"Nah," Megan said, leaning back slightly, "don't give me crazy. I've seen crazy. This isn't crazy. You just need to figure out what you want. And then find a way to get it."

With a quiet voice, Manley suddenly admitted, "I wanna wake up with him. Every day. And I want to fall asleep with him every night."

"So that's settled, then", Megan said matter-of-factly. "And your secret's safe with me." She smiled warmly at Manley before falling silent.

"Which one?" Manley asked.

"All of them," Megan replied calmly. "I'll have to give Faris something, but he doesn't have to know it all."

Manley eyed Megan sidelong. "He probably knows anyway. We're pretty close."

"I know," Megan acknowledged with a knowing smile. "But he isn't going to hear certain things from me."

Manley looked back out at the tranquil water for a moment, then turned her gaze back to Megan. "You got another one of those?" She gestured to her empty bottle.

Now it was Megan's turn to raise an eyebrow. "And just when I thought you were done, you surprise me again." She handed Manley a second bottle, a subtle grin playing on her lips. Apparently, she wasn't as surprised as she said she was.

Manley deftly opened it with her teeth. "On a good day, you'd never know I had two of these." She took a long sip, the bitterness of the gin mingling with the saltiness of the sea air. Despite knowing she might regret it later, she didn't care. There were four people at the house who could take care of her when she was drunk.

"Enjoy", Megan said and opened another one for herself.

On a particularly nice afternoon about two weeks after their arrival at the beach house, Manley and Blake were sitting on the patio, in the shade, looking out to the sea. Earlier, they had indulged in a refreshing dip in the water. Blake had devoted his time to vigorous swimming, maintaining his fitness, while Manley had simply stood in the water, letting it sway her from side to side. Though when Blake had come back, he had wrapped her up in an embrace that her doctors would probably not have approved of, an embrace that involved hands under the surface and things they did with them. Their security detail was calmly looking out to the sea. If they noticed or suspected anything, they remained discreet, wisely choosing not to betray any knowledge. They probably knew better than to grass Manley and Blake up. By now, everyone had cooled off, savouring the gentle breeze that caressed their skin, warming them after their time in the water.

At least, that was what Blake thought, until Manley suddenly broke the tranquillity. "I know it was you." Her eyes remained fixed on the sea, revealing nothing more.

Blake turned to her, a frown creasing his forehead. "What?" He wasn't sure what she meant; it couldn't possibly be what he thought he had heard.

"I know it was you. You killed Claver." She paused, letting the words hang in the air, her gaze steadfastly on the ocean. "You didn't have to do that. You're a lawyer. If this gets out, you'll never work as a lawyer again. You shouldn't have risked your career for me." Her voice fell silent, her head still unmoving, eyes locked on the endless horizon. There. She had said it.

Blake didn't attempt to deny it; he knew better than to try. "Who told you?" he asked softly, reaching for her hand and taking it gently, his eyes avoiding hers.

"Owen."

Of course. He should have known. The privateer had been present when Blake had shot Claver. It was no surprise that Owen had revealed Blake's role in Claver's death, perhaps seeking some form of redemption. Blake recalled the agony Owen's presence had caused Manley on that dreadful day at the hospital — her confusion, disappointment, and rage had been obvious to all. Owen had needed to atone, at least in part, and so he had confided in her about Blake's actions. "I see."

"He told me when you were out of the room with Faris. He thought I needed to know." She swallowed, her gaze still fixed on the water. "Why didn't anybody else tell me? Why didn't you say anything?"

Good question. Thankfully, Blake had already come up with an answer, having pondered this very dilemma for the past few days. "I was going to tell you. I just hadn't found the perfect situation, and now that we're having this conversation, I'm beginning to realize that there'll never be the perfect time to tell you."

He gently moved his thumb across her hand, finding connection in the simple, reassuring touch. "I'm sorry for not telling you. I should have, and I should have told you right away when you woke up in the hospital. I'm not sorry about killing him. I'd do it again if I had to, even though it wasn't something I planned." He could even justify this in court, if it ever came to that. Claver had attacked them, and it had been a matter of self-defence. At least, that was what Blake kept telling himself to justify what he did.

Deep down, he knew that it wasn't entirely true. When he saw the chance to exact revenge on the man who had harmed the woman he loved, he had snapped. He had done something that went against all his principles, everything that he believed in. And he had thoroughly enjoyed it. He had felt pleasure paying the villain back for what he had done to Manley, even though Blake had only glimpsed her injuries until then. Claver had technically been unarmed, his blaster lying abandoned on his desk. Blake remembered running towards him with steady, deliberate steps and shooting Claver when he made a move towards his weapon. Blake wouldn't have needed to shoot him in the chest. He could have aimed for his leg or hand or anything else. But he went for a clear shot at his heart. It had been a matter of instinct, an impulsive decision that bypassed rational thought.

The lawyer in him had wrestled with the idea of turning himself in for days. The man seeing his chance at a life of happiness alongside this extraordinary woman had silenced him, firmly telling him to mind his own business. No one would ever know. He was confident that neither Owen, nor Haylen, nor Darra would breathe a word of this to another living soul. They probably understood his motives. Blake wasn't certain what they had conveyed to Faris, nor what Faris had officially documented regarding Claver's death.

"I see." Manley's gaze remained fixed on the sea, and then she abruptly shifted the conversation. "So, what does this mean? Are we going back to our old lives? Are we doing anything new?"

Blake sighed. "Honestly, I don't know. I've taken a leave of absence for this month and the next. Lannister and his team are handling my clients for now, and beyond that, I have no idea what's going to happen. What I'll do with my office. I don't have a plan. Do you?" Then it dawned on him. She wasn't talking about her plans, but about their plans as a couple. He decided not to highlight this realisation. Who knew if she might change her mind once he pointed it out?

Manley shook her head. "No, I don't. I really don't. Faris sent a message to the Faction, telling them I'd join them later. I haven't heard back, but I guess they'll wait. They probably know what happened." The Faction wasn't known for long, detailed messages that anyone could intercept. They would wait and approach her in a secure manner when they deemed it necessary. One thing was certain, though. She was not going back to ISA. Faris would have to lead the agency without her, she was done with that. She had been looking forward to her new role, and she knew she would have unlimited resources for whatever the Faction needed her to do. Who wouldn't dream of a job like that?

She took a deep breath and turned to Blake, her eyes filled with a newfound determination. "There's something I need to do. I need to see my parents. They still believe I'm dead, and I can't go on pretending. I need to see them."

She recalled the desperate moment when she had pleaded with Faris one last time to see her parents, about six months after her escape from Claver's mansion. She had known, deep down, that he couldn't grant her request, but she had needed to ask. She had to make sure that she had exhausted every possibility, that there was nothing left to grasp from her old life. But now, the charade they had been playing was no longer necessary. The Claver family was gone, and the other captors from the complex were behind bars. There was no longer any need to shield her mom and dad from danger. They were safe now.

Blake nodded, his expression one of understanding and support. "I get it. I guess we'll have to talk to Faris about it."

Manley sighed. Right. Faris would have to be involved. The thought of that confrontation wearied her, but she knew she had to face it. Perhaps, just perhaps, there was a way back to at least this part of her old life.

* * *

Manley felt sleep slip away with an unsettling swiftness. It was still dark outside, the morning several hours off, yet her body insisted on waking. The daytime rest, though crucial for her healing, left her nights fragmented and restless. But it was necessary. She couldn't risk any delay in the healing process. Denying herself her usual rigorous muscle training and cardio was testing her patience, pushing her to the brink of frustration. As she lay there pondering her sudden wakefulness, she sensed Blake stirring behind her. He must have felt her restlessness, for he turned and wrapped his arm around her, propping himself up against her back.

"So you can't sleep, either," he murmured.

She snorted softly. "Nope."

Blake took that as an invitation to make the most of their sleeplessness. He lowered his head to her neck, kissing her passionately. With her movements restricted, Manley decided to let him indulge in what he excelled at. His hands—those wonderful hands—glided over her skin, causing shivers of pleasure. After a while, he whispered, "Do you want to sneak outside and have definitely no sex on the beach?"

A grin spread across her face as she turned to look at him, a task made challenging by her immobile shoulder. "No, I don't."

His amusement was palpable. "Too comfortable to get out of bed?"

She shook her head immediately. "Definitely not. I've done this before." She glanced at him, half-expecting to see a frown as he imagined her with another man, but it didn't seem to bother him. "I'm not doing that again. There's gonna be sand everywhere, and I mean *everywhere*."

She took another breath, her tone turning more resolute. "If we're definitely not going to have sex, it'll happen here."

Blake lifted his hand off her body, a playful smile spreading across his lips. "I can certainly live with that. I don't really like sand everywhere." With that, he resumed what he had been doing, his touch both deliberate and teasing. He was acutely aware that their security detail was just around the corner, stationed in the small corridor outside the room. Knowing that they were probably listening made this a little more exciting. "What I do like is this," he murmured, his hand now softly touching sensitive spots on her body. "And this."

He kissed her again, pushing his own body up against hers. Just when it seemed they could bear it no longer, Blake pulled back, his arms wrapping tightly around her. His embrace was firm, reassuring, a silent promise of unwavering support and love. It took them a long while to fall asleep.

Haylen North was feeling confused. She found herself on approach, scheduled for a visit with Manley for the second time within weeks. She felt an odd sense of foreboding, a persistent feeling that something would go wrong, despite her careful preparations. She had informed the security team at the beach house ahead of time, notifying them that she was bringing

Manley's blasters. She had retrieved these from the safe in Manley's hotel room during her own investigation. Security, understandably, might be uneasy about anyone bringing weapons, even if they belonged to their subject. As she piloted her Drekar, she touched down in the clearing designated as her landing spot. The late afternoon sun cast long shadows, adding a sombre tone to the scene. She grabbed the bag containing Manley's blasters and exited the ship. The beach house stood quiet, with only one security guard visible, standing watch at the entrance.

Approaching the porch, the guard met her with a direct gaze. "I'm gonna have to take these off you," he said, pointing to the bag with the blasters.

Haylen chuckled, handing over the bag. "I figured. Take them for safekeeping. But expect her to demand them back."

The guard nodded and gestured toward the house. "They're in the living room. It's the one straight down, looking out."

She acknowledged him with a nod and made her way inside. The layout was straightforward: a small bedroom to the left, the kitchen to the right, a small room for appliances, and another room likely designated for additional security and medical personnel to have some private space, and the large room towards the sea. As she entered that living room, she found Manley and Blake ensconced on a large lounger, gazing out at the sea. Manley looked utterly at home in Blake's arms. They turned their attention to her as she stepped into the room. Manley sprang up like a bolt of lightning, rushing to embrace her. Blake, slower to rise, nodded at Haylen with a warm smile.

"It's good to see you up and about," Haylen whispered in Manley's ear as they hugged.

"Thanks," Manley replied, her smile radiant.

"I brought your blasters," Haylen announced, watching as Manley's face lit up with a mixture of relief and joy. "Had to hand them over to security, though."

"And I thought I'd never get them back! When Faris had someone pick up our things from the hotel, the blasters were gone. I guess we never talked about them." Manley was visibly relieved, her fingers twitching with the familiar desire to hold the weapons she knew so well. She had taken those weapons to the hotel for a reason—they were extensions of herself, tools she trusted implicitly. She was glad she didn't have to invest into any new ones.

Haylen settled into an armchair, the soft leather creaking slightly under her weight. "I guess we didn't." She observed Manley, noting the marked improvement in her appearance. Although she still wore the splint, the dreaded plastic cage encasing her shoulder, she seemed far more animated and alive than during the last visit. Owen and Faris had mentioned it would be at least two more weeks before she could rid herself of the contraption, but at least she had avoided surgery. "Please don't take this the wrong way—but you look so much better than the last time I visited."

Manley grinned, a lightness in her eyes. "Yeah, you didn't exactly catch me on my best day last time."

Blake turned his head, his expression amused. "That's a nice understatement."

"I'm very good at that, in case you haven't noticed." Manley's tone was playful, clearly enjoying the banter.

"Oh, I've noticed," Blake replied, his amusement growing.

"I'm also very good at getting what I want," Manley added, her gaze locking with Blake's. In that moment, she seemed to forget Haylen's presence, especially when Blake's hand began inching toward her waist.

Blake kissed her, a tender yet possessive gesture. "I know that, too," he murmured when he pulled back. Then he turned to Haylen, who had been watching the exchange with a smirk of growing amusement. "So, how have you been?"

Haylen shrugged, leaning back in the armchair. "Not too bad, I guess. I slept for a day or two when we got out of the mansion. Had a couple of drinks with Darra and Owen. Acquired a few smaller jobs that kept me close to Enkil. Guess I'm back in business."

"So you're not going home? I mean, you'd probably never have to work a day in your life, would you?" Blake's question hung in the air, a knowing smile tugging at his lips as if he anticipated her response.

"Nope." Haylen fumbled with her belt, her fingers betraying a hint of agitation. "I don't wanna be sitting around all day, spending Daddy's money. Which is too much to spend in a lifetime, anyway. I can pick and choose my jobs thanks to that money. I'll take it from here and see where I might end up. The North imperium is in good hands with the people leading the companies right now."

"Sounds legit," Blake responded, giving her an approving smile.

Manley had remained quiet during their exchange, an uneasy feeling creeping up on her. She sensed that Haylen was holding something back. She loved how Haylen and Blake got along, and knew they had been quite the team during the search for her, but something felt off. Taking a leap, she asked, "Haylen, are you saying goodbye, too?"

Haylen's eyes widened in surprise. "How—never mind." She drew a deep breath, realising that her tension had not gone unnoticed by Manley, who always saw more than she let on. "Yes, I'm saying goodbye for now. I'll work through my jobs and take care of a couple of things. And then I will come back, and we'll have that drink we've been talking about." She watched as Manley's expression sank. Her friend still sat nestled in Blake's embrace, his protective presence supporting her. "It's not goodbye forever. I promise."

"It'd better not be," Manley said, her face morphing into a frown. This wasn't what she had envisioned when she heard Haylen was coming. She had wanted to spend a fun day on the beach with her friend, not hear about another departure. Owen had left just a couple of days ago, and now Haylen was leaving, too. "You do realise that I'm not too fond of that idea, don't you?"

Haylen nodded, a mischievous glint in her eye. "I figured you wouldn't like this very much, which is why I was glad the guards took the blasters from me." She broke into a grin.

Manley sighed dramatically. "Like I'd shoot you. I mean, of course I could, but can you imagine the paperwork?" She grinned back, the familiar banter lightening the mood. "As long as you'll be back, I'll be fine. It's not like I'm totally on my own here." She glanced at Blake, then back at Haylen. "Now, what do we do?"

Blake motioned toward the kitchen. "What about dinner?"

"Now you're talking," Manley said, looking content again.

Blake stood, carefully removing his arm from around Manley's back. "I'll see what I can find. There's gotta be some pasta left in the fridge," he said, then headed off to the kitchen to start putting a meal together.

Manley and Haylen found themselves alone in the room. The silence between them now was no longer uncomfortable but filled with unspoken understanding. Finally, Manley broke the silence, her voice soft. "I'll miss you."

Haylen nodded, her expression serious. "I'll miss you too." She didn't say how much. Over the past few weeks, rummaging through Manley's past, she had grown closer to her friend than she had ever anticipated. Haylen felt a deep sense of connection, something she hadn't allowed herself to feel in a long time.

She felt like she owed Manley a piece of her own past, the burden she had always felt as the sole heir to the North empire. It wasn't until recently that she had grown comfortable to using the advantages her late father's companies and funds gave her. Now, she was still trying to find a purpose for all that money. There had to be something good she could do with it, something meaningful. She didn't need much for herself, just enough to maintain her lifestyle. The rest—there had to be a way to put it to some good use.

The redhead lounging on the couch opposite Haylen cast a sidelong glance toward the beach, tilting her head slightly. "I love the feel of the water on my feet. Care to join me?" she inquired. With a nod, Haylen rose to her feet, and Manley led the way. They passed the second security guard, who was perched on the front patio with a commanding view of the ocean. Manley acknowledged him with a brief nod. "We'll be down by the water for a bit," she said. The guard, dressed in the standard black uniform, nodded back but remained at his post. Manley was confident that the house's security was impenetrable, reinforced by the measures Faris had put in place. Even if someone dared to breach the perimeter, these highly trained agents would neutralize the threat in mere seconds. At least, that was what Manley's professional experience assured her.

Reaching the shoreline, Manley felt a sense of relief as the pleasantly cool ocean water swirled around her ankles. She glanced back to see Haylen remove her heavy boots, her gaze fixed longingly on the water. "I can fetch some swimwear from the house if you want," Manley offered.

Haylen hesitated briefly before making up her mind. "No need. Blake's seen a naked woman before, hasn't he?" she replied, a mischievous smile playing on her lips.

"Indeed, he has," Manley responded, choosing to leave it at that. Everyone knew that she didn't only play cards with Blake when they were alone.

"A towel would be nice, though," Haylen added as an afterthought.

"I'll get us some," Manley said, heading back to the house. She fetched two large, unused towels from the bathroom and then made a detour to the kitchen, where Blake was busy preparing a delicious-smelling pasta dish. "Could you untie my dress for me? I'll go for a swim with Haylen," she requested.

"Swim?" Blake echoed, motioning for her to turn around, so he could untie the green dress she had chosen for the day. Manley had developed the habit of wearing her beachwear beneath her dresses, so she wouldn't have to change every time she went into the water.

"You know what I mean," she teased. "I want to stand in the water and pretend I could actually swim." She planted a quick kiss on his lips before heading back outside. By the time she returned to the water, Haylen had already discarded all her clothes and was joyfully splashing in the gentle waves.

"I can't remember the last time I've actually been in the water on a planet," Haylen shouted, her voice brimming with joy.

Manley stepped cautiously into the water. The sea was calm today, presenting no real threat of slipping, but she wasn't inclined to take risks. With her arm immobilized in the splint, any fall could be disastrous. If she fell, she might not have been able to get back up herself.

"We should've done this earlier," Manley mused aloud.

"We should've done a lot of things," Haylen replied, her tone turning reflective. "Like paying closer attention to the woman who helped us clear out Ortiz and Claver. In the beginning, we had no idea where to start looking for you. And Faris wasn't exactly forthcoming."

Manley nodded. "I heard about that. Blake mentioned Faris lied. He was protecting himself. I can't even blame him. Everything connected to the Claver family was a mess, one we should've cleared up long ago. We thought we were safe until Owen pulled us into his investigation."

Haylen had found a place beside her in the water. "Honestly? I don't think we could've found you without the breadcrumbs Claver left. He might have been a narcissistic psychopath, but at least his trail led us to you." She paused, her voice softening. "And Faris came around just in time. Your rescue wouldn't have gone so smoothly if Henders hadn't been able to extract you."

Manley took a deep breath, savouring the salty air. "But it did. In the end, we were all fortunate that things unfolded the way they did."

Haylen chuckled. "Indeed. But I would've loved to see the look on that guy's face when you took his blaster and cornered him." She found a place close to Manley. Both women began to bask in the warmth of the sun with their eyes closed.

"That was satisfying. Not in the strictest sense of the word, but in that moment, I knew I might actually stand a chance," Manley said, a note of pride colouring her voice.

"And before you ask—no, I have no idea how I walked out of there on my own two feet with all these injuries. I've heard that question more times than I can count, and I still don't have an answer. I guess I seized the one chance I had, and I really didn't want to fail." She moved her right arm through the water, steadying herself against a slightly larger wave. She glanced at Haylen. "Who did you shoot? In the leg? You mentioned it at the hospital."

Haylen glanced back, trying to suppress a grin but failing miserably. "Ah, that." She sighed, her expression a mix of amusement and exasperation. "Quincy Murkle. The hotel manager. He refused to give us the security tapes showing four musclemen carrying you out of the hotel. They paid him to look the other way. That shot was necessary."

"I see." When she had first met Haylen a few months ago, she could never have imagined the North heir wielding a weapon and shooting someone for information. Haylen had been busy finding her own place in the world, determined not to be defined solely as the North heir. But that girl seemed light years away now. Haylen had evolved from an insecure teenager into a confident woman who knew exactly what she wanted. In an afterthought, Manley asked, "Did Blake shoot anyone else?" She left out the obvious—that he had shot Claver.

"Not that I know of. He was playing the silent thug when he was with me. He didn't even touch his blaster until we were heading for the mansion." Haylen eyed Manley from the side. Was her friend still trying to determine whether or not she should trust Blake? Or was she trying to come to terms with everything that had happened? She decided to keep her thoughts to herself. Manley didn't need another person to tell her that Blake was serious about her. Why else would he have travelled across the sector, risking his own life to find her? She was convinced that Manley would see all of that in her own time.

They nearly missed Blake calling them for dinner, so absorbed were they in the gentle rhythm of the ocean. The security guard coaxed them out of the water and back to the house. Together, they gathered around the table to enjoy the meal Blake had prepared. The smell of his cooking wafted through the air, tempting their senses. As they took their first bites, they were pleasantly surprised by the depth of flavour in the vegetables he had made along with some creamy sauce and rice. Manley couldn't help but marvel once again at Blake's hidden talents.

Blake, seated across the table, noticed the small, contented noises Manley made while savouring her food. She probably wasn't even aware of it, but he heard them clearly. A glance from Haylen, accompanied by a knowing smile, confirmed that she had noticed as well. Both of them remembered the conversation about Manley's eating habits from the beginning of their journey together. Those endearing little sounds were a good sign, indicating that despite her injuries and the turmoil they had faced, Manley was gradually finding her way back to normalcy.

Later that night, when Haylen had said her goodbye, Blake found Manley sitting on the porch, her feet in the sand. She didn't seem to hear him, and she was looking out at the ocean in the darkness. Her body seemed relaxed, and her breathing was quiet. He would have given a lot to know what she was thinking about. He decided not to ask and quietly stepped beside her. She looked up to him and smiled, reaching out for him with her good hand. He sat down behind her, supporting her back and wrapping his arms around her. He breathed a kiss on her neck and wondered what tomorrow would bring.

Chapter 15

Day 44

Manley was sitting in the darkness on the edge of her bed, her gaze wandering aimlessly over the sprawling cityscape that lay before her. The glittering lights of cars and ships created a sparkling mosaic connecting sky and ground. The sky above was a tumultuous sea of thick, black clouds. Rain was softly hitting the floor-length glass wall at the front of the room, and she could hear thunder roll in the distance. It felt strange to be back here, in this apartment that had been her sanctuary for fifteen years. Once, she had called it home; now, it felt like it belonged to a stranger. How could six weeks have turned her life so completely upside down?

She glanced back at Blake, who was sleeping soundly, his presence a fragile anchor in the storm of her thoughts. Tomorrow, she would face her parents for the first time in nearly two decades. She had no idea what she wanted to tell them, how she could justify what happened so many years ago. She had no idea how her parents would take it. And she had no idea how she would take it herself. The pain she had caused them — unintentionally, but deeply nonetheless — loomed large in her mind. And though she knew others were to blame as well, she was scared to admit her part of the journey.

The decision to declare her dead had been made by ISA without consulting her, a cold bureaucratic act that had ripped her from her old life. For her parents, that bureaucratic act had translated into a grievous loss. And Claver, the man at the centre of her troubles, was dead, beyond any reckoning or retribution. Manley knew she couldn't let the current state of things stand, especially now that the Claver family was gone.

For years, she had avoided even the thought of venturing close to her parents. She had relocated to the other side of the city, choosing a place she knew they would never frequent. In hindsight, it baffled her that she hadn't simply left the planet the moment she regained control over her life. From her flat, she could see the hills of the suburbs where she had grown up, yet she had always kept herself at a safe distance from that part of the city. Until tomorrow. Tomorrow, she would return and attempt to mend the breach she had created, if her parents would allow her to.

Her father, she hoped, would be glad to see her. Her mother, however, was a different story — she might meet her daughter with anger and rage, and Manley could hardly blame her. She had missed curfew by seventeen years, three months, and thirteen days. Her mother's wrath, if it came, would be well-deserved. But eventually, Manley believed, she would come around. At least, she always had during the first seventeen years of Manley's life.

She looked around her apartment in silence, absorbing the familiar yet soon-to-be distant surroundings. Once she started her new job with the Faction, she wouldn't return here. She would sell the flat; she needed to be closer to their headquarters on Myrto. There wasn't much to transport to a new place. Her childhood had been abruptly severed years ago, and she had started her new life with nothing but the essentials that Faris had provided her with. Over the years, she hadn't accumulated much — her apartment was stark, almost barren, save for the basic furniture and the contents of her walk-in wardrobe. She had never seen the point in collecting things, given that she was rarely home. In recent months, especially while working with Owen, she had often slept at her office in the ISA headquarters. She usually ate out, and souvenirs from her missions never interested her. It wouldn't be too hard to leave this place, would it?

And yet, this flat had been her sanctuary for fifteen years. Whenever she needed solitude, she had retreated here, basking in the peace and quiet it offered. Never had she let any of the men she had been with cross this threshold. The only man to have ever set foot in this apartment, apart from delivery personnel, was Faris. He had come to inspect the place before she bought it, and since then, he had been the sole visitor she had entertained here. Until now.

Blake was sleeping right behind her. They had chosen to come here for the night instead of a hotel after finally leaving the beach house. She knew this place could be monitored more easily; fewer people went in and out of the building, and all who did were checked and accounted for. She might only have been safer within ISA headquarters, but her apartment was as close to safety as it could possibly get outside the ISA building.

She was suddenly startled by a noise behind her, and her well-trained instincts flared into action. She was on the verge of leaping up to defend herself when she realised it was Blake, merely shifting in his sleep. Only, he wasn't asleep any more. She saw him move closer, a sleepy smile curling on his lips. His hand reached out for her, and she turned to him, allowing his arms to envelop her. He was naked, again. She shivered softly as his skin pressed against hers.

Blake, always careful to avoid putting pressure on her injured left side, gently pushed her down onto the bed with both hands on her shoulders, motioning her to lie still. The thunder rolled again, a distant, soothing rumble. Blake didn't say a word; he didn't need to. His mischievous smile spoke volumes, and she instantly knew what he was going to do. Her heart quickened at the thought, and a familiar tingling sensation began to rise below her stomach.

For the past few weeks, she had felt completely disconnected from herself. It was only in moments alone with Blake that she reclaimed a sense of normalcy, a semblance of the woman she had been before the nightmare began. Connecting with him, skin on skin, grounded her, pulling her back from the abyss of trauma and memories. Manley closed her eyes, arching her head back in excitement as he sat over her, making her wait just a moment longer. He bent down and kissed her, long and hard, before his lips began exploring her body. Each touch, each kiss, was deliberate, a methodical release of the tension that had built up over the weeks. If ever there had been a time to let go, this was it.

Blake made very sure that Manley didn't move more than necessary. While their first two nights had been reigned by passion and burning desire, tonight he chose a gentler approach. The splint was finally gone, replaced by a small sling she wore during the day to minimize movement until the bones strengthened, but he would not be the one to add to her discomfort. He was confident she would make it up to him some other day when she was fully healed. The doctors had explicitly advised against any "intimate exertion," as they put it, but here they were, defying orders again.

Blake grinned and looked up at Manley's face. She met his gaze, smiled, and reached for his face with her right hand, pulling him close while carefully placing her left arm by her side. He positioned himself beside her right side, his left hand trailing down her body to strip away the soft fabric around her hips. She kicked it off impatiently, eagerly anticipating more.

Blake had all the time in the world. He propped himself up on his left elbow and let his other hand roam down her body towards her legs. "Is this really what you want?" he asked quietly, his fingers softly teasing her. He already knew the answer; her body was speaking for her. She didn't say a word, nor did she need to. Her hand moved towards a part of his body that seemed to defy control, and while he let her touch him for a moment, he savoured the sensation, relishing being right here, right now. He had been longing for this night as much as she had. Six long weeks of celibacy were about to end.

He slid down from the bed, his hands still moving over her body, eliciting soft moans from her. He knelt in front of her, propped up her legs, and gently but firmly pulled her closer to the edge where she had been sitting just a little while ago.

Everything between them felt just as it had five weeks ago before she had been kidnapped on Nergal B. The sling lay discarded on the side of the bed, and though Manley's face still bore the faint remnants of bruises inflicted by Claver's henchmen, the attraction between her and Blake remained undiminished. They had spent countless nights in tight embraces, holding back from acting on their desires, so she could heal properly. Tonight was the first night they were truly alone, just the two of them, without any security detail lurking around the corner.

They knew Faris had the apartment monitored by various measures, but cameras were not among them. And even if cameras had been present, neither Blake nor Manley would have given a damn. Faris had stationed two agents in an empty apartment at the other end of the hall, and someone was undoubtedly watching the security footage from the hallway live. None of that could make Manley and Blake keep their hands off each other tonight.

A good while later, Blake and Manley lay flat on their backs. Blake felt pleasantly exhausted, the result of maintaining his fitness with running and swimming over the past four weeks. Manley, however, felt the strain in every muscle, despite having been the more passive participant. Her thorax and lungs ached from laboured breathing, her throat was parched, and her legs throbbed from their unusual position. Yet,

Manley hadn't felt this good in weeks. A surge of euphoria coursed through her, making her feel invincible, as if she could conquer anything that lay ahead. Intellectually, she knew she was riding a hormonal high that wouldn't last, but she was willing to enjoy that ride for as long as it lasted. Tomorrow promised to be emotionally exhausting.

Listening closely to her body's signals, she recognised its craving for more, despite the fatigue. The painkillers she had taken before bed were still numbing any potential discomfort. She would have to come off those eventually, but the doctors had agreed that healing would work a lot faster when she wasn't in pain. She rolled over to her right side and began to climb over Blake.

"Where are you going?" he asked, planting a soft kiss on her leg as she manoeuvred over him.

"I need to get a drink. What about you?"

He nodded. "I'd say yes, but you can't carry two glasses." He grinned and sat up, acutely aware of his own and her nakedness.

She rolled her eyes, turning to walk to the kitchen with him. "You know, I could have had my water in the kitchen and then brought you a glass with my good hand," she said, her voice carrying frustration. She hated still being dependent on help for everyday tasks, though the nurse's visits were now limited to administering painkillers.

"You could have," Blake said with a mischievous grin spreading across his face. "But that would have robbed me of the pleasure of watching your naked back." He heard her inhale sharply as he paused right behind her. She chose not to respond further.

Manley retrieved two glasses from the cabinet, filled them with water, and handed him one without meeting his gaze. The kitchen counter remained bare; Manley rarely used it these days. It was becoming increasingly difficult for her to feign indifference toward repeating their recent escapade. He was so close — his skin against hers, his breath warm on the back of her neck. His fingers grazed her hips lightly, sending small, electric jolts through her. Her exhaustion was subsiding, replaced by a craving that had built up over six weeks of restraint. Despite their creativity at the beach house, nothing compared to the real thing. Now that she had tasted it again, Manley found herself eagerly anticipating the next time.

Blake seemed to share her sentiments. Suddenly, he grasped her waist firmly with both hands, turned her around, and sat her on the kitchen counter. His lips found hers with an urgency that took her breath away. He also kissed a few other parts of her body. Manley closed her eyes, surrendering to the sensation.

Just when she thought she couldn't endure any more, she set down her empty glass a bit harder than intended, slid off the counter, and swiftly headed for the bathroom. "Be right back," she managed to say, her breath slightly uneven. She closed the door behind her, leaning against it for a moment, relishing the solitude. She closed her eyes, allowing herself a moment to collect herself. Her body trembled with exhaustion and exhilaration, but it felt so damn good connecting with him again on the physical level. Her physical desire was contrasting the emotional work they had pursued at the beach house over the past month.

They had delved deep into each other's stories, unravelling their pasts and exploring their future together. Through it all, both had yearned in equal measure for the physical intimacy they had just shared. While Manley couldn't speak for Blake, she knew, with every fibre of her being, that she wanted him again, desperately.

Blake smiled after Manley in the enveloping darkness. He had a hunch of why she had left, a memory from six weeks ago flashing vividly in his mind. It was back at the hotel, when they had been this close to tearing each other's clothes off over the bottle of champagne on the balcony of his room. He had left in a hurry because his body had given him certain unmistakable signs that the taunting situation was way too hard. He had left abruptly then, the mutual tension between them proving too intense to bear. Now, as he stood in the quiet kitchen, he couldn't help but wonder if this time, it was Manley who needed to reclaim control over the overwhelming sensations stirring within her.

Blake just couldn't shake the question: Why? Why did she think she needed to restrain herself now? Hadn't he shown that he could navigate their passion without risking her path of healing? Perhaps it wasn't about him at all. Maybe it was a deeper fear of losing control, coming from her harrowing captivity in Claver's underground bunker.

The thought softened his smile, understanding the complexity of her emotions. He silently walked up to the bathroom door. He would welcome her there when she opened it, and they would see where things would take them from here. Minutes passed in silence, the darkness enveloping him like a comforting embrace. Finally, he heard the soft click of the bathroom lights switching off and the gentle creak of the door opening.

When Manley saw Blake standing there, patiently waiting for her, she cast her caution aside in an instant. Briefly, the memories of Claver's bunker flickered in her mind, but she banished them with practised ease. In general, the idea of losing control didn't seem too attractive right now. But it was different with Blake. With a determined resolve, she moved towards him, surrendering to the powerful pull of desire that had simmered between them for too long. Damn precautions; she deserved this.

She rushed towards him, giving in to desire. She wrapped her good arm around him, feeling his hands meet at her back, their touch igniting a fire within her. Blake guided her gently, manoeuvring until her back met the cool concrete wall behind her for support. Their kisses grew deeper, each moment more passionate and demanding than the last.

Manley faced a choice — to cling to him or to satisfy him with her hand. Opting for the latter, she revelled in the intimacy, knowing he wouldn't leave her side. With expert ease, Blake lifted her effortlessly and carried her to her bedroom. In his arms, she felt anything but fragile, despite the weight she had lost during her captivity and in the hospital.

At least now, he didn't need to worry about figuratively breaking any of her bones. Gently laying her down on the pillows, Blake snuggled up behind her, his free hand exploring her body with purpose, his touch feather-light on her left arm and shoulder. Manley melted into his embrace, enjoying the pleasure of skin against skin. Their bodies moved in sync, passion reigniting and building until finally, spent and exhausted, they collapsed together. Blake didn't let go; he held her tightly, pulling the duvet over them both. His head rested softly against hers, his words a tender whisper amidst the distant rumble of thunder, "This was long overdue, my dear."

"It was," she whispered softly, her voice carrying the weight of longing and contentment intertwined. "Incredibly overdue."

She kept her eyes closed, unwilling to let go of the warmth and intimacy. Opening her eyes felt like an invitation to the harsh reality awaiting her — the daunting prospect of facing her parents after so many years apart, the responsibilities that awaited her outside this sanctuary with Blake.

In this moment, she didn't want it to end. She yearned to stay here with Blake forever, shielded from the demands of the world outside. The thought of diving back into her duties—chasing criminals, making decisions about her future with the Faction—felt threatening. She knew these decisions loomed, but for now, she craved this intimate connection, the safety of Blake's embrace. She could take her time with decisions about work. And she would certainly not start that new job before she had healed properly. She knew she would need to be on top of her game if she started to work for the Faction. Manley could still feel Blake's warmth enveloping her, his touch a steady reassurance against the uncertainties that lay ahead. His hand rested gently on her belly, a familiar gesture that had comforted her through weeks of recovery and rediscovery. She knew she would lean on that hand again tomorrow, perhaps more times than she could count.

Chapter 16

Day 45

It was done. Manley sat in the back of the giant black car the agency had provided, granting her the one wish she had named in the aftermath of her kidnapping. The vehicle was parked at the side of the road in one of the city's more pleasant neighbourhoods. The sunshine outside, punctuated by a few wispy clouds, cast a serene, almost idyllic glow over the scene. Last night's thunderstorm was gone, only the wet grass reminded of it. Towering trees lined the road, creating a natural boundary between the street and the opulent properties of Enkil society's elite. A gentle breeze rustled through the leaves, yet the air retained a crisp freshness.

Blake sat beside her, patient and silent, waiting until she was ready. In the passenger seat, Faris knew better than to say a word just yet. Manley's gaze was fixed on the empty space before her. She had been determined to come here, and now that she was, she wasn't so sure any more that this was a good idea. She couldn't even bring herself to look at the house. Seventeen years had passed since she last walked through that door, and her parents believed she was dead. They were convinced she had died in the woods outside the Claver estate, a belief carefully orchestrated by Faris and ISA.

Daxton Faris observed his former protégé in the rearview mirror. Her face had mostly healed, though a few lingering bruises cast darker shadows on her left side. These marks, too, would fade with time. He remembered the frail young woman he had picked up in the woods back then. Manley looked a lot like her today. Scared, haunted, tortured. Right now, his former right hand seemed to be stuck between a rock and a hard place. He knew that she desperately wanted to get out the car and tell her parents that she had been alive all this time. She seemed paralysed, caught between a desperate need to rush into her parents' arms and a crippling fear of the confrontation that awaited her. He knew that this visit, however necessary, would not be without pain. There would be tears, and possibly recriminations, and there was only so much she could take at the moment. Faris cleared his throat softly. "Manley?"

She didn't react. Her eyes remained fixed on the seat in front of her, showing no indication that she had heard him.

"Manley," Faris repeated, a little louder this time.

She blinked and met his gaze in the rearview mirror. "Yes?"

Faris scratched his head, pondering his next words carefully. "Do you want me to go in first and explain? I could tell them why we put you into the program. I can take the yelling and the blame. I've seen this before." He waited, almost sure that she would agree to let him assume responsibility for this.

Manley looked helpless, her eyes darting to Blake for support, her uncertainty etched in her frown.

Blake nodded encouragingly. "This might be a good idea, you know? That way, they might be a little less mad when you come in. Maybe you ringing the doorbell isn't exactly something they'd take well initially?" He touched her hand softly, reassuring her that whatever she decided would be fine with him.

Now this was something Manley hadn't thought about. In her mind, she had envisioned herself ringing the bell, her mother opening the door, and then staring at her in utter shock. If Faris could soften the blow by preparing her parents, would that be okay? Would they be able to forgive her? Would they be mad? Would they want her to leave? Maybe they wouldn't want to see her at all, needing time to adjust to the fact that the daughter they had believed dead for seventeen years was sitting just outside. Maybe they wouldn't even recognize her. And what about Darren? She would have to explain what she witnessed back then, how long it took her to seemingly heal, and the fresh wounds from recent events. It was all connected, and she would have to expect them to be okay with all of that.

The thought of burdening them with so much was overwhelming. Yet, she had come this far. She had asked for the car, the security detail, Faris' company, and now she was here, just outside the house where her parents still lived. She willed herself to rejoin the conversation and looked Faris in the eye. He had offered to help, and she wanted him to help. "Yes, please. Go and explain." She said nothing else but held her gaze steady, her determination returning.

Faris nodded, breaking eye contact, then turned and exited the car without haste. He didn't look back at Manley, fearing he might catch a glimpse of her crying, even through the dark, tinted windows. He couldn't afford that right now; he needed his mind clear. This was familiar territory for him, though usually, his visits involved delivering the devastating news of a loved one lost in action. He had been to this very house before, telling the Carter family that their only child had been killed by an unknown assailant. He recalled with painful clarity how Mrs. Carter had screamed and cried, her hope brutally extinguished by his sharply phrased words. He had described finding Amy's body and the necessity of using DNA from the database to identify her. Mrs. Carter knew what that implied: her daughter's body had been ravaged by animals and likely violated by humans who did not deserve the name. The anguish and grief had nearly destroyed her. Faris had seen it in her eyes, the light snuffed out, and he feared she might not survive another year. Amy's father, on the other hand, had silently closed his eyes and then turned to comfort his wife. His true thoughts remained a mystery, though Faris noted how much smaller and quieter Mr. Carter seemed when he left.

Now, Faris stood once more at this house, ready to reveal a truth that would upend the grief they had lived with for sixteen and a half years. He was about to tell Mr. and Mrs. Carter that he had lied to them, that their teenage daughter, now a grown woman, was alive and sitting in a car outside. He took several deep breaths, steeling himself, and raised his hand to ring the doorbell. He was wondering why he had volunteered for this, and then he remembered again. He owed it to Manley, and he owed it to himself and her parents.

For a few moments, nothing happened, and Faris half-wondered if the intel he had received about the Carters being at home had been incorrect. But then, a figure appeared behind the tinted glass of the large wooden door. A woman opened it, her grey hair bound into a loose ponytail at the back of her head. She looked a lot like Manley. She looked up at him, and then several things seemed to happen at once. Faris saw that she recognized him — this had to be Mrs. Carter. He would not have recognised her; too much time and too many faces lay between these two encounters. But he knew the look on her face. This woman vividly remembered him and their last encounter, and as her expression shifted from surprise to something between anger and rage, he knew this was the right house.

"You," she said coldly, standing in the doorway, not inviting him in and blocking the entrance.

Faris had expected this. He completely understood why she didn't invite him in. He was the one who had told her that her child was dead. "Yes, Mrs. Carter. It's me." He stood his ground.

"What do you want?" she shot at him.

"I have something for you. Can we go inside?" Faris was on uncertain ground here. He didn't know for sure that she would let him in. He was running out the clock, hoping that eventually Mr. Carter would appear. He had been the quiet one during their last encounters and might be able to diffuse some of the tension.

Mrs. Carter looked him in the eye. "What could you possibly give me that wouldn't make things worse?" She pursed her lips, waiting for his answer, never breaking eye contact.

But of course, Faris had prepared for this day. "I have new details about Amy's passing. We finally have a suspect." He hadn't closed his mouth yet when he saw the change in her posture. And while what he had told her as bait wasn't exactly the truth, it served its purpose. Mrs. Carter's stance softened, and she looked a lot less threatening now. He knew that this was a piece of news she had been waiting for, for so many years. He almost felt bad for her.

"You do?"

Faris nodded. "May I come in, please?" He pointed to the back of the house, half-expecting her to shoot him when he wasn't looking.

Mrs. Carter hesitated but then nodded, stepping aside to allow him entry. She suddenly felt sick. When Amy had been found, there hadn't been sufficient proof implicating anyone specific. While they suspected her death was connected to Darren's near the Claver family mansion, they had never been able to prove it. "Let's go in there," she said, pointing to the salon to their right.

Faris approved her choice. If she passed out from shock, at least it would be in a room with a thick carpet instead of the tiled kitchen. He had seen this happen more than once — not in the Carter mansion, but in other homes when he came with bad news. Though he wasn't carrying bad news today, he knew his visit would stir deep emotional turmoil.

Mrs. Carter motioned him to sit in one of the cushioned armchairs opposite the couch. "Arthur!" she called.

After a minute of silence, Mr. Carter appeared in the doorway, his feet in country boots and his hands dirty from garden work. His face displayed the same range of emotions Faris had seen on his wife's face. Faris half-expected a punch to the face and wouldn't have been surprised; he might have even welcomed it as a form of penance. But Mr. Carter, despite his rugged appearance, restrained himself. "Good afternoon, Mr. Faris," he said politely, without a trace of the anger Faris anticipated. Ignoring his dirty boots and weathered hands covered in mud and bruises, he came in. He knew that if Faris was here, something serious was up, and it concerned Amy. He was about to hear it right now.

The Carters took their seats on the soft, green couch opposite Faris, looking at him expectantly. Though he had prepared for this moment, Faris suddenly felt uncertain about how to break the news. Thankfully, Mrs. Carter intervened.

"You mentioned a suspect in Amy's case," Mrs. Carter said, her voice trembling as she nervously fumbled with her hem and hands.

Faris nodded. "I did. We have confirmed that Mr. Claver and his soldiers were involved. Although we couldn't prove his connection to Amy's death back then, we have the evidence now." He paused, allowing the gravity of the news to settle. He knew they must have heard about Claver's suicide on the news, and Mr. Carter had had business dealings with him for many years.

Then Faris dropped the bomb. "There's something else I need to tell you. When I informed you that Amy was dead, I lied. She was alive seventeen years ago, and she is alive now." He watched as disbelief and shock washed over their faces. The Carters gasped in unison, staring at him in shock. He could only imagine what his words meant to them: the betrayal of a lie sustained for so long and the heart-wrenching realisation that they had missed half of their daughter's life. The looks they gave him were a storm of emotions they couldn't yet articulate. He was grateful he could see any blow coming and that the Carters apparently were not carrying blasters in their home.

"But you said... She was... How..." Mr. Carter was the first to speak. He grabbed his wife's hand, who seemed too stunned to speak. He looked at her, then back at Faris, and then at the empty space between them, his mind struggling to catch up.

"It's complicated," Faris began, his voice steady despite the tumult of emotions swirling within him. "Claver shot Darren; that much we knew back then without being able to prove it. I was the one who found Amy three days later, in the woods, running away from something. It was more of a coincidence — she bumped into me out there. She didn't speak a word and seemed totally shell-shocked."

As he watched tears start to brim in the Carters' eyes, he forced himself to continue, deliberately shutting out his emotions, even though his own words drew him back into the past. "We knew something was seriously wrong and took her into witness protection. I was personally responsible for her. It took her months to interact with people again in a socially acceptable way, and despite our efforts, we didn't get any closer to arresting Claver for murder."

When Faris paused to breathe, Mrs. Carter blazed at him, finally finding her voice. "So you lied to us. You lied to our faces. You told us our baby girl was dead, and you lied. Man, you've got some nerve coming here and telling us that."

Faris nodded, acknowledging the fury in her voice. "I know, and I'm sorry. It was necessary to protect her and to protect you. Claver would have come after all of you if she had returned home. He wasn't exactly known for taking prisoners."

"You can't know that!" Mr. Carter's hands were now trembling with a mixture of rage, shock, and exhilaration. Faris understood where this was coming from. Claver had been Carter's business partner for most of his career. They had even been friends, and Carter couldn't imagine his friend coming after him. Mrs. Carter was staring silently at Faris now, her eyes darkened with unleashed, unbridled fury. She clenched her jaw, likely imagining how far she might get if she tried to wring his neck.

"In fact, I do know," Faris began, his voice steady as he revealed the painful truth. "We intercepted transmissions and conversations in the days following Darren's death. It was clear Claver wanted Amy dead because she had witnessed two murders and managed to escape. She had run at the first chance, and she ran for days, and she ran into me. We needed to protect all of you, knowing you had business ties with Claver," he explained.

Mrs. Carter stood and walked toward Faris, her eyes blazing with anger as she loomed over him. "You looked me in the eyes and told me she was dead. You convinced me not to see her again because she was supposedly mutilated by animals. You lied to me. You asked me not to see her because she wasn't dead, and you didn't have a corpse I could say goodbye to."

Faris stood his ground, allowing her fury to wash over him. She had every right to be out of her mind with rage. He couldn't fathom the agony of losing a child, living without them for seventeen years, and then discovering they were alive despite everything. He met her gaze calmly, refusing to be provoked by her anger. There was nothing to forgive from his side of the table. "That's correct."

"There is a headstone in her name. We buried her coffin. We still visit it every week to place fresh flowers, so everyone knows we still miss her. That we haven't moved on from losing our only child." Mr. Carter's voice was flat, like he was reciting a grocery list, but Faris could see the pain in his eyes. Mr. Carter clenched his jaw, his fists trembling. He looked like he might rip his boot off and hurl it at Faris's face at any moment.

"I know. I'm sorry," Faris said, his voice heavy with remorse. There was nothing more he could say that would lessen their pain or make up for the years of deception.

Mrs. Carter moved back to the couch, her eyes never leaving Faris. She shot the only question that mattered to her. "Where is she?"

"Mrs. Carter... You should know..." Faris tried to stall. He needed a little more time to prepare them for the state their daughter was in now. He couldn't confront them with the fact that Manley had been kidnapped by Claver's son and injured badly in the process. But Mrs. Carter wasn't giving him much choice.

"WHERE IS SHE?" Her voice thundered through the room, startling even her husband with its volume and determination.

Faris realised he had no more room to manoeuvre. He had to get it over with. "She's outside, in the car I came in. She'll be here in a moment. But," he added quickly as Mrs. Carter began to rise from her seat, "she's recently been in trouble, and she is still healing from a couple of injuries. I'm telling you this, so you're not too shocked. She still has some bruises on her face, and her arm is in a sling because she broke a few bones." He paused, watching as the Carters looked at each other, their faces showing stunned expressions. "We'll explain everything later." There was a few moments of silence, broken only by the loud ticking of the grandfather clock at the other end of the room. Finally, the spell broke.

"Can... Can we see her? We'd really like to see her," Mr. Carter said quietly, holding his wife's hand again.

Faris nodded. "Of course. I'll go get her." Without waiting for a reply, he left his seat, walked through the hall, and stepped out of the house. He knocked gently on the tinted car window where Manley was sitting. "Now might be a good time as any. They've asked for you."

Inside the car, Manley blinked, her heart suddenly pounding in her chest. She had waited for this day for 17 years. So many days and nights she had imagined meeting her parents again. So many nights she had cried herself to sleep in those first few years, imagining the day she would lie in her mother's arms again, holding her father's hands. Faris had made it possible now. The Claver family was gone; Blake had killed the last one. No Claver would ever come after her or her family now. Faris had told her parents what they needed to know for now. They would have more questions, she was sure of that. Seventeen years needed to be explained, especially how she was ripped from her former life and turned into ISA top agent Dana Manley.

She shivered slightly, not daring to look at Blake. She knew he would encourage her to get out of the car, to go and confront the one part of her past that she could not live without. She also knew that she would have to explain him, and that her parents might compare him to Darren. They had not agreed to her relationship with Darren back then, and they might not agree to their long-lost daughter running off with a lawyer she had just met, either.

She took a few deep breaths, trying to calm herself. It was futile. She felt tears brimming in her eyes, and she knew they were going to fall. There were so many emotions she felt at once. She longed to see them as she had never longed to see anybody. She dreaded seeing them as she had never dreaded seeing anybody. And she loved the idea of seeing them again as she had never loved seeing anybody else. How could she ever explain? How could they ever understand? Manley bit her lip. She had to do something. She gathered up all the strength and determination she still had left and pushed the car door open in one swift motion.

The sunlight was blinding as she stepped out, illuminating her like a spotlight on a stage. The cool breeze ruffled her hair, and she took a moment to steady herself. Blake was beside her in an instant, his presence a comforting anchor. He didn't say a word, but his hand on her back was all the support she needed.

The neighbourhood still bore the familiar semblance of seventeen years past, save for the trees in the gardens and along the road, which had towered with time. She was transported back to the moment outside Claver's mansion when she first noticed how the trees on her rescue route had grown, marking the passage of years. The same transformation had, unsurprisingly, occurred around her childhood home. Vividly, she recalled the last time she had left this house, standing silent and steadfast against the majestic backdrop of the mountains. Claver's mansion lingered somewhere in those distant hills. Her parents' house, constructed of dark red brick, had once been her sanctuary until the day she stormed out, seventeen years ago. It was a fateful day, marked by a fierce argument with her mother. She had tried, in vain, to make her understand why she had to marry Darren immediately, and not wait for a year or two. In hindsight, the argument seemed trivial compared to the monumental events that unfolded later that day. She remembered vividly what she wore: a light white shirt paired with a green skirt, an outfit that revealed more than it concealed. The thought of letting her own daughter, should she ever have one, leave the house dressed like that was unimaginable to her. But back then, she had been a headstrong teenager, brimming with attitude and a very scant understanding of the vast world around her.

Manley stood, her feet heavy with the weight of memories, and took a few tentative steps towards her parents' house. Her gaze remained fixed ahead, though she was acutely aware of Blake stepping out of the car and Faris trailing behind her. She followed the narrow footpath that led to the front door, each step feeling like a journey through time. As she reached the threshold, she hesitated, knowing that crossing it would be a point of no return. She knew all too well what awaited her on the other side of that door. The surge of emotions, the flood of memories, and the reunion with her parents would be overwhelming for them all. With a deep breath, she steeled herself for what was to come.

Faris and Blake refrained from hurrying her along. They knew it would be futile to try. They had an idea of the difficulty Manley faced, returning to a life she had believed lost for seventeen long years, though none could truly comprehend the turmoil within her at this precise moment. None of them had walked in her shoes, not now, not seventeen years ago. Faris, however, was confident she would not retreat from the challenge ahead, no matter how much time she needed to summon her resolve. He had witnessed her confront daunting tasks before, and each time, she had accomplished what was necessary.

He remembered vividly when she had been tasked with eliminating a pirate lord. She had found the man dining with his family, surrounded by six children of various ages, his wife and three sisters. She had to pose as a business associate sent by an ally and bide her time until she caught him alone. She had hesitated, unwilling to execute the deed in front of his wife and children. Even so, the horror of her actions were still horrendous when they discovered his lifeless body moments after she had slipped away. Today, Manley would once again do what had to be done.

Her decision came quicker than anticipated. After a minute or so, she drew a deep breath and stepped inside. The layout of the house was still so familiar, each detail etched in her memory. Without hesitation, she walked into the salon on her right, the very room where her parents had once entertained visitors like Faris. Her mother and father sat on the couch, holding hands, their expressions haunted as if they had seen a ghost. They did not look quite as she remembered. Her mother's hair had turned white, and she wore it a lot shorter than before. Her father appeared to have aged far more than the seventeen years that had passed. While he was cleanly shaven, the lines in his face were so much deeper than she remembered him. His skin seemed to be thinner, as was his whole frame. They were dressed casually — her mother in a buttoned green dress that accentuated her eyes, her father in rugged pants and working boots, suggesting he had just come in from the garden.

Arthur and Anne Carter stared at the woman who had just entered their salon. Her hair, tied in a messy bun, was a striking red, though the dye had begun to grow out, revealing nearly an inch of auburn roots that spoke of neglect and urgency for a proper cut. Her face bore the faint remnants of deep bruises that had almost healed. Her left arm was in a sling, and a dark blue wool coat was draped over it with careful precision. Her feet were clad in black, flat leather ballerinas, and she wore a knee-length dark blue dress with small sleeves that perfectly complemented her eyes and slender figure. But it was her eyes that struck them most—the same eyes their little girl once had. Those blue eyes, which had often looked at them with wonder and, at times, hatred, now seemed both resolute and uncertain.

For a few moments, no one moved. Time appeared to stand still in this moment, the moment Amy Carter returned home as Dana Manley. Anne and Arthur felt overwhelmed with memories of the day Amy hadn't returned from her afternoon with Darren. They remembered the frantic calls to the police the following day when there was still no sign of their beloved daughter. They recalled the police inquiries about Claver, the devastating news that there had been an incident at the Claver mansion, that Darren had been killed, and Amy was nowhere to be found. The fear that had grown with each passing day, week, and month was seared into their memories. They also remembered Faris' visits. He had told them he was assigned to the case, searching for her, though they now understood he had been there to prepare them for the worst. And now, here she was. Despite the grown-up appearance, the dyed hair, and the different clothes, there was no doubt this was their long-lost daughter.

Anne Carter was the first to regain her composure. She jumped up, crossed the room, and enveloped her daughter in a gentle embrace, mindful of the injured arm. Whatever had happened, and she was determined to find out, she wouldn't add to the pain her daughter had clearly endured. The accumulated tension of years and moments drained from her body, and she began to sob. Amy was back. The child she had believed dead for nearly seventeen years stood in their salon, alive and almost well. Arthur Carter took a few seconds longer to rise from the sofa, seemingly pulling himself out of the avalanche of memories that had crashed upon him. He quietly joined his wife and daughter in their embrace, his sobs mingling with theirs. Silently, he wrapped his arms around them, holding them close.

Faris and Blake could only watch from the hall. They stood at the foot of the stairs, feeling slightly out of place in this intimate tableau. They were spectators in a drama that required no audience. Faris placed a gentle hand on Blake's shoulder and silently gestured toward the back of the house, where he knew the kitchen was located. Blake nodded, closed the entrance door quietly, and walked to the back. Faris followed, the click of the door shutting behind him audible louder than usual in the charged silence of the house.

In the kitchen, Faris scanned the countertops until his eyes landed on an expensive coffee machine nestled in the corner by a window overlooking the meticulously tended garden. "Coffee?" he asked Blake, already moving to inspect the machine.

Blake nodded. "Yes, please. Although I wouldn't refuse a really stiff drink, either."

Faris understood the sentiment, but they needed to stay sharp. He wasn't expecting trouble today, but his years of leading ISA had taught him to always be prepared. He hadn't anticipated that his very first mission would go so disastrously wrong, and even now, seventeen years later, he was still dealing with the fallout. He began preparing the coffee, the familiar motions grounding him amidst the chaos of emotions and memories. This was getting to him a lot more than he had anticipated. As the rich aroma of freshly brewed coffee filled the kitchen, Faris contemplated the hours ahead, uncertain what he would discuss with the lawyer to fill the time.

Blake, sensing his thoughts, broke the silence. "Faris, how did we get here? And I'm not talking about the car outside," Blake asked quietly.

Faris shrugged and placed a large mug of steaming black coffee in front of Blake. The delicious aroma was a lot better than the bitter, brown liquid they had often endured in spaceports and other far-flung locales. "You fell in love. It happens," Faris said simply. After a few contemplative moments, he added, "And there's a couple of really fucked-up people with sick minds in this part of the galaxy." He carefully took a sip of the hot beverage.

"You tell me. It'd be interesting to compare notes, I guess," Blake said. He gripped his mug firmly and met Faris's gaze with unwavering intensity. "Have you?"

Faris returned the look calmly. He had known this moment would come eventually. Blake's question was inevitable, especially after witnessing the way Faris had behaved around Manley, the worry etched on his face, the subtle touches that spoke volumes. Now that Blake was aware of their shared history, it was natural for him to wonder if there had ever been anything romantic between them. "I might have, back then, yes. I wasn't sure what I felt. I was hardly out of my teens myself. And I'm still not sure today about back then. But today, I can tell you that I love her like the sister I never had—nothing more."

He paused, taking another sip of his coffee, letting the warmth ground him before he continued. "There was a moment, fifteen or sixteen years ago, when things could have gone either way. She came into my office after work, and we chatted and had a drink. It was one of those moments you see in movies. There was a weird tension in the air, and I'd be lying if I said I didn't think about kissing her. She must have sensed something because she left, and it's never felt like that again. I care about her deeply, yes. And I guess I always will. But not the way you do."

Faris held Blake's gaze, his words carrying the weight of long-buried truths. This was as close to a confession as he would ever come. It wasn't the whole truth because, for a time, he had wished that things had gone differently in his office that day. But they hadn't, and since then, he had never seen Manley with the same man more than twice. She had never been in a relationship worthy of the name since joining ISA, at least not to his knowledge. If she had confided in anyone about a man she liked, it would have been him.

Blake looked down at his coffee, absorbing the revelation. "Thank you. I appreciate your honesty." His posture relaxed slightly, and he seemed lost in his thoughts.

"You're welcome," Faris replied, his own gaze dropping to his mug. The kitchen was filled with the aroma of coffee and the joined silence of understanding.

Both men remained silent for a while, each lost in contemplation. Blake wondered how two people could be as close as Faris and Manley had been for years without ever crossing the line into romance. He had crossed that line the night he met Manley and several times since. Perhaps that was something unique to their circumstances, a rare and intense connection that defied his usual experiences. He had picked up women for easy nights on occasion, seen some a few times before retreating from anything resembling serious dating. But whatever had transpired the day he met Manley had irrevocably changed both their lives.

Faris, on the other hand, reflected on the impending change in his life. Things would never go back to the seamless cooperation he and Manley had enjoyed for so long — working together to take down the scum of society, understanding each other without words. She was leaving, clearly headed for a life with Blake, something she had not seen coming. Despite the physical and psychological trauma she had recently endured, she seemed content with him. That would have to be enough for Faris, too. She deserved happiness more than anyone he knew, even if it meant they would be working on opposite sides of the law whenever they met again.

The only sound in the salon on the other side of the wall was the quiet sobbing. Manley felt rooted to the spot, a strange mix of feeling out of place and finally at home at the same time. How she had longed for this day. Her gaze was fixed on the wall before her, but she could hardly see through the tears. Her sobs blended with the cries of her parents. Her mother had wrapped her arms around her carefully, mindful of the arm in the sling, while her father held her tightly from behind, one arm draped around her mother in a comforting embrace.

Time seemed to stand still. None of them could later say how long they stood like that. The shadows cast by the furniture had shifted noticeably by the time Anne Carter finally released her daughter. She took Manley's hand and gently guided her to the sofa where she had been sitting earlier. Her father sank into the lounging chair beside her, and her mother slid down to the floor, wrapping her arms around

Manley's legs and resting her head in her daughter's lap.

It was Anne who found her voice first, and it quivered with emotion. "Where have you been, young lady?" she asked quietly, her attempt at levity bringing a weak smile to Manley's lips.

At least she knew where she had inherited her sense of humour. She wanted to say "I'm sorry," but her voice felt foreign to her, small, unsure. She cleared her throat loudly and whispered, "I'm so, so sorry, Mom..." Then she turned to her father and repeated the phrase. She knew no words could ever make up for what they had gone through. They had lost their only child, grieved her, buried her in their hearts for so long. Now she was here, trying to explain that it had all been for their own good. Could any amount of explaining truly recap the past seventeen years in a way that would allow them to forgive?

Arthur Carter, a man of high logic and steely composure, took Manley's hand and whispered, "What happened? Talk me through it."

His eyes were brimming with tears, and Manley struggled to remember if she had ever seen him cry before. The phrase was hauntingly familiar, echoing the recent past. Back at ISA's hospital wing, Faris had asked her to recount the details of her kidnapping. Then, a concise answer had sufficed for the events of those horrible days. But putting the last 17 years in a coherent narrative seemed an insurmountable task. She was momentarily transported back to the time she had first run into Faris, her mind then a jumble of shock and unanswered questions. Softly clearing her throat, she met her father's gaze. "This isn't going to be easy."

"I know," he said, his voice trembling as he nodded for her to continue.

Manley took a determined breath and started. "That day, Darren and I witnessed two men being killed in Claver's mansion. I managed to get away and ran. Three days later, I ran into Faris." Her parents exchanged anxious glances, but she pressed on. "He took me to ISA headquarters. I was traumatised, and they put me into witness protection. The investigation didn't lead anywhere, so ISA decided to have me declared dead, hoping it would take you off Claver's target list."

She drew quick breaths, gathering her strength. "A year later, I joined ISA and became an agent. That's what I've been doing for the past 16 years until recently. I was just about to change my job when I got kidnapped on Nergal B." She prayed silently that her parents wouldn't press for details about her previous job or her intended future. That was a conversation she was not ready to have. "My friends found and rescued me, and now that all the Clavers are dead, there's no more reason for witness protection."

Her parents listened intently, their expressions a mix of shock, pain, and a flicker of understanding. Manley knew her brief recounting didn't do justice to the years she had lived through. Seventeen years deserved more than the few sentences she had used to summarize her life.

"What happened to your arm? And your face?" Anne Carter's voice quivered, her eyes searching her daughter's expression for answers. The torrent of information Manley had just shared swirled in her mind, too much to process all at once. But above all, Anne needed to know that her daughter was okay, or at least on the path to recovery. Amy looked like she had been through hell, and the sight tore at her heart.

Manley had anticipated this question. She had braced herself for it. There was no need to delve into all the gruesome details of her time at Claver's mansion. She would share them later, if necessary. For now, a summary would suffice. "While I was in captivity, I tried to escape. Let's just say my captors didn't appreciate my attempt. They outnumbered me. On a good day, I could have fought my way out without so much as a scratch." She could see tears appear again in her mother's eyes while she spoke. She wished she could spare her parents the unimaginable, searing pain of imagining some villains beating up their daughter, but there was just no way. Her own eyes began to mist up again, and her heart ached.

Anne Carter nodded tearfully, the mental images of her daughter being beaten causing her almost physical pain. She was still struggling to reconcile the face of the teenager she had known with the woman sitting before her. "I see." She paused to gather her strength, then asked, "Is it going to heal? Does it hurt much?"

Manley nodded. "It's healing. I've come a long way. Faris had me checked out at the ISA hospital for a week. I'm closely monitored, under medication, and in no pain. I've already spent four weeks at a beach house, resting with Blake." She waited. She knew her parents would ask about him soon enough.

"Blake?" Her father asked, a mix of curiosity and protectiveness in his voice. "Who's he?"

Oh my, here we go, Manley thought, steeling herself. "I met him on my holiday on Nergal B. We really hit it off, and I like him a lot. He went looking for me after I was kidnapped. My friends joined him, and they found me together. So, this isn't just a one-time thing."

She hoped that they would keep in mind that she was a grown-up, despite their memories of a sullen teenager from seventeen years ago. She could not have a discussion about how you didn't jump into being with someone you barely knew now.

Her father scrutinised her, noticing the spark of joy that lit her eyes when she spoke about Blake. It made him happy, but he also needed to reconcile the fact that his little girl was now a grown woman with desires and decisions beyond his control. He hesitated, then said, "I see." After a brief pause, he added, "Is he good to you? Is he for real?"

Manley nodded with a small, reassuring smile. "He is. You'll meet him later; he came along today. I'm not sure where he is right now, but he'll hang around until we go back to ISA."

"So you'll be leaving again," Anne Carter stated quietly. Letting her baby girl go again today would require all her willpower, now that she finally had her back.

With a deep breath, Manley answered, "Yes. But only for today. I will be back tomorrow. That is, if you'll have me."

"If we'll have you? Are you crazy?" Her mother jumped up, shouting, and sat beside her on the sofa, clutching her hand tightly. "Of course, we'll have you!

You could stay up in your room if you wanted, but I understand if you need to get used to the idea." Though Anne Carter would have liked nothing better than to tuck Amy in upstairs in her old teenage room, which was practically untouched apart from the occasional dusting, she figured her daughter wouldn't appreciate being held in a confined space again so soon.

Manley nodded, her throat tightening with emotion. "We'll see about that in a little while." She swallowed hard and added, "Could we have a drink? My throat feels so dry."

Immediately, her mother jumped up, eager to help. "I'll go get you something." She took the shortcut at the back of the room. When she opened the kitchen door, she was surprised to see Faris sitting there with another man, steaming coffee mugs in their hands. She couldn't help but remark sarcastically, "I see you've made yourselves at home."

The man opposite Faris jumped to his feet, setting his mug down with a soft clink before extending his hand with a warm smile. "Mrs. Carter, I'm Michael Blake. Your daughter and I..." His voice faltered briefly, searching for the right words. "We met during her holiday, and I've grown quite fond of her. I'm truly sorry for everything you're going through."

Anne Carter regarded him, a hint of amusement twinkling in her eyes, though she maintained her composure. "Thank you," she replied, clasping his hand briefly in a formal shake. "Now, if you'll excuse me, I'll fetch something for her to drink." She deftly poured a glass of water, balancing it in her right hand while closing the tap with her left. Without another word, she gracefully exited the kitchen. She delivered the glass to Amy and settled back onto the sofa. "Your... Blake is in the kitchen with Faris," she informed her daughter calmly.

Manley's face lit up, and she set the empty glass down, declaring, "I'll be right back," as she practically ran towards the kitchen.

And while her parents remained sitting in the salon, looking at each other in a new bout of confusion, Manley felt an overwhelming urge to hug both Blake and Faris for their unwavering support in facing her past. She could have chosen to escape, to leave her old life behind without looking back, and everyone would have understood. Instead, Faris and Blake had stood by her, encouraging her to return. Pushing through the swinging kitchen door, Manley found Blake still standing, his earlier encounter with her mother lingering in the air. Faris rose swiftly as he noticed her, and without hesitation, she hurried towards Blake, her steps resolute and focused. He enveloped her in a wordless embrace, sheltering her from the world, and she closed her eyes, revelling in the comfort of his arms.

Blake felt her melt against him, her breath ragged as though she had just completed a marathon. He could sense the storm of emotions raging within her as she confronted her past with her parents. Over the past weeks, he had witnessed her vulnerabilities, anticipating that today, emotions would overflow, perhaps repeatedly. Supporting her firmly with his arms, he guided her to a nearby chair and settled her onto his lap for comfort. She wrapped her right arm around him silently, resting her head against his shoulder.

Across the table, Faris observed the scene. He knew well the emotional turmoil Manley was navigating. She sought confort in Blake, finding safety and reassurance in his presence. Manley appeared utterly drained, her body limp in Blake's embrace, her coat slipping from her shoulders. Faris gently retrieved it, draping it over a chair back. In a soft voice, he murmured, "I'll give you two some space. I'll wait outside in the car."

Blake nodded gratefully, acknowledging the unspoken support Faris offered by stepping away. Just as Faris turned to leave, Manley's weak voice stopped. "Don't," she whispered, lifting her head from Blake's shoulder to meet Faris's gaze with weary eyes. "Thank you for making this possible. Thank you for taking the blows." She wondered what her mother had said to Faris; perhaps she would ask him another time. With a shaky motion, she reached out to Faris, who approached her swiftly, and rose to embrace him unsteadily.

Faris instinctively enclosed her in a protective embrace, making sure he held her firmly and tenderly. "You're welcome. It was something I could finally do," he murmured, knowing she understood the depth of his words. So many times back then, she had asked him to her parents again, and every time he had had to say no. He was so glad that he could grant her this wish now. Leaning in, he rested his head gently atop hers, pressing a soft kiss onto her hair.

Blake observed the exchange with a momentous pang of jealousy tightening his chest. The familiarity in the way Faris held her, and how she leaned into him, unsettled him despite earlier assurances about their relationship. Faris's tender gesture of kissing her hair felt like a poignant reminder of their history together. Though Faris held her securely around the waist, steadying her, it was clear she had sought him out for support. And yet, she had come running to him, not to Faris. She had come to him, looking for support. Blake repeated this realisation in his mind as he watched her break away from Faris's embrace.

Anticipating her need, Blake moved swiftly behind her, guiding her back to the chair where they had been seated moments ago. Meanwhile, Faris lingered at the kitchen door, turning back to say softly, "I'll wait outside. Take your time." With those words, he departed, leaving a brief silence in his wake.

For a heartbeat, the kitchen remained still until the quiet was interrupted by the arrival of Manley's parents from the salon.

"You're still here," her mother remarked, her voice carrying a mixture of surprise and curiosity.

Manley nodded quietly, her body still and her gaze lowered. "I'm sorry," she murmured, feeling the weight of their unspoken expectations and her own tumultuous emotions. Her apology hung in the air, adding to the complexities of family dynamics and their unresolved past.

Mrs. Carter settled onto the chair beside Blake, her eyes softening as she observed the way he cradled her daughter with such tenderness. "We were just worried about you. But you're in very good hands, I can see that."

It was evident that he shared her own concern and worry, and she found a bit of peace in seeing Amy in his caring embrace. This day had been overwhelming beyond measure. When Faris had appeared at her doorstep, she had been ready to shut him out, weary of more devastating news. Yet, against all odds, he had brought a glimmer of hope after seventeen long years — revealing not only who was responsible for Amy's supposed death but also that she was alive and now here in their kitchen, embraced by a stranger who seemed to offer her comfort.

Anne Carter couldn't shake the surreal feeling of seeing her grown daughter, who had been estranged for so long, now finding comfort in the arms of someone new. The reasons for their separation, supposedly for their safety, still seemed incomprehensible to her. It would take time to fully grasp the enormity of those lost years and the pain they had all lived with.

Offering Amy a weak smile, she suggested gently, "Would you like some fresh air? Out in the garden?"

Manley smiled and nodded. "That sounds nice."

"I think I have some cookies somewhere..." Anne began to fuss around the kitchen, her voice trailing off uncertainly. "And I'll make us some tea. And coffee. Who wants coffee?" Her nervous energy betrayed her uncertainty about what to do next.

Her husband intervened, turning her around with a gentle touch. "You go outside. I'll get the drinks." With a subtle nudge, he guided mother and daughter out of the kitchen.

Manley, her mother, and Blake returned to the salon, where Anne opened the patio doors leading to the garden terrace. A cosy seating area surrounded a glass table, inviting them to relax. Anne gestured for Manley and Blake to take a seat. "Have a seat, I'll be right back." She disappeared back inside to assist her husband with the coffee tray.

Returning with him a moment later, Anne set the tray down on the table and inquired, "Tea or coffee, Amy?"

Manley didn't react, she was still looking at the garden in deep thought.

"Amy?" Mrs. Carter looked genuinely puzzled.

Seeing her confusion, Blake interrupted gently, coming to Amy's aid. "Mrs. Carter, do you remember when Faris mentioned the witness protection program?"

Anne Carter nodded slowly, a flicker of realization crossing her features as she started to connect the dots.

"She had to assume a new identity," Blake continued, his voice steady. "She's been using the name Dana Manley all these years."

Anne and Arthur Carter exchanged a meaningful glance, silently communicating thoughts that Blake could only guess at. He reached out, touching Manley's arm to draw her attention back to the present. She seemed momentarily lost in thought, as if awakening from a daydream. "I just explained about the name," Blake added softly, his eyes meeting hers with warmth. "They didn't know."

Manley mirrored her parents' earlier confusion. "What name?"

"The Manley name you've been using for seventeen years," Blake clarified with a gentle smile directed at her. He turned to the Carters, his smile widening slightly. "I guess Faris forgot to mention that."

The Carters nodded in unison, their expressions softening with understanding. "He did," Mrs. Carter acknowledged, her voice tinged with empathy. "But it makes sense that she couldn't keep her original name, doesn't it?"

Feeling suddenly weary, Manley reached for a cup of coffee with her uninjured hand, mindful of the arm in the sling. "At least I got to choose it myself," she murmured, her voice carrying a mixture of resignation and a hint of bitterness. "Faris had ISA create a whole backstory for my alias. I had to memorise every detail."

Mrs. Carter nodded in sympathy and moved to sit in the chair beside her daughter. Blake promptly vacated the seat on the other side, silently offering it to Mr. Carter. After all, Blake would be taking Manley home later, making sure she was cared for throughout the day. Or night. Or both. He bit his lip to hide a grin that was trying to find his face.

"Faris kept me out of official business. My name only appeared in internal documents; I never attended formal occasions for years. That's how I remained undetected for so long," Manley explained, her voice tinged with a mixture of relief and apprehension. She wasn't entirely sure why she was telling her parents these details now, but perhaps it was a tactic to sidestep the many questions she knew they must have had.

"No one outside the agency knew I still existed. Until Landon Claver somehow found out. He—" Manley began, only to be interrupted by her mother's sudden realisation.

"Landon Claver? Didn't you go to school with him?" Mrs. Carter's eyes widened with recognition, piecing together the fragments of memory.

Manley closed her eyes briefly, steeling herself against the flood of memories and emotions that threatened to overwhelm her. When she met her mother's gaze again, her expression was guarded but resigned. "Yes, I did. He was Darren's best friend."

"What did he do?" Anne Carter's tone turned investigative, her familiar determination evident on her face.

Manley knew she was treading on dangerous ground. The information she held was classified, and revealing more could jeopardise not just herself but others as well. "You must have heard about the incidents involving Senator Ortiz and Claver Sr. a few weeks ago," she replied carefully, taking a sip from the expertly brewed coffee in front of her. Oh, the joy of real coffee, made expertly by her father.

Arthur Carter nodded solemnly, his expression reflecting genuine sympathy. "It's terrible that he felt he had no other choice but to take his own life."

"I don't think you even know the half of it," Manley began, catching herself before revealing too much. She hesitated, realising her father couldn't possibly comprehend the extent of Claver's involvement in the stealthy activities that had remained hidden from public view for so long. Much of it had been deliberately kept out of the media, for reasons that were painfully clear to her.

But her words hung in the air, landing heavily on her parents' ears. "How would you know anything about that?" her father demanded, a hint of anger showing on his face.

Manley and Blake shared a silent exchange, their eyes meeting briefly in understanding, though it only served to deepen her parents' confusion. "Claver had more secrets than you could imagine," Manley continued carefully, choosing her words with deliberate caution. "We had gathered enough evidence to corner him, but instead of facing justice, he chose to end his own life."

There was a brief pause as Manley assessed her parents' reactions, gauging how much more she could disclose without risking their emotional well-being. When they remained silent, she felt compelled to elaborate. "I headed the team that found him dead. Landon thought I had something to do with his death. But I didn't." She admitted that it had to be hard for her parents to find another angle on Claver than that of the long-term business partner and friend that her father had lost.

She could see the turmoil brewing in her mother's eyes, a storm of emotions swirling beneath the surface. "You were involved in that dreadful affair?" her mother asked, looking terrified. A million things seemed to go on in her mind at the same time.

Manley chose to simplify her response, aware that the full truth could overwhelm them. "Sort of. It was an ISA investigation," she explained, omitting her leadership role in the operation alongside Faris and Owen. Some details were best left unsaid, especially when they involved the complexities of covert operations and the toll they took on those involved.

Anne and Arthur Carter struggled to grasp the magnitude of the events that had unfolded before their daughter's return. "You investigated Kirk? And Landon kidnapped you because he thought you killed his father?" Anne asked, her disbelief etched into her frown.

"In a nutshell," Manley replied wearily, feeling the weight of the day's revelations pressing down on her. She took a deep breath, trying to steady herself.

"Listen, I don't think we should delve into all of the difficult details today. There will be plenty of time for that," she suggested gently, hoping to spare her parents and herself further distress.

Her parents exchanged a guilty glance, realising they had conjured up painful memories and complex emotions. They nodded in agreement, silently acknowledging the need for a gradual unpacking of the past.

An hour later, as the sun began to dip below the horizon, Manley and Blake prepared to leave the Carter's house. Blake gently insisted it was time to depart, noticing the strain in Manley's posture, her trouble sitting upright and the tension in her neck, evidence of the physical toll the day had taken on her. They promised to return the following day to continue their conversations.

Manley could see the struggle in her parents' eyes as they reluctantly bid her farewell for the night. She understood their reluctance to let her go, but she couldn't stay any longer. Exhaustion weighed her down after the emotional roller-coaster of the day. Faris had waited patiently in the car throughout their visit, and now he chauffeured them back to Manley's flat on the other side of the city. Manley managed to make it inside on her own feet, though her steps felt heavier than usual. Once inside, she leant against the wall, sliding down until she sat on the floor, her arms wrapped tightly around her knees.

"I can't do this again tomorrow," she whispered softly, her head resting sideways against her knees. The pain her parents felt seemed to add to her own.

Blake settled down beside her, his arm instinctively finding its place around her back. "You can do this.

And you will," he murmured softly, his voice a steady reassurance in the quiet of her flat. "You've come so far. Turning away now would be the hardest thing for you."

Manley felt his words resonate deep within her. This journey, fraught with pain and revelation, held the promise of healing—for herself and for her parents. With a determined effort, she gently pushed herself upright, gently warding off Blake's supportive gesture. "I'm okay. I'll go take a shower," she insisted, needing a moment of solitude to collect her thoughts.

Blake, who was an attentive observer, knew by now that this was a way of coping with stress for her. "I'll see if I can order us some food. You must be hungry," he suggested, knowing her tendency to downplay her needs.

Manley managed a weak smile. "Maybe a little." And since she was the queen of understatement, and he knew it, she was sure that he would order a meal that could feed at least a party of four. He did not disappoint her. As she indulged in a lengthy shower, letting the warm water wash away the remnants of the day's tension, Blake took care of their meal. By the time she emerged, feeling refreshed and renewed, the aroma of pizza, steak, pasta, and an assortment of desserts greeted her. Blake had thoughtfully laid out the meal on the bed, creating a makeshift dining experience in the comfort of her bedroom. He even took care of cleaning up afterward, leaving her to relax and unwind.

As the last rays of sunlight filtered through the windows, casting a warm glow over the room, Manley and Blake finally settled into bed. Blake wrapped his arms around her gently, holding her close as they both fell asleep.

Over the next week, Manley and Blake continued their daily visits to her parents' house, gradually unravelling the narrative of Manley's life that had been hidden for seventeen years. She recounted her journey into ISA, carefully leaving out the more gruesome details that she knew her parents would find too distressing. She shared stories of her training, how Faris had discovered her talent during shooting practice, and the defining moments alongside Owen in uncovering the conspiracy involving Kirk Claver and Gavin Ortiz. Despite the shock of learning about their old friend's criminal activities, Anne and Arthur Carter believed their daughter's account, but still struggling with the newfound complexities of her life.

After another intense lunch filled with revelations and cautious questioning, Manley and her mother went outside for a breath of fresh air. Left alone in the kitchen, Blake couldn't shake the feeling that he had suddenly changes places into a scene from a suspenseful movie. The quiet intensity in Arthur Carter's gaze as he studied Blake hinted at an impending conversation, one that Blake sensed would be important. Sure enough, Arthur motioned for Blake to take a seat and handed him a glass of what appeared to be whiskey. Blake accepted it graciously, taking a small sip and placing it back on the table, hoping it would suffice to show appreciation without committing to drinking it all. He met Arthur's gaze, deciding it was better to approach the situation head-on rather than defensively. "What's on your mind?"

Blake asked, keeping his voice steady despite the tension in the room.

Arthur Carter gave him a measured look, acknowledging Blake's directness with a nod. "Alright, young man. I never thought I'd be having this conversation, but here it is. What is it with you and her?"

Blake held Arthur Carter's gaze steadily, understanding the weight of the conversation they were having. It was a rare moment for him, having never before found himself in a situation where he needed to discuss his intentions with a woman's parents. He could sense Arthur's concern, a mixture of protective fatherly instincts and a genuine desire to make his daughter was happy and safe.

"If you mean what my intentions with her are..." Blake began, choosing his words carefully. He saw Arthur nod, his expression tinged with a hint of awkwardness. "My intentions are sincere. I want to spend the rest of my life with her, if she'll have me," he declared earnestly. He paused, allowing his words to sink in. He watched as Arthur's scepticism softened into a semblance of approval. "Why else would I go and chase her all over the sector?" he added with a hint of humour, hoping to lighten the mood while making his point clear.

Arthur took a moment, contemplating Blake's words as he stared into his glass. "You have a point." He looked down at his own glass and spoke on quietly and with paternal concern. "It's been a while since I've done this. The last man who wanted her is dead, and she died for us, then. I know it won't happen again like this but I... I just want to know she'll..." His voice trailed off.

Blake listened attentively, sensing Arthur's worry and the importance of his daughter's happiness to him. "She won't disappear again," Blake reassured him firmly. "I'll make sure of that. She deserves a life free from danger and uncertainty. We'll come back here, time and again."

Arthur's concern shifted, manifesting in a more direct question. "How do I know you won't leave her?" he asked.

The question hung in the air, and Blake was prepared for it. He understood Arthur's need for reassurance, especially after everything Manley had been through. "I pursued her from the moment I met her," Blake explained. "I didn't chase her down out of curiosity or whimsy. I knew she was someone special, someone I couldn't let slip away. I'm not letting her go, ever," he affirmed, leaving Arthur no room for doubt, making it very clear that he wasn't just messing around with his daughter. It hit him. Lannister had been right, he was going to spend the rest of his life with her.

Arthur nodded thoughtfully, admitting to himself that Blake's words made a lot of sense. "But you hardly know her," he challenged, a hint of scepticism still lingering. He had already seen how his beloved daughter and Blake doted on each other, no more proof was needed, actually. Yet Blake didn't seem thrown off by the question.

Blake shook his head. "Not true. Yes, we hit it off on the physical level at first. We clicked. And then we spent those four weeks at the beach house. We didn't have much else to do except talk and talk because she was still healing. I think I know her better than my own life now." It wasn't just knowing her favourite foods or her favourite music—it was about understanding the scars she carries, the resilience that defined her. There were not enough words in the universe to explain this to her father. He went out on a limb. "Yes, I've slept with your daughter before getting to know her entirely. Several times, and we both enjoyed it very much. But putting things this way round doesn't make them wrong." He wasn't quite sure if it was clever to refer to their sex life so openly with her father, but he felt he was running out of options here.

Arthur's expression broke into a big, friendly smile. "It's okay, Michael. I couldn't be a dad for 17 years, I think I have to do some catching up. And please", he added, "please don't ever talk to me about what you're doing in the bedroom again. I might have to punch you. My imagination can do without the specifics. She's still my little girl."

For a split-second Blake wondered if he should tell the man that what he didn't want to hear about didn't only take place in the bedroom, but he thought better of it. Instead, he just replied with a smile, "Understood, Sir." It was probably for the best if Anne and Arthur didn't know too much about the things Manley and Blake did when they were alone.

Later on that same day, they had all retreated to the salon as the air outside was cooling down. And while they were chatting over coffee, Manley sat back on the sofa, her mind swirling with thoughts and emotions. Each new detail and disclosure added layers to her already complex story for her parents. There was so much going through her head. The things her parents told her. The things Blake told them about himself, about her. The things she needed to say, today or some other time. She sighed softly, feeling the exhaustion settle in again. Right now, it all felt too much. But she knew that the feeling would recede with a good night's rest.

Without a word, she rose from the sofa, her eyes fixed on the patio door leading outside. The cool afternoon air brushed against her skin as she stepped onto the terrace, seeking the quiet of the garden. An image had formed at the back of her mind, and she wasn't sure how it ran along with the life she had been leading, or the things she had gone through these past few weeks, or the plans she had recently made for the years to come. She had seen a woman with auburn hair wearing a blue summer dress made of very light fabric, standing behind a garden swing and pushing a little girl with golden curls up until she squealed with glee. A man with blond hair was sitting on a picnic blanket, his back to her, with a little boy on a lawn as green as she could imagine. The little girl looked a lot like Blake, and the little boy had her own auburn hair, and he was quietly playing with his dad.

The gentle breeze outside enveloped Manley as she closed her eyes and took a deep breath. It was calming, grounding, and in that moment, she felt Blake's reassuring presence behind her. Of course he was there, steadfast and patient, giving her the space she needed yet ready to catch her. Of course he was. She shivered. This wasn't going as planned. Again. She shivered slightly, the unexpected rush of emotions stirring within her.

She turned around to him and studied him carefully, without a word. He was just standing there, hands in his pockets, waiting if she had something to say. His hair wasn't quite as orderly as when they had arrived here. He had a habit of running his hands through it nervously when he thought no one was watching. His expression was friendly, a nearly imperceptible smile tugging at his lips. Their eyes locked and he returned her gaze, not in a demanding way, just looking at her. Manley reminded herself to breathe, overwhelmed by the realisation of how far he had gone to find her, with the unwavering support of her friends. She had so much to tell him, and yet didn't know where to start.

It was obvious to her that she wouldn't say goodbye to him after all that had happened. She knew deep in her heart that she couldn't. Without a word, she walked up to him and rested her head against his chest, gently placing moving her hands to the comforting embrace of his back. In response, Blake enveloped her in his arms, holding her close. His kiss on her hair sent a wave of warmth through her, familiar and reassuring, evoking memories of their first kiss in the hotel corridor. It seemed ages ago, yet it had only been little over two months. The lifetime ahead of her seemed to linger just beyond the horizon, and she suddenly knew that it was going to hold other things than she had thought. Maybe there wasn't going to be a new job at the Faction for her, at least not for now. She needed to be with Blake, to heal, to find her real place in the world. And she knew she wasn't going to have to find that place on her own. Blake would be by her side, supporting every decision she made, even if he insisted being involved in them.

A faint, weary smile played on Manley's lips as she savoured the moment. Maybe this was exactly what she needed right now.

Coming soon

Manley: Grounded

The next chapter:

Ex-ISA agent Dana Manley finds herself in the aftermath of a holiday gone wrong. Badly injured and fighting the demons from her past, she is on her road to recovery when a mysterious stranger shows up on her doorstep and invites her to a mission that sounds just a little too easy. Manley being Manley, she agrees to go hunting with her new partner Raine Burton and finds herself in a situation that demands a great deal of her and Michael Blake, who is still by her side. New secrets and turns of events leave little space for planning their future...

Manley moaned, feeling a little anger rise. Who the hell was at her door? No one knew she lived here, except for her parents and Faris. Her parents had not ventured to this part of town yet since her reunion with them. And Faris never came without calling first. Could this be the literal neighbour asking for an egg? She felt Blake's fingers moving up her leg while he was still kissing her, and they were driving her crazy, inching their way up to the more sensitive areas of her thighs.

The doorbell rang in staccato for at least a minute while Manley and Blake did their best to ignore it. At last, Manley rolled out from under Blake, fumbling for a sheet from the bed and her blaster from inside her nightstand. She quickly wrapped the sheet around her body, shushing Blake with an index finger on her lips, and walked towards the door briskly.

Blake considered stopping her for a second. This was the first time he saw her carrying a weapon, and the blaster looked like it was just a metal extension of her hand. She held it naturally, and he had the feeling that Faris's words "She could probably shoot us with a blaster from her hospital bed" hadn't been exaggerated. Then he went after her, following her into the narrow corridor. The bell rang again.

Manley tapped the security display beside the entrance door. The tiny camera built into the wooden exterior over the steel case showed a woman. She was a little less tall as Manley but just as slim. Her long, black hair was in an artful crown on top of her head, making her appearance a little taller than it was. Her eyes were dark, too, and she hardly wore any make-up. Her eyes were crowned by half-circles of black paint, and her lips wore a light shade of pink. She wore something long and dark, but it was hard to figure out what it was from the camera angle. She looked serene, as if she had been expecting Manley not to open at the first ring of the bell. When her hand reached for the bell button again, Manley stepped back from the door and opened it quickly. In one swift movement, she swung up the blaster and looked her visitor in the eyes. "Come in. Quietly."

The woman in black didn't seem surprised about this half-hearted welcome. She implied a nod, keeping her hands quiet and where Manley could see them. Manley appreciated that and gestured her to walk into the room where she had just been trying to have a good time with Blake. The woman gave Blake a good look from head to toe while she walked past him. He suddenly wished he had gathered up a sheet, too. The woman made him feel a little uncomfortable, though he couldn't quite pinpoint why. Women had seen him naked before, and never had he felt anything but amused by it. When he was about to walk after the visitor, he caught Manley's eye, and she motioned him to stay where he was with a slight movement of her eyes, all the time aiming the blaster at the woman in black. Manley went after her alone.

The woman had stopped in the living room, turning back around to Manley slowly and deliberately. "Bad time, is it?" she asked, smiling.

Manley cocked an eyebrow. "What makes you think that?" She motioned her visitor towards the couch facing the glass wall and followed her.

"Just a hunch." The woman stopped at the couch, looking at Manley curiously. "I am unarmed, if that is a question."

Manley smiled at her. "You probably know who I am. I can't take your word for that."

The woman smiled, slowly raising her hands, so the naked agent in the sheet could see them even better. She was wearing a fluttering dress of several layers. Layers that could have held any number of weapons. "Please, feel free to check."

"Who are you?" Manley asked. She was really curious who dared to come into her apartment unarmed.

The woman in the black dress kept on smiling. "I'm glad that you're asking. I wouldn't have been surprised if you just hit me." After a pause of breath she added, "My name is Raine Burton, and Howard sends me."

There was a long moment of silence in Manley's living room corner. Manley's thoughts were racing. Howard. He was the head of the Faction, the one representing the organisation.

The man she was looking for was standing at the bar. He was wearing a simple black t-shirt, clinging to his well-trained torso and tight black pants, showing off his very attractive behind. He wore a five-o'clock shadow of a beard that was greying already, as did the very short hair on his head. On an earlier mission, years ago, Manley might have been tempted to use that attractive behind for her own satisfaction before turning him in, but that would never happen now. If anything, she was going to use

Blake's very attractive behind upstairs in their room. But Arlo Zane didn't know that. In fact, he didn't know at all that he was being watched. Manley slowly rose from the couch she had been lounging on with Raine and expertly straightened the glittering red dress she was wearing. She walked to the empty spot on Zane's left side and waited for the bartender to order a drink. When he addressed her, Zane turned towards her, noticing her for the first time. His eyes widened, and his strained expression changed towards a smile. He leant on his right elbow and watched her. Manley saw all of that from the corner of her eye, not giving him a clue that she had registered him. When the bartender had placed her glass of gin and tonic in front of her, she took a sip, then seemingly looked at Zane for the first time. She gave him a curt nod and was about to turn back to the table when he finally took the bait.

"What's a pretty lady like you doing alone in a place like this?" he asked, giving her a smile. Manley cocked an eyebrow.

"If this is your best pick-up line, it's no wonder you're standing at a bar, trying to impress a woman." Then she turned and made another step towards Raine who was watching this with growing amusement. She was expecting him to stop her.

"I'm sorry", Manley heard Zane say behind her when she had barely taken two steps. "The ladies in this place usually aren't as classy as you clearly are."

She almost ignored the cheap compliment but turned around to meet his gaze. "I bet you're not giving the ladies in this place enough grace, Mr…" Manley threw out another piece of bait. "Zane. Arlo Zane." He stretched out his hand, clearly expecting her to shake it. Manley frowned visibly. "I see", she snarled, rolling her eyes ever so slightly. That guy was clearly acting out. She watched him pull back his hand. "And what are you up to, Mr. Zane?" she asked without giving her own name away.

Coming in early 2025

www.ingramcontent.com/pod-product-compliance
Lightning Source LLC
LaVergne TN
LVHW020311200726
843507LV00012B/2061